Beyond The Edge of Lies

M. Lea

M. LEA BOOKS

First edition 2025

ISBN: 979-8218802738

Contents

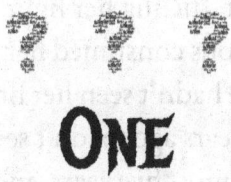

ONE

S he had done everything right. She had worn her vest, checked the corners, and kept her back to the wall on the stairs. So, how the hell had he shot her?

Lying on the dirty warehouse floor, she felt the warm stickiness of blood as it pooled between her shirt and her vest. Panic clawed at her as she struggled to breathe, her instincts screaming at her to move, to fight back against the darkness creeping in around her. Pain shot through her with every movement. She clenched her teeth against the pain.

"Man, the fuck up, Algatta," she spat as the cold concrete pressed into her hips, causing her to shiver.

Footsteps echoed in the distance. She had to focus. It could be him, and he may be returning to finish what he started. Drawing on every ounce of strength left within her, she turned her head, trying to peer through the dim light filtering through the filthy windows.

Her hand trembled as she pressed it against her side, her teeth gritted in pain as she suppressed a scream. The warmth of her blood seeping through her fingers, slippery and thick, filling the air with a metallic stench, added to her fear. The pain was all-consuming, an almost unbearable agony, unlike anything she had ever felt. 'I am not going out like this,' she cursed, determination fueling her fight to stay alive.

Guilt of past decisions consumed her as she lay there, fighting to stay awake. She hadn't seen her brother Paul since their father's funeral two years ago; hadn't seen Paul's wife and her best friend Anna in almost five years, and had missed the birth of her niece, and now she might never get the chance to meet her. Tears streamed down her face as she realized how much time she had wasted. Her heart ached as she thought about her former partner, Renee, and her dad, both of whom had been shot and killed in the line of duty. She wondered if they had had this same fear and pain before they died.

"What's running through your head?" a low, menacing voice cut into her thoughts. A looming figure appeared as she opened her eyes. He was tall and bulky, a dark hat pulled low on his head, shadowing his face. "Does it hurt, Detective?" he asked, as he kneeled and pressed his knee into her chest.

"You fucking bastard," she spat.

"Algatta?" he said, glancing at the name tag on her vest. "That name rings a bell, any connection to James Algatta?"

Gasping for air as his knee pressed even harder, she wheezed, "Fuck you."

"You wouldn't be his daughter, Paxxton, would you?"

"How?" Paxx gasped. "How do you know...?"

"Oh, how did I know your old man?" he replied, standing up and dusting off his knees. "I knew your father quite well. He always kept me on my toes. Although the last time I saw James, he looked like you do now." He laughed as he walked away, adding, "When you meet your dad on the other side, tell him I said hi."

"Who?" Paxx demanded, her voice trembling with anger.

"Tell him Mr. Black said hi; he'll know who I am." With that, he strolled away, a low chuckle echoing in the open space.

"Paxx."

She heard her partner call out from somewhere in the building. "Rowan," she called out, the sound barely audible even to her ears. "Rowan," she repeated louder, a cough wracking her as warm liquid escaped her lips. "Damn it."

"Paxx," Rowan called again, closer now. Soon, the sound of hurried footsteps approached her.

"Rowan," she cried once more.

"Officer down! Officer down! I need immediate medical help at 12th Avenue Warehouses! Officer down, we need backup!" She heard Rowan's voice as he frantically called out on the radio. "Paxx, stay with me, shit, breath Paxx, breath. Paxx! Look at me!" He touched her face, drawing her back from the edge and forcing her to focus on him. As she blinked against the dim light, his features came into focus.

"Rowan..."

"I'm right here, you're going to be okay."

"Mr. Black..." The name slipped from her lips before she could stop it.

"Who?" Rowan's brows drew together as a shadow passed over his face.

"Mr. Black, he knew my dad, Rowan; he killed him," she gasped, words tangled between breaths. "He... he wants me to tell dad hi."

"Not today, partner, that will have to wait."

3

"I don't want to die," she whispered as panic surged in her chest.

"You will not die, Paxx," he said, lifting his radio back to his lips. "This is Officer Rowan Taylor. Where is the fucking ambulance?"

The dispatcher's reply was muffled as Paxx drifted in and out of consciousness. "Stay with me," Rowan murmured as he leaned closer, their foreheads almost touching.

Paxx opened her eyes surprised at their closeness. "You're not going to kiss me, are you?" She asked, trying to laugh, only to cough and expel more blood.

"Will it piss you off enough for you to fight?"

Despite the searing pain threatening to drown every trace of reason, Paxx nodded. As the distant wail of sirens grew louder, she felt herself slipping once again, clinging desperately to life. Then everything faded into nothingness. But with so many words left unsaid, true love unknown, and a niece she'd never met, she wasn't ready. 'Fight,' she whispered.

Flashing lights and blaring sirens filled the darkness. Where was she? What was happening?

"Detective Algatta, can you open your eyes?" A woman's soft yet urgent voice cut through the chaos.

"I need more gauze," a man stated firmly.

"Stay with us, Detective," the woman urged.

"Stay," Paxx murmured.

"That's right, Detective, stay with me." The woman's green eyes smiled as Paxx focused on her, feeling a soft touch on her cheek.

"You have beautiful eyes," Paxx whispered.

"Thank you. Keep looking into them."

"Paxx, my name is Paxx."

"Paxx, Good, that's good, Paxx. My name is Riley. Keep your eyes on me Paxx focus on me. Let's speed things up, Jones," she said, addressing the driver.

"Riley."

"I'm right here, sweetie," she reassured, squeezing Paxx's hand.

"Please don't let me die." Paxx begged as her grip slackened, and her eyes closed.

"Come on, Paxx, we are almost there."

Paxx fought to stay alive with every ounce of remaining strength inside her.

———◦———

O verhead, Paxx grimaced at the bright lights that cut through her closed eyelids and the pungent scent of disinfectants mingled with the constant beeping of machines.

"Get me more gauze, and for fuck's sake, clear the way. What's the status on an operating room?" A stern male voice demanded.

"Doctor, the operating room won't be ready for twenty minutes," another voice, this time female, called out.

"She doesn't have twenty minutes," the man snapped in frustration. "We have to stop this bleeding."

Paxx tried to open her eyes, but they felt too heavy. She sensed the urgency in the room as hurried footsteps echoed around her.

"What's her status?" came yet another voice, this one softer but laced with concern.

"Critical," a deep voice replied. "We're losing her."

A rush of panic surged within Paxx; she couldn't leave yet, not when she had so much left to do.

She felt pressure and the chilling touch of gloved hands working over her, each movement radiating urgency as muffled voices enveloped her once again.

"The bleeding's slowing."

"Not nearly enough," the voice replied sharply.

She felt an odd warmth spreading through her body, but couldn't tell if it was real or another figment of this surreal experience.

"Stay with us, Detective," the same voice pleaded again.

"I'm... here," she tried to reply, but no words came; only a faint, feeble gasp escaped.

"Get me that suction," a man ordered again.

Paxx could sense the frantic energy pulsating around her, the people hustling to save her life while she teetered on the edge of two worlds.

"We have to operate now!" another voice demanded.

"Detective, stay with us; you have to fight." These were the last words Paxx heard as the pressure shifted away, as did the chaos surrounding her senses. Something covered her nose and mouth, and then the world faded as she succumbed to the anesthesia.

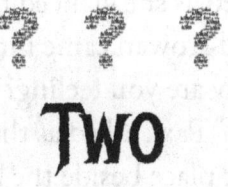

TWO

Beep, beep, beep, the sound kept time with Paxx's heart-beat. Silence surrounded her, except for the persistent beeping. Where was she? Paxx attempted to open her eyes, but her eyelids felt heavy.

"Paxx, can you hear me?"

"Here," Paxx tried to respond, but something in her throat choked her.

Then she felt a hand on hers. She tried to close her hand around it, but the black engulfed her again.

———◇———

Coughing, she was coughing. Damn, it hurt.

"Take it easy. I'm going to remove the tube from your throat," a gentle voice assured her.

"Not as heavy now," Paxx thought, as she opened her eyes. The room was dimly lit and cold. A woman with soft features and a warm smile came into view.

"Welcome back," the nurse whispered.

"Where am I?"

"You're in the hospital, sweetheart."

7

"What happened?"

The nurse hesitated as she glanced toward the door. Paxx turned her head, and Rowan came into focus.

"Hey, partner, how are you feeling?"

"What happened?" Paxx asked as the nurse stepped away, and Rowan took her place beside the bed.

"You were shot, Paxx; we nearly lost you."

Scenes of chaos and pain flashed through Paxx's mind. "Did you try to kiss me?" Paxx coughed, remembering his face close to hers as she lay on a cold concrete floor.

"You remember that?" he chuckled. "I wasn't going to kiss you; I was about to resuscitate you, but luckily, you came to." His smile narrowed his eyes, and a sigh escaped his lips.

"How did I get shot? Who did it? Did you catch them? Dad, Mr. Black," Paxx bombarded him with questions.

"Take it easy, Paxx. You need to stay calm."

As the nurse returned, everything faded back into the abyss.

———◆◇◆———

Beep, beep, beep. When Paxx opened her eyes this time, the light was brighter and hurt her eyes. "Rowan," she whispered.

"He's not here."

She gasped at the familiar voice. "Paul?" Paxx asked, not trusting her ears.

"Yes, sis, it's Paul," He replied as he approached the bed.

Paxx's eyes flooded with tears as she lifted her hand. Paul took it as he leaned over and kissed her on the forehead.

"After you were shot, Rowan called me and..." he trailed off, his voice cracking.

"I'm alright, little brother; it's so good to see you."

"It's good to see you, too, sis."

"Mom?" Paxx blurted out without thinking.

"She's not coming; I'm sorry, Paxx."

Paxx closed her eyes, not surprised that her mother wasn't coming, but still disappointed.

"I'm glad you're here."

"Me too. Can I get you anything?"

"Water," she said as she tried to sit up. "Fuck," she cried out as pain shot through her stomach.

"Easy, you have had major surgery; you need to take it slow," Paul said as he picked up a cup of ice and placed a hand on her shoulder.

"How long have I been here?"

"Three days," Paul replied, shaking ice into her mouth.

"Three days? I need to leave," she exclaimed, attempting to sit up once more, but falling back on the pillow in pain.

"You've got to calm down!"

"Paul, the man who shot me, he knew Dad," she said, each word laced with pain as she clutched her chest. "He killed Dad."

"What? What makes you say that?"

After drawing a ragged breath, she continued, "He told me to tell Dad hi when I saw him on the other side. Paul, he said his name was Mr. Black."

"Mr. Black," Paul said as he sank into a chair beside the bed. "Mr. Black."

"Paul, who is Mr. Black?"

"Paxx, you know who Mr. Black is. He is the serial killer that Dad hunted for over two years before his death. 'Mr. Black' was the crude nickname given by the media because, after his crimes, he left a black rose dipped in the blood of each victim at the scene."

"Paul," Paxx said, her voice thick with hurt and anger, "I don't remember."

"How often did you talk to Dad in the last year of his life, Paxx? You were dealing with..." Paul trailed off, not wanting to open old wounds.

"Renee," Paxx sighed, "I was dealing with Renee's death."

"Paxx, you lost not only a partner, but a friend."

"Yeah, and her husband lost his wife while her kids lost their mother. That was no excuse for me to..."

"Stop it!" Paul growled. "I know what Renee meant to you, Paxx, and how it affected you, and so did Dad. It's difficult to move on when the person you love, someone you had relied on for almost three years, is shot and dies in your arms."

"I was too late, and I lost her, and then I missed spending the last year of Dad's life with him." She said, fighting back tears as an old wound gaped open in her chest, "And then I lost myself," Paxx whispered, as she closed her eyes.

"I get it, sis. So much happened all at once. You came back; Paxx, you found your way back."

Paxx remained silent as memories of her partner's murder and her father's death played in her mind. She had tried drowning her guilt and pain in alcohol, but the self-recrimination persisted. Why hadn't she been faster? Why hadn't she saved Renee? Despite killing the bastard who had shot Renee, and then stood over her while she begged for her life, she couldn't stop Renee from dying in her arms. Then, not even a year later, as she was finding her way toward sobriety, someone killed her father in the line of duty, and the police never caught the culprit. She had fought desperately to stay afloat, clinging to anything or anyone that might numb the pain, even if only for a few hours.

Paxx took a shaky breath, then opened her eyes and blinked away the memories. "They never found any leads on Dad's killer."

Paul's expression darkened, haunted by their father's unsolved murder. "I kept in touch with his partner, Ian, for over a year, but with no new leads after a year, the department stopped investigating."

"What about Mr. Black?"

"Mr. Black's been on the run for the past two years," Paul replied. "After Dad died, he vanished."

Anger and frustration bubbled up inside her. "Well, he's back. Shouldn't someone have kept me in the loop? I could've helped!"

"You were in no shape to help anyone. You were barely holding it together after Renee died."

"Bull shit!" she snapped. "It's clear now why they've consistently refused any transfer requests to the homicide division. And, it's not because I'm valuable in narcotics; it's because they didn't want me stirring up trouble. You left ten years ago, up and moved to Chicago. And when Dad died, Mom didn't even care enough to show up at his funeral. She never even called me. Did she call you?"

Paul's silence told her she had. "Mom lives in Chicago, Paxx."

"You have been in contact with her over the past ten years and never told me?" Paxx said as anger and hurt boiled to the surface.

"Paxx..."

"No!" she cut him off, her voice strained from both pain and emotion. "I can't."

"I am going to be honest with you, Paxx, and you are going to be pissed and hurt." He took a deep breath before continuing, "After Mom left, she kept in touch with me; whenever I went away on what you and Dad thought were 'boys' trips with friends, I was going to see her."

Paxx stared at him in disbelief. His words bore into her like a flaming arrow, driving in deep, searing everything in its path. "Why, Paul? Why didn't she want to see me?"

"When you came out to them, and they didn't support you, you were so angry, and then she left Dad. She knew you would never forgive her, and she couldn't accept your lifestyle. Paxx, she felt it was best to stay away." Paul sank deeper into the chair as his heart broke at the pain and hurt he was causing his sister.

A heavy silence filled the room as Paxx absorbed his words. "After she left, I soon understood why," Paxx sighed. "I never realized how much she shielded us from, how blind I had been to his drinking and rage. You never flinched; you always stood up to him, even at fifteen. I was the older sister, yet I relied on you to stand in the gap between us."

Moving forward in his chair, Paul took her hand once more and said, "Don't you remember why I stood up to him? And why, for so long, you stayed away from him?"

Paxx closed her eyes, willing the memory not to return. "It's been twenty years, Paul; I've spent most of those years fighting hard to forget."

"That night, when I heard you screaming and rushed into the house, you were in the living room wearing nothing but a bloodied, torn T-shirt. Your nose was broken and bleeding, and the rage in your eyes terrified me," Paul said, catching his breath. "Paxx, I knew that if I didn't intervene, you would kill him."

"He had no right," Paxx growled.

"No, he had no right to hit you or try to ... Paxx, it was his house, and he had warned you about bringing girls home when he wasn't there."

"You always brought girls home, even when he was there. You were only fifteen, and you could fuck any girl you wanted with him sitting in the living room watching TV." Paxx shook her head, adding, "And if I would have brought boys over, he'd likely have given them a beer and told them to enjoy themselves. I never forgave him for that night. I became a cop to spite him, and I'm a fucking good cop, no thanks to him."

"You're a great cop, Paxx; everything I learned, I learned from you, not him. And it wasn't fair that Mom abandoned you." Paul stood and began pacing beside her bed. "Please believe me. I tried to convince her to contact you. But she couldn't get past thinking she had failed you."

"Failed me?"

"Paxx, when you came out to them, and he tried to 'fix' you, she knew." Paul turned to face her, tears streaming down his cheeks. "The black eye and busted lip; he did that to her because she said she was leaving him and taking us with her."

"Then why did she leave me there? Leave us?" Paxx couldn't hold back the tears.

"You had six months of school left, and the last time he went to your room, and you fought him off, he beat the shit out of her. She knew you could take care of yourself."

"I was so scared," Paxx whispered.

"Paxx, you've always been stronger than you believe. You have fought through so much, overcome so much."

"You married Anna and moved on, and built a new life. I haven't had a relationship last for more than a couple of months. Paul, I am thirty-eight years old and still terrified of letting anyone in too deep."

"Paxx, I haven't moved on. I think about what happened every day. It's taken me years to figure out how to cope without drowning in it. Paxx, your anger and grief, you need to face those feelings instead of burying them under alcohol, work, and fear."

"And how do I do that?"

"Start by allowing yourself to grieve. It doesn't make you weak; it makes you human."

She knew those words were true, but they terrified her. She wanted to believe that she could fight against the shadows creeping into her mind, but how? Where would she even begin?

"You don't know how hard that is for me."

"I do, believe me. But you have to let someone in, open your heart. Paxx, you need to trust someone. I would never have made it without Anna."

"Anna, how is she? And the baby?" A sense of regret and shame over their infrequent contact washed over her.

"They are great; Embry is already walking everywhere," Paul said, his face lighting up as he mentioned his wife and daughter.

"I'm happy for you and glad you have them."

"There is someone for you, too, Paxx, but you have to be open to finding them."

"Vulnerability is not one of my strong suits."

The door creaked, and Rowan looked in.

"I heard you were awake," he murmured.

Paxx managed a small smile. "Hey."

Rowan stepped closer, glancing at Paul before fixing his eyes on Paxx. "How are you doing?"

"Still here," Paxx answered, trying to keep the weariness out of her voice.

"You're tougher than nails."

"I'm tired, but I'm trying. Rowan, have you met my brother, Paul?"

"Only over the phone."

Paul stood and offered Rowan his hand. "Thank you for calling."

"I was afraid she wouldn't make it, so I looked through her phone and found your number."

"Well, I'm grateful you were there for her."

"Yeah, Rowan, I owe you my life."

"That's what partners do; they look out for one another," Rowan said as he met Paxx's gaze, a strange glint in his eyes.

Paxx shuddered, shifting in bed and drawing a shaky breath, breaking away from his unsettling stare, and asked, "So, when are we starting the search for Mr. Black?"

"I have a sketch artist coming over tomorrow to get a description from you; we will move forward from there," Rowan replied.

"Rowan, it's been three days; you haven't been looking for him?" Paxx said, her tone mixed with frustration and annoyance.

"We've pulled video from every camera around the warehouse. Unfortunately, most of the cameras in that vicinity are out of order, damaged, or fake, so our best lead so far only shows someone's back."

"Damn it," Paxx muttered, her frustration and anxiety causing her blood pressure to spike, which set off an alert on the machine.

Moments later, the nurse from earlier entered the room, her expression irritable. "Gentlemen, I think she's had enough for today. Let's let her rest."

Paul and Rowan nodded, exchanging looks, not wanting to cross the petite yet intimidating nurse. "Yes, ma'am," Paul said as he leaned over and kissed Paxx on the forehead. "I will be back tomorrow and bring Anna and the baby."

"They're here with you? I would love to see them."

"Anna insisted on coming; she has missed you," he said as he stepped away from the bed.

"I have missed her too," Paxx replied, her thoughts drifting to her best friend from high school. Anna had always supported her in every way, listened to her frustrations about life, and later fell in love with Paul, who took her away to Chicago.

"Ok, out you go," the nurse said as she ushered the men to the door. Once they were gone and the room fell silent again, Paxx stared out the window at the gray clouds in the sky.

? ? ?

THREE

O utside, as the clouds darkened, the steady beeping of machines receded, becoming a gentle backdrop as Paxx let herself drift into sleep. She embraced it, longing for a temporary escape from the burdens of her thoughts. As she drifted deeper into sleep, images of happier times with Paul and Anna flitted through her mind. Alongside these memories lurked the dark shadow of the moment she'd chosen distance over closeness, letting fear dictate her choices.

Paxx jolted awake, blinking at the plain, white ceiling overhead. When she glanced out the window, she saw that the clouds had gathered, and a light rain pattered gently on the glass, echoing the uneasy rhythm of her heartbeat.

There was a knock on the door before it opened. A nurse peeked in, this one more cheerful than the last.

"How are you feeling?" she asked before checking Paxx's blood pressure and pulse.

"Tired, how long have I been asleep?"

"You were asleep when I came on shift, and that was almost seven hours ago. I will look at your chart," she smiled. In the corner, at a small desk, the nurse logged into the computer. She entered Paxx's vitals and then commented, "Looks like you slept about twelve hours."

"Twelve hours? Is that normal?"

The nurse returned to the bed and replied, "You have had a major injury; you are on some strong pain meds, and the more you can rest, the faster you heal."

Paxx smiled at the short, gray-haired nurse, her soft voice comforting her.

"Are you hungry? Do you think you can try some Jell-O?"

Nodding, Paxx became aware of her hunger.

"Great! I will put in an order of Jell-O for you. I will be right back, and if you're up to it, a couple of people are waiting to see you."

"Send them in, please," Paxx said, hoping it was Paul and Anna.

As the nurse disappeared through the door, a moment later, Anna entered the room, holding a beautiful toddler with fiery red hair.

Paxx couldn't hold back the tears as their eyes met. "Hey, you."

"Hey you," Anna responded as she handed the baby to Paul and rushed to Paxx's bedside. "Can I hug you?"

Paxx only nodded, opening her arms. Anna leaned in, and the two cried as they held onto one another.

"I missed you so much," Anna said when they parted.

"Me too, I didn't realize how much until I saw you."

They gazed at one another for several minutes, wiping away each other's tears.

"Anna, I'm so sorry; I was selfish and hurtful to you. It's unforgivable."

"Paxx, I forgave every word the moment you said them," Anna reassured her with a gentle kiss on her cheek. Hearing the toddler giggle, she said, "Paxx, I want you to meet Embry Paxxton Algatta."

Paxx stared at Paul and Anna as tears ran heavier down her cheeks. "You named your daughter after me?"

"Of course, we did," Anna chuckled as she took Embry from Paul and sat her on the edge of the bed.

"She's beautiful," Paxx said with a mix of excitement and exhaustion, as her trembling hand reached out to touch tiny fingers.

Embry wrapped her little fingers around Paxx's as a big smile spread across her face.

"You've got your momma's red hair and green eyes. Daddy's gonna have his hands full." Paxx laughed, glancing up at Paul.

"The nurse said we can't stay very long; they need to take you for some X-rays or something," Paul said as he picked up Embry.

"Will you come back?"

"Paul is going to keep Embry this afternoon so I can return. We can catch up." Anna explained, planting another kiss on Paxx's cheek.

"I would like that. Thank you for bringing her by. She is perfect."

"We are staying for a while," Paul said. "You will get to see her a lot."

"Where are you staying?"

"We are in a hotel a few blocks away."

"Why don't you stay at my house? I will be here for a while; you would do me a big favor if you would water my plants and occasionally give Jimmy a break from caring for the horses." Paxx implored.

"Paxx, are you sure?" Paul asked. "And you have horses?"

"I'm sure. There are three bedrooms, and it's a little way out of town, so it's quiet. Yes, horses, and you are more than welcome to ride if you'd like. Please make yourself at home when you get there." Paxx's heart brimmed with hope at the thought of them accepting her invitation.

Paul exchanged a glance with Anna, who nodded. "Okay, if you're sure."

"I'm sure, I should have a bag somewhere with my keys inside. Call Rowan and swing by the precinct to pick up my Jeep. I assume you are renting a car?"

Paul nodded.

"You can use my Jeep, and there's also a truck in the garage, which I use to tow the horse trailer. Feel free to use that as well."

"Paxx," Paul protested.

"No argument. I am thrilled you are here, and I want you to stay as long as you can." Paxx closed her eyes as a wave of nausea swept over her.

"Paxx, honey, are you alright?" Anna asked, concern lacing her tone.

Paxx nodded. "I'm fine, but could you please send the nurse in?"

Paul left the room, returning in a moment with the nurse.

"I will see you later, okay?" Paxx murmured, "I love you."

"We love you, too, and I will be back in a few hours," Anna assured her as they left the room.

Once they were gone, Paxx looked at the nurse and said, "I think I am going to be sick."

"I came prepared," the nurse said as she raised the head of the bed until Paxx was in a semi-sitting position before handing her a small bucket.

———◆———

O ver the next four hours, Paxx ate some Jell-O and toast. She also underwent an X-ray and an MRI. When Anna returned, Paxx was asleep, so she settled in a chair by the bed with a book until Paxx awoke.

"Hey, you."

"Hey, you," Anna replied, closing her book. "How are you feeling?"

"I've been better. Did you get settled at the house?"

"We are going to go tomorrow morning. Embry fell asleep on the way to the hotel, so we let her sleep. Can I get you anything?"

"No, just stay with me, we have a lot of catching up to do."

Over the next three hours, Anna shared stories about life in Chicago while Paxx recounted her own experiences, both the highs and the lows. Their conversation flowed easily, as if no time had passed since they last spoke.

As she stood and pulled on her jacket, Anna said, "God, I've missed this."

"Me too. Will you come back?"

"We will be back tomorrow unless you need us sooner."

"Alright, and please, make yourself at home. You know all my secrets, so nothing is off-limits to you. Paul might want to keep a respectful distance from my personal space in my bedroom." Paxx teased with a wink. "Otherwise, both of you are welcome to anything I have."

Anna giggled. "I will steer him clear of your bedroom. Thank you again, Paxx."

"I'm glad your both here."

"Me too," Anna agreed as she said goodbye and left the room.

??? FOUR

I n the days that followed, Paxx gradually regained her strength, each day bringing a little more vitality back to her frail form. Eventually, she found herself able to sit up for short periods, her resilience shining through. On the sixth day after the event, a gentle knock on the door interrupted Paul, Anna, and Paxx's conversation. "Paxxton Algatta?" a pleasant voice called from the doorway.

Turning her head, Paxx locked eyes with a striking redhead. A tight ponytail pulled her hair back, revealing a delicate rose tattoo below her left ear. Her bright green eyes, accentuated with dark mascara and eyeliner, sparkled, and her full, dark pink lips curved into a smile as she stepped further into the room.

"I'm Paxxton," Paxx stammered.

"Good morning. I'm Jaylee Pittmore, and I'll be your physical therapist while you're here."

"Good morning."

From the couch, Paul cleared his throat as he stood up. "We'll leave you to your therapy," he said with a smile as Anna slipped on her jacket and assisted Embry with hers.

Anna approached the bed, leaned down to kiss Paxx's cheek, and whispered, "She's gorgeous."

Paxx nodded and returned the kiss. "I'll see you later."

Once they had left, Jaylee explained the series of exercises they would be undertaking and outlined her hopes for what Paxx could achieve with each session. Paxx's gaze drifted to a gold band on Jaylee's left ring finger, a detail that brought a flash of disappointment.

As Jaylee led Paxx through various stretches, their eyes would occasionally meet, sparking an unexpected connection they both felt. Paxx focused on her breathing, trying to overcome the discomfort of each stretch, but she couldn't help but steal glances at Jaylee.

"Okay, let's try to stand for a moment. I've got you," Jaylee said, her voice steady and encouraging. With a gentle grip around her waist, Jaylee helped Paxx shift to the edge of the bed. The effort was monumental, and sweat beaded on Paxx's brow as she edged forward.

As she stood, Paxx wrapped her arms around Jaylee's shoulders, breathing in her perfume's fresh, earthy scent and the soft smell of lavender in her hair.

"You're doing great! Are you alright?"

"It feels... different from what I thought it would."

"What do you mean?"

"I expected recovery to feel like a burden. But right now, with you here, it's not so bad," Paxx admitted, heat creeping into her cheeks as she sat back down.

"I'm glad you are comfortable with me; that will help you get through the hard things we will tackle."

"When are you coming again?" Paxx asked as Jaylee began picking up her supplies.

"Tomorrow morning, someone will bring you to the therapy room," Jaylee said as she slipped on her jacket. "I will see you in the morning, Paxxton."

"Paxx. You can call me Paxx."

"Alright, Paxx, but I must admit, I like Paxxton," she said with a wink.

"In that case, you can call me Paxxton."

"Then, Paxxton, I will see you in the morning."

"Bye," Paxx said as Jaylee left the room.

As she ate dinner and watched TV, Paxx couldn't get Jaylee out of her mind. She wore a ring; she must be married. Paxx tried to convince herself that what she sensed between them was wishful thinking as she tried to focus on the episode of Law and Order on television. Finally, she couldn't keep her eyes open as the day's excursion settled into her weak muscles.

That night, she dreamed of a dark figure as he stood over her, laughing as she lay on a cold concrete floor, bleeding. Each time she awoke, she pressed the morphine button, hoping to ease the mental pain as much as the physical. When she awoke the last time, the sun was already brightening the sky.

Picking up her phone, she called Rowan, frustrated when he told her they had no breaks in the case and that the composite drawing the sketch artist had done was leading them nowhere.

———◦◦———

At eight o'clock, a hospital orderly arrived and wheeled her to an elevator that took them up one floor to the therapy room. The room was brightly lit, filled with workout equipment. Cushioned tables lined one wall, the orderly helped her onto a table, leaving once she was situated.

"Good morning, Paxxton," Jaylee's soft voice interrupted Paxx's thoughts.

"Morning."

"How are you feeling this morning?"

"Sore and tired," Paxx said, closing her eyes against the bright lights.

"You didn't sleep well?" Jaylee asked as she began massaging Paxx's legs.

Paxx shook her head, keeping her eyes closed.

"I'm sorry, let's begin with some light leg stretches," Jaylee said as she lifted Paxx's left leg, bent it, and pressed it toward her stomach, making Paxx wince. "You have some beautiful ink," Jaylee commented on the colorful tattoos that covered Paxx's arms.

"Thank you."

"You have more?"

Meeting Jaylee's gaze, Paxx responded, "Yes, a few. What about you? Is that rose your only one?"

"I have to cover them up while at work, but I have a few."

"What do you do away from here?" Paxx asked, breaking the tension that had risen between them.

Jaylee glanced at her, a hint of surprise in her expression. "Oh, just your typical stuff. I like to read and mountain bike; I am a physical trainer at a gym a few times a week."

"Do you have kids?"

"No, do you?"

"No, I have a niece; she was there yesterday with my brother and sister-in-law."

"She's beautiful."

"What about your husband? What does he do?" Paxx asked, opening her eyes as Jaylee paused, moving her leg.

"I'm not married."

Paxx's eyes drifted to Jaylee's hand, where the gold band shimmered.

Noticing Paxx's glance, Jaylee smiled and held up her hand, wiggling her fingers as she teased, "It keeps the guys from asking me out."

"Oh, that's clever."

In the days that followed, Anna and Paul visited often, and Paxx grew increasingly thankful for her second chance. With each session of therapy, she felt her strength coming back. Her and Jaylee exchanged stories and laughter during the sessions and as their personal boundaries started to fade, the sessions became moments that both Paxx and Jaylee eagerly anticipated. The days slipped by until one afternoon, meeting Paxx's gaze, Jaylee said.

"You're stronger than you realize, Paxxton, you have made great progress. This is our last session; your discharge is scheduled for tomorrow."

Paxx was surprised by the sudden feeling of loss in her chest. "I know this is probably a hard no, but can I call you?"

"I would like that."

❓ ❓ ❓
FIVE

Paul and Anna arrived at the hospital at ten a.m. the following day. Anna carried a gym bag containing Paxx, a change of clothes.

"Thought you might like some sweats and a T-shirt," Anna said as she set the bag on the foot of the bed.

"Thank you, I would. Anna could you stay and help me? Paul, could you excuse us for a moment? I still can't lift my arms over my head without severe pain."

"Of course, Embry and I will wait in the hallway," he replied, holding Embry's hand as they sauntered out the door. Her short legs were wobbly, but determined.

"He's an amazing dad," Paxx smiled.

"He sure is."

As Anna was helping Paxx with her socks, a soft tap came from the door. Jaylee peered around the door as it opened, her long red hair cascading in loose waves around her shoulders. "Good, you're still here."

"Come in," Paxx replied, unable to hide the happiness in her voice.

"I will leave you two alone; see you at the Jeep," Anna said, winking at Paxx before exiting the room.

Jaylee picked up Paxx's tennis shoes and helped her put them on before tying the laces. When Jaylee looked up. Paxx reached down to tuck a few stray strands of her hair behind her ear.

"Are you alright?" Paxx asked as Jaylee rose, her expression uncertain.

"Paxxton."

Paxx froze, dropping her hand to her lap. "I'm so sorry I have misread this," she said, her cheeks flushed with embarrassment.

Placing her hand on Paxx's cheek, Jaylee leaned in closer. "No, I want to be sure I haven't."

Clasping Jaylee's scrub top, Paxx drew her closer. "You haven't," she whispered, and as their lips met and they shared a delicate kiss that quickly deepened. Paxx's lips parted, inviting Jaylee's tongue to explore, sending shivers of passion between them.

Jaylee moaned softly as she leaned in further, intensifying the kiss. After a moment, Jaylee broke the kiss. "I have wanted to do that for days."

"Since the first time I saw you," Paxx admitted as she leaned back, searching Jaylee's eyes for any sign of hesitation or doubt. Heat and want burned in Jaylee's eyes, kindling Paxx's desire.

"Really?"

"When you walked in on the first day and said my name, I was instantly smitten. And you make scrubs look incredibly sexy."

Jaylee's heart skipped a beat as a shiver ran down to her lady parts. "You make my knees weak, Paxxton."

Drawing Jaylee closer, Paxx wrapped her arms around her waist while Jaylee ran her fingers through Paxx's hair. "Jaylee, I don't want to rush this or overwhelm you, but I want to spend time with you."

"Rush this, please," Jaylee pleaded as she captured Paxx's lips again, surrendering to the heat and passion of their embrace.

With a gasp, Paxx pulled away, clutching her stomach as a sudden, intense pain pierced her side.

"Paxxton," Jaylee gasped as she stepped back and lifted Paxx's shirt. The bold colors of bruising that covered her mid section caused Jaylee's eyes to glisten with tears. "I had no idea it was this bad."

"I'm sorry, you take my breath away," Paxx replied, taking slow, shallow breaths.

"Very funny," Jaylee said as she released the hem of Paxx's shirt and kissed her. "I'll take things slow until you're healed."

"Good idea," Paxx replied as the door opened, and a nurse with a wheelchair entered the room.

"Ready to go home?"

"Ready," Paxx smiled as she stood up and, with Jaylee's help, moved to the wheelchair.

Paul was waiting with Anna and Embry in the Jeep outside the hospital. He opened the passenger door as the nurse wheeled Paxx out of the hospital, followed by Jaylee, carrying her bag.

After some effort, Paxx settled into the Jeep. Jaylee stepped close, pulling the seatbelt across Paxx and clicking it into place. "Talk to you soon."

Paxx cupped her face in her hands and kissed her, a gentle kiss that left them both longing for more.

Handing her phone to Jaylee, Paxx said, "Enter your number, and I'll text you my address. I'll be around for at least the next few days, so let me know when you can drop by." Jaylee took the phone and input her number as Paul settled into the driver's seat.

"I never asked where you work," Jaylee remarked as she returned the phone.

"I'm a detective with the Ivan Hope police department," Paxx replied, as a frown crossed Jaylee's face. "Does that bother you?"

"No," but the look in her eyes told Paxx something different.

"Jaylee, are you alright?"

"Yeah," Jaylee replied, pressing their lips together once more, "It will be okay. We just need to talk."

"I will tell you anything you want to know," Paxx assured as Jaylee stepped back and closed the door.

"Call me when you get home and settled."

"I will."

As the Jeep pulled away, Paxx glimpsed Jaylee in the side mirror. Her heart pounded from their kisses, and excitement and nervous anticipation fluttered in her stomach.

"Everything alright?" Paul asked as they merged onto the main road.

Paxx turned to him, forcing a smile. "Yeah, you know, everything's new."

"New is good."

"How are you feeling?" Anna asked from the back seat.

"I am a little sore, it's nothing I can't handle."

They arrived home about twenty minutes later. Paxx's old farmhouse stood welcoming beneath the mid-day sun. Paxx smiled at the garden spot she knew Anna had tended to while she was in the hospital, and she felt a swell of gratitude for her family's support. Once inside, Paul carried a sleeping Embry to the bedroom while Anna helped Paxx get comfortable on the couch, draping a blanket over her lap.

"Can I get you anything?"

"Some water would be great," Paxx replied, leaning back against the soft cushions.

After Anna left for the kitchen, Paul returned to the living room. "What's going on between you and your physical therapist?"

Paxx's cheeks flushed; it felt strange to put words to what had happened between them so quickly. "I don't even know if anything is happening with us.".

"You look like you're smitten with her, and she is definitely smitten with you."

"I might be," she confessed, biting her lip nervously. "But I could tell she has questions about my job... and I don't want to scare her."

Before Paul could respond, Anna returned with a glass of water and handed it to Paxx. "I think you two look great together."

Paxx took a sip and felt the coolness soothe her throat as she reached for her phone and hesitated before typing a message to Jaylee.

'Hey! I'm home. Let me know when you're free, and I'd love to talk more.'

Biting her lip, she hit send. Moments later, a reply came. *'Glad you're home! Let me know when I can swing by.'*

'Now,' Paxx replied, attaching a pin to her house location.

'Are you sure you're up for the company?'

'I'm not up for company, but I am up for seeing you.'

"I am making Fajitas for dinner," Anna said from the kitchen. "Why don't you invite Jaylee?"

"Okay," Paxx agreed as she typed another message.

'Anna is making Fajitas; she wants you to come for dinner.'

Several minutes passed before Paxx's phone buzzed with a message.

'Rain check for dinner, but call me before you go to bed.'

Disappointed, Paxx replied.

'Okay, talk soon.'

Jaylee replied with an emoji, blowing a heart kiss.

Paxx's disappointment eased a little as she returned the same emoji.

"She says raincheck on dinner," Paxx said as she stood and walked to the kitchen. "Can I help?"

"You can sit down and relax," Anna said as she sautéed onions in a small skillet.

"I need to get up and moving," Paxx replied, getting a beer from the fridge. "I have to get back to work. It's been over two weeks, and Rowan says they still have no leads."

"Do you think that will change when you get back?" Paul asked as he entered the room.

"It might," Paxx said as she sat on a bar stool in front of the kitchen island. "I want this guy worse than anyone else."

"Paxx, he avoided the cops for two years after killing Dad; he's probably in Canada by now," Paul stated, his frustration mounting. "You need to take time and heal."

Paxx slammed her beer down on the counter, a surge of frustration and anger bubbling to the surface. "I can't sit around while he's out there, Paul! Not after everything he's taken from us."

Anna glanced over her shoulder, her brow furrowed as she stirred the sizzling onions. "You need to take care of yourself, too, Paxx."

"I have to do this?" Paxx's voice trembled, betraying the turmoil inside. "For the past eighteen days, I have replayed him shooting me, standing over me, confessing to Dad's murder over and over in my head, trying to figure out why he was even there. We were there looking for a meth lab, a drug distribution site. Why would a serial killer, gone for two years, be there?"

"What kind of headspace are you in right now?" Paul asked.

When Paxx didn't answer, Paul continued, "Exactly why you shouldn't rush back."

Paxx took a deep breath and ran her hands through her hair. "I know, but how do you find peace when everything feels so... unsettled and out of control?"

Anna turned off the burner and stepped closer, wiping her hands on a towel. "Sometimes peace comes from accepting what you can't control."

Paxx sighed and took another swig of her beer, but it tasted bitter on her tongue. "It's hard to accept when I feel so powerless."

"I don't want to see you go down into a dark place again," Paul said as he wrapped his arms around Paxx, pulling her into a gentle hug.

Leaning into his embrace, Paxx found solace in the familiarity of her brother's arms. "I don't want that either, I'm not sure I'd survive it."

Pulling back, Paul met her eyes with genuine concern. "Then take your time healing both your body and your mind."

Paxx helped Anna set the table for dinner, and they chatted about trivial things as they ate. Paxx chuckled when Paul attempted to coax Embry into trying a sautéed onion, but his efforts made her grimace at the taste.

"Tell us about this house," Anna said. "How many acres do you have?"

"Fifty," Paxx replied

"It must have cost a fortune," Paul said.

"Actually, I bought it on the courthouse steps for next to nothing."

"Really?" Anna asked, "How long have you lived here?"

"I have lived here for eight years, but bought it ten years ago. Authorities confiscated the property in a major drug bust in 2009; it sat vacant for three years before going up for auction in 2014. Given its history, the considerable amount of work needed to be done, and location, I was the only bidder, so I bought it for next to nothing." Paxx sat back as she looked around the bright space.

"What all did you have to do to get it livable?" Paul asked.

Paxx smiled as she began the story. "I figured I would have it torn down and build a small cabin. I brought in an inspector to evaluate it, and he told me the structure was solid, but it needed to be completely renovated. So, I hired a crew to strip it down to the studs. When they finished, you could stand at the front door and see the back pasture."

"Wow, do you have pictures?" Anna asked.

"In one of the spare bedrooms," Paxx sighed as she stood. "Come on," she said, leading them from the living room down the hall. Opening a door, she brought them into a roomy spare bedroom. "This is a picture of the original house," she explained, pointing to a framed photo on the wall. Then pointing to another large frame on the wall, this one of a set of blueprints, she added, "And that's the floor plan I designed for the remodel."

"How many square feet is this place?" Paul asked.

"Around three thousand, not including the garage and sunroom additions."

"That's a tremendous amount of work," Paul replied as he studied the blueprints.

"Took two years, all my saved vacation time, and most of my savings."

Looking shocked, Paul asked. "You did all of this yourself?"

Turning and exiting the room, Paxx spoke over her shoulder as they returned to the kitchen. "I had help, I hired a plumber and an electrician, and with the help of several friends and friends of friends, we did ninety percent of the interior. After two years, several calls for favors, and several favors done, it was finally finished."

Paxx caught Anna's mischievous grin. "Favors?"

Catching her meaning, Paul picked up Embry. "I'm going to give Em her bath so you ladies can discuss favors."

Paxx and Anna laughed as he rolled his eyes and left the room.

"So, tell me about the favors."

"Would you mind if I told you all the smutty details in the morning? I'm exhausted."

"Of course not, but I want all the juicy details in the morning over coffee."

"You got it," Paxx smiled as she excused herself and made her way upstairs.

? ? ?
SIX

S he winced with each step up the stairs, her hand pressing against her side. Once inside her room, she closed the door, undressed, and stood before the full-length mirror hanging on the back of the door.

The soft, dim light illuminated her bruised and swollen midsection. She ran trembling fingers along the edges of the bruises and over the bandage, wincing at the tenderness. Her eyes, once a vibrant shade of blue, now appeared bloodshot and encircled by deep, shadowy rings, a testament to countless sleepless nights steeped in pain and anxiety. Even her ordinarily well-kept short hair had become a tangled, limp mess, needing a trim and a color touch-up.

In the attached bathroom, Paxx turned on the shower and adjusted the water to a warm temperature. After covering her bandage with a waterproof bandage, she stepped under the soothing spray, closed her eyes, and exhaled a ragged breath. Though the warm water provided some relief to her aching body, it couldn't wash away the emotional turmoil that had been building inside her over the past two weeks. Tears streamed down her face, and sobs racked her body as she allowed herself to break down in the solitude of her home. "I guess thinking you're going to die has this effect," she murmured between sobs, desperately trying to piece together the fragmented events that had brought her to this moment.

After her shower, Paxx dried herself, taking special care around her midsection as she dried and redressed the red and swollen incision. Pulling on a pair of lounge pants and a T-shirt, Paxx sat on the edge of her bed and texted Anna.

'Are you busy? Can you come up for a few minutes?'

'Be right there.'

A soft knock on the door pulled Paxx from her thoughts. "Come in."

Anna slipped into the room, her face etched with concern. "Hey, you okay?"

Paxx patted the bed beside her, and Anna sat down, their shoulders brushing against one another. Her friend's comforting warmth made Paxx lean in.

"I... I don't know," Paxx admitted, her voice trembling. "Everything is crashing down on me all at once."

Shifting sideways on the bed, Anna wrapped her arms around Paxx's shoulders, drawing her closer. "I'm here, talk to me."

Once again, emotion overwhelmed Paxx, and she buried her face into Anna's shoulder and cried. Each sob sent a sharp pain through her abdomen.

"I keep replaying it all in my mind. The shooting, the hospital, the fear... Anna, I thought I was going to die."

"I know, sweetie. Paul and I were so scared." Anna murmured, tears streaming down her cheeks as she held Paxx, soothing her with gentle strokes through her damp hair.

Paxx drew in a shaky breath, her fingers clutching Anna's shirt. "I keep seeing him, Anna. The man who... who did this to me. Every time I close my eyes, he's there, his face hidden in shadows."

"You're safe now," Anna murmured, her lips brushing against Paxx's temple. "You're here, you're alive, and you're going to be alright."

Paxx pulled back, in the dim light she could see the worry etched in her friend's features, her brow furrowed with concern. A warmth spread through her chest despite the pain, a warmth she had not felt in years. "Anna, I'm so glad you're here. I've missed you so much. I don't know how I'd get through this without you. You and Paul, you're the only family I have."

"I'm glad I'm here too. This may not be the best time, but I need to talk to you about something."

"Sure, anything."

With a hesitant tone, Anna began, "Paul and I have been talking, and we're considering moving back here."

"Really? When?"

"You would be okay with it?"

"Of course, I would."

"We have a lot to do before we can move. Paul has put in for a position at the county sheriff's office, and..."

"And?"

"I'm pregnant, and I want to work from home," Anna said, placing her hands on her stomach.

Unable to hold back her tears, Paxx looked at Anna with overwhelming joy. "Congratulations! Having you here would make me happier than anything."

"Really?"

"Really, and you can stay here as long as you want. There is an old homesite on the far side of my property. It's only a concrete slab, but it has all the utilities run to it. You can build whatever you want on it, or I can build a small cabin, and you can have this place; it's too big for one person anyway. Or there is a small apartment in the barn loft."

"Slow down, Paxx, we are not coming back to blow up your life."

Taking a deep breath, Paxx looked at Anna. "You would not be blowing up my life; if anything, you would bring some peace and steadiness to it. I want you here. I know we cannot occupy the same space for a long period, but we could make it work for six or eight months. When are you due?"

"December."

"Okay, then we have until November, actually October, if we want to beat the possibility of an early winter to have you settled somewhere."

"Paxx, are you sure?"

Looking into Anna's eyes, Paxx confirmed, "I'm sure."

They embraced once more, crying and laughing at the refreshing feeling of belonging.

"I'm so happy," Paxx declared as she released the embrace.

"Me, too."

"Anna, thank you for listening and being here for me."

"Always. Do you need anything?"

"No, I'm going to call Jaylee."

"Okay, I'll be up in a flash if you need me," Anna said as she opened the door and left.

Paxx picked up her phone from the nightstand and dialed Jaylee's number, sighing as the call went to voicemail. After leaving a brief message, Paxx took two pain pills, slid down, and closed her eyes, only to be startled a few minutes later by the sound of her phone ringing. Without checking who was calling, she pressed the answer button.

"Hello."

"Did I wake you?" Jaylee's soft voice asked.

"It's alright, I'm glad you called."

"How are you feeling?"

"I'm pretty sore; I managed a shower; it's a good thing my hair's short, so it didn't take much to wash it, but raising my arms is a killer." Paxx laughed, then winced at the pain it caused.

A long silence filled the call before Jaylee asked, "Paxxton, what happened?"

"I figured you knew since you had access to my medical records."

"I only get PT orders, not the specific reason patients need it."

Hesitating, Paxx said. "I was shot in the line of duty."

"I thought cops wore bulletproof vests?"

"I was wearing one, the perp shot me in the side where there is little protection."

Paxx could hear Jaylee gasp, and the distinct sound of crying soon filled her ear. "Jaylee."

"Paxxton, I don't..."

"It's okay, Jaylee; being in a relationship with a cop is hard. I understand if it's too much for you." Paxx said, wiping a tear from her cheek as a familiar ache returned to her chest.

"How long have you been a cop?"

"Seventeen years. I have been a narcotics detective for the past eight years."

"Seventeen years. Wow, I haven't even been out of high school that long."

"How old are you?" Paxx asked, realizing their ages had never been discussed.

"Twenty-nine, how old are you?"

"Older than you are," Paxx replied with a sigh.

"You can't be that much older; I'd guess around thirty-two or thirty-three."

"Add another five," Paxx replied, anticipating the inevitable remark about her age and the stresses of her job.

"Well, you are very sexy."

"Thank you, but I saw myself in the mirror this evening, and I am anything but sexy." Paxx laughed before moaning as the pain flared up again.

"There's something I need to tell you, Paxxton."

"Let me guess, I'm too old for you, and my career choice is a problem."

"No, you're not too old for me. Your career choice is scary, but I can handle it."

"Okay," Paxx said, confused.

"My brother is in prison; he is serving a twenty-year sentence for first-degree murder."

"Tell me what happened," Paxx urged when Jaylee fell silent.

"My mom and I came home late from shopping one day. Frank, that was my stepdad, was drunk, and he started hitting my mom, so I called Jasper to help. When Jasper got to the house, Frank was on top of me trying to...anyway, Jasper pulled him off and beat him so severely that he died a few days later in the hospital."

"Jaylee, I'm so sorry," Paxx whispered, tears welling in her eyes.

"My mom and I testified that Jasper was trying to save us, but because he had a record, he ended up in prison. I understand if you want nothing to do with me."

"Jaylee, it doesn't matter to me what's in your past, and your brother saved you and your mom. I want to see you, and I want to have a relationship with you."

"Paxx, I'm worried about you; your breathing sounds labored."

"I've overdone it a little today. You could come over and sleep beside me. Make sure I make it through the night."

"I could, but aren't your brother and sister-in-law staying with you?"

"Yes, but they are downstairs, and it is my house."

"It would be the responsible thing for me to do."

"I would sleep better knowing you were watching over me."

There was a brief silence before Jayle said, "I would hate for you not to rest well."

"Then I will see you in about thirty minutes?"

"About that, do you need me to bring you anything?"

"Just you," Paxx said in her most seductive tone.

"See you soon then," Jaylee replied, and the call ended.

Pulling up Anna's name on her phone, Paxx sent her a text message.

Jaylee is coming over; please send her up when she arrives.

Paxx watched the three dots as they showed Anna was typing a reply.

'Is everything alright?'

'It hurts to breathe; she is worried. I'm sure it's from moving around more today than I have in over two weeks.'

'Okay, I will send her up, but please be careful.'

Paxx smiled at Anna's implication.

'We are not going to have sex.' Paxx replied with a smiley face emoji.

'Okay, if you say so.'

???

SEVEN

Paxx drifted in and out of sleep until she heard her bedroom door open.

"Are you awake?" Jaylee whispered as she stepped into the room.

"Not really."

Paxx could hear Jaylee undressing, and a smile spread across her face as Jaylee slipped under the covers and turned to face her.

"Hi," Jaylee breathed.

"Hi."

"How are you doing?"

"I'm tired and sore. The pain meds don't seem to help much."

"Have you tried applying heat or ice?" Jaylee suggested, running her hand down Paxx's arm before placing it tenderly on her side.

"No, honestly, I've been pretty emotional, so I wanted to lie down for a bit," Paxx sighed, tucking a stray lock of hair behind Jaylee's ear while her thumb caressed her cheek. "You're so beautiful."

Jaylee moved closer, pressing her body against Paxx. "Is this alright?"

"Yes," Paxx affirmed as she met Jaylee's lips in a soft kiss. "Is that okay?"

"Yes, but that is all we can do; I don't want to hurt you."

Paxx smiled against Jaylee's lips, igniting a warmth within her that momentarily distracted her from the dull ache in her body. "I could get used to this."

"Don't push it, okay? I'd hate to be the reason you end up back in that hospital bed."

"I promise. You being here makes everything feel better."

They lay together for a while, enjoying the closeness. Paxx focused on the steady rhythm of Jaylee's breathing, a calm, grounding beat amid the surge of pain rushing through her body.

"Tell me something," Jaylee whispered, breaking the silence, "What made you want to become a cop?"

"My dad was a cop and always pushed my brother to follow in his footsteps. When I mentioned I wanted to be an officer, maybe even a detective, he said that women had no business wearing a badge."

"Paxx, I'm so sorry."

"You called me Paxx."

"I guess I did," Jaylee replied with a chuckle. "So, you joined to spite him?"

"In a sense, yes. When I was seventeen, I came out to my parents; they were less than thrilled. My dad had been abusive toward my mom most of my life, mostly mentally and emotionally, but he would hit her occasionally. Once Paul turned fifteen, he grew a foot and put on muscle from playing football, so he started stepping in when dad would drink too much." Paxx closed her eyes, deciding whether to confide in Jaylee things that very few people knew.

Jaylee sensed Paxx's hesitation. "You can trust me, Paxx; I want to know you, all of you."

"Paul was out with friends the night I came out, so he wasn't there when my dad entered my room after I'd gone to sleep. He was drunk, and as he yanked the covers off my bed and started unbuckling his belt, he said, 'I'm going to show you what women are supposed to like.' He held me down while he tried to..." She paused, closing her eyes against the memory. "Luckily, he was too drunk to get it up; he tried to touch me instead, but I fought him off."

"Paxx, I'm so sorry," Jaylee whispered, wiping a tear from Paxx's cheek.

"He tried again a week later, but I kneed him in the groin, and after he left my room, he brutally beat my mom. Three days later, she packed up and left, and divorced him six months later. I haven't talked to or seen her since." Paxx turned, lying on her back, staring at the ceiling. "From that moment, I decided I'd become the best cop and detective I could, no matter the sacrifices or the cost."

"I'm sorry about your mom. I'm not that close with my mom, but I know she's there if I need her," Jaylee said, propping herself up on her elbow as she looked into Paxx's eyes.

Paxx shrugged, the pain in her heart worse than it had been in a while.

"You must have seen some horrible things on the job," Jaylee murmured, steering the conversation away from Paxx's mom.

"Yeah, there are things I wish I could unsee, but saving someone or giving them hope makes it worthwhile."

Jaylee nestled closer, resting her head on Paxx's shoulder. "I get that. Sometimes it feels like the world's burden is too heavy, and people need someone to lean on," she whispered, absently caressing Paxx's breasts through her shirt.

"If you keep doing that, I am going to return the favor," Paxx whispered as she turned back on her side, placing her hand on Jaylee's chest.

Jaylee's breath caught at the touch. "Maybe we could just explore one another," she whispered against Paxx's lips while moving her hand lower.

"I will caution you that what lies below my waist is very eager for you, but keep going,"

"Me too."

Paxx's hand trailed down Jaylee's shirt, coming to rest on her hip and pulling her closer.

Jaylee's breathing faltered when Paxx's hand slid beneath her shirt, fingers gently exploring the contours of her toned abs. They lingered momentarily at her belly button ring before moving up to her chest, where Paxx's thumb lightly grazed the ring on her nipple.

"Aren't you full of surprises?" Paxx whispered against her ear. "I want to see you."

Jaylee sat up and with trembling hands, pulled her shirt over her head. Her chest heaved as she tried to slow her breathing, while Paxx's eyes roamed over every inch of her upper body. The hunger in Paxx's eyes excited her.

Paxx gasped as soft moonlight filtered through the window, casting a gentle glow on Jaylee's milky white skin accented by light freckles. Her thick red hair cascaded over her tattooed shoulder, partially veiling one of her firm, ample breasts, the silver nipple ring catching the light with each rise and fall of her chest. Paxx didn't rush to touch her; instead, she let her eyes savor every detail of Jaylee's exquisite form before cupping one of her breast. "I was wrong, you're not beautiful; you're absolutely gorgeous."

Jaylee's heart raced at the weight of Paxx's words, the sincerity in her tone sending a shiver straight to her core. "You think so?"

"I don't think it; I know it," Paxx replied, her thumb brushing across Jaylee's sensitive skin. "You are the most beautiful woman I have ever seen. You're a work of art."

With a sly smile, Jaylee leaned in closer. "You're not so bad yourself," she murmured, letting her hand glide along Paxx's side. "I could give you more of an honest opinion if I could see more of you." She could feel the tension in Paxx's muscles, a mix of excitement and uncertainty, as she helped her pull her shirt over her head.

Paxx caught Jaylee's gaze as she gasped at the bruising and swelling covering her stomach.

"Paxx, you're absolutely stunning," she whispered as she ran her fingers lightly over Paxx's stomach before leaning down to press soft kisses along her abdomen.

"Jaylee," Paxx whispered, her voice catching as the warmth of Jaylee's lips sent shivers dancing down her spine. "I..."

Before she could finish, Jaylee pulled back, her eyes searching Paxx's. "What is it?"

Paxx hesitated, battling the swirl of emotions that threatened to overwhelm her. "I've never let anyone get this close before."

The vulnerability in her tone was unmistakable, as her defenses quivered on the verge of collapse. Jaylee knew Paxx was not referring to a physical closeness as she eased herself out of the warm blankets, her bare feet padding across the cool hardwood floor. She made her way to the other side of the bed, crawling underneath the covers until she was next to Paxx. She cuddled against Paxx's back, wrapping an arm around her and drawing their bodies together, feeling the gentle rhythm of Paxx's breathing against her breasts as they pressed against her back. The curve of Paxx's hips fit perfectly into hers. "Let's just be close tonight." She whispered as she settled a hand on Paxx's breast. She smiled at its softness and weight, delighting in the tender sensation as she cupped it.

Paxx leaned back into her embrace, savoring the delicate contact. "You are driving me crazy."

"Good," Jaylee replied before trailing tender kisses along Paxx's neck and shoulder.

"Thank you for being here."

"There is no place I would rather be."

Paxx felt warmth bloom inside her from Jaylee's words, but as she closed her eyes and slipped into sleep, she held onto her doubts; they were shields forged from past hurts, and she wasn't sure she was ready to cast them aside yet.

???
EIGHT

A s they had over the past two weeks, vivid and haunting dreams of Mr. Black tormented Paxx as she slept. This time, she found herself standing at her father's casket, staring down at his lifeless body. Suddenly, his eyes flew open, meeting hers with a cold, empty gaze as he warned, "Mr. Black will come for you." Gasping, Paxx jolted awake, sitting up with tears streaming down her cheeks.

"It's okay, Paxx, you're okay, I'm here," Jaylee's soothing voice reached Paxx's ears as she wrapped her arms around her trembling body.

Paxx shivered uncontrollably, feeling as if the temperature in the room had plummeted. As quickly as Jaylee appeared, she was gone, only to return a moment later with a shirt. She guided Paxx's arms into the sleeves and pulled it over her head before sitting beside her on the bed. "Paxx, honey, talk to me."

"He killed my dad," Paxx choked out through sobs, leaning into Jaylee.

Jaylee wrapped her arms around Paxx, trying to be gentle. The warmth of her embrace steadied the tremors racing through Paxx's body.

The remnants of the dream clung to Paxx as reminders of her father, and the dark figure haunted her thoughts.

"Take a deep breath, in and out, nice and slow," Jaylee whispered, brushing a stray lock of hair from Paxx's face.

"It hurts," Paxx admitted as she held a hand to her chest, trying to focus on the rhythm of her breathing. "I can't shake it off. It felt so real," she murmured, her voice muffled against Jaylee's shoulder.

"You're safe now. Do you want to talk about it?"

Paxx nodded her head, motioning for Jaylee to lie beside her. Once they were facing each other, Paxx shared the details of her nightmare. "The man who shot me...he told me he's the one who killed my dad two years ago."

"Oh my god, Paxx."

"I'm sorry," Paxx whispered, pulling away.

"Sorry for what?"

"I'm not this person," Paxx blurted out in frustration. "I'm strong and resilient, and I don't break down and get scared by dreams."

Cupping Paxx's cheek in her hand, Jaylee met her eyes with understanding. "Paxx, the same man who confessed to killing your father, shot you, and you almost died. It's okay not to be okay."

"I feel like I've dragged you into a hornet's nest filled with all my drama and shit."

"You didn't drag me into anything. I met a beautiful, intelligent, strong woman, and it's my choice to be with you. I'm not just here for your sexy body, Paxx; I'm here for your heart."

"My heart is pretty fucking messed up right now."

"I know it is, but that doesn't mean it's not worth it. Paxx, I know you're worth it."

Paxx let the words sink in, the warmth of Jaylee's hand grounding her as the remnants of her nightmare faded. Outside, the first light of dawn crept through the windows, casting a gentle glow across the room.

"I... I don't want to burden you with all of this. You deserve someone whose life isn't chaotic."

"Listen to me, we all have our shit. Yours happens to come with a side of trauma, and I want to help you carry it. I chose to be with you even before I knew everything you were dealing with. Your struggles don't define you, Paxx."

The honesty in Jaylee's eyes made Paxx's chest tighten with emotion. Taking a deep breath, she glanced away, biting her lip as she tried to manage her swirling thoughts. Could she let someone in like this? Wouldn't it push Jaylee away in the end?

"I don't know how to do this," Paxx admitted, vulnerability creeping into her voice.

"Do what?"

"Lean on someone, confide in someone; hell, I don't even know how to be in a relationship that lasts more than a couple of months."

Holding Paxx's hand and intertwining their fingers, Jaylee reassured her, "We will take it one step at a time."

Jaylee pulled Paxx close and wrapped her arms around her, feeling the heat of her body radiating through the thin fabric of her shirt. She could feel Paxx's heartbeat quicken as she pressed their bodies together. Their lips met in a soft, lingering kiss that tasted of desperation and need.

"I have to go to work," Jaylee whispered against Paxx's lips.

"Right now?"

Looking at the clock on the nightstand, Jaylee frowned. "It's six thirty; my first client is at eight. I need to leave in the next thirty minutes."

"Thank you for staying with me last night," Paxx said as she moved her hand over Jaylee's arm, tracing the dark purple dragon sitting on a stack of books tattooed on her arm from her elbow to her shoulder. "This is beautiful, I love dragons."

"Thank you. It was dark last night, so I didn't see the rest of yours."

"Once the bruising on my stomach is gone, you will see them better. I have one on my thigh, but if you touch me there, I won't be able to let you leave."

"Can I see it? I promise I won't touch."

"Not yet; it goes with the one on my stomach. It loses some of its flair by itself."

"Well, the ones on your arms are gorgeous," Jaylee complimented as she ran her fingers over the bold-colored multiple rose and vine tattoo that covered the upper half of Paxx's left arm.

"I dated a tattoo artist about eight years ago for a short while; she gave me my first tattoo as a gift."

"Wow, this is some gift."

"That wasn't my first one."

"What was your first?"

Lying back, Paxx lifted her shirt to reveal a tattoo between her breasts, a heart pierced by a sword, with bright red droplets of blood running from the blade's tip down her abs, fading into the dark bruises.

"I didn't see this last night," Jaylee said, moving to touch it. Paxx pulled her shirt down, covering it before she made contact. "If you touch me there, I will come undone. I am so turned on right now."

Jaylee's breath caught in her throat at Paxx's admission, a mix of surprise and exhilaration coursing through her. She leaned closer, her voice low. "What if I want to see you come undone?"

"You're playing with fire, you know."

"Maybe I like the heat," Jaylee replied, smirking as she let her fingers dance along Paxx's arm again. Each touch felt electric, igniting the air between them.

"You'd better go before we start something we can't finish," Paxx murmured reluctantly, brushing her thumb over Jaylee's cheekbone.

After one last lingering kiss that burned on their lips and left a sense of longing behind, Jaylee slipped away from Paxx's embrace and dressed.

Paxx watched each slow movement, frowning as Jaylee covered more and more of her well-toned body. "You're driving me crazy."

"Good, then you will want me to come back." Jaylee smiled as she pressed another kiss to Paxx's lips before turning away from her.

As she reached for the door handle, she turned back one last time, a silent promise hanging between them that this wasn't over.

"Can I call you between clients?" Jaylee asked as she opened the door.

"Of course," Paxx replied with a smile.

As the door closed behind Jaylee, Paxx lay back on the pillow, her head and heart spinning in joy and dread. "What are you doing, Paxx?" she muttered as she crawled out of bed. Turning on the shower, she pulled off her shirt and stepped under the spray, turning it to its coldest position. "This is not a good idea, not now," she chastised herself.

After the cold water had dulled the burning heat between her thighs, she adjusted the temperature to warmer. Once out of the shower, she brushed her teeth, changed into loose sweats and a T-shirt, and headed downstairs for coffee.

？ ？ ？
NINE

A s Paxx descended the stairs, the aroma of coffee wafted through the air. She found Anna already in the kitchen, leaning against the counter with a steaming mug in her hands.

"Good morning." Anna greeted Paxx as she entered the kitchen.

"Morning," Paxx replied with a smile.

"So, tell me about last night, I heard Jaylee leave a bit ago."

Paxx shrugged. "It was nice to have her here; she calms me."

"And?"

"And nothing; we talked and slept."

"Paxx."

"We talked and slept topless, but nothing happened. I am way too sore to receive any, and she deserves my very best, and I hurt too much to give it right now. So, nothing happened."

"Give it time; you will be fit as a fiddle before you know it," Anna chirped, handing Paxx a cup of steaming coffee.

"Anna, I really like her, but I'm not sure if now is the right time to start something with her. I don't just want to have sex with her. We have a connection unlike anything I have ever felt. I'm tired of one-night stands and coyote mornings; I want something that lasts, and I want to be with someone who means something." Paxx sighed as she sat at the table, wrapping her hands around the warm cup.

When Anna didn't respond, Paxx looked up and saw tears streaming down her cheeks.

"Anna."

"Paxx, I have never heard you talk about settling down. Being in a committed relationship is a big step for you, and I am so happy for you."

"I'm not saying I want to get married, but I do want to build something real with one person." She recalled the heat of Jaylee's skin, the undeniable spark that deepened with every moment spent together. Yet, doubts still lingered. "Jaylee feels... different." Paxx whispered, "I need to figure out if I'm ready for this." Paxx sipped her coffee, savoring the warmth as it spread through her.

Silence settled over them as Paxx processed that thought, the caffeine warming her from the inside out while the icy tendrils of doubt melted away a little more with each passing second.

"Don't overthink it; take it as slow as you need to. But you need to talk to her honestly about your wants and fears. Be honest about your job and everything," Anna said, gesturing toward Paxx's injury. "By the way, I set my computer up in your office to finish some work this morning and saw your whiteboard. Are you going to tell Paul that you have been investigating your dad's death for the past two years?"

"You didn't tell him about it?"

"It's not for me to tell. Paxx, I realize we haven't seen each other in almost ten years and haven't talked as often as we should have, but you can still trust me. You never stopped being my best friend. You can still confide in me. I will always keep your secrets."

"I have missed you so much, Anna," Paxx said through tears. "You have never betrayed my trust, and you kept my secret about being gay for two years before I came out, and after I told my parents, you were there for me in the brutal aftermath. You have always been and will always be my best friend, no matter the distance and no matter how much or little we talk." Paxx said as she stood and embraced her. "I love you, and I always will."

"I love you, too, sweetie, and I am so glad I'm here. We still need to talk about that whiteboard in your office, but first, you promised me smutty details about the remodel."

Refilling their coffee cups, they sat at the table, and Paxx picked up where she had left off last night, leaving little to the imagination.

"So, the house has been christened from the studs to the last picture hanging on the wall." Paxx laughed. "The upstairs is the only untouched part of the house."

"Really?"

"I like my space to be my space, uninhabited by anyone but me."

"And Jaylee?"

"We didn't have sex, but she is the first woman to be in my bed." Paxx felt heat rise in her cheeks as she spoke.

"Paxxton Rae Algatta, are you blushing?"

The heat in Paxx's cheeks intensified as she looked away. "Maybe," she admitted, trying to hide a smile behind the rim of her coffee cup. The warmth of the brew on her lips was comforting, yet the blush was a vivid reminder of how Jaylee made her feel. Setting her cup down, Paxx bit her lip, the memory of Jaylee's kiss stirring butterflies in her stomach. "I... I haven't felt this way about anyone in...well, ever. Anna, it scares me."

"You're allowed to feel scared, Paxx. It means you care. You've built so many walls for so long; it's time they start coming down."

Paxx looked into Anna's eyes, searching for reassurance. "It feels different. Like there's something real between us, and that's terrifying."

"That makes it worth pursuing! Real connections are rare and precious. Take your time, be honest, and let it unfold naturally." Anna replied, reaching across the table to squeeze Paxx's hand. "Don't let fear deter you from exploring something potentially amazing."

As they sat and chatted about everything from their past to current events, Paxx felt herself relaxing into the moment. Laughter filled the kitchen as they shared stories and teased each other until they were both ready for a coffee refill.

With their mugs filled and their spirits lifted, they returned to the table and settled. The atmosphere shifted when Paxx brought up the whiteboard again.

"Hey, what do you think I should do about Paul?"

"Well... honesty is always the best policy, right?"

"I guess so," Paxx replied. Deep down, she knew she needed to tell him, but feared how he would react.

"Paxx, maybe he can help."

"Yeah." Paxx stared into her coffee cup as if seeking answers in its depths.

"Paxx, you need answers; you both need answers, especially now. You deserve to live your life without fear."

As they sat, the front door opened, and an excited Embry toddled into the kitchen. "Momma, Momma, donuts!" she squealed as she climbed onto Anna's lap.

"You got donuts?" Paxx laughed as she absorbed Embry's excitement.

Embry nodded as she pointed her little hand toward her daddy. "Daddy, donuts."

"Can Aunt Paxx have a donut?" Paxx asked.

She nodded as she met Paxx's eyes and smiled. "Paxx donut."

Tears came to Paxx's eyes as she stared at Embry's bright, cheerful face. "You are the prettiest thing I have ever seen," Paxx whispered as she held out her hands.

"Can you sit on Aunt Paxx's lap and eat your donut?" Anna asked Embry, who hesitated at Paxx's invitation.

With a nod, she climbed off her mother's lap and walked over to Paxx, holding her arms up. Paxx looked at Anna, knowing she couldn't lift her. "Let momma help you," Anna said as she stood and picked Embry up, setting her on Paxx's legs. "You have to sit still, okay."

Embry nodded as she patted the table with her hands. Paul set out paper plates and donuts in front of them, and Paxx laughed when Embry offered her the first bite.

After taking a small bite of Embry's chocolate donut, Paxx moaned in gratitude. "That is yummy, Embry. Thank you."

Embry giggled as she took a bite of her donut, mimicking Paxx's moan. "Yummy," she squealed.

After finishing their donuts and coffee, Anna picked Embry off Paxx's lap and carried her to the bathroom to wash the chocolate off her hands and face.

"Paul, she's precious." Paxx gushed.

"Maybe you should think about having one."

Paxx shook her head. "No, thank you. I am not built to be a parent; I will enjoy being an aunt, though."

"What if…"

"Don't even say it, Paul."

Holding up his hands in surrender, Paul laughed. "I want to talk to you about something," he said, turning serious.

"Yeah, me too, you first."

"Anna talked to you last night about our moving here?"

A broad smile brightened Paxx's face. "Yes, she did."

"Are you okay with that?"

"Of course, I am."

As Anna returned to the kitchen, and with a triumphant tone, Anna declared, "I told you she'd be thrilled."

"Yes, you did, my love."

Turning his gaze to Paxx, Paul asked. "Now, what did you want to talk to me about?"

"Let me show you," Paxx replied as she stood and motioned for him to follow. Entering her home office, Paxx pulled the 3 X 6 whiteboard away from the wall.

Paul gasped at the information covering the surface: suspects' names, locations, timelines, speculations, and theories laid out in extensive detail.

"Paxx, I thought you didn't know much about Dad's murder. How long have you known about Mr. Black's involvement?"

"To anyone outside this house, I don't, and I wasn't a hundred percent sure until I got shot, and he told me," She confided. "I'm a detective, Paul, and so are you. Are you saying you haven't been searching for answers?"

Paul looked at her; the sudden fear in his eyes made Paxx shiver. "If you have put all of this together, I'm not sure you getting shot by Mr. Black is just a coincidence."

Paxx felt the weight of Paul's words settle in the air. She swallowed hard, her heart racing. "What do you mean by that?"

Paul took a step closer, and his brows knitted together. "I'm saying Mr. Black must know you are onto him."

"Why would he come after me? I barely have any concrete evidence."

"You've got more than enough here to raise suspicions, more than Dad's partner has. If Black realized you're on his trail..." His voice trailed off, leaving the implication hanging in the air.

Paxx inhaled sharply, her mind racing through every conversation she had eavesdropped on, every unguarded moment she'd observed over the past two years. "I can handle this, Paul," she insisted, her voice firmer than she felt. "I've been doing the legwork for over a year, and I won't back down."

Paul crossed his arms over his chest, frustration flickering in his eyes. "It's not about backing down, Paxx! It's about being smart!" He continued to look over the board. "These names, I recognize some of these. Ian, you think Dad's partner might be involved?"

Paxx glanced over the whiteboard filled with notes and half-formed thoughts and fell silent for a beat before speaking again. "I think it is a possibility; Paul, think about it. Ian and Dad were the only two on that side of the building when Dad was shot. Ian said Dad was barely hanging on when he found him. I looked at the autopsy report; Dad's injuries were severe, but had he gotten to the hospital sooner, he would have lived. Why did it take Ian so long to get to him, to call an ambulance?"

Paul's eyes narrowed as he absorbed her words, the tension in the room thickening. "You're right. If Ian was around when it happened, if he was the only one there besides Black... You think he set Dad up?"

"We can't ignore that possibility, there are too many unanswered questions. And Ian, well, has always been unpredictable. I've seen him act like a friend one moment and like a snake the next."

Paul rubbed the back of his neck, pacing as he processed what she was saying. "If you think this is true, we need to find a way to prove it without putting you in danger."

Anna's voice broke through their conversation. "Hey! You two!" She peeked around the door frame, Embry now asleep in her arms.

"We were just..." Paul stammered.

"I know, I saw it yesterday."

"Why didn't you tell me?"

"Not mine to tell; Paxx needed to be the one to tell you, to ask for your help," Anna replied with a wink in Paxx's direction.

"Are you asking for my help, Paxx?"

"Only if you're willing, but if you believe Black knows I'm investigating and that his shooting me isn't a coincidence, it might not be safe for you to get involved," Paxx said, her tone solemn as she shifted her gaze between him and Anna.

"Let Anna and I discuss it and mull it over for a bit," Paul replied, looking at his wife.

Paxx nodded in acceptance. "Take all the time you need."

The tension in the room eased as they stepped away from the whiteboard. Paxx felt a mix of relief and anxiety, relief at sharing her investigation with Paul, but anxiety about what this could mean for all of them.

"Let's take a break from this for now," Anna suggested. "Why don't we go sit on the porch? It's a beautiful morning."

Paxx nodded gratefully, following Paul and Anna out of the office. The warm sunlight and gentle breeze helped calm her nerves as they settled into the porch chairs. They sat in comfortable silence for several moments, each lost in their thoughts.

After about thirty minutes, Embry began stirring, and Paul stood and stretched. "Anna, we need to run some errands."

Looking at her watch, Anna agreed.

Paxx stood and followed them into the house. "I need to go upstairs and spend at least twenty minutes on the treadmill. I have to regain my strength so I can return to work."

"Don't overdo it," Anna said as Paxx walked past.

"I won't."

? ? ?

TEN

After a thirty-minute stretching session, Paxx panted heavily and grumbled about the treadmill's sluggish speed.

"I brought you some water," Anna announced from the doorway.

Stepping onto the sides of the treadmill, Paxx pressed the end button on the display. "Thank you," Paxx replied, taking the bottle. "You weren't gone long."

"We had a quick errand to run. Are you doing okay?"

Paxx nodded as she took a long drink from the water bottle. "I only managed twenty minutes." She winced as she pressed a hand to her heaving chest.

"It will take some time to rebuild your strength and stamina," Anna said, looking around the large room full of various workout machines and weights. "This is amazing."

"It's my favorite room in the house and you are welcome to use it anytime you want."

"Thank you, I have missed going to the gym since we arrived."

"I don't like gyms; too much scrutiny and judgment," Paxx remarked with a smirk.

"Please, you're gorgeous and in great shape."

"I work hard to keep this body in shape, and once the guys find out I have no interest in them, it's no longer enjoyable."

"I can see that happening," Anna shrugged. After a moment, she asked, "Have you heard from Jaylee?"

"Not yet. My phone is in the bedroom; this is a phone-free zone to avoid distractions."

"That's a good policy to have. I think I'll try to squeeze in a workout while Embry is napping."

"Bring up the baby monitor so you can hear her if she wakes," Paxx advised, settling herself at the leg press machine.

"Paul is reading in the bedroom. He will get her if she wakes up, but I need to change clothes. I think I brought some shorts." Anna said as she turned to leave.

"Get some of mine; we are still the same size."

"We are not the same size; I had a baby at thirty-six, and now I am three months pregnant with another."

"You are still the sexiest girl I have ever met." Paxx winked.

"Sexier than Jaylee?"

"Okay, you are tied for the sexiest girl I have ever met."

"I am honored to be in league with her; she is smoking hot," Anna said as she wiped her brow and fanned her face.

"Yes, she is."

Paxx struggled through light leg exercises for the next ten minutes while Anna ran on the treadmill.

"I need a shower," Paxx said, standing up and wiping the sweat from her brow.

"I'm going to do another half mile," Anna said, barely winded.

"Take all the time you need, and by the way, those shorts look really good on you," Paxx said with a sly smile as she left the room and walked across the hall to her bedroom. Once inside, she closed the door, stripped off her clothes, and headed to the bathroom, grabbing her phone off the dresser as she went. After turning on the shower, she looked at her phone and saw a missed call and message from Jaylee and a missed call from Rowan.

Pulling up the message from Jaylee, she frowned when she read it.

'Is everything alright? I hope I didn't make you uncomfortable last night or this morning.'

Before responding, she listened to her phone message.

"Hey, gorgeous. I wanted to call to say hi and see how you're feeling. I enjoyed staying with you last night, and I hope we can do it and more again soon. Call me back."

Looking at the time of the call and the time of the message, Paxx understood why Jaylee was worried. How had she not noticed her call come in three hours ago? Looking at the side of the phone, she cursed as she pushed up the ringer button. Pulling up Jaylee's number, she called her. After four rings, the call went to voicemail. Instead of leaving a message, Paxx texted her.

'I'm Sorry I missed your call. The ringer on my phone was off, and I just finished a workout. Please call me.'

As she hit send, the phone rang, displaying Jaylee's name.

"Hey," Paxx answered, "I sent you a text."

"Hold on," Jaylee said as the line went quiet. "I'm back; I read your message. I didn't want to come off like a stalker by calling and texting two hours later; I was worried I had done something wrong."

"No, you did everything right. Actually, I...I want to talk to you."

"Okay, is everything alright?"

"Yes, but I don't want to talk over the phone."

"Are you free for dinner? Can I take you out?"

"I would like that. Can you pick me up? I'm not yet cleared to drive".

"Of course. My last client finishes at three, so how about I pick you up around five?"

"Five works; I'm about to step into the shower, so six hours should be plenty of time to make myself somewhat presentable."

"A shower, huh? I wish I were there with you; I could wash your back, among other things."

"You drive me crazy."

"Good, I can't wait to see you, all of you."

"If you keep talking like that, I'm going to take a cold shower."

"It's a good thing I have to meet my next client, but I can't wait to see you."

"Me too. See you at five."

"See you at five," Jaylee confirmed before ending the call. Paxx placed her phone on the vanity and studied her reflection in the mirror above the sink. Although her eyes weren't as bloodshot as they had been the day before, the dark circles beneath them drew a weary sigh from her. Shifting her gaze between the phone and the mirror, she smirked, picked up her phone again, and snapped a photo of the tattoo nestled between her breasts, revealing just enough cleavage to tease.

With a hesitant breath, she sent the image to Jaylee along with the caption, *Just to get you by.'*

After setting her phone aside, Paxx opened the glass shower door and stepped into the lukewarm spray. Once done, she dried off and picked up her phone. Tapping the message icon, she opened Jaylee's reply.

"Fuck me," Paxx whispered as she looked at the image of a dark-haired, big-busted woman riding a red firework tattoo. The angle of the image left little to the imagination as it showed Jaylee's high inner thigh, with the tip of the firework pointing to the black lace at the crotch of her panties.

Paxx's heart sped up as she gazed at the photo. "She may be more than you can handle, Paxxton Algatta," Paxx whispered to herself as she texted a response.

'You are still full of surprises.'

'I hope I never stop surprising you,' Jaylee responded, punctuating her words with a heart emoji.

'Something tells me you won't,'

'Gotta go, see you soon.'

'See you soon.'

After getting dressed, Paxx went downstairs and heard raised voices coming from the kitchen. As she approached, she recognized the voices of Paul and Rowan, though their conversation was too muffled to decipher.

"What's going on?" she inquired as she entered the room.

Both men fell silent and turned to look at her. "Rowan was asking when you were returning to work," Paul explained, his tone unconvincing. "I told him you're nowhere near ready yet."

Anger flashed in her eyes. "I will decide when I am ready to go back. You weren't talking about that, though."

Rowan raised his hands in a gesture of frustration but remained silent.

Turning away, Paxx entered the living room and settled on the couch. She grabbed a book from the side table and pretended to read while listening to Paul and Rowan's lingering voices. After a few minutes, Rowan entered the living room and sat in the chair across from her.

"How are you feeling?"

"Still sore. What have you found out?"

"Captain Kimble made me step away and told me to let special crimes handle it."

"What?" Paxx growled. "Have you talked to anyone there? Who caught the case? Do they have any leads?"

"Thompson and Darby caught the case, and I haven't been able to get any information from them." Rowan spat. "I have been trying to locate the informant who gave me the bad intel about the warehouse."

Paxx recalled how she and Shannon Darby had met over drinks once. Darby had wanted something more, but Paxx wasn't interested in dating a coworker. She liked Darby, and she thought she was sexy as hell, but just because the woman was sexy didn't mean Paxx was going to sleep with her.

Studying Rowan's face, Paxx felt a deep-seated skepticism about his honesty. Ever since she'd been shot, a nagging feeling had taken hold; he was clearly hiding something. She scrutinized his expression, noticing a flicker of doubt as he shifted in his seat. Leaning forward, with her arms crossed over her chest and pain still lingering from her injury, she demanded, "You're telling me you haven't been able to get anything? A name? A location?"

Rowan sighed, running a hand through his well-groomed hair. "I'm doing everything I can, Paxx. You know, it's not always simple." He paused, a pained look crossing his features. "Thompson and Darby are keeping quiet; they've got strict orders."

Uncrossing her arms, Paxx leaned back against the back of the couch, her gaze fixed on Rowan's tense posture. "You've been working with Thompson and Darby for years. They trust you. Why can't you get anything out of them?"

Rowan ran a hand through his hair again, frustration etched across his face. "The higher-ups don't want us poking around, and I don't want to ruffle any feathers when things are already shaky."

"And what about the informant? Any leads?" Paxx muttered, her mind racing as anger boiled inside her.

"Nothing solid yet. He's using his usual ghosting tactics, moving location, and changing phones. It's like trying to catch smoke with your bare hands." He leaned forward, the intensity in his voice palpable. "I will find him."

Paxx nodded, choosing her following words carefully. "Rowan, if there's anything you're holding back, you need to tell me. My life is on the line here."

"I've been reaching out to old contacts, but most of them are either dead ends or too scared to talk." His brow furrowed as if he were weighing what to say next.

"Is there someone you haven't contacted yet? Someone you suspect might know something?" she pressed.

Rowan hesitated before responding, his tone laced with uncertainty. "There's one guy. He's not exactly reliable, but... he might have some info."

Paxx raised an eyebrow skeptically. "Why haven't you reached out to him yet?"

"I wanted to make sure we had something substantial before involving him," he said defensively.

"Fine," she conceded, each word feeling forced. "Just keep me informed."

"You're not cleared for duty yet!" Rowan shot back, locking eyes with her. "I'm not even supposed to discuss this with you!"

"If you were in my position, would you want me to withhold information from you?"

"No."

"Then why are you here?"

"I don't know," he admitted, frustration mounting in his voice, "Actually, I do know why I'm here, I'm here because I know you; when your partner was shot, you spiraled down so far that for the first six months of me being assigned to you, I was afraid I would find you dead from either drinking too much or something worse. When your dad was shot, you became an unreliable loose cannon again. And because you just got shot!" he snapped back, his frustration exploding. Paxx flinched at the sharpness of his tone. "I refuse to stand by and watch you destroy yourself, your career, or my career chasing after this guy. You need to focus on getting better Paxx before jumping back into danger."

"You don't get to decide that for me, I will not sit around while someone gets away with trying to kill me." She rubbed her temples, trying to quell the headache that was forming behind her eyes. "I won't let this case go cold like my dad's did because you think it's safer."

The tension between them crackled like static electricity; Rowan stood up and turned toward the kitchen. "I'll see what I can find out," he said over his shoulder, sounding defeated. "Paxx...promise me you won't do anything reckless while you're healing. I can give you updates but let me handle it for now."

She hated being sidelined, and unanswered questions and uneasy thoughts gnawed at her insides.

Before Rowan took two more steps, Paul entered the room and surveyed them both with a raised eyebrow. "You two, okay? You looked like you were about ready to throw punches just now."

Paxx shot him a look that said more than words ever could; she wasn't in the mood for anyone else's opinions right now.

"We're fine," Rowan stated while gesturing at Paxx with an exaggerated flair, as if handing the baton of responsibility over to Paul.

Paul frowned but didn't press further; instead, he leaned against the doorframe with arms crossed.

"I'll call you when I have some information," Rowan said as he opened the front door and walked out.

Once Rowan was gone, Paul asked. "Are you alright?"

"He's hiding something," Paxx replied, meeting Paul's gaze. "What were you two really talking about?"

"He doesn't want you digging into this," Paul admitted as he sat in the chair Rowan had vacated. "Wants me to steer you away, keep you out of it."

"I guess he doesn't know me as well as he thinks he does," Paxx smirked.

"No Paxx, he does know you and that's why he's worried."

Paxx offered a small smile that didn't quite reach her eyes. "I have you and Anna here, hopefully for a very long time. You two will keep me in check."

"We'll sort everything out in the next few days. And yes, we'll make sure you stay in line." Paul stood up and asked, "Do you want a sandwich?" as he walked toward the kitchen.

"That sounds good, thank you," Paxx replied, laying her head back on the seat and closing her eyes, trying to calm herself. Her phone rang from the table beside her, interrupting her thoughts. She reached for it with shaky fingers and saw another message from Jaylee.

'Can't stop thinking about you.'

Paxx hesitated before responding, weighing her options. She knew she had to make a tough decision. Her fingers trembled as she typed the words, unable to shake off her intense attraction towards Jaylee.

'Me too. Especially after your last photo.'

After a moment's hesitation, she added another message.

'Can I take a rain check tonight? I'm not feeling up to going out.'

'Are you okay? Is your pain getting worse?'

Paxx sighed. Her reluctance to hurt Jaylee and put her in danger while tracking the shooter weighed heavily on her. After deleting three different drafts, all of which felt cold and dismissive, Paxx finally settled on a response:

'I need some time. I'm sorry.'

'No, I'm sorry, I moved too fast.'

Reading Jaylee's words filled Paxx with a sadness that brought tears to her eyes.

'You did nothing wrong. This is all on me and my need to find the person who shot me. I don't want to endanger you.'

She hit send before she could second-guess herself.

"Here you go," Paul said, breaking her out of her thoughts as he returned with two plates, setting one on the coffee table in front of her. "Are you alright?" he asked, noticing the tears in her eyes.

Paxx wiped away a stray tear and nodded. "I'm fine," she whispered as she picked up her sandwich. "Thank you." She took a bite, trying to push away the heaviness in her chest.

ELEVEN

Paul and Paxx ate in the quiet of the living room. Relief spread through them when Anna and Embry entered, breaking the silence. Paxx's heart ached with a tinge of sadness at the thought that she had missed the first two years of her niece's life. But joy quickly replaced any sadness as Embry bypassed her father and made a beeline for her.

Embry reached out her arms towards Paxx, demanding to be picked up. Anna chuckled as she lifted Embry and placed her on Paxx's lap.

"Hey, sweet girl," Paxx said happily.

The toddler pointed at Paxx's plate, which was almost empty except for a few leftover chips. "Want!"

Paxx glanced at Anna and Paul for approval before picking up a chip and offering it to Embry. The toddler shook her head and pushed Paxx's hand towards her mouth. "Eat," she commanded with a giggle.

Remembering their game from earlier that day, Paxx took a bite of the chip and exclaimed, "Yummy!" before offering the rest to Embry, who eagerly took a bite. This time, however, Embry's green eyes widened in surprise at the unexpected tangy flavor of salt and vinegar.

Undeterred, Paxx grabbed another chip and repeated the process. Embry took another bite and grimaced, but this time, she excitedly exclaimed, "Yummy!"

They all laughed as Embry ate two more chips, each followed by a grimace and a happy squeal.

"You ready for some lunch, little one?" Paul asked as he stood and took Embry from Paxx.

While Paul took Embry to the kitchen, Anna sat beside Paxx. "What's wrong?"

Paxx shook her head. "Nothing."

"Come on, Paxx; you can't hide things from me. Tell me what's going on."

Unable to speak, Paxx handed Anna her phone after scrolling past the revealing pictures.

After reading the messages between her and Jaylee, Anna said, "Paxx, you can't stop living just because you got shot. You should embrace the chance to be with someone who is obviously crazy about you." Anna gasped as she scrolled the message up before Paxx could stop her. "Nice tattoos, both of you," she teased with a wink.

Swiping her phone from Anna's hand, Paxx felt heat rise in her cheeks. "I can't let anything happen to her," Paxx replied, not addressing the tattoo comment. "If I don't walk away now, I may not be able to if things get bad."

Turning sideways, Anna replied, "Sweetie, I know we haven't seen each other in person for several years, and when we talk on the phone, it hasn't been about intimate things for a while. But I know you, and the way you talked about her this morning and the look on your face now shows that Jaylee means something to you. Paxx, don't let that bastard win by taking away the best thing that has ever happened to you."

Wiping away tears, Paxx leaned her head back, "Anna, I feel broken and vulnerable; this," she pressed a hand to her chest, "this is not me, these feelings, I don't get these feelings. I have always been a hard ass, and I know it. I have purposefully kept myself out of relationships. Hell, I'm the fucking queen of one-night stands and quickies in a bar bathroom. I don't know how to feel this way."

Paxx's confession did not surprise Anna. "Have you told her that?"

"Not the part about the one-night stands and bar antics, but I did tell her I didn't know how to have a relationship."

"What did she say?" Anna pressed.

With another sigh and the wiping of more tears, Paxx answered, "She said we would take it one day at a time."

Anna smiled and kissed Paxx on the cheek. "Then don't give in to fear, Paxx. Take it one day at a time. As I mentioned this morning, be truthful with her."

As Paxx accepted Anna's hug, Embry raced back into the living room and patted her legs. "Play"

"Yes, sweet girl, let's play," Paxx replied as she carefully slid off the couch onto the floor.

For the next forty-five minutes, Paxx and Embry sat on the floor and played with blocks and dolls until Paxx was so sore she could not get up. "Sweetie, Aunt Paxx needs to lie down for a bit."

Embry stood and walked over to the couch and patted a cushion. "Night, night!"

With Anna's help, Paxx stood and then lay on the couch, picking up the TV remote off the end table.

"Want to watch cartoons?" Paxx asked as Embry climbed onto the couch, nestling between her legs.

"Coco!" Embry squealed, clapping her hands in delight.

Paxx gave Anna a puzzled look as she turned on the TV. Taking the remote, Anna punched in the show name and pressed play. Paxx couldn't help but smile as she watched Embry's excitement.

<hr>

P axx woke up drenched in sweat, her chest heavy and her ribs and stomach aching. Opening her eyes, she smiled at Embry, asleep on her chest with sweat dampening her hair. "You're a little heater," Paxx whispered, careful not to wake her.

Hearing voices in the kitchen, Paxx covered Embry's exposed ear and called out in a loud whisper, "Anna." After a minute without a response, she called out again, a little louder, "Anna."

Anna emerged from the kitchen doorway, smiling at the sight of the two of them.

"She's like having a heating blanket on my chest," Paxx grinned.

"I know; she can crank out some heat," Anna said as she walked closer.

A movement from the doorway caught Paxx's attention, and she froze as Jaylee entered the living room.

"Hi," Paxx said, surprised.

"Hi," Jaylee responded with a soft smile.

Picking up Embry, Anna said, "I will leave you two to talk," then winked at Paxx before heading off to join Paul in the office.

Grimacing as she sat up, Paxx met Jaylee's gaze. "What are you doing here?"

Nodding toward the office, she replied, "I called while you were asleep, and Anna answered your phone. She invited me for dinner and said you needed to talk to me."

Shaking her head with a smile, Paxx replied, "I need to change my shirt; let's go upstairs."

"Okay," Jaylee said as she offered Paxx her hand.

As they climbed the stairs, Paxx could feel Jaylee's eyes on her back, and the urge to turn around and kiss her was overwhelming. Once they were upstairs, Paxx heard Jaylee close the door behind her.

"Jaylee," Paxx whispered when she felt her step close and wrap her arms around her waist.

"Paxx, talk to me," Jaylee whispered against her neck.

Paxx turned to face her, and they melted into each other's arms without exchanging words.

"I'm so sorry, Jaylee; The last thing I want to do is hurt you."

"Paxx, I am here for you, and I am here with you. Please don't shut me out."

"Jaylee, you don't know me, the danger you may be in by being with me, the danger I am in everyday when I go to work," Paxx said harshly as she turned away.

"Stop," Jaylee demanded sharply.

Paxx stood still, bowing her head and closing her eyes as she fought to remain strong.

"Paxx, look at me."

Paxx didn't move, afraid she would crumble if she turned around.

"Paxx, please look at me."

Taking a deep breath, Paxx slowly turned, tears welling as she met Jaylee's gaze. "Jaylee, I don't know how to..." she began before her voice trailed off.

"How to what, Paxx?"

"How to explain what I feel, what I fear, and who I am?" Paxx whispered, feeling a wave of shame envelop her.

"Just tell me as plainly as you need to and don't overthink it," Jaylee urged, wiping a tear from Paxx's cheek.

"When I texted you and told you I needed time, my heart ached like nothing I have ever felt. The pain in my chest intensifies with the thought of you getting hurt because of me. I don't know how to have a relationship or be with just one person."

"Is that what you want? Is that what your heart wants?"

"If I say yes, will it scare you?"

"Would it scare you if I confessed that I began falling for you the first week after we met?"

The surprise in Paxx's heart showed through her eyes, as she nodded hesitantly.

"Well, then, we are both scared," Jaylee smiled, "But are we more scared of being together or being apart?"

For a long moment, their gazes locked, neither daring to be the first to break the silence. Finally, with a slight nod, Paxx admitted, "Apart, but I have never been," she paused, "I have never been faithful. When I started feeling something for someone, I would fuck it up by sleeping with someone else. I don't know how much I can give you."

Moving closer, Jaylee pressed their lips together. "Paxx, I don't care about your past. I don't want this to end. I only want three things."

"What three things?"

"I want you, I want trust, and I want us," Jaylee replied deepening the kiss.

Paxx fumbled with Jaylee's pants, pushing them down her hips.

Once freed from her pants, forgetting Paxx's injury, Jaylee gripped her hips firmly and pulled her close.

Paxx gasped sharply at the piercing pain, clutching her stomach with one arm and cursing under the strain of fighting back tears.

"Fuck, I'm sorry, Paxx," Jaylee cursed, pressing her hands to her mouth.

"Just give me a minute," Paxx wheezed. "We are going to do this; I want to do this."

"We can't do this yet," Jaylee whispered, her voice full of concern. "I am going to run a bath for you," she said as she as disappeared into the bathroom. Turning the water on she began filling the oversized clawfoot tub with warm water.

"Only if you join me." Paxx grinned as she began undressing, her eyes fixed on Jaylee.

"Of course, I will," Jaylee smiled back, unbuttoning her blouse and letting it and her bra fall to the floor.

After applying a waterproof bandage over Paxx's stitches, Jaylee stepped back to admire Paxx's body, arching an eyebrow at the dragon tail tattoo that trailed from her bruised stomach, wrapping around her thigh several times before ending at her knee. "Stunning," she whispered before stepping into the tub, sighing as the warm water embraced her. Paxx followed suit, settling between Jaylee's legs and leaning back against her chest.

"You are the first person besides me to sit in this tub," Paxx said.

Jaylee's hands roamed over Paxx's toned arms, tracing the defined muscles and tattoos beneath her fingertips. "Really?" she replied, her voice low and husky with desire.

Paxx nodded, turning her head to meet Jaylee's lips in a tender kiss. "You are also the first person to share my bed with me," she whispered. "And hopefully, the first person I make love to in that bed."

Jaylee's heart swelled with Paxx's words as she nuzzled her neck. "You've never had other women here?"

"I have had women here before, but they never came upstairs."

Curious, Jaylee pressed, "May I ask why not?"

"I wanted to save this space for someone special, for me and someone who means something to me."

Realizing the depth of Paxx's words, Jaylee's emotions surged. "I'm honored to be here with you, to be the first," she said, kissing Paxx's neck.

Paxx's voice thinned to a whisper, laden with emotion. "And if I want you to be the only one?"

Running her hands from Paxx's arms down to her thighs, Jaylee whispered. "Then I want to be the only one."

Sitting up, Paxx turned to face Jaylee, guiding her onto her lap.

"Paxx," Jaylee whispered.

"I just want to hold you," Paxx replied, her lips brushing against Jaylee's chin before trailing down to her nipple ring and teasing it with her tongue.

A sharp gasp escaped Jaylee's lips at the sensation. "That really turns me on," she admitted, feeling a surge of desire between her legs.

Paxx smiled against Jaylee's breast before taking it into her mouth again and sucking hard, causing Jaylee to moan with pleasure. "Let me love you," Paxx said, her voice a low growl as she teased Jaylee's nipples with her teeth and tongue and caressed her back, moving lower and lower until she cupped Jaylee's ass in her hands.

Jaylee shook her head, even as her desire grew stronger by the moment. "Not until I can love you back." she sighed as she wiggled out of Paxx's embrace.

Paxx watched her with a blend of astonishment and hunger. "Are you sure?"

"Yes! I'll wait until you heal. But once you're healed, if your brother- and sister-in-law are still here, you're coming to my place."

Paxx's expression shifted from surprise to anticipation. "Oh yeah, why is that?"

Jaylee's smile turned seductive as she replied, "Because I suspect it will be at least another week, probably two, before you are pain free. And in another two weeks, we'll be so wound up that we might not resurface for days". She leaned in closer until their lips were barely an inch apart. "When that time comes, we'll do things to one another that will make our toes curl, and our eyes roll back."

Paxx groaned as she wrapped her arms around Jaylee's waist once more, pressing their bodies together. "Promises, promises," she murmured against Jaylee's lips before capturing them in a burning kiss that ignited a fierce passion within her. The water's warmth enveloped them, but the heat of their connection ignited them. Jaylee melted into her embrace, feeling each pulse of desire as they lost themselves in each other.

Breaking the kiss, Paxx panted against Jaylee's lips, "We should probably get out before my pain is no longer an issue and I can't control myself."

"Agreed," Jaylee replied breathlessly, already yearning for the moment they could fully surrender to their desires.

? ? ?
TWELVE

"Earlier today, you said you had just finished a workout. What gym do you go to?" Jaylee asked as they dressed.

"The gym across the hall." Paxx smiled as she slipped on a pair of socks.

"You have a gym?"

Standing, Paxx opened the bedroom door and motioned for Jaylee to follow her.

Walking across the hall, Jaylee gasped as she entered the large room with multiple workout machines and free weights inside. "This is amazing; the gym I pay out the nose for every month isn't this nice."

"I don't like public gyms, so over the years, I have gradually added equipment until I have everything I want."

"You know, I am a personal trainer specializing in sports injuries. I would be more than happy to help you with your rehab."

"I think that sounds like a wonderful idea," Anna said from the doorway.

Paxx turned and beamed at the two women. "I feel like I am being ganged up on," she laughed. "But yes, I will take all the help I can get to get healed and back on the streets."

"Good," Anna smiled. "Dinner is ready, so come and eat."

As they ate at the large kitchen table, Paxx smiled at Paul, Anna, and Jaylee, enjoying each other's company.

"I heard from the county today," Paul said as he sat back from his plate.

"And?" Paxx asked.

"And I got the job. I start in three weeks."

"Three weeks?" Paxx asked.

"That gives us enough time to return to Chicago, pack the house, and get it on the market." Anna replied.

"That is great," Paxx smiled. "You can store things in the barn loft; it's clean and temperature-controlled; all that's in there are a bunch of boxes filled with Dad's things."

Paul and Anna looked at each other before Paul said, "We found a house and twenty acres a mile away. We put in an offer this morning. We should hear something tomorrow."

Paxx smiled as she processed her emotions. "That's where you went this morning?"

Paul and Anna nodded.

"Good, at least you will be close."

Paul leaned forward, a hint of excitement dancing in his eyes. "It's got a big backyard, perfect for the kids."

"I can finally have that garden I've always wanted!" Anna's enthusiasm was contagious, and Paxx's smile grew even wider.

"Kids?" Jaylee asked, glancing over at Embry.

"Due in December," Anna said with a smile, patting her stomach.

"Congratulations!"

"Thank you,"

"That sounds perfect for you two," Paxx said, her heart swelling with warmth. She loved seeing her brother and Anna so happy.

"Before long, Embry will be riding her bike over to Aunt Paxx's, talking you into all sorts of mischief," Anna laughed.

As laughter filled the kitchen, Paxx gazed out the window at the sunset, painting the sky in shades of pink and orange. She felt a flicker of hope amid the uncertainty of her own journey. Each shared moment with her loved ones seemed to heal the wounds of distance and time, stitching together the frayed edges of her spirit.

As dinner progressed, conversation flowed easily, but Paxx couldn't shake off the heaviness in her chest. They discussed future plans, but she knew deep down the reality of the challenges ahead. The thought of her physical and mental rehabilitation was daunting enough, but what weighed on her mind even more was the possibility of her father's killer, the man who had shot her, walking free once again. Once more, fear pervaded every aspect of her existence.

"Are you alright?" Anna asked as they began cleaning up the dishes.

"I just need a minute," Paxx replied as she stepped outside onto the porch and let the cool evening air envelop her. In the distance, she could hear crickets chirping. Leaning against the railing, she breathed the crisp air, trying to clear her muddled thoughts. The sky had deepened to a dusky purple, and stars were twinkling in the vast expanse above. She took a deep breath, inhaling the scent of mown grass and blooming wildflowers. It was easy to get lost in such beauty, yet her thoughts kept dragging her back to the shadows lurking in her mind.

"Hey," Anna's voice broke through her thoughts as she stepped onto the porch, a concerned expression on her face. "I thought you could use some coffee."

Paxx turned and forced a smile. "Yeah, thank you. I just needed a breather," she said as she took the steaming cup.

Anna leaned beside her, gazing at the horizon and admiring the beautiful sunset. "Talk to me if something is bothering you."

"It's just... everything feels overwhelming," Paxx admitted, glancing sideways at her sister-in-law. "I need answers."

Anna nodded in understanding. "It's okay to feel that way; you're going through a lot."

"I have to catch him and keep us safe," Paxx said, her voice cracking as she spoke.

"Paxx, you're not alone in this fight. We will all face it together; that man has taken so much from you and Paul, but he won't take the strength of our family."

Tears pricked at Paxx's eyes as she absorbed Anna's words. "Thank you."

. "What's going on?" Paul asked as he stepped out onto the porch

"Oh, just girl talk," Anna replied.

Paul raised an eyebrow but didn't press further; instead, he leaned against the railing beside them, his body relaxed but his eyes keenly observant. "I think Jaylee wants to come out and talk to you," Paul said, breaking the silence. "She's lovely, Paxx, and she cares about you."

"I'm glad you both like her," Paxx smiled. "I care about her, too."

"Let's go back in," Anna suggested as she took Paul's hand.

Paul nodded, kissing Paxx on the cheek. "We're here if you need us."

"I know and thank you both for being here and helping me get through this."

Paul and Anna retreated inside, and a moment later, Jaylee's soft voice spoke from behind her. "Hey, gorgeous, what are you thinking about?"

Paxx shrugged. "It's been a long time since I've had family around."

Standing beside her, Jaylee asked, "Are you okay with them moving back?"

"Of course," Paxx smiled as she swept a strand of hair behind Jaylee's ear. "I couldn't be happier."

Seeing the uncertainty in Paxx's eyes, Jaylee asked, "But?"

"I'm not the person I was ten years ago before they left. Not all bad, but not exactly good either."

"I don't know who you were ten years ago, but the person you are now..." Jaylee smiled as she laced their fingers together. "The person you are now is pretty freaking amazing."

"You just think that because you want to use my gym."

"Oh, I want to use something alright, but baby, it's not your gym." Jaylee said with a sly, seductive grin, as she moved closer,

They laughed as their lips met, their passion drawing them close. "Come upstairs," Paxx whispered. "I don't want to wait; I'll be fine."

Jaylee pressed her hips against Paxx's and ground against her. Paxx winced as she stepped back. "You are not fine, and I don't want you back in the hospital. We are going to wait."

"Will you stay? No messing around, I promise."

"I can't tonight, I have to wash my scrubs, and I have an early morning tomorrow. I can be here by four tomorrow, and we can start your rehab."

"That sounds good, but now, can I just hold you for a bit?"

Jaylee wrapped her arms around Paxx's waist, resting her head on her chest, and whispered, "I'd love for you to hold me."

For the next half hour, they stood on the porch, enveloped in each other's arms, exchanging gentle kisses and soft touches.

Once Jaylee left, Paxx lay in bed, staring at the ceiling, reflecting on how much had happened in such a short time. The shadows of uncertainty from her shooting still lingered, threatening to overshadow the joy she felt in moments like tonight. Jaylee's presence, along with Paul and Anna's impending move nearby, offered a glimmer of hope, renewal, and strength.

? ? ?

THIRTEEN

F or the next two weeks, Jaylee showed up every other day to put Paxx through a rigorous, and sometimes painful physical rehab session. Despite the discomfort, Paxx could feel herself growing stronger and more mentally resilient with each passing day. Meanwhile, Paul and Anna had left for Chicago, planning to return within a week to complete the purchase of their new house.

One afternoon, unable to concentrate on the book she was reading and frustrated that Rowan still had provided no leads or updates, Paxx picked up her phone and called Georgetta, a tall, blonde, blue-eyed bombshell who worked in the crime lab. As soon as Georgetta answered, Paxx turned on her seductive charm.

"Hey George, how are you doing?"

"Good. Paxx, is so good to hear your voice. How are you doing, by the way?"

"Slowly healing but making it. Can you tell me what they found on the bullet that shot me?" Paxx asked, jumping right in.

"Paxx, this is not your case, and besides, I'm still mad at you for not calling me."

Paxx cringed at the recollection of one night a few months back after too many drinks she and Georgetta had had an intense and passionate one-night stand the one time she broke her rule about not getting involved with coworkers. And now, she regretted her promise to call her. "Yeah, sorry, I've been busy."

"Well, I forgive you, but I would really like to get together again," Georgetta purred into the phone.

"I'm seeing someone," Paxx blurted out before thinking.

"Really? Is it serious?"

Paxx smiled as her thoughts drifted to Jaylee. "Yeah, I think it is."

"How about that, I never thought I would see the day when Paxx Algatta would be in a serious relationship."

"You and me both," Paxx laughed. "I guess getting shot and almost dying changes your perspective on things."

"Yes, I imagine it would. Congratulations, and tell this woman who has stolen your heart that hearts will break all over Chandler County now that you are off the market."

"Well, I don't think hearts will break but thank you."

"I can guarantee pussy's will be frowning." Georgetta giggled.

Paxx shook her head, stifling a laugh. "You can take up the gauntlet, George. You are more than qualified."

"Mmmm, now you're just sucking up, but I like it, so what is it you want to know?"

"Can you tell me about the bullet that shot me? Is it connected to any other cases?" Paxx asked, getting back to business.

"Just a minute. Let me pull it up. I did nothing on this case, so I don't know anything off the top of my head." Georgetta said as she began typing on her computer. Paxx patiently waited as she listened to the soft tapping of keys.

"Fuck me," Georgetta whispered after several minutes.

"What is it?" Paxx asked, confident she knew the answer.

"The bullet recovered is from a gun that was used in five homicides in the past three years," Georgetta said as she continued typing. "Three of the victims are from right here in Chandler County."

"Who are the victims?" Paxx asked, sure her father's name would be among them.

As Georgetta rattled off five names, Paxx jotted them down in her notebook, surprised when none of them were her father.

"Are you sure that's all of them?" Paxx asked, confused.

After a minute more of typing, she replied, "That's it."

"That can't be, can you look up the ballistics report for my dad's case? Double-check to make sure it's not the same gun."

"Just a minute," Georgetta said as she resumed typing. "Same caliber Glock 19, but different gun," she confirmed after reading the report.

"Thanks, George, I appreciate it."

"You sure you don't want one more mind-blowing round before you settle down?"

"Thanks for the offer, but I'm going to focus on just one woman and see where it goes."

"Good luck, and I will keep the rest of the women warm for you if you change your mind."

"Enjoy," Paxx replied, smiling as she disconnected the call.

Placing her phone on the couch, Paxx looked over the notepad filled with the names Georgetta had given her.

She tapped her pen against the notepad, her mind racing. She leaned back against the couch, her gaze drifting to the window as if expecting answers from the outside world. The sun had disappeared behind a dark cloud, casting long shadows across the living room.

Her phone buzzed, breaking her reverie. She glanced down at the screen to see Paul's name. A small smile crept across Paxx's lips as she swiped to answer. "Hey!" she greeted.

"Hey! How's it going?" Paul's bright and warm voice melted some of Paxx's tension away.

"Just finished a call with a friend at the crime lab," Paxx replied, glancing at the notepad again. "Got some interesting info about my shooting."

"Oh? Good or bad?"

"Depends on how you look at it. The bullet they pulled from me links back to five unsolved homicides... three of them here in Chandler County. Paul, Dad wasn't one of the victims."

A moment of silence stretched between them before Paul spoke again, concern lacing his tone. "Have you looked into who the victims were?"

"I just got their names," Paxx said, trying to sound casual despite her racing heart. "I need to dig deeper to see if there's any connection."

"We are all packed and will pull out in a few minutes," Paul said as she heard Embry jabbering in the background. "Should be there the day after tomorrow."

"OK, I have a doctor's appointment to get released on Friday, so hopefully, I'll be finished before you arrive. Drive carefully and be safe."

"We will, and good luck," Paul replied before disconnecting the call.

Paxx walked onto the porch, looking out over the open pasture. She inhaled, taking in the day's warmth, but her thoughts quickly returned to the names and the lives lost. Who were they? What tangled web connected them all? Looking down at her notepad, she flipped to the page where she'd scrawled Georgetta's list. The names blurred as she read through them again: Fiona Reed, Ebony Moss, Tressa Nguyen, Jordan Blackstone, and Mallery Hanks. Each name felt heavy with untold stories. Running her fingers along the paper, she knew she needed to sort this out, and it couldn't wait.

Back inside, she grabbed her laptop from the coffee table, opened it, and typed in the first name: Fiona Reed. The soft whir of the machine filled the silence as the screen lit up. A search engine popped up, and she clicked through various links: news articles, social media profiles, obituaries, all potential leads.

Paxx read Fiona's story, about a twenty-six-year-old single mother found dead in an alley and felt a twist in her stomach. She continued her search, piecing together the details of each victim. Ebony Moss was a promising jazz musician whose death had shocked her family. Tressa Nguyen, who had been gunned down right at her doorstep, was known for her charitable work for refugee organizations. Jordan Blackstone was starting her career as a pediatric nurse before her life was taken. Mallery Hanks, a high school basketball coach just days away from marrying her college sweetheart, had met a tragic, brutal end on a snowy February night.

Hours slipped by as Paxx delved deeper into each case, jotting down details, connecting dots, and printing out every crucial article she could find. These victims were either local to Chandler County or had significant ties here; their deaths had sent shockwaves through families, neighborhoods, schools, and even local businesses. Paxx leaned back in her chair, rubbing her temples as fatigue washed over her. The list before her looked innocent enough on paper, yet it held so much darkness within it, a fallen testament to lives lost too soon. Still, a more pressing question gnawed at her mind: Why were these names connected to her shooting? The victims linked to Mr. Black, and these victims didn't share the same modus operandi.

She glanced at the clock on the wall; it was later than expected. Just as she began closing tabs on her browser, a message from Rowan pinged on her phone.

'Hey Paxx! Sorry, I haven't gotten back to you earlier! Got some leads to share when you're free?'

'Let's talk tomorrow.'

'OK.'

Standing, Paxx stretched her arms above her head, bent over, and placed her palms on the floor. A week and a half of rehab had made a world of difference in her pain level. Smiling, she picked up her phone and pressed Jaylee's number.

"Hey, gorgeous," Jaylee answered.

"Hey, Beautiful. When will you be finished this evening?"

"I just finished; I am on my way home. Is everything alright?"

"Yes, everything is fine. Can you come over?"

"Let me go home and shower, and then I will pick up some food. I can be there in about an hour or so?"

"Sounds great. See you then," Paxx replied as she ended the call.

❓ ❓ ❓
FOURTEEN

Anticipation bubbled within Paxx as she awaited Jaylee's arrival. She arranged plates and silverware on the dining-room table. She lit two candles, placing them in the center so their warm light enveloped the space with a romantic ambiance.

Upstairs, Paxx's hands trembled as she lit candles around the bedroom, their gentle light throwing subtle shadows on the walls. She smoothed the sheets and fluffed the pillows, determined to make this special evening perfect. Every tiny detail, from the soft lighting to the inviting bed, added to the growing excitement that pulsed through her body.

"Algatta, you have gone sappy," she laughed to herself.

By the time Jaylee knocked on her door an hour later, Paxx felt a mixture of anxiety and excitement coursing through her veins. Opening the door revealed Jaylee with two bags and an eager smile.

"Food's here!" Jaylee chirped. "And I brought drinks, too."

Paxx stepped aside to welcome her in. "Perfect timing," she said, striving to keep her voice steady as she admired Jaylee's flushed cheeks from the cool evening air and the sparkle in her eyes.

Jaylee set the bags on the table and glanced around, her smile widening. "Wow, look at you! Trying to set a romantic scene?"

Paxx felt a blush creep up her neck. "I thought it'd be nice to eat by candlelight; make it special."

Jaylee's expression softened as she pressed a gentle kiss against Paxx's lips. "I love it," she murmured, returning the smile as she unpacked the food. The soft, flickering candlelight enhanced the intimate atmosphere with an air of seduction.

A blend of excitement and possibility hung in the air as they ate and talked. After clearing the table, moving closer and drawing Jaylee into a warm embrace, Paxx whispered, "Let's go upstairs."

"Are you sure? How's your pain?"

"I'm sure."

Hand in hand, they ascended the stairs; Jaylee gasped as she entered the bedroom, bathed in the soft, warm, sweet aroma of flickering candles as they cast dancing shadows on the walls and ceiling. Before Jaylee could turn around, she felt Paxx behind her, her hand brushing the hair away from her neck, exposing the soft skin. Then Paxx's lips brushed against her neck. Jaylee melted against her as Paxx's fingertips traced down her arms. She shivered with fiery desire, causing her breath to hitch as Paxx kissed her neck, teasing her earlobe with her lips before running her tongue over her delicate skin, leading to the softness of her neck where her pulse thumped with urgency.

"Tell me what you want."

"I want everything you want to give."

"I want to taste you," Paxx confessed, her grip tightening on Jaylee's hips as if trying to steady herself amid tumultuous waves of desire.

Jaylee turned to face her, and their lips met in a slow, deep, sinful kiss. Heat spread between them like wildfire as their tongues danced together, tasting, teasing, promising untold pleasures yet to come.

"You're wearing too many clothes," Paxx growled, breaking away to tug Jaylee's shirt over her head. Jaylee laughed, a low, wicked sound that made Paxx's blood boil. She reached behind her to unclasp her bra, letting It fall away, revealing firm, full breasts, tipped with rosy nipples that stood erect with desire.

Paxx lowered her head and took one nipple into her mouth, swirling her tongue around it before giving it a playful nip with her teeth. Jaylee gasped, arching her back as Paxx lavished attention on the other. Running her fingers through Paxx's hair, Jaylee pulled her closer, moaning with pleasure.

"Paxx, please," Jaylee begged, her voice hoarse with desire.

Paxx was happy to oblige. She slid a hand down Jaylee's body, cupping her through the thin fabric of her pants. She could feel Jaylee's heat radiating through the material, her core aching and wet with desire. Paxx murmured against her breast, rubbing small circles over Jaylee's clit. "Do you like that?"

"Yes," Jaylee gasped, hips bucking against Paxx's hand. "God, yes."

Paxx smiled, increasing the pressure as she felt Jaylee's orgasm building, her muscles tensing as she approached the

M. LEA

edge. But Paxx wasn't ready to let her fall just yet. She pulled away, leaving Jaylee panting and gasping for breath.

"What...what are you doing?"

"Taking my time, I want you to enjoy every single moment of this," she whispered as she slowly pushed Jaylee's pants down over her hips. Jaylee's heavy breathing and the tantalizing sight of her black lace panties threatened to undo Paxx's sanity altogether. Unable to resist her growing desire any further, she knelt before Jaylee, her breath hot against her skin.

Paxx traced her tongue over the delicate skin below Jaylee's navel, pulling her lacey panties down her thighs. Paxx followed their path with her tongue, leaving a trail of warmth in her wake. Her fingers danced over Jaylee's inner thigh, pausing to admire the intricate tattoo that adorned her skin. Paxx kissed the image, then let her tongue linger, her touch light and exploratory. A hum of delight escaped her lips when Jaylee moaned with desire as Paxx's tongue continued its journey, following the rocket's direction, and dipped deep between her thighs, exploring the hidden depths with tender curiosity.

Jaylee gripped Paxx's shoulders as her knees weakened. Paxx wrapped an arm around her thighs as she delved deeper into Jaylee's sweet sex. With skillful fingers and a tongue that knew just how to please, Paxx brought Jaylee to the brink of ecstasy again, and again, only to pull back at the last second and leave her begging for more.

"Please, I need more."

Paxx's fingers returned to caress Jaylee's swollen heat, stroking and massaging in rhythm with her tongue until

104

Jaylee could no longer hold back. With a loud cry, she climaxed, her juices flowing as Paxx savored every drop. As the intense waves of pleasure subsided, Jaylee collapsed onto the bed, her breath coming in ragged gasps. She reached up to draw Paxx close until their lips met and she tasted her juices on Paxx's tongue.

"You're amazing. Jay, are you okay?" Paxx asked, placing her hand on Jaylee's cheek and wiping away a tear.

"Yes, I have never felt so exquisite, you knew exactly what I needed and wanted."

Paxx swallowed hard, her mouth dry as she fought to find words. "Fuck, Jaylee, I need you."

Jaylee's heart raced, and the urgency in Paxx's voice ignited a fire deep inside her. She could feel the heat radiating off Paxx's body. "You have me," she replied breathlessly, rolling over on top of her.

Jaylee's hands roamed over Paxx's body, exploring every curve with a fierce possessiveness that sent Paxx's pulse soaring while Jaylee tugged at Paxx's clothing, desperate to feel her bare skin against hers. The soft flickering light of the candles danced across Paxx's exquisite body as drops of sweat glistened on her skin. Her small, perky breasts, topped with hardened nipples, begged to be touched. Jaylee's hands explored every inch of her body, tracing the smooth lines of her breasts down to the gentle flare of her hips. Paxx's body trembled with anticipation as Jaylee's touch ignited a fire within her.

Paxx shivered with pleasure as Jaylee's lips found hers, plunging her tongue deep into Paxx's mouth in a hungry kiss that set every nerve ending alight. As Jaylee's hands continued to explore Paxx's body, she could feel herself growing wetter and more aroused by the second. Jaylee moved lower, and her lips found Paxx's collarbone, neck, and breasts. She teased and tormented Paxx with her tongue, her teeth, and her lips, driving her wild with pleasure.

Jaylee kissed and licked her way down Paxx's stomach, admiring the colorful dragon tattoo that covered her stomach, now visible that the bruising had all but disappeared. "Gorgeous," she whispered against her naval before continuing her descent. Paxx's breath came in ragged gasps as Jaylee's tongue explored her delicate folds, first teasing and then plunging deep. Moans of pure pleasure escaped her as Jaylee's fingers slipped inside, stroking and exploring with such expert skill that it sent a rush of heat through her veins. Clutching the sheets, Paxx's fingers squeezed and released as Jaylee repeatedly brought her to the precipice of climax.

"Oh, god, Jay, don't stop," Paxx pleaded breathlessly.

Jaylee sent Paxx over the edge, drawing out every last shudder and shiver until Paxx lay breathless and spent. As Jaylee kissed her way back up her body, Paxx lay back against the pillows, her body slick with sweat and the aftermath of pleasure. She looked at Jaylee with awe and adoration, her heart filled with a fierce love that threatened to consume her. 'This was what it meant to truly pleasure someone,' Paxx thought as she tried to slow her breathing.

"Fuck, Jay, I never knew it could be like that."

"Neither did I, and I want more."

"Me too."

The night lingered as they lost themselves in the pleasure of each other's bodies. They explored every inch of one another, and their desire and taste for one another was insatiable.

As dawn broke, they lay intertwined in each other's arms, their bodies utterly spent.

"Jay, can I tell you something?" Paxx whispered.

Kissing the curve of Paxx's breast while her fingertip traced the outlines of the tattoo on Paxx's stomach, Jaylee replied, "Anything."

"I was really nervous last night."

Pushing up on her elbow, Jaylee said, "Really? Me too."

"You were?"

"I was afraid I wouldn't live up to all the buildup and excitement we'd created over the past three weeks."

Paxx pulled her closer and kissed her. "I worried I wouldn't be able to take things slow enough to give you everything I wanted to," she admitted, her gaze dropping.

"You gave me more than I ever imagined," Jaylee whispered, drawing her body closer. "Please look at me."

Paxx met Jaylee's gaze, feeling vulnerable by the intensity of their connection.

"I want us to be completely open and honest about everything. I know you're more experienced than me. I've only been with three women, including you, and my first experience was hardly meaningful, since neither of us knew what we were doing. I have never been with a guy and have little experience with..." Jaylee paused, "with toys."

"I never would have guessed that I'm only your third lover, you are amazing, no one has ever taken the time to make love to me like that before. It's always been rough and fast. But with you, I want to slow down and savor every touch, every taste. Jay, I don't want rough and fast with you unless that is what you want."

"I want you, Paxx, and I want all of you in every way."

"I will give you anything sexually you need, want, or fantasize about." Then, pressing her lips against Jaylee's ear as if someone would hear, Paxx whispered, "And if you want to try some toys, I can accommodate that."

Jaylee moaned, understanding the toy she was speaking of as Paxx pressed and moved her hips against her. "I don't think I'm ready just yet," she whispered, "but when I am, I want that, with you." With that, Jaylee rolled them over and straddled Paxx. The spark of excitement lighting Paxx's eyes sent a jolt of electricity through her.

"God, you're beautiful," Paxx whispered while sitting up and delicately tracing the curve of Jaylee's collarbone with her tongue. Jaylee felt herself melt under Paxx's tender touch, a sensation unlike anything she had ever known.

"Don't stop," she breathed heavily, arching into the exploration.

They spent the morning tangled in each other's arms, learning and discovering new things about each other's bodies and exploring new sensations and desires. By midday, despite the mild temperature outside, they spread a blanket in front of the lit fireplace downstairs in the living room. They snuggled close, basking in each other's warmth and eating leftover Chinese food from the night before. But soon, their hunger for one another grew too intense to ignore. They abandoned their plates, letting their desire consume them as they devoured each other with uninhibited passion, lost in their world of pleasure and desire.

As evening settled, Paxx could feel the lingering effects of their intimate escapades in her throbbing abdominal muscles. Upstairs, Jaylee drew a bath, filling it with warm water and a few drops of calming essential oils. They both eased into the tub, surrounded by calming music as they relaxed.

Paxx murmured as Jaylee leaned back, nestled in her arms, "My final checkup is tomorrow."

"Well, if you get enough rest tonight and regain your strength, I'm sure they will clear you for duty."

Paxx chuckled, "Yes, it has, thanks to you. I'll have to retake my firearm qualification test. Still, if all goes well, I should return to full duty by next Tuesday."

Jaylee nodded but remained silent.

"What's wrong?" Paxx asked, noticing Jaylee's sudden change in mood.

Jaylee shook her head and muttered, "I hadn't thought about you being back on the job, potentially facing danger again."

Paxx tightened her arms around Jaylee as she kissed her cheek. "I will be fine, don't worry."

Paxx's careless dismissal of the dangers that come with her job sent a sharp and searing pain through Jaylee's chest. An overwhelming fear gripped her as she pushed herself out of Paxx's embrace, covering her naked body with a towel as she stepped out of the tub and into the cool bathroom air. Paxx remained seated momentarily before standing up and grabbing a towel to cover herself. She followed Jaylee into the bedroom. "Jay, you knew I would have to go back eventually. It's my job."

"I know, I never expected it to hit me so hard. I'm sorry."

Paxx wrapped her arms around Jaylee from behind, trying to comfort her. "Don't apologize. I know firsthand what it's like to have loved ones in law enforcement."

Tears streamed down Jaylee's cheeks as she turned around. "Paxx, your father died in the line of duty, and you were nearly killed," Jaylee's voice cracked with emotion as she continued, "I will deal with this, and hopefully, it won't take long for me to relax and not worry, but it's hard knowing that the woman I love is putting herself at risk."

Paxx stood and stared into Jaylee's tear-filled green eyes. Fear and longing filled her chest.

"I'm sorry, I didn't mean to scare you by saying that."

"You didn't scare me by saying that, Jay, I have waited since I was sixteen to hear those words. For the last twenty-two years, I have longed for someone who truly meant them to say those words to me. And I know you mean them. I could feel your love with every touch and kiss we shared last night and today, and if I'm being honest, I felt it soon after we met." Paxx took a deep breath before continuing, "I have never said those words romantically to anyone, never felt them toward anyone. Jaylee, when we were together last night, I wanted you to feel how I felt and truly feel about you."

Stepping closer, Jaylee pressed her hand against Paxx's chest. "I felt you, Paxx. I felt your heart."

"I love you, Jay," Paxx murmured against her lips.

As their towels fell to the floor, they sealed their love with a heated passion that burned hotter than anything they had experienced yet.

？ ？ ？

FIFTEEN

T he following morning, Paxx awoke to the sound of an incessant buzzing. Fighting out of a deep sleep, she reached for her phone, which lay on the bedside table. "Hello," she said groggily as Jaylee nestled closer to her.

"I've been trying to call you since yesterday morning," Rowan's irritated voice growled on the other end.

Looking over at Jaylee's peaceful face, Paxx smiled as she said, "I was deeply involved in something yesterday and didn't have my ringer on."

"You told me to call you yesterday and give you the new information I found."

Paxx fought the urge to tell him to fuck off and hang up. "Give me half an hour, and I will call you back."

"Fine," Rowan snarled before the line went dead.

"Do you have to get up?" Jaylee asked as her fingers began stroking Paxx's inner thigh.

"I have to call him back in half an hour," Paxx murmured as she slid down and met Jaylee's mouth hungrily.

"Thirty minutes," Jaylee whispered breathlessly as they intertwined, quickly bringing each other to the peak of pleasure.

Twenty-eight minutes later, while Jaylee showered, Paxx prepared coffee and called Rowan.

"Hey, what did you find?" Paxx asked as soon as the call connected.

"I found Mr. Black."

"You found Mr. Black? Rowan, did you catch him?"

"Not exactly, Paxx. He was caught eighteen months ago."

"What? How did that happen?"

"He's in the Pennsylvania State Prison."

"Since when? Are you absolutely sure it's him?"

"Positive. The Pennsylvania state police arrested him after a woman he tried to assault shot him. The police found a black rose in the bag he brought to the scene. His name is Clancy Devonshire, and his fingerprints and DNA link him to all of Mr. Black's murders."

"Rowan, if he's in prison, then who shot me?" Paxx questioned, her legs trembling as she struggled to process the information. She pulled a chair from under the table and sat down.

Rowan's tone softened as he asked, "Are you sure the man who shot you claimed to be Mr. Black?"

Paxx fell silent, replaying the incident in her mind. "Yes, Rowan, I'm sure."

"You were in pretty bad shape when I found you, Paxx."

"I didn't imagine it, Rowan," Paxx growled, anger rising. "I know exactly what I heard."

"Okay," he replied defensively.

"If not him, then who would try to kill me and claim to be the same man who killed my dad? Whoever it was obviously didn't know Mr. Black is in prison," she barked, pressing a hand to her forehead in an effort to quiet the dizzying rush in her head and stomach.

"I don't know, Paxx, when do you think you'll be cleared to come back?"

"I have my last appointment today at one," Paxx said, glancing up as Jaylee entered the kitchen. "Once cleared, I'll re-qualify at the range, and if everything goes well, I should be back on duty by Tuesday or Wednesday."

"I'll keep digging and see what else I can uncover," Rowan promised.

"I've got some information on the gun that shot me; it's connected to five unsolved homicides." She sighed as Jaylee rested a worried hand on her shoulder.

"What? When were you going to tell me? Where did you get that information from?"

"I only found out recently, and I wanted to do some research before I spoke to you."

"You should have told me, Paxx, I'm your partner!"

"You made it clear you weren't involved in the case anymore."

"Yeah, but you still should have let me know."

Paxx clenched her jaw, feeling Rowan's frustration through the phone. "I'm sorry," she said, forcing the words out even though she felt anything but sorry. She could hear him pacing, the sound of his footsteps echoing in her ear. "I wanted to be sure I understood everything before coming to you. I didn't want to cause a panic without knowing the full picture."

"Panic? You think this is about panic?" Rowan shot back. "This is about your safety. Do you understand how dangerous this is?"

"Yeah, I do," Paxx replied, crossing her free arm across her chest as if that could shield her from the gravity of their conversation. Jaylee's gentle touch had faded into the background as tension filled the space. "I can't go around spreading half-formed theories without proof."

"So, what's your plan?"

"I'm still working on that," Paxx admitted, guilt gnawing at her. "I'll have everything ready to show on Tuesday when I return to work."

Jaylee knelt between Paxx's knees, her face lined with concern as she placed her hands on Paxx's thighs. The warmth of her touch calmed Paxx even as tension buzzed all around.

"Alright," Rowan finally conceded with a sharp exhale. "But you need to keep me in the loop."

"I have to go, another call's coming in," Paxx said, ending the call abruptly. She tossed her phone onto the table, bent over, and buried her face in her hands, taking deep breaths as rage threatened to consume her.

Jaylee wrapped her arms around Paxx, pressing her cheek against her head and rubbing soothing circles on her back. "Talk to me."

"Give me a minute."

"Okay."

After several minutes, Paxx finally felt some semblance of calm. Sitting up, she met Jaylee's worried gaze. "Coffee, first?"

"Coffee first," Jaylee agreed as she stood, poured two cups, and placed them on the table. She then retrieved a container of cream from the fridge and a spoon from a drawer.

Pouring creamer into both steaming cups, Jaylee stirred the mixture before sliding a cup over to Paxx, who picked it up and took a sip.

"How much did you hear?"

"Not much," Jaylee replied as she sat down.

"My dad's killer is in prison."

"That's great," Jaylee exclaimed excitedly, then frowned. "That is good, right?"

"He's been in prison for the last eighteen months."

"Wait, what? But... how is that even possible?" Jaylee asked, frowning as she tried to untangle the conflicting information. "If he's in prison, then who shot you?"

"Exactly, who the fuck shot me, and why would they want me to think it was him?"

Jaylee pulled her phone out of her scrubs pocket and began typing.

"What are you doing?"

"I'm getting someone to cover my clients this morning."

Paxx covered her phone with her hand. "You took yesterday off, I don't want you to miss two days of work. I'm fine."

"Yesterday, I was already off, so I didn't miss anything, I only have two clients this morning and I want to be here with you. You know the things girlfriends do for each other."

"I have never had a girlfriend," Paxx's face contorted with anger and pain. "You don't have to babysit me, I told you, I'm fine." But it was a lie. Deep down, Paxx knew she wasn't fine.

Tears streamed down Jaylee's face as she stood frozen, unable to comprehend Paxx's anger and dismissal.

Watching Jaylee's disappointed expression made Paxx instantly regret her words. But pride kept her from apologizing or reaching out to comfort her even though she wasn't angry at Jaylee. The past few weeks' events had cracked something open inside her, unraveling all the carefully constructed walls she had built around herself. This morning's situation with Rowan, the haunting memories of her shooting and the weight of the new information began to affect her. As much as she wanted to apologize and explain, Paxx couldn't bring herself to open up.

"Please, just talk to me," Jaylee pleaded, reaching for Paxx's hand.

But Paxx pulled away, her body tense and closed off. "Jay, I..." Paxx started, but the words caught in her throat. Paxx watched Jaylee's expression shift from worry to hurt and frustration. She wanted to take back her harsh words, apologize, and make things right between them. The thought of opening up and admitting just how much she needed someone in this chaotic mess terrified her.

Jaylee took a step back, a little more distance than before. "You don't have to pretend you're okay with me," she said softly, her voice steady despite the hurt lingering in her tone.

"I'm not pretending," Paxx insisted, but even she could hear the weakness in her words. She rubbed the back of her neck, feeling the tension coil tighter. "It's just... everything is so fucking messed up right now."

"Then let me help, you're going through a lot, but you don't have to carry it all alone."

Paxx looked down at her coffee cup, swirling the liquid inside it as if looking for answers in the murky liquid. The truth clawed at her insides; She knew she needed Jaylee's support. Still, vulnerability felt like a threat when everything around her was already in chaos.

Paxx finally met her gaze, the vulnerability and fear shining through. "I know I'm being a jerk, but I don't want you to get hurt because of me. It's dangerous, and I don't want you involved."

Jaylee's eyes hardened at Paxx's words. "I am with you, Paxx, so I am involved. Is this how it will always be? When things are good, you'll want me around, but when shit hits the fan, you'll push me away?"

Paxx stood abruptly as if she had been struck, knocking her chair over.

"I know all of this is overwhelming, but if the last several weeks meant something, if what you said to me yesterday meant something, anything, then you wouldn't be pushing me away, not like this."

Paxx felt tears prickling at the corners of her eyes as Jaylee's words hit home. She wanted to pull Jaylee close and tell her everything, but fear still gripped her.

"I was completely honest with you when I told you I didn't know how to be in a relationship; I didn't know how much I could let you in," Paxx said as she took a deep breath and glanced away momentarily before meeting Jaylee's eyes again. Fear and insecurity gnawed at her insides, whispering doubts and insecurities into her mind. "He thinks I made it all up... what I heard that night," she finally admitted, trembling with frustration.

118

"Who?"

"Rowan," Paxx spat as the anger bubbled back up as she spoke. "I know what I heard, Jaylee. He said he was Mr. Black!"

"Maybe he's just frustrated about how things are, and maybe he feels out of control since he doesn't know everything," Jaylee suggested. "I completely understand how he feels."

"Jay..." Paxx trailed off, unsure how to articulate the tangled emotions swirling inside her head.

"What?"

"I just feel alone in this."

"But I am here," Jaylee said hurtfully, "Paxx, I am right here."

Paxx met Jaylee's gaze, pain and regret filling her chest. "I'm sorry, I have to do this on my own."

"This isn't just about you anymore, Paxx. Don't shut me out."

"I'm not shutting you out," Paxx replied, though it sounded weak even to her ears. "I just... I told you I don't want you to be part of this mess. It's dangerous."

"Dangerous, Paxx, life is dangerous! What happened to you is beyond awful and scary, and now you're telling me you'd rather face whatever comes next alone? That doesn't make any sense."

The truth hit Paxx hard. Wasn't that what she had been doing all along, treating every danger as something she had to shoulder by herself? The thought shamed her, and silence filled the space between them for a moment as they both wrestled with their emotions.

"Maybe I'm scared," Paxx finally admitted, her voice barely above a whisper. She felt fragile admitting it but knew it was a truth that needed to surface. "Scared of needing someone and then losing them, too."

Jaylee stepped closer, reaching out to grasp Paxx's hand. "You will not lose me because you let me in, you'll only lose me if you push me away."

Paxx's heart pounded at Jaylee's touch, and doubt clawed at the edges of her determination as images from the past flooded back, the chaos, the pain of loss, and she flinched.

Gripping her hands tighter, Jaylee said, "Paxx, I am not one to mince words or beat around the bush; I am tired of being alone. I love you with everything in me, which means I stand by you in and through everything life throws at you, both within and outside of us. Look at me," Jaylee demanded as Paxx kept her gaze averted. "Look at me," she said again.

Finally, Paxx met Jaylee's eyes, their sadness and determination searing her heart.

"Do you love me?" Jaylee asked, searching Paxx's eyes for the truth she wasn't sure Paxx could voice.

"I..." Paxx trailed off.

"I will make this very simple; all I need is a yes or no. Yes, and I am here no matter what, and for the rest of my life. No, and I will walk out that door and never bother you again."

The thought of Jaylee walking out the door and never seeing her again made Paxx's knees weak, but the idea of her staying and something awful happening to her caused her head to swim.

"Jay, I," Paxx whispered as Jaylee released her hands and turned to walk away.

Jaylee reached the front door before Paxx cried out, "Yes, please don't go, Jay, yes, I love you and I don't want to be alone anymore either," She sobbed as she crumbled to the floor.

Jaylee rushed to Paxx, falling to her knees and enveloping her in a fierce embrace. "I'm sorry I had to do it that way, Paxx."

Paxx held onto Jaylee as she wept, her tears chipping away at the hardened walls surrounding her heart. "I love you so much, Jay. It hurts inside from how much I love you. I can't lose you."

"You won't lose me, Paxx; I am here."

"You already know me so well," Paxx said, meeting Jaylee's eyes. "Did you mean what you said about being here for the rest of your life?"

Jaylee wiped tears as she pressed her lips to Paxx's. "I want to be here as long as you want me."

"I think we need to talk seriously," Paxx said as she stood up and grasped Jaylee's hands.

"Was that too much too soon?"

"I'm still processing; let's talk about that later. First, let me apologize for doing the same thing I always do when I get scared. Please be patient with me. I have never had anyone stand up to me before."

"You're not the only badass in this relationship, Paxx; I can hold my own."

"I know you can. And when we fight, because let's face it, we will. It will be fierce."

Pulling Paxx into her arms, Jaylee said, "And when we make up from those fights, Katy bar the door, because it's going to be one hell of a ride."

"Fuck yeah, it will," Paxx growled as she pressed their lips together, quickly they removed their clothes before clearing off the table in a frenzy of desire.

? ? ?
SIXTEEN

J aylee drove Paxx to her doctor's appointment at half-past twelve, their fingers intertwined on the center console. As Jaylee waited in the reception area, Paxx disappeared through a door and emerged twenty minutes later with a bright smile.

"Good news?" Jaylee asked as they headed towards the elevator.

"I got a clean bill of health."

"That's great. I know you've been looking forward to returning to your normal routine," Jaylee said as they stepped into the elevator.

Paxx turned towards Jaylee after pressing the button for the ground floor and embraced her, grateful they were alone. "I am ready, but I wouldn't trade these past few weeks with you for anything," Paxx whispered before kissing her deeply.

As the elevator descended, Jaylee felt the warmth of Paxx's embrace radiating through her. When the doors opened with a soft chime, they reluctantly separated, but Paxx kept hold of Jaylee's hand as they stepped into the bustling lobby.

As they reached the door leading outside, Paxx hesitated, glancing over at Jaylee. "You know, I really couldn't have done this without you. Your support... it means everything."

Jaylee's heart swelled at the sincerity in Paxx's gaze. "We're a team," she replied, squeezing Paxx's hand tighter. "Besides, you're stronger than you think."

As they climbed into Jaylee's car, Paxx's phone rang. Pulling it from her pocket, she smiled at Anna's name on the screen.

"Hey, you," Paxx answered.

"Hey, you, how did your appointment go?"

"I'm cleared for active duty, no restrictions."

"That's great, how's Jaylee?"

"She's here with me," Paxx said as she pressed the speaker button.

"Hi, Anna," Jaylee greeted. "When will you be back?"

"We just pulled into the title company parking lot. Our signing is in twenty minutes, we are exhausted."

"I'm sure you are," Paxx said. "Where is the title company? Do you want us to come and get Embry? We can take her home."

"You don't mind?"

"We would love to," Jaylee agreed.

"That would be a big help; she's getting a little cranky from being in the car for the past three days," Anna said as Embry fussed in the background.

Anna gave them the address, and ten minutes later, Paxx and Jaylee swapped keys with Paul and Anna before driving a van full of boxes and a happy Embry home. Once they arrived home, Jaylee fixed lunch while Paxx and Embry played with blocks on the living room floor. After they ate lunch, Jaylee watched cartoons with Embry on the couch while Paxx cleaned up the dishes.

"How did she do?" Anna asked Paxx as she entered the kitchen.

"She was great," Paxx answered as she pressed the start button on the dishwasher.

"It looks like she and Jaylee are getting along well," Anna said as she leaned against the counter.

"Aunt JJ is a natural."

"Aunt, JJ, huh."

"I called her Jay, so Embry started calling her Aunt JJ."

"How are you two doing?"

"Anna, it's amazing," Paxx whispered, "Unlike any relationship I have ever had. She doesn't back down, and she calls me on my shit."

"I'm so happy for you, Paxx; you deserve to be happy, and you need someone who calls you on your shit."

"Agreed." Paxx replied. "How are you doing with the move?"

"It's a little overwhelming, but I'm happy to be here with you, and Paul is excited about his new job."

"I'm thrilled you are here, but why do I feel like something is bothering you?"

Averting her gaze, Anna said, "I'm worried about you getting involved in your dad's case, in your case. I don't want you to get hurt again, or worse."

"I have new information about all that; where's Paul?" Paxx asked as she walked toward the living room.

"He went to lie down; he wouldn't let me drive, so he has only slept a few hours over the past few days."

"Poor guy, and I will fill you both in later, why don't you nap? Jaylee and I have Embry."

Anna nodded thanks, then disappeared into the bedroom.

"Paul asked if I would trade him vehicles," Jaylee smiled from the couch, where Embry was curled up in her lap, nearly asleep.

"I don't blame him; who wouldn't want to trade a minivan for a sleek, sexy black Camaro SS?" Paxx laughed.

"Oh, I don't know," Jaylee smiled seductively, "I'm looking forward to riding around in your Jeep naked."

Paxx raised an eyebrow as she smiled, "If you're going to be naked in my Jeep, we will need to take it off-road."

Jaylee stifled a laugh as Embry moved onto her lap, nestling closer. "I meant your Jeep will be naked."

Paxx gazed at Jaylee on the couch, Embry nestled in her arms. "Jay, do you want kids?"

Jaylee looked up at Paxx, then back down at Embry. "I have never given it much thought, and I'm not sure I am wired to raise kids. Do you want kids?"

Paxx shook her head. "I think I am happy being an aunt."

"Then I am happy being an aunt, too."

Paxx settled on the couch beside Jaylee, trying not to disturb Embry's sleep. "I never thought I would have that conversation with someone."

Jaylee leaned against Paxx, laying her head on her shoulder. "Me neither, but I'm glad we can be open and honest with one another."

"Me too," Paxx said as she kissed her forehead. "Do you mind if I go work in my office? I need to put some things together for Tuesday."

"Go ahead; I'm going to sit here, watch TV, and enjoy holding this little one," Jaylee said, pointing the remote at the TV and changing the channel from cartoons to a home makeover show.

Paxx stood, leaned down, and kissed Embry on the head, then Jaylee on the lips. "I love you."

"I love you, too."

I n her office, Paxx began compiling all the information from her conversations onto index cards and the clean side of the whiteboard. Each victim received a column and a note card. Once Paxx had organized all the victims, she began searching for links between them. Three hours later, the opening of the office door interrupted her thoughts.

"What ya doing?" Paul mumbled.

Turning to face him, she responded. "I'm trying to connect the victims of my shooter."

"I've been thinking about that, and without knowing the specifics, what are the chances each victim has a different shooter?" Paul asked as he rubbed his three-day beard.

Paxx leaned back in her chair and closed her eyes. "That would certainly explain the randomness of the shootings. I've spent the last three hours trying to place these people at the same gyms or grocery stores, but I keep coming up empty."

"Paxx, you are a narcotics detective; how many drug busts have you made over the past eight years? How many heavy hitters have you sent to prison? It's not out of the question that one or more want your head on a platter."

Paxx's brow furrowed in confusion as she looked at Paul. "But why tell me they were Mr. Black? Why confess to killing Dad?" she asked, her voice trembling with emotion.

Paul's eyes met hers, his expression grave. "I don't know, but I think we should talk to Mr. Black and see what we can find out."

Paxx nodded, deep in thought. "I could push back returning to work a few days."

"We have painters coming Monday to start painting the house, so we won't move in until next weekend. I don't start at the sheriff's office until a week from Monday; we could fly out Sunday afternoon, go to the prison Monday, and catch a red-eye back Monday night."

Paxx's mind raced with all the possibilities and potential obstacles. "We need to call the prison and see if we can even talk to him."

"I did that on the way back from Chicago, after you texted me about him being in prison. I called in a favor; we have an appointment Monday at nine."

Relief flooded through Paxx's body as she stood and embraced Paul. "Thank you, Paul."

"We both need to put this behind us, and you need to focus on the job, not a ghost."

A small smile tugged at Paxx's lips as she looked at her brother. "I am so glad you are here."

"Me too."

"Dinner's ready!" Anna's cheerful voice rang out from the kitchen, interrupting their conversation.

As they sat down to eat, Paul explained the details of their plan for the upcoming week; Jaylee volunteered to stay at the farmhouse with Anna and Embry while Paul and Paxx were out of town, allowing them to focus on their task without worrying about leaving Anna and Embry alone.

Paxx enjoyed every bite of her meal but kept glancing at Paul, who seemed lost in thought. She couldn't shake off a feeling of unease about their upcoming trip, as so many unknowns awaited them.

"Paul?" Paxx ventured cautiously as Anna and Jaylee cleared the table. "Are you feeling okay about this? I mean... It's not just another case for us."

His gaze snapped back to her, and he took a deep breath. "Yeah, I am. It's just... heavy stuff we're dealing with, but we'll get through it together."

Paxx respected Paul's determination but detected underlying unspoken issues. She squeezed his hand across the table.

"You're right, It's just... I want us to be prepared for anything."

"Trust me, we'll tackle whatever comes our way."

Later that evening, after everyone had retreated to their respective corners of the house, Paxx found herself alone in her office again, staring at the mess of notes and index cards scattered across her desk like chaotic thoughts begging for order. The clock ticked in the background, the rhythmic beat echoing her racing heart.

Inhaling, she pulled out one note card detailing a victim's connection to T.C. Hines, a local dealer whose name had cropped up during interrogations before but had led nowhere significant.

"Maybe I should dig into this guy more..." Paxx mumbled aloud to herself before reaching for her laptop.

As she began typing, footsteps echoed outside the door before Jaylee appeared in its frame. Her silhouette, backlit by hallway light, made Paxx's heart skip a beat.

"Hey, gorgeous, thought I'd check on you."

"I'm okay, just trying to make sense of everything." Paxx gestured toward the mess on her desk in mild frustration.

"You're like a real-life version of Christine Cagney," Jaylee teased as she moved closer to Paxx's side.

"A much less glamorous version." Paxx sighed but couldn't suppress a smile. The closeness sent an electric thrill through her as Jaylee perched beside her on the edge of the desk.

"A very sexy version," Jaylee said seductively.

Stepping in front of her, Paxx placed her hands on Jaylee's hips. "I just worry..." she started hesitantly. "What if I uncover something that puts us all at risk?"

Jaylee reached out and brushed a thumb against Paxx's cheek. "We will deal with it."

A few moments later a knock came from the door, followed by Anna's voice breaking through their escalating heat. "Paxx, can I come in?"

Paxx smiled at Jaylee with a reluctant sigh before leaning back and fastening Jaylee's pants, which she had undone. "Come in."

"Oh, shit," Anna said from the doorway, "I interrupted you."

Jaylee pushed off the desk. "It's okay; we will continue our conversation later." She smiled and winked at Anna as she walked by.

"I'm sorry," Anna frowned once Jaylee was gone.

"Don't be," Paxx smiled reassuringly.

"Can I talk to you?" Anna asked as she sat in the arm-chair in the corner of the room.

"Of course," Paxx replied as she sat in the desk chair, rolling it over in front of her. "What's up?"

"I need you to talk to Paul while you are gone."

"Okay, about what?"

Anna took a deep breath and closed her eyes as she responded. "While we were back in Chicago, Paul asked me again if we," Anna motioned between them, "had ever been together."

"Again, what? Why would he think that?"

Anna continued looking at her hands as she spoke. "I never told you this, and please don't be mad at Paul, but we moved to Chicago after we got married because he thought we had been involved."

"Anna, look at me," Paxx said as she grasped her hands. "You did tell him nothing ever happened, that we have always just been friends, right?"

"I told him, but I don't think he ever really believed me. And now that we are back, he is distant; I see him watching me around you and Jaylee."

"I will talk to him, but it might slip that..."

Anna smiled, remembering when they first met, and Paxx kissed her. Anna remembered laughing hysterically until Paxx was so pissed that she wouldn't talk to her for a week. But after Paxx's embarrassment had worn off, they became inseparable.

Another knock came from the door; this time, Paul peeked his head in, a frown covering his face at their proximity. "What are you two doing?"

"Paul, come in here a minute," Paxx said as Anna's eyes widened in fear.

Paxx patted Anna's knee reassuringly.

"What's up?" Paul asked as he stepped inside.

Paxx's smile grew wider as she turned to face Anna. "I was just telling Anna how happy I am that you're here, remember when you and Anna got married? That was the happiest day of my life. My best friend, who supported me through high school and coming out to our parents and joining the police academy, and my brother, who always had my back. You two were the most important people in my life, and when the two of you got together, it made me so happy. Then you moved away, and I lost both my brother and sister. For ten years, I've felt so empty. But now," tears started forming in Paxx's eyes, "I have my sister and brother back, a beautiful niece, and another little one on the way. And I'm in love with an amazing woman with whom I want to spend the rest of my life with."

Paul and Anna both wiped tears from their eyes as Paxx spoke. "Paxx," Paul whispered.

"I'm not finished," Paxx interrupted. "I love you both so much, and sometimes I feel you think something besides friendship went on between Anna and me. Paul, Anna and I have always only been friends, she is the straightest straight girl I know." Paxx laughed, "I love her, Paul, but only as a sister, nothing more."

Paul sighed as he grasped Anna's hand, interlacing their fingers. "I'm sorry; I should have just asked ten years ago and now."

"I can understand you wondering," Paxx said slyly, "She is smoking hot and totally my type."

"We agree on both accounts." Paul smiled. "Now it's late, and I want to take my wife to bed."

"And I have a gorgeous woman waiting for me upstairs; I don't want to keep her waiting any longer," Paxx said, turning off the light and following them out the door.

"Thank you," Anna whispered as she hugged Paxx.

"Anytime," Paxx whispered back with a wink.

Once Paxx locked up the house and turned off all the lights, she climbed the stairs and quietly opened the bedroom door. Jaylee lay snuggled under the covers, soft sounds of sleep escaping her. Paxx brushed her teeth and stripped off her clothes before sliding under the covers and nestling against Jaylee's back. Jaylee turned over and snuggled into Paxx's arms, their naked bodies intertwining.

"Hey, gorgeous," Jaylee murmured as she kissed Paxx's neck.

"I didn't mean to wake you."

"You didn't wake me, I was just resting until you got here."

Time passed unnoticed as they lost themselves in each other. Every touch was electric, and every whisper seductive. Eventually, they settled into a comfortable silence, the soft rhythm of their breaths blending as they lay intertwined under the covers.

"Hey," Paxx murmured after some time had passed.

"Yeah?" Jaylee replied sleepily.

"I love you," Paxx confessed quietly, feeling the weight of those words settle comfortably in her heart.

Jaylee smiled against Paxx's shoulder. "I love you, too."

Paxx welcomed the warmth spreading through her chest as she listened to Jaylee's gentle breathing.

❓ ❓ ❓
SEVENTEEN

On Saturday, Paul and Paxx made the final preparations for their flight and overnight stay in Pennsylvania on Sunday and Monday. Jaylee went to work early to accommodate a few extra clients who had missed their appointments the day before. Meanwhile, Anna left Embry with Paul as she went to town, stopping at the grocery store and post office to register a change of address and restock Paxx's pantry and refrigerator.

"I have found nothing that ties Mr. Black to the gun that shot me or any of the other victims," Paxx said, leaning back in her chair at the dining table in frustration.

"What about that dealer, Hines?"

"He is a small-time weed dealer. Ebony and Mallory bought from him, but I can't connect anyone else to him."

"Who does he get his products from?"

Looking through her notes, Paxx frowned. "I haven't been able to connect him to anyone yet."

"We are going to get answers, and we will find closure," Paul said as he picked up a fussy Embry.

Paxx couldn't help but smile at the sight of Paul with his daughter. She stood up and walked over to the refrigerator, pulling out a juice bottle and filling Embry's sippy cup. "I know we will," she affirmed, handing the cup to Paul.

"I'm going to put her down for a nap," Paul said as he carried Embry out of the kitchen.

Paxx nodded as she put a kettle of water on the stove for tea. Pulling a cup from the cabinet, she heard the front door open. Soon, Anna entered the kitchen, carrying bags of groceries.

"Is there more?" Paxx asked as she turned off the burner.

"Yes," Anna responded as she set the bags on the counter.

Once the groceries were in the house and put away, Paxx made two cups of tea, and she and Anna went out onto the porch and settled on the swing.

"Did you buy out the entire store?" Paxx asked as she handed Anna a steaming cup.

"We have eaten all of your food, so I wanted to restock everything, plus a few things Embry likes."

For the next hour, they talked about paint colors for the new house, and Paxx told her she would like to turn one of the spare bedrooms into a kid's room with a crib and a toddler bed.

"That would be lovely."

"I figure Embry could stay with Jaylee and me while you are in the hospital having this little one," Paxx said as she rubbed Anna's belly.

"Embry would love that. Can I ask you a personal question?" Anna said, her tone turning serious.

"What personally don't you know about me?"

"Are you and Jaylee serious, like forever serious?"

Paxx met Anna's gaze as she replied, "I think so. I asked her about kids yesterday, and she said she didn't think she wanted any, which is good because neither do I. We agreed that being aunts to Embry and this next one was enough for us."

"Do you think you will marry her?"

Paxx laughed. "I think that is a long way off. I enjoy her being here and love waking up next to her, but I don't want to move too fast. Anna, this is my first committed relationship. I want to be sure, and I want her to be sure before we jump into the deep end."

"Have you had your first fight?"

"Yes, we discussed my return to work; she is scared, just like you are. Yesterday, we had a very heated discussion that ended with her nearly walking out the door." Paxx sighed. "I can't lose her, Anna. I have never felt a connection like this before, and except for you, I have never loved another woman as much as I love her."

"Then you better ensure she knows it and see if she feels the same way," Anna said, patting Paxx's leg.

"She does, she told me yesterday that she would stay forever if I wanted her to."

"What are you two smiling about?" Paul asked as he entered the room.

"Oh, Paxx's hot girlfriend and Paxx's plans to make an honest woman of her." Anna laughed as Paxx slapped her leg.

"Is that so?" Paul asked, sitting on a rocking chair. "Am I going to have a sister-in-law?"

"Not anytime soon," Paxx replied as her phone rang; pulling it from her pocket, she said, "Speaking of the hottie."

"Hi, beautiful," Paxx greeted.

"Hey, gorgeous, what ya doing?" Jaylee chirped.

"I am sitting here talking to Paul and Anna. Are you finished for the day?"

"No, I have one more therapy client and two appointments at the gym. I'm sorry, but I probably won't finish until after seven."

"That's okay, are you still coming over. I want to see you before I leave tomorrow."

"Yes, I have a bag packed, and I will come straight there after the gym."

"Great, then I will see you in a few hours."

"See you in a few hours; I love you."

"I love you, too. Be safe," Paxx responded without hesitation as she ended the call.

"You love her," Paul said. "I don't think I have ever seen you so happy."

Paxx met Paul's gaze and felt tears well up in her eyes. "I do, Paul. I am so in love with her, and that is why I need to get closure, not only in Dad's murder, but in my shooting. I want to start a life with her without all this baggage."

"We will, Paxx, I promise."

Paxx grinned at Anna. "Would you mind cutting and coloring my hair?"

"I put my haircutting supplies in my suitcase when we packed everything, I figured you would be tired of this mop on your head soon." Anna tussled Paxx's hair as she stood. "Do you have color?"

"I do," Paxx said as she stood and headed upstairs. "Do you have a cap and hook?"

"Yes, I do."

Paxx settled into a kitchen chair. Anna plugged in her clippers and went to work to get Paxx's hair back to the way she liked to wear it. Two hours later, Paxx smiled at her reflection in the mirror, admiring the blonde highlights in her dark hair and short haircut.

"Anna, you should open a salon," Paxx said as she entered the living room.

Anna shook her head. "Five years of standing all day, cutting and coloring people's hair was enough for me. I will stick to supplies and consultations."

"I'm glad the company you work for is letting you stay on and work remotely," Paxx said as she ran her fingers through her hair.

"They have been wanting to expand west; they think with me here, maybe it will be an incentive for companies to use them."

Before Paxx could respond, giggling echoed through the living room as Paul and Embry entered. Embry rubbed her eyes and clutched a stuffed bear larger than she was.

"There's my girl!" Paxx exclaimed as she knelt to scoop Embry into her arms. The little one squealed in delight, wrapping her chubby arms around Paxx's neck.

"Did you have sweet dreams?" Paxx asked, peppering kisses on Embry's face.

Embry nodded, a big grin lighting up her face, but she couldn't articulate her excitement beyond an excited babble.

Anna watched them with affection. "You're a natural with her."

Paxx felt a surge of pride at the compliment.

Just then, the front door opened. "Hi, everyone," Jaylee smiled, tossing her bag aside and shedding her jacket as if leaving behind the weight of the day.

Paxx's heart raced at the sight of her, how her fire-red hair cascaded around her shoulders, and how that smile made everything brighter even after a long day at work.

"Hey there," Paxx greeted as Jaylee approached them. "You finished early."

"And you got a new do, very sexy," Jaylee said with a wink as she admired Paxx's hair. "My last client rescheduled for Monday," she explained, leaning in to kiss Paxx before tickling Embry. "Did you miss me, little one?"

"Yay!" Embry cheered, reaching out for her.

Jaylee laughed as Paxx handed Embry over to her, and they twirled around in an impromptu dance that filled the room with joyful giggles. At that moment, Paxx's heart swelled with love seeing the happiness radiating from both girls reminding her why she needed to fight hard for closure. She wanted to create happy memories without fear hanging over their heads.

After a whirlwind of hugs and stories about the day, most of which revolved around various antics involving crayons and Playdough, Paul excused himself and went to the office.

As the three women and Embry gathered in the kitchen discussing dinner, Paxx felt an overwhelming urge to draw Jaylee close. She reached out and took Jaylee's hand in hers.

"You look tired."

Jaylee shrugged, but when their eyes met, Paxx could see it all, the exhaustion behind those sparkling green eyes and genuine warmth as Jaylee whispered back, stroking Paxx's hair, "Not tired enough not to be happy that I'm here."

"What do you all want for dinner?" Anna interrupted as they were leaning in for a kiss.

Paxx held up her hand as if to pause the moment as she continued leaning in, meeting Jaylee's lips. "I'm glad your home."

"Me too," Jaylee purred, kissing her once more.

"Paxx, Paxx," Embry's excited voice echoed as she patted Paxx's leg. Looking down, Paxx and Jaylee laughed as Embry blew them both kisses. Bending over, Paxx picked her up, and she and Jaylee kissed each of her cheeks as she squealed with delight.

"What do you want to eat, Embry?" Paxx asked as she turned to face Anna.

"Cheese," Embry said as she pointed to a box of shells and cheese on the counter.

"Yummy, cheese," Paxx laughed.

"I need a shower," Jaylee said tiredly.

Leaning closer, Paxx said, "If you will wait until after dinner, I will join you."

"If you don't think I smell too bad, I will wait."

Pressing her lips against Jaylee's ear, Paxx whispered, "I think you smell delicious."

Jaylee giggled, kissing Paxx's cheek.

As Anna stood over the stove cooking chicken, Paxx and Jaylee took turns holding Embry while they prepared mac and cheese and tossed a quick salad together.

After dinner, Paul cleaned the dishes while Anna bathed Embry. Meanwhile, Paxx and Jaylee retired upstairs.

"How was your day?" Paxx asked Jaylee as they undressed and stepped into the shower, the hot water enveloping them.

"It was okay; a couple of patients were kids with severe disabilities and helping them is both gratifying and challenging." Jaylee stood under the water, letting it wash away the day's stress while Paxx massaged her shoulders, causing her to moan in gratitude.

"Did you bring enough clothes for the next few days?" Paxx asked, pressing her lips to Jaylee's collarbone.

Leaning back into her, Jaylee sighed, "No, I will go by my apartment tomorrow after I drop you off at the airport."

"You could bring things to leave here if you want," Paxx suggested. "You could bring a toothbrush, deodorant, and some clothes."

"Are you asking me to move in?"

Paxx shrugged. "I'm saying if you want to leave things here, I will give you a key."

Looking over her shoulder, Jaylee raised an eyebrow, the steam from the shower swirling around them like a gentle fog. "A key? That sounds a little serious, don't you think?"

Paxx chuckled softly, her fingers still kneading Jaylee's shoulders. "Maybe. But it's just an invitation to make this place feel like home for you, too. It doesn't have to mean anything more than that if you don't want it to."

Jaylee let the warmth of the water seep deeper into her muscles. The thought of leaving some of her things at Paxx's felt both thrilling and peaceful. "It would be nice to have some of my things here, but... moving in sounds like a big step."

Paxx stepped closer, their bodies almost melding together under the cascading water. "I'm not rushing you; just think about it." She paused, brushing a damp lock of hair behind

Jaylee's ear, her touch lingering. "You already spend so much time here. It would just be practical."

Jaylee turned to face Paxx, her heart quickening at their closeness. "Practical?"

"Yeah, practical until we are ready for permanent."

"Okay," Jaylee said slowly, "Let's make it practical until it becomes permanent."

"I love you," Paxx whispered, pressing their lips together.

"I love you, too."

The warm water from the shower rained down upon their naked bodies as they stood close together, their slick skin pressed against each other. Paxx's hands explored Jaylee's curves, her fingers tracing the outline of her breasts and teasing her hard nipples. Jaylee let out a soft moan as Paxx's touch sent shivers down her spine. In return she explored Paxx's toned physique, she felt the strength and smoothness of her muscles under her touch.

As they continued to caress and explore each other, their movements becoming more urgent and intense, loud moans and pleas for more filled the air, their bodies shuddering with uncontrollable pleasure. They stood in each other's arms, their bodies trembling as the water rained down on them.

"That was amazing," Jaylee panted, trying to catch her breath.

"You're amazing," Paxx replied.

? ? ?
EIGHTEEN

"**P**axx, your phone's ringing," Jaylee said as she stretched across Paxx's body, picking it up off the bedside table.

Handing the phone to a groggy Paxx, Jaylee settled herself atop her, pressing her lips against her collarbone before moving down and pulling a nipple into her mouth, causing Paxx to gasp as she answered the phone.

"One minute, sir," Paxx said into the phone as she pushed the mute button. "Jay, this is my Captain. Can you go easy for a few minutes?"

When Jaylee moved to get up, Paxx wrapped her arm around her waist and said, "Don't go anywhere. You're not finished; I just need a few minutes."

Pressing their lips together, Jaylee smiled, "No, we are not finished."

Taking a deep breath, Paxx released her, then unmuted the phone and continued the conversation with Captain Kimble.

"Yes, sir, I will be at the shooting range on Tuesday morning. I am ready to be back, sir." Paxx said as she ended the call, just as a knock came from the bedroom door. "Just a minute," Paxx called out as she pulled on a robe and peeked her head into the bathroom, where Jaylee was running water into the bathtub; the scent of jasmine and honeysuckle filled the air.

"I'm not ready for you yet," Jaylee smiled as she approached the door.

Paxx raised an eyebrow. "Someone is at the door. Don't come out uncovered."

"Okay," Jaylee smiled as she pushed the door closed.

Crossing the room, Paxx opened the door; Anna stood outside, tears streaking her cheeks.

"Anna, what's wrong?"

"Paxx, it's your mom."

"My Mom?"

"Paul is on the phone with the hospital in Chicago, her housekeeper found her this morning."

"Her housekeeper, what happened?" Paxx asked, confused, as she pulled on a pair of lounge pants and a T-shirt, unconcerned about dressing in front of Anna. Opening the bathroom door, Paxx sighed at the sight of Jaylee lighting candles around the tub. "Jay, something has happened. I will be downstairs." Before Jaylee could ask questions, Paxx rushed downstairs with Anna, where Paul sat on the couch, his head in his hands.

"Paul," Anna said as she approached him.

Looking up, his eyes filled with tears as he shook his head.

"Paul, what happened?" Paxx asked, staring at him.

"The doctor said she had a stroke."

"How bad?"

"She had to be intubated," Paul said shakily. "Paxx, they are not sure...."

"How long?" Paxx interrupted.

"They don't know when or if she will wake up," Paul answered.

Paxx began to pace as she felt her anxiety rise. She wrung her hands until Jaylee appeared and wrapped her arms around her, calming her.

"What do we need to do, Paul?" Jaylee asked calmly.

"We have to go," Paxx whispered. "I have to see her; I have to talk to her."

Anna picked up her phone and began securing plane tickets for four adults and one child.

"Jay, do you want to go?" Paxx asked as she leaned into Jaylee's arms.

"Do you want me to be a part of this family?"

"Yes."

"Then I am going."

"Thank you," Paxx said, laying her head on Jaylee's shoulder. The tears that fell and the pain in her heart surprised her.

"Our flight leaves in four hours," Anna said as she hung up. "Paul, if you start packing, I will cancel your and Paxx's Pennsylvania flight."

Paxx straightened a new concern, twisting inside. "Paul."

"Let's get to Chicago and check on Mom. If she is stable, we will fly to Pennsylvania tomorrow, see Mr. Black, and then return to Chicago. Anna and Jaylee can stay with Mom and keep us informed about her condition," Paul assured Paxx, grasping her hands.

Paxx nodded, then followed Jaylee upstairs to pack.

Once in the bedroom, Jaylee asked, "Paxx, honey, what can I do to help you right now?"

Paxx sat on the edge of the bed, a blank look on her face. "I never thought I would see or talk to her again. Jay, when she left me twenty-one years ago, I swore I would never forgive her or speak to her ever again."

Sitting beside her, Jaylee said, "Paxx, you need closure."

"I can't forgive her for what she did, Jaylee," Paxx growled as she stood and began pacing.

As Paxx continued her restless pacing, her anger and frustration mounting, Jaylee stood, embraced her, and calmly spoke. "Paxx, I didn't say forgive her, I said you need closure, in whatever form that comes in."

Paxx stiffened as she met Jaylee's understanding gaze. "Help me."

"I will be with you the entire time if you want me."

"I want you," Paxx murmured as she pressed their lips together. "I'm sorry about messing up your romantic bath."

"You didn't mess up anything. We have time, and you need to relax now more than ever." Jaylee grinned as she led Paxx into the bathroom, where candles still burned and steam rose from the tub. "Besides," Jaylee continued, her voice lightening the mood as she gently guided Paxx toward the tub, "this might be the last chance we have to unwind before everything gets chaotic."

Paxx managed a small laugh, the tension easing slightly. "You're right. I could use a little distraction."

As Paxx settled into the warm water, the fragrant steam enveloping her, Jaylee sat on the tub's edge, her fingers lightly trailing across Paxx's shoulders. The flickering candlelight danced against the bathroom walls, casting calming shadows.

"Close your eyes."

Paxx obeyed, letting herself sink deeper into the soothing heat of the water. She took a deep breath, imagining they were still in that moment of bliss from earlier, before life had intruded with its harsh realities.

"How are you feeling?" Jaylee asked quietly after a few moments.

"Scared," Paxx admitted, her voice shaky. "I thought I was past all of this... that I'd moved on."

"You've been strong for so long," Jaylee replied, her tone sincere. "It's okay to feel this way. You're human."

The warmth of Jaylee's presence grounded Paxx. Every soft stroke of her fingers reminded Paxx that she wasn't alone in this fight. "What if she doesn't wake up?" Paxx whispered, opening her eyes to meet Jaylee's gaze.

"She will. And you'll have an opportunity to say what you need to say."

"But what if it's too late for those words? What if..."

"There are no 'what ifs. You're going to Chicago to see your mom; whatever happens next will unfold as it should. You deserve that chance."

Paxx took another deep breath, steeling herself against the wave of emotions threatening to pull her under again. "You really think so?"

"I know so." Jaylee smiled reassuringly and leaned down for a lingering kiss that radiated warmth through Paxx's entire being.

Reluctantly breaking away from their kiss, Jaylee grabbed a washcloth from the rack next to the tub. Dipping it into the bathwater, she washed Paxx's shoulders and back.

"What are you doing?"

"Just taking care of you."

As she surrendered to the tender care of Jaylee's hands, the worries of potential heartbreak eased. "Join me," Paxx said, taking Jaylee's hand.

Jaylee slowly undressed and stepped into the tub. Sitting in front of Paxx, she caressed her legs. Paxx released her tension as they sat, enjoying the tranquil atmosphere, until Anna walked in without knocking.

"Hey! Are you two, oh!" Anna froze mid-sentence, wide-eyed at the sight of Paxx and Jaylee in the tub with only bubbles covering them, an amused grin plastered on their faces.

"Can't a girl have a quick bath in peace?" Paxx retorted with mock indignation.

Anna shook her head but couldn't hide her smile. "I just wanted to let you know I booked your flight to Pennsylvania."

"Thank you."

Anna rolled her eyes as she crossed her arms over her chest. "You're going to have to get out of there eventually!"

Paxx sighed as Jaylee giggled.

"Seriously, though, we need to figure out where we will stay once we land."

"Okay," Paxx reluctantly agreed, realizing reality was beckoning again. She rose from the tub, letting the water cascade off her skin while wrapping herself in a towel.

As Anna retreated, Paxx reached for a clean towel from the rack nearby and handed it over to Jaylee.

"Thank you," Jaylee said heavily.

"What's wrong?" Paxx asked, noticing the change in her demeanor.

Motioning to the door, she asked, "Have you and Anna ever been together?"

"You mean romantically?"

Jaylee nodded, feeling foolish.

"Why do you ask?"

"You got out of the tub, and she didn't even flinch at seeing you naked," Jaylee said, almost ashamed.

"Anna is like my sister, and no, we have never been romantic. But we have done everything else together that sisters and best friends do. So, she has seen me at my best and my worst." Paxx replied, wrapping her arms around Jaylee and kissing her tenderly.

Jaylee smiled, a sigh of relief escaping her lips. "I'm sorry for jumping to conclusions."

"Don't be. Paul wondered the same thing." Paxx laughed as she pulled a suitcase from her closet, retreated into their bedroom, and began rifling through clothes. Her heart beat with anticipation and anxiety about seeing her mother again after such a long time.

"Really?" Jaylee asked, following Paxx into the bedroom.

"Yes, really," Paxx replied as she packed her suitcase.

"We will need to stop by my apartment so I can get some clothes, all I have here is sweats and scrubs," Jaylee said as she dressed.

Paxx chuckled as she caught Jaylee's confused stare.

"What are you laughing at?"

"I just realized that I have never seen you in anything but scrubs or sweats, both of which you look very sexy in, by the way."

"I can say the same thing about you: sweats, lounge pants, and your birthday suit, all of which are very becoming on you."

"We have nowhere to go but up in our wardrobe selection." Paxx smiled as she disappeared into the bathroom, reappearing moments later dressed in jeans, and a Nebraska Cornhuskers T-shirt.

"Very sexy," Jaylee grinned as Paxx wiggled her ass.

"Why, thank you, ma'am."

"Are you two ready to go?" Paul's voice called from downstairs.

Opening the bedroom door, Jaylee called back, "Coming."

Paxx closed her suitcase and followed Jaylee downstairs, where Paul stood holding Embry while Anna packed the diaper bag.

"I thought she was potty trained?" Paxx asked, confused.

"Have you ever tried to get a two-year-old to use an airplane bathroom at thirty thousand feet?" Anna quipped.

"Nope, and understood," Paxx replied with a nod. "We need to stop by Jay's place so she can get some clothes."

"JJ," Embry giggled, reaching out her arms to Jaylee.

"I figured as much," Paul said as he handed Embry to Jaylee.

After loading the bags into the minivan, they drove into town, stopping at Jaylee's apartment building, where she and Paxx went in to pack a suitcase.

Jaylee guided Paxx through the apartment, and Paxx took in the small kitchen with its dining table and two chairs tucked in the corner. The space melted into the cozy living room, where a plush burgundy loveseat sat with plump cushions and soft fabric. Above it hung a large, framed picture of a majestic mountain range at sunset, the vibrant pinks and purples of the sky painting a beautiful contrast against the darkening landscape. A sleek flat-screen television was mounted on the wall above the electric fireplace entertainment center, opposite the loveseat. Paxx took a moment to absorb the atmosphere of the apartment. Bookshelves lined one wall in the living room. "I love that you have all these books," Paxx said, running her fingers along the spines. "What's your favorite?"

"It's hard to choose just one, I like Patricia Cornwell, Jae and Sue Grafton."

Paxx chuckled, her heart warming at Jaylee's excitement. "A strong female lead who knows what she wants? I can totally see you liking that."

"What about you? What's your go-to read?"

"Hmm..." Paxx tapped her chin playfully before answering. "I don't read a lot, but I do like a good lesbian crime fiction novel once in a while. I like Carsen Taite and Jae's Conflict of Interest and Next of Kin, which are two of my favorites."

Jaylee raised an eyebrow. "Books about cops make sense."

"This is a nice place," Paxx said as they walked through Jaylee's apartment.

"Thanks. I've tried to make it feel like home. It's not much, but it's mine."

As they entered the bedroom, the simple yet elegant platform bed, adorned with a black-and-white checked bedspread and an array of fluffy, colorful pillows, drew Paxx's attention. Against one wall stood a vintage dresser with ornate handles that caught the light, adding a touch of elegance to the space. Paxx noticed feminine touches everywhere she looked, which added a delicate charm to the apartment.

With careful consideration, Jaylee placed her most essential items in her bag: a blend of comfortable clothes for everyday wear and something a bit more elegant for dinner. Her hands moved, folding each item carefully before placing them into the bag. Returning through the apartment, Jaylee checked the windows and balcony door while Paxx carried the suitcase to the front door. Outside at the minivan, Paxx felt anticipation bubbling inside her, a mixture of excitement about the trip and trepidation about seeing her mother after so long. She glanced sideways at Jaylee as they climbed into their seats, and the warmth radiating from her made everything feel less daunting.

"Are you okay?" Jaylee whispered when she noticed Paxx's pensive expression.

Paxx took a deep breath and nodded as she fastened her seatbelt. "Yeah...just trying to wrap my head around everything." She tried to sound casual, but knew Jaylee could sense her unease.

Jaylee smiled reassuringly and squeezed her hand tightly. Even though the past held painful memories and unresolved issues, having Jaylee by her side brought a sense of security and strength she had never felt.

"Paxx," Jaylee began, her voice cutting through the tension, "I know this trip might bring up a lot of emotions for you. Just know that I'm here for you, no matter what."

"Thank you, Jay, I really appreciate you being here with me through all this."

? ? ?

Facing Demons

Facing your demons is the only way you stop them from
having power over you!

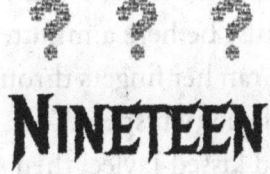

NINETEEN

The flight to Chicago went by quickly, even though Paxx wanted it to slow down. Once they had landed and collected their luggage, Paul went to the rental car desk to retrieve the keys. While they waited, Anna took Embry to the restroom, and Jaylee and Paxx guarded the luggage.

"I think it would be best if I could shower and freshen up a bit before going to the hospital," Paxx said when Paul returned with the rental van.

"I agree," Anna nodded. "And Embry needs to have her clothes changed. That last yogurt pack landed more on her shirt than her mouth."

Paul agreed and drove the twenty-five minutes to the hotel. Once checked in, they rode the elevator to the fourth floor, where they found their way down the hall to their adjoining rooms.

"See you in an hour," Paul said as he opened his and Anna's door. "I will call and check on Mom and let you know if we need to leave earlier."

"Okay," Paxx replied as she followed Jaylee into their room.

"Do you want me to unpack while you shower?" Jaylee asked Paxx.

M. LEA

Paxx sat on the edge of the bed and pulled Jaylee close, wrapping her arms around Jaylee's waist and laying her head against her chest. "Just be here a minute," Paxx murmured, smiling when Jaylee ran her fingers through her hair.

"I'm right here," Jaylee whispered.

Paxx stood up and kissed Jaylee; then she undressed. "I'm going to freshen up and change into something nicer."

"Okay," Jaylee smiled as she also undressed.

After a quick shower together, they each dressed in slacks and button-down shirts; as Paxx gelled and styled her hair, Jaylee applied eyeliner and mascara.

"You are so beautiful," Paxx said, looking at Jaylee in the mirror.

Jaylee smiled at their reflections. "You make me feel beautiful."

Turning, she leaned into Paxx, their arms encompassing one another. "I love you," she purred.

"I love you, too," Paxx responded, tightening her hold.

"Are you ready?" Jaylee asked as they broke the embrace.

"As ready as I will ever be, I suppose," Paxx replied, sitting on the bed and pulling on her boots.

Just then, a soft knock sounded from the door that connected their room to Paul and Anna's. Paxx opened the door, smiling at Embry standing on the other side.

"Paxx, Paxx," she squealed, holding out her arms to be held.

Laughing at her excitement, Paxx picked her up. "Are you ready to go, sweet girl?"

"Bye-bye," Embry mumbled, opening and closing her hand in a cute wave.

"We are ready if you are," Paul said from the other room.

The drive to the hospital took less time than they expected. Paul pulled up to the entrance, dropping the others off before parking the van. Paxx entered the hospital, Jaylee holding her hand, the sounds and movement of the bustling lobby filling her senses. Embry squirmed in Anna's arms, and she tried her best to keep her entertained as they waited for Paul near the information desk. Paxx glanced around; the antiseptic smell and fluorescent lights made her hands tense. She felt Jaylee squeeze her hand, and Anna gave her a reassuring nod, as if they both understood the nerves she didn't admit to having.

Together, they took the elevator to the sixth floor. The corridors were quieter here, punctuated by the soft rhythms of machines and distant voices. Paxx and Jaylee stood outside her mother's room in the ICU while Paul and Anna went in. Jaylee gripped her hands and spoke with soft encouragements as they waited.

"Paxx," Paul said from the doorway, "You need to come in."

"Is she awake?" Paxx asked hesitantly.

Paul shook his head. "No."

Closing her eyes and taking a deep breath, Paxx interlaced her fingers with Jaylee's and entered the room. Paxx's heart raced as she took in the sight of her mother, the woman who she remembered being radiant and beautiful, now lying pale and fragile beneath the hospital sheets. Tubes snaked across her body. Their purpose was essential and suffocating as machines beeped rhythmically.

Jaylee squeezed her hand tighter. "You've got this," she whispered, though the words felt inadequate in the face of such vulnerability.

Paxx approached the bedside, her breath hitching at the sight of her mother's stillness. "Hey, Mom," she said softly, forcing a smile that didn't quite reach her eyes. "It's me, Paxxton." She reached out, brushing a few strands of grey hair away from her mother's forehead.

"You okay?" Anna asked, stepping next to Paxx at Jaylee's urging.

Paxx nodded, but kept her gaze on her mother. "I'm trying," she replied, feeling like she was looking at a stranger. "I don't even recognize her, Anna," Paxx muttered as tears rose. "The last time I saw her, she was young, and despite what Dad put her through, she was strong and beautiful."

"It's been twenty years, Paxx," Paul said from the other side of the bed.

Looking up at him, anger flared deep within her. "It's not my fault that it has been twenty years since I've seen her." Paxx spat.

"I didn't say it was your fault," Paul said calmly.

"I can't do this," Paxx murmured as she turned and left the room.

"I'll go," Paul said when Jaylee moved to follow her. Catching Paxx down the hall, Paul gripped her arm to stop her. "Paxx."

"Paul, I thought this would be good for me, for her, but all I feel is anger," Paxx said without turning around.

"You knew this would not be easy, but you're here, and she may never wake up, so talk to her, tell her about your life and Jaylee." Paul sighed, "Paxx, tell her about your anger; you need to leave it with her and stop carrying it around."

"Will she even hear and comprehend what I say?" Paxx whispered, turning to face him.

"We have to believe that she will," Paul replied, pulling her into his arms.

Paxx nodded against his shoulder as they turned back toward the room.

Taking a deep breath, Paxx wiped her eyes and squared her shoulders. The warmth of Paul's embrace lingered as they walked back toward the room. Each step felt heavier, and her heart pounded a steady rhythm of uncertainty.

"I don't know how to do this," she murmured, more to herself than to him.

"Just be honest," Paul encouraged. "She needs to hear from you."

Paxx nodded, but doubt still clouded her mind. As they reached the door, a sense of dread washed over her. The machines inside continued their relentless beeping, a reminder of her mother's fragile state.

Jaylee stood by the doorway, her eyes brimming with tears and understanding. Paxx could see the supportive glimmer in them. "I'll be right here if you need me," she whispered, squeezing Paxx's hand before stepping back.

"Hey... Mom," she whispered again, her voice cracking under the weight of emotions. She reached out, gripping her mother's hand, her fingers trembling slightly at the touch. "It's me, Paxxton."

Silence enveloped them as she waited for a response that would not come. Paxx swallowed hard and fought against the swell of tears that threatened to spill. "Mom..." she tried again, struggling to find the right words. It had been so long since they last spoke, and all that remained was a gaping open wound. "It's been so long..." Her chest ached with emptiness; "I wanted you to know I turned out okay...I'm a narcotics detective now, and I love my job. I own a house with some acreage, and even though you may have disapproved of my lifestyle, I have the most amazing girlfriend." Paxx paused as she looked over at Jaylee with a soft smile.

With each word she spoke, she released years of pain and hurt. "But mom, you weren't there for me when I needed you! You missed my high school graduation, my graduation from the police academy. You missed so fucking much!" The frustration flooded through her as words spilled out unfiltered. "I don't even know who you are; I feel like I am looking at and talking to a stranger," Paxx's voice cracked with emotion as she turned to look at Paul, who gave her a comforting nod. "It makes me so angry." Tears spilled over as she struggled to hold back the flood of emotions. Paxx paused, overwhelmed by it all. Her voice was softer when she continued, "I need you to wake up; I need to know you hear me." The heart monitor beeped beside them as Paxx poured out all the words she had been holding for too long.

After several moments of silence, Jaylee stepped up beside Paxx and rubbed her back. Turning away from the bed, without speaking, Paxx exited the room. Walking down the hall, she entered a restroom and closed the door behind her. Running cold water in the sink, Paxx filled her hands and splashed water on her face, still fighting to keep her emotions in check.

"Paxx, are you okay?" Anna asked from outside the door.

Pulling towels from the dispenser, Paxx opened the door as she dried her face. "Yeah, I'm fine," she said unconvincingly.

"You know what fine stands for, don't you?" Jaylee asked from behind Anna.

Anna and Paxx looked at Jaylee in confusion as they shook their heads.

Jaylee counted each letter on her fingers, saying, "Fucked up, Insecure, Neurotic, and Emotional."

"I'd say that sounds about right," Paxx laughed as she stepped into Jaylee's open arms.

"The doctor's in her room," Paul said as he hurried to them.

Hurrying back to the room, Jaylee took Embry from Anna and stood close to the door as the doctor spoke.

"Her vitals are good, and the brain scan we did this morning looks promising." The doctor said.

"Do you have an idea when she might wake up?" Paul asked.

"Hard to say, but from what the tests say, I am confident she will," he nodded.

"My sister and I need to fly to Pennsylvania tomorrow morning if you think she is out of the woods."

The doctor looked at Paxx and Paul, and he said, "Her condition could change at any time, but I don't see any reason you shouldn't go. Will you be gone long?"

"Just a day, hopefully," Paul replied. "My wife Anna and Paxx's girlfriend Jaylee will stay here."

"Good," the doctor nodded, "Then they can keep you informed if things change."

After a few more questions, the doctor left the room.

At six o'clock, they left the hospital to eat and then returned to the hotel for the evening.

"We fly out at eleven tomorrow morning," Paul said as they rode the elevator up to their rooms. "I'd like to go to the hospital before we leave. Is eight-thirty alright with you?"

Paxx and Jaylee agreed and said goodnight as they entered their room.

"How are you doing?" Jaylee asked once they were alone.

"I just want to crawl into bed with you and forget where we are for the next ten hours," Paxx murmured, pulling Jaylee into her arms.

"How about you crawl into bed, and I give you the best massage you have ever had?" Jaylee whispered as she began unbuttoning Paxx's shirt.

Smiling seductively as she unfastened her pants and pushed them down over her hips, Paxx agreed. "I won't argue with that."

"Good."

As Paxx settled on the bed, Jaylee dug into her overnight bag and pulled out a bottle of massage oil.

"What's that?" Paxx asked.

"Oh, just a little something I brought to help relax you." Her smile was warm and reassuring as she pulled off her pants and climbed onto the bed in just her lace panties. She straddled Paxx's hips and poured some oil into her hands, and then, with skilled fingers, Jaylee worked the warming oil into Paxx's tense back, kneading and soothing her stiff muscles.

Paxx let out a soft moan as Jaylee's hands worked their magic. The tension in her shoulders melted away under the skillful touch. As Jaylee's fingers trailed down her spine, Paxx felt a different heat building within her.

"That feels amazing," she murmured, her voice muffled by the pillow.

Jaylee leaned in close, her breath warm against Paxx's ear. "I'm just getting started," she whispered.

A shiver ran through Paxx's body at the suggestive tone. She turned, glimpsing Jaylee's face in the dim light. The desire in those green eyes made Paxx's heart race.

Jaylee's hands slid lower, down the curve of Paxx's back, tracing the dip of her waist like she was memorizing every inch of her. The oil made her skin gleam under the dim light, and Jaylee's breath hitched just a little as she let her palms glide over the swell of Paxx's hips. "You're fucking perfect," Jaylee whispered, her voice rough now, like she was already imagining what came next.

"Don't stop," Paxx breathed.

"You want me to keep going?" she asked, her voice a low purr that sent shivers down Paxx's spine. Paxx nodded, unable to form words.

Moving down, Jaylee began kneading the muscles of Paxx's calves with a firmness that made Paxx whimper. Her fingers trailed higher, needing her thighs as her thumbs traced the sensitive skin of Paxx's inner thighs, and Paxx spread her legs wider without even thinking about it. Jaylee hummed as she leaned down, pressing a hot, open-mouthed kiss to the small of Paxx's back.

Moving up, Jaylee continued kneading Paxx's firm ass and lower back before working her way back down to her inner thighs. Paxx's breath caught in her throat as Jaylee's fingers teased her sensitive flesh. She arched her back, begging for more. Jaylee obliged, her touch growing bolder as she traced lazy circles along Paxx's inner thighs.

"Is this okay?" Jaylee murmured, her voice dripping with desire.

"God, yes," Paxx gasped, turning her head and meeting Jaylee's heated gaze over her shoulder. "Please, don't stop."

Jaylee's lips curved into a wicked smile. She leaned down, pressing a trail of passionate kisses along Paxx's spine. Her hands never ceased their ministrations, alternating between firm kneading and feather-light caresses that left Paxx trembling.

As Jaylee's fingers slipped between her folds, her fingers moved, teasing and exploring Paxx's most sensitive areas. Paxx's breath came in ragged gasps as waves of pleasure coursed through her body as she gripped the sheets and buried her head in the pillow.

"Jay, please," Paxx begged.

Jaylee slid two fingers inside, curling them to hit that perfect spot. Paxx cried out, her back arching as Jaylee began a steady rhythm. Jaylee slid her other hand underneath Paxx to circle her swollen clit as she nipped and kissed her ass.

The dual stimulation was too much. Paxx felt herself climbing higher and higher, chasing that elusive peak. Jaylee's movements became faster and more insistent.

"Let go," Jaylee urged.

Paxx buried her face in the pillow as the waves of pleasure washed over her. Her body trembled and shook, each sensation rocking her to the core. Jaylee's touch was gentle yet powerful, guiding and igniting her every step of the way. As

Paxx reached the peak of bliss, she was surprised to feel tears streaming down her cheeks. Her sobs echoed through the room, racking her body with overwhelming emotion.

Concerned, Jaylee wrapped her arms around her and whispered soothing words into her ear. "Baby, what's wrong? Did I hurt you?"

Paxx shook her head, turning onto her side and curling against Jaylee's warm body. "No," she choked out between sobs. "I just... I've never felt like this before."

Jaylee kissed away the tears from Paxx's flushed cheeks and held her close, whispering reassurances and love into her ear.

After a few moments, Paxx's sobs turned into quiet sniffles. She looked up at Jaylee with watery eyes. "I'm sorry," she whispered hoarsely. "I don't know what came over me."

Jaylee shook her head, leaning in to kiss Paxx tenderly. "Don't apologize," she murmured against Paxx's lips. "Sometimes, release can bring unexpected emotions. Do you want to talk about it?"

Paxx nuzzled into the crook of Jaylee's neck. "It's just... I've never felt such a strong connection with anyone before."

Jaylee's heart swelled with love for the incredible woman in her arms. She kissed Paxx, wiping away any remaining tears.

"You are incredible, Paxx," Jaylee breathed against her lips. "You are strong, beautiful, and so damn brave."

As they lay in each other's embrace, Paxx traced her fingers along Jaylee's jawline, marveling at her familiarity and comfort with this woman who had entered her life only a short time ago. Every touch, every kiss, every moment shared between them felt right.

? ? ?

TWENTY

P axx's sleep was unsettled and broken. She woke several
times to Jaylee's calming voice and gentle caresses. As
the sun shone through the hotel curtains, Paxx awoke, a fierce
dread and fear consuming her. Sitting on the edge of the
bed, she flinched when Jaylee kissed her shoulder and ran her
fingers down her back.

"Paxx, baby, what's wrong?" Jaylee asked, sitting back on
her heels.

"I need some space," Paxx said as she stood.

"Okay, but please don't shut me out."

Turning, Paxx met Jaylee's gaze. Jaylee stifled a gasp at the
wild look in Paxx's eyes.

"I feel a little out-of-control right now."

Jaylee moved to the edge of the bed, reaching out her hand.
"What can I do to help you?"

Paxx swallowed hard as she whispered, "I'm afraid to touch
you."

With confusion, Jaylee dropped her hand, stood, and then
slowly moved toward her. "Why?"

"Jaylee, stop," Paxx said, holding up her hands and stepping
back.

"Paxx, talk to me. What's happened?"

Pinching the bridge of her nose, Paxx asked, "How many times did I wake up last night?"

Jaylee shrugged, "I don't know, three or four, maybe."

Without meeting her gaze, Paxx asked, "Did I touch you?"

Still confused, Jaylee replied, "Yes."

As tears welled in her eyes, Paxx whispered, "Did I force myself on you?"

Stepping closer, Jaylee said, "Paxx, you could never force yourself on me."

As she tried to step away, Jaylee placed her hands on Paxx's hips, holding her in place. "Paxx."

Standing with her arms at her sides, her body slumped, Paxx asked, "Did I hurt you?"

"Of course not," Jaylee said reassuringly.

"It must have been a dream," Paxx sighed, relief filling her.

"Paxx, what did you think you did to me?"

"I... we..."

"You what?"

"We had sex," Paxx started, "But it was rough, hard sex like I used to have with women before I met you."

Not loosening her hold, Jaylee asked, "Were you having sex with me or someone else?"

Paxx gasped as she met Jaylee's gaze. "It was with you! Jay, I haven't thought about anyone else since we've been together."

Jaylee grinned seductively at her defensiveness. "So, are you saying you want our sex to be rougher, harder?"

"I never want to hurt you," Paxx whispered as she cupped Jaylee's face.

"Just because it's hard and rough doesn't mean you will hurt me," she murmured against Paxx's lips.

"Are you saying you do not oppose me being more aggressive?" Paxx asked, sliding her arms around Jaylee's shoulders.

"I am saying if you need something a little more aggressive, then we can explore that," Jaylee smiled slyly.

Paxx's eyes widened as Jaylee's words sank in, her body trembling with fear and desire. "Jay..." she started, but Jaylee silenced her with a kiss, deep and hungry, her tongue sliding against Paxx's with a ferocity that left them both gasping for air.

Jaylee broke the kiss, her hands gripping Paxx's hips as she ground against her, the friction sending sparks of pleasure racing through their bodies. Stepping away, Jaylee slowly removed her shirt. "Do you want me, Paxx?" she asked, her voice low and sultry.

Paxx moaned softly, her hands gripping Jaylee's hips. "Yes," she whispered, her voice trembling with need. "God, yes."

Jaylee grinned, her hands sliding up to cup Paxx's tits, her thumbs brushing over her hard nipples. "Then take me!" she demanded, her voice a sultry command that sent shivers straight to Paxx's core. "Show me how much you want me."

Paxx paused, her heart pounding as she looked into Jaylee's lustful eyes. Then, with a growl of desire, she surged forward, capturing Jaylee's lips in a kiss of all teeth and tongue. Her hands fisted in Jaylee's hair, pulling her closer as she pressed her against the wall, their bodies grinding together in a desperate rhythm.

Jaylee moaned into the kiss, her hands sliding down to grip Paxx's ass, pulling her closer until there was no space left between them. "Fuck, yes," she gasped as Paxx's lips trailed down her neck, leaving a trail of hungry kisses and bite marks.

Paxx's hands roamed over Jaylee's body with a feverish urgency, brushing over the soft curve of her tits before sliding down to the waistband of her panties. "I need to touch you." She growled, her voice thick with desire.

Jaylee nodded, her breath coming in ragged gasps as Paxx's fingers slid beneath the lace, stroking the slick heat between her thighs. "Fuck, yes," she cried out, her hips bucking against Paxx's hand as she sank into the pleasure.

"You feel fucking amazing," Paxx whispered, her lips trailing fervent kisses along Jaylee's collarbone as she set a relentless rhythm with her fingers, hitting all the right spots. Paxx's other hand slid up Jaylee's outer thigh, her nails digging into the soft flesh as she pulled her leg up to her waist and leaned in closer, her breath hot against Jaylee's ear. The sound of their ragged breaths and the slick movements of Paxx's hand filled the intimate space between them.

Jaylee's nails dug into Paxx's shoulders as she arched into the touch, wrapping her leg around Paxx's waist as her body trembled with the force of her pleasure.

"Are you alright?" Paxx whispered breathlessly.

"Don't fucking stop," Jaylee begged, her voice a needy whimper that sent a surge of heat through Paxx's body.

Paxx complied, her fingers moving faster as she pressed her thumb against Jaylee's clit, stroking it in tight little circles that had her moaning loudly. "Come for me, Jay," Paxx demanded, her voice low and commanding, as she thrust her fingers deeper, faster, pushing Jaylee over the edge.

Jaylee's body convulsed as the pleasure washed over her in waves, her orgasm crashing over her with a force that left her shaking and gasping for air. "Fuck," she moaned, her legs giving out as she sank into Paxx's arms.

Paxx held her close, her breath coming in ragged gasps as she pressed soft kisses to Jaylee's neck. "Fuck, I love you," she whispered, her voice shaky with emotion.

Jaylee smiled as she wrapped her arms around Paxx, holding her close. "I love you, too."

Moving to the bed, they collapsed in each other's arms, their breathing slowing as they kissed. Swiping hair away from Jaylee's eyes, Paxx asked, "Are you okay?"

"Paxx, that was fucking amazing; you can take me like that anytime."

Paxx felt a surge of relief and desire at Jaylee's words. She pulled her closer, nuzzling into her neck. "I was so worried I'd hurt you or push too far."

Jaylee ran her fingers through Paxx's hair. "You didn't hurt me at all. I trust you completely." She tilted Paxx's chin until their eyes met. "And I want all of you, the gentle and the rough."

Their lips met tenderly, then slowly built in intensity. Jaylee rolled them over, so she was straddling Paxx, her eyes dark with renewed desire. "Now it's my turn to show you how much I want you," she purred, grinding their centers together.

Paxx's breath caught at the feeling of Jaylee's wetness moving against her and Jaylee's hands roaming over her body. She arched into the touch and moved her hips in rhythm with Jaylee, desperate for more. A sharp knock at the door between their room and Paul's startled them before they could continue.

"Shit," Paxx said as Jaylee slid off her and under the covers. Paxx stood and pulled on her robe before crossing the room and opening the door.

Paul stood on the other side of the door, a knowing smirk on his face. "Since you are up, the hospital called, and mom's awake."

Looking back at Jaylee, who was waiting impatiently in bed, Paxx smiled. "We are up but not finished."

"You have forty-five minutes to finish, shower, and get dressed; we are leaving at seven-thirty," Paul said as he shut the door.

Shutting the door on their side, Paxx removed her robe and returned to the bed. "Now, where were we?"

"Right about here," Jaylee purred as she captured Paxx's mouth with hers and slid her hand between Paxx's thighs. Jaylee's touch was demanding, sending shivers of pleasure through her body. She tangled her hands in Jaylee's hair, pulling her closer for a deep, hungry kiss.

"God, Jay," Paxx moaned against her lips. "Please..."

Jaylee grinned wickedly, her fingers teasing Paxx's entrance. "Please, what? Paxxton, tell me what you want."

Paxx whimpered, her body trembling with need. "I want you. Please, Jay, I want you."

Hungrily, Jaylee set a relentless pace that had Paxx crying out. With every stroke of Jaylee's fingers and every kiss shared between them, Paxx felt herself spiraling over the edge. A wave of heat engulfed her as she surrendered completely to the pleasure building within, each contraction drawing her deeper into bliss.

As an overwhelming rush that sent shockwaves through her body, Paxx cried out in pleasure as it pulled her under its intoxicating grip. She clung tightly to Jaylee, feeling every tremor ripple through them both until they were finally left panting in each other's arms.

"Holy fuck, we have to do this more often," Jaylee breathed as she gazed into Paxx's wild, satisfied eyes.

Paxx grinned at Jaylee's newfound enthusiasm. "You like that?"

"Hell yeah, I do," Jaylee said before her voice lowered, and she continued. "I need to tell you something about my past relationship."

Paxx sat up. "You can tell me anything."

Taking a deep breath, Jaylee sat up and faced Paxx, intertwining their fingers. "My last relationship was with a woman in her forties; our relationship was..." She paused, trying to find the right words. "Our relationship was strictly sexual and, more to the point, it was about me satisfying her."

Paxx brushed the hair from Jaylee's face. "Honey, I'm so sorry."

Meeting her gaze, Jaylee said, "After four months of her directing my every move, I got sick of 'do it like this, not like that' and her constant degrading and correction. And then I met you. The first day I walked into your room, the way you looked at me was the last time I saw her, and it was to tell her it was over."

Paxx's heart swelled with pride and love as Jaylee spoke. "Jay," she whispered.

"Paxx, until we were together, I had never felt pleasure, I had never had an orgasm, I thought I had, but after being with you, I knew I had found someone who wanted me to be happy, wanted me to be fulfilled."

"I want you to be happy, Jay, and I want to fulfill all of your desires," Paxx said as she pressed their lips together. "Never let me take advantage of you like that."

"I know you never will, Paxx, and you have already fulfilled my deepest desire simply by loving me," Jaylee whispered as she melted into Paxx's embrace.

? ? ?

TWENTY-ONE

Paxx and Jaylee rushed to the shower at ten after seven, giggling. Jaylee told Paxx, "Turn around and look in the mirror."

Turning around and looking over her shoulder, Paxx's eyes widened, and a smile spread across her lips as she admired a large hickey on the left cheek of her ass. Meeting Jaylee's amused gaze, Paxx said, "I expect a matching one on the other cheek when I get back."

Looking at her watch, Jaylee sighed, "Too bad we are out of time; otherwise, I would make them match right now."

"You drive me crazy," Paxx laughed as she pulled Jaylee into the shower.

After a quick shower, they dressed before Paul knocked on the door again.

"Are you two ready?" he asked, hopeful, as Paxx opened the door.

"Just gotta put my boots on," Paxx exclaimed as she sat on the edge of the bed.

"Did you remember everything for tonight and tomorrow?" Paul inquired, glancing around the room.

"Oh shit," Paxx cursed under her breath.

"I'll grab your toiletries," Jaylee called out from the bathroom, where she was putting the finishing touches on her makeup.

After slipping on her boots, Paxx quickly packed a change of clothes and the toiletry bag Jaylee handed her into a small carry-on bag.

"Where's Anna and Embry?" Paxx asked as she slung the bag over her shoulder.

"Anna took her downstairs for breakfast," Paul replied, leading the way down the hall to the elevator.

The echoes of their hurried footsteps filled the dimly lit hall, filling Paxx with a sudden wave of anxiety. The past few days' events had left her on edge, and now they were rushing off into the unknown. As they stood in the elevator, Paxx gazed at Jaylee, who seemed unfazed and composed as always. Paxx admired her figure, accentuated by slim-fitting black slacks and a form-fitting light green sweater that hugged her curves in all the right places. Perfectly applied makeup adorned her flawless complexion, highlighting her piercing green eyes. Her fiery red hair cascaded around her shoulders in tight curls.

Paxx felt underdressed and out of her league in her simple attire: tight black jeans and a button-down white shirt. She had taken the time to tame and style her usually unruly hair and apply a touch of mascara and eyeliner. Still, she couldn't help but feel inadequate next to Jaylee's effortless beauty.

"You okay?" Jaylee whispered, sensing Paxx's unease.

Paxx nodded, forcing a smile. "Yeah, just... nervous, I guess."

Jaylee squeezed Paxx's hand, sending instant calmness through Paxx's body. "It's going to be alright," she murmured, her voice low and soothing.

The elevator doors slid open to the bustling hotel lobby. Anna and Embry were waiting near the entrance. Embry's face lit up as she spotted them and waved enthusiastically.

"There you are!" Anna called out, relief evident in her voice. "We were starting to worry."

"JJ," Embry squealed, reaching for Jaylee.

"Good morning, sweetie," Jaylee smiled, taking Embry from Anna.

"I'll go get the van," Paul said as he exited the doors and walked to the parking garage.

While they waited, Jaylee babbled with Embry as Anna pulled Paxx aside.

"So, this morning was pretty passionate?" Anna asked with a knowing grin.

Heat rose in Paxx's cheeks. "You heard us?"

Laughing, Anna replied, "I think the entire floor heard you. What did you do to that lucky woman?"

Looking at Jaylee, Paxx said, "It's not what I did to her, Anna; it's what she's done to me."

Anna's eyebrows shot up, her grin widening. But before Anna could respond, Paul pulled up in the van. The crisp morning air hitting Paxx's face cleared her thoughts. Jaylee settled Embry into her car seat before sliding in next to Paxx. The drive to the hospital was a blur of nervous energy as Paxx's mind raced with uncertainty and fear of seeing her mom awake. She tried to focus on the warmth of Jaylee's thigh pressed against hers, anchoring her to the present.

Placing her arm on the back of the seat behind Paxx, Jaylee rubbed her shoulder, leaned over, and whispered in her ear. "I love you, and I will be right by your side if you want me there."

Tilting her head so their heads touched, Paxx said as she intertwined their fingers. "I love you, too, and always want you by my side."

When they arrived at the hospital, they found a spot in the parking garage before heading inside. Jaylee and Paxx walked hand in hand toward the entrance, with Paul and Anna leading the way. Embry playfully blew kisses at them from her father's arms, causing giggles from both Jaylee and Paxx.

They stepped into the elevator and watched as the numbers lit up above the door, signaling their ascent upward. The doors opened on the fifth floor to a busy corridor filled with nurses and guests, beeping machines, and the pungent smell of disinfectant.

As they approached their mother's ICU room, a new wave of anxiety washed over Paxx, causing her to pause. Looking back at her, Paul halted and turned to face her. "Do you want me to go in first?"

Paxx nodded and gripped Jaylee's hand tightly.

Paul and Anna disappeared into the room. Jaylee rubbed Paxx's forearm with her free hand. "Paxx, sweetie."

Meeting Jaylee's concerned gaze, Paxx smiled, then leaned in and pressed their lips together. "I'm alright," she murmured.

After several minutes, Anna walked out of the room with Embry in her arms. "I'm going to take Embry to the bathroom; you two go in."

"Is she awake?" Paxx asked.

Anna nodded. "She is groggy but awake."

"Did you tell her I was here?"

"Yes, Paul told her."

"Does she want to see me?" Paxx asked hesitantly.

"Paxx, please just go in." Anna encouraged.

As Anna walked away, Paxx and Jaylee entered the room.

When she saw Paxx, tears filled her mother's eyes and spilled onto her cheeks. "Paxxton," she said hoarsely.

Without letting go of Jaylee's hand, Paxx slowly walked to the bed. "Mom," Paxx murmured.

The silence in the room was palpable as Paxx stood, staring at her mother's frail form in the hospital bed. The beeping of monitors and the soft sound of the oxygen machine filled the silence. Jaylee squeezed Paxx's hand, offering support.

"Oh, Paxxton," her mother whispered again, her voice cracking with emotion. She raised a hand towards her daughter.

Paxx hesitated, then stepped forward, gently grasping her mother's hand. The contact flooded her with memories of childhood, both happy and painful. She swallowed hard, fighting back a surge of emotions that threatened to overwhelm her.

Paul cleared his throat and excused himself, leaving Paxx alone with her mother and Jaylee.

"Who's this?" her mother asked, her gaze shifting to Jaylee.

Releasing Jaylee's hand, Paxx wrapped her arm around her waist. "This is my partner, Jaylee," Paxx said proudly.

Releasing Paxx's hand, her mom extended it to Jaylee. "It's nice to meet you, Jaylee."

Jaylee took her hand and smiled. "It's lovely to meet you, Mrs. Algatta."

"Oh, dear, I haven't been Mrs. Algatta in years; please call me Patsy."

"Yes, ma'am," Jaylee said, releasing her hand.

"Paxxton, can we talk?"

"I think we need to."

"Are you okay?" Jaylee asked Paxx. "I can wait in the hall to give you two some privacy."

Stepping away from the bed, Paxx kissed Jaylee and nodded. "Thank you, I love you."

"I love you, too."

After Jaylee exited the room, Paxx pulled a chair beside the bed. "Paxxton," her mom began. "I heard everything you said yesterday." She paused as tears ran down her cheeks, and the beeping of one machine increased.

"Mom," Paxx began.

"Don't," Patsy said. "I have no excuse for leaving and not contacting you for twenty years. I am ashamed and so very sorry."

Paxx felt hot tears run down her cheeks as years of anger and hurt rose to the surface. "Why did you leave me? Why didn't you ever call or write to me?"

"Once I left, I was so relieved to be away from your father, but as time passed, I was too ashamed to face you."

"You left Paul to protect me from Dad, and you left me to fend him off when Paul wasn't around."

Patsy flinched at Paxx's words, her face crumpling with guilt and sorrow. "I know," she whispered. "I was selfish and weak, and I convinced myself you'd be better off without me, that Paul would protect you. Paxx, I was wrong, so terribly wrong."

Paxx clenched her fists, fighting the urge to lash out further. "Do you have any idea what it was like? To wake up one day and find out your mother had abandoned you? To face Dad's rage alone?"

Tears streamed down Patsy's face. "I can't imagine the pain I caused you. I've regretted my decision every day since."

"Then why didn't you come back?" Paxx demanded, her voice rising as she stood, scraping the chair across the floor. "Why didn't you call, write, or do anything to show you fucking cared?"

"I'm so sorry, Paxxton," Patsy reached out, her frail hand hovering between them. "And I know sorry doesn't begin to cover it, but I truly am. If I could go back..."

"But you can't," Paxx interrupted, her words sharp. "You can't," Paxx sighed. "I don't want to argue; what's done is done, and nothing can change the past. I came because I wanted you to know I have a great life. I have finally met the love of my life, and I wanted to meet her. Paul and I have to fly to Pennsylvania in a few hours, so I will let them come back so you can visit and see Embry." Paxx turned toward the door and then paused after a few steps. Looking at her mom over her shoulder, she said, "I hope your recovery goes well; maybe you can come visit Jaylee and me once you're better."

"Do you mean that?" her mom asked shakily.

"Yes," Paxx replied before exiting the room.

Paxx stepped into the hallway, her heart pounding and her emotions swirling. Leaning against the wall, she took a deep breath, trying to calm herself. Jaylee appeared beside Paxx, wrapping her arms around her and holding her close. Paxx buried her face in Jaylee's neck, inhaling her comforting scent.

"I've got you, sweetie," Jaylee murmured.

"Paxx, are you alright?" Paul asked.

Straightening up, Paxx nodded, "Did you hear any of that?"

"All of it."

"Paul, I can't forgive her, but I don't want to be the one walking away from a relationship."

"I'm proud of you, Paxx," Paul smiled as he embraced her. Releasing her, he looked at his watch. "We have to be at the airport in an hour and a half; Anna and I will visit a little longer."

Paxx nodded. "Jaylee and I will be in the waiting room."

As Paxx and Jaylee walked down the hall, Jaylee stole glances at Paxx, her mouth turned up in a sweet smile.

"What are you smiling at?" Paxx asked.

Stopping at a restroom, Jaylee pulled Paxx in, locking the door behind them. Turning to face her, Jaylee pressed Paxx against the door. "You have found the love of your life?" she purred against Paxx's ear.

Paxx shivered at the feel of Jaylee's warm breath on her skin. "Yes," she whispered, her hands instinctively finding Jaylee's hips. "I have."

Jaylee leaned in and kissed Paxx's forehead, cheek, and lips. The kiss was tender and comforting, a physical reassurance of her presence and support.

When they parted, Paxx rested her forehead against Jaylee's. "Thank you for being here with me."

"I will go anywhere with you."

"Can I ask you something?"

"Of course, anything."

"Be honest when you answer."

Jaylee nodded, "I will."

Paxx paused, unsure how to approach the question.

"Paxx, what is it?" Jaylee urged.

"Are you proud to be seen with me?" Paxx finally blurted out.

Jaylee stepped back, confused. "Of course, I am. Why would you ask me that?"

Paxx motioned up and down Jaylee's body and then up and down her own. "Look at you; you're gorgeous, dress fashionably, and have perfect makeup and hair. I dress comfortably, and I have never been one for much makeup."

Jaylee's eyes softened as she cupped Paxx's face in her hands. "Oh, sweetie, you're gorgeous, inside and out. Your strength, your kindness, your intelligence, those are the things that make you irresistible to me. I love the way you dress. It's authentic and uniquely you. And your natural beauty doesn't need any enhancement; you are smoking hot."

Paxx's eyes welled with tears, overwhelmed by Jaylee's sincerity, and then her voice turned mischievous. "Have you ever had sex in a hospital bathroom?"

Jaylee's eyes widened, a spark of desire igniting within them. She bit her lip, glancing around the small bathroom before gazing at Paxx. "No," she admitted, her voice low and husky. "But there's a first time for everything."

With a swift movement, Paxx stepped forward, pressing Jaylee against the sink. Her hands found Jaylee's hips, gripping them tightly.

Jaylee leaned in, her lips brushing against Paxx's ear. "Are you sure about this?" she whispered, her breath hot against Paxx's skin.

Paxx nodded, her heart racing. "Yes," she breathed, her fingers unfastening Jaylee's pants. "I want you."

Jaylee's breath hitched as Paxx's fingers unfastened her pants. The cool air of the bathroom clashed with the heat radiating between them. Paxx's lips found Jaylee's neck, trailing hot kisses along her sensitive skin.

"We have to be quiet," Jaylee whispered, her hands tangling in Paxx's hair.

Paxx hummed in agreement, her fingers slipping beneath the waistband of Jaylee's panties. Jaylee bit back a moan as Paxx's fingers dipped lower, and just as Paxx's fingers met Jaylee's wetness, a sharp knock on the door made them freeze. "Fuck them," Paxx breathed as she continued her exploration of Jaylee's center, "I'm not stopping."

Another sharp knock came, "Be out in a minute," Paxx called out as Jaylee tightened around her fingers.

"Right there, Paxx," she moaned against Paxx's ear. "Fuck, right there."

Paxx quickened her movements, she could feel Jaylee's body tensing, teetering on the edge of release.

"Let go," Paxx whispered, her lips brushing Jaylee's ear. "I've got you."

Burying her face in Paxx's shoulder, with a muffled cry, she came undone, her body shuddering against Paxx as waves of pleasure washed over her. Paxx held her close, supporting her trembling form as she rode out her climax.

As Jaylee's breathing slowly returned to normal, she lifted her head from Paxx's shoulder, her eyes dark with lingering desire. "That was…"

"Incredible," Paxx finished, a satisfied smirk on her lips.

"Fucking incredible," Jaylee agreed.

Turning the water on, Paxx washed her hands while Jaylee straightened her clothes and fastened her pants.

When they opened the door, two women met them, smiling as they entered the bathroom. "It's our turn," one said as she pulled the other in and closed the door.

Jaylee and Paxx exchanged surprised looks. "I guess we aren't the only ones who need a fix." Paxx laughed.

As they took seats in the waiting room, Jaylee leaned over and whispered, "Fucking incredible," into Paxx's ear.

"I'm glad you liked it," Paxx whispered back.

In about ten minutes, Paul and Anna appeared in the doorway, Embry asleep in Paul's arms. "Are you ready?" he asked.

Standing, Paxx nodded. "Ready."

"Are you feeling okay, Jaylee?" Anna asked. "You look a little flushed."

As they walked by, Jaylee pointed to the bathroom and scoffed, "The bathroom was really hot."

??? TWENTY-TWO

O nce at the airport, and after fifteen minutes of farewells, Anna and Jaylee left Paul and Paxx. They watched the van vanish before turning into the terminal. After a brief stop at the ticket kiosk, Paul and Paxx waited for their turn to go through security. Paxx fiddled with the strap of her carry-on bag, taking a deep breath to focus her scattered thoughts on why they were there. As they inched closer to the security checkpoint, a nagging feeling told her that something was off.

"You okay?" Paul asked, his brow furrowing with concern.

Paxx forced a smile that didn't quite mask her unease. "Yeah, just... pre-flight jitters, I guess."

Paul studied her face, clearly not buying it. "Come on, Paxx. I know you better than that. What's really going on?"

"What if Mr. Black doesn't give us any answers?" Paxx asked, "What if he can't?"

Furrowing his brow, Paul asked, "What do you mean if he can't?"

"Paul, he obviously did not shoot me, and I have a gut feeling he didn't shoot Dad either."

"Why do you think he didn't shoot Dad?"

185

"Think about it: after almost two years away, why would he come back to Chandler County just to kill Dad?"

Paul's brows knitted together as he thought over her words, and they placed their bags on the security belt.

Once through the metal detectors and after retrieving their bags, Paxx continued, "It doesn't add up, Paul. It just doesn't make sense."

After handing their tickets to the gate attendant, they walked silently down the corridor to the plane. After stowing their bags and buckling their seatbelts, Paul said, "Hopefully, we will have some answers tomorrow morning."

"Hopefully," Paxx sighed as she pulled out her phone, sending a quick text to Jaylee. *'Getting ready to take off. I love you.'*

Immediately, the three dots appeared, signaling Jaylee's response.

'I love you too; please be safe.'

'See you tomorrow,' Paxx responded

'Can't wait.'

Leaning back in her seat, Paxx closed her eyes as the flight attendant reviewed the safety protocols. As the plane took off, Paxx gripped the arms of her seat, the uneasy feeling from earlier returning.

When the plane reached cruising altitude, she relaxed. She glanced over at Paul, who had already pulled out his laptop to review what looked like case files. Although she admired his dedication to their mission, she couldn't shake the persistent doubt that had taken hold.

"Paul," she said, leaning closer to him. "What if we're walking into something bigger than we realized?"

He looked up from his screen, his eyes sharp with focus. "What do you mean?"

"I can't explain it, but I feel like we're missing something important. Like, there are pieces to this puzzle we haven't even seen yet."

Paul closed his laptop, giving Paxx his full attention. "You've always had good instincts, sis. What's your gut telling you?"

Paxx bit her lip, "I don't know; the other day when I was talking to Rowan, he was overtly vague, and that's not like him; he is cautious, but if it is something that he believes in or affects someone close to him, he usually jumps in head first, no matter the cost."

"You think he is hiding something from you?" Paul asked.

Paxx pinched the bridge of her nose and squeezed her eyes shut. "He let Captain Kimble pull him off the case and has refused to push Special Crimes for information."

"Paxx," Paul began.

"Paul, I was shot over a month ago, and he still has no information. If your partner got shot, would you just stand by and let someone else handle it?" Paxx asked, finally looking at him.

Paul sighed as he shook his head. "No."

"I don't know a cop that would, unless..." she trailed off.

"Unless they had something to hide."

"Unless they had something to hide."

For the last thirty minutes of the flight, they sat in silence, each lost in thoughts of potential scenarios and solutions.

As they disembarked and made their way through the bustling airport, the weight of their conversation hung between them. Paxx's mind raced with unsettling possibilities. Noticing the tight set of Paul's jaw and the furrows in his brow, she knew he was as troubled by their discussion as she was.

They stepped out into the crisp air after stopping at the rental car desk to pick up their keys. Paxx felt a shiver run down her spine, which had nothing to do with the temperature.

"Where to now?" Paul asked, his voice low and gravelly.

Paxx pulled out her phone and double-checked the hotel address they had been given. "The hotel is about 20 minutes from here." Glancing at her watch, Paxx said, "It's three o'clock; we should probably eat and rest before tomorrow's... meeting."

"Agreed. I want to do more research on the evidence found when they arrested Mr. Black," Paul said as they walked toward the rental car parking lot.

"We should probably start calling him by his real name," Paxx said. "I don't think calling him Mr. Black will get us in to see him tomorrow," she smirked.

"Agreed," Paul said as he unlocked the car doors.

"So, you look into Clancy Devonshire, and I will look deeper into T.C. Hines and his connection to the rest of the victims connected to the gun," Paxx said as she pulled her vibrating phone from her pocket.

A text from Jaylee lit up the screen. 'Landed safely?'

Paxx replied: 'Yes, heading to the hotel now.'

'Miss you.'

'Miss you too.'

Following dinner at an Italian restaurant, they proceeded to the hotel and checked into neighboring rooms. They kept the connecting doors open and got to work on gathering information that could aid them in their upcoming interview with Clancy Devonshire, also known as Mr. Black.

As the night wore on, Paxx paced the length of her hotel room, her eyes burning from staring at her laptop screen for hours. She paused by the window, gazing at the unfamiliar city skyline, its lights twinkling like distant stars. The uneasy feeling in her gut had only intensified since their arrival.

"Hey, Paxx," Paul called from his room. "I think I found something."

She hurried through the adjoining door, hope and trepidation mingling in her chest. Paul was hunched over his laptop; the screen's glow illuminated his face.

"What is it?" she asked, leaning over his shoulder.

"I've been digging into Devonshire's past, and there's a gap in his history. About two years before the first murder attributed to Mr. Black, Clancy Devonshire disappeared from social media, his bank accounts were all closed, and his house went into foreclosure." Paul relayed as he read information from his computer.

"So, what happened over nine years ago to make him disappear?" Paxx questioned.

Paul continued scrolling through media pages and Clancy's friends' Facebook pages. Suddenly, he stopped, his hand hovering over the keys. "His family died," Paul said in a soft, shocked tone, his expression turning somber.

"Family? How?" Paxx asked, leaning closer.

Paul continued searching. "This article says that in December 2014, just outside Yellow Creek, Pennsylvania, his wife and two children were found dead in a car that had careened off the road and into a ravine,"

Paxx read over Paul's shoulder, "Clancy wasn't in the car, and nobody heard from him for the next three years." Standing straight, Paxx sat on the edge of the bed. "That might explain why he is here in Pennsylvania," Paxx observed. "He is from here; can you see who his friends and family are? Maybe with whom he corresponded with the most?" Paxx asked.

Paul clicked some more keys before shaking his head, "There is a man who claims to be Clancy's brother-in-law, Theodore Hines." Paul said as he pulled up his profile page.

Standing to look over Paul's shoulder again, Paxx gasped quietly. Then, without a word, she quickly disappeared into her room, and the sound of papers rustling and strong cursing echoed through the open doorway. When she returned, she held a photograph in her trembling hand. Holding it next to the glowing screen, Paul could see the same man captured in both images. The resemblance was uncanny, down to the most minor details. His piercing blue eyes, chiseled jawline, and tousled brown hair were identical in the photo and on the screen before them.

"Who is that?" Paul asked.

"T.C. fucking Hines!"

"The drug dealer?"

"That's why I can't find anything on him; I didn't realize the T stood for Theodore," Paxx said as she continued pacing, her hand running through her hair in frustration.

Paxx's mind raced as she paced the room, connecting the dots. "This changes things Paul. T.C. Hines isn't just some random drug dealer, he's Clancy Devonshire's brother-in-law. And if he's involved..."

Paul leaned back in his chair, rubbing his temples. "It means this goes deeper than we thought. But why? What's the connection between Hines, Devonshire, you, and Dad's shootings?"

Paxx stopped pacing and turned to face her brother. "I don't know, but I bet Rowan does. Or at least, he knows more than he's letting on." She looked at her watch, checking the time. "It's late, but I need to call him."

"Paxx, wait," Paul said, standing up. "We don't know who we can trust right now. Let's see Clancy tomorrow and see if he can shed some light on this before we start pointing fingers. And honestly, I want to look Rowan in the eyes when we ask him what he knows." Paul growled.

"I agree, and goddamn it, if he is involved in any of this," Paxx seethed but didn't finish as her phone began ringing from the other room.

Rushing to answer it, Paxx took a calming breath at Jaylee's name on the screen. "Hey, beautiful," Paxx greeted.

"Hey, gorgeous," Jaylee replied.

"Hold on just a minute," Paxx said as she returned to Paul's door. "It's Jay. I will see you in the morning."

Looking at his watch, Paul cursed, "Shit, I was supposed to call Anna half an hour ago."

"You better call her now and whisper sweet nothings to her." Paxx laughed as she closed the doors between their rooms.

"I'm back," Paxx said into the phone as she undressed for bed.

"Are you going to whisper sweet nothings to me?" Jaylee asked in a sultry tone.

"Mmmm, I was thinking we would just get naked and have FaceTime sex," Paxx purred.

"I'll show you mine if you show me yours," Jaylee teased, accepting the challenge.

Paxx pressed the FaceTime button, angling the camera so that when Jaylee answered, she could see Paxx's naked body in the full-length mirror she stood in front of in the bathroom.

Jaylee's eyes grew wide as the call connected, revealing Paxx's bare form on the screen. Her full lips parted, a quiet, longing moan slipping out. "God, you're fucking gorgeous," she breathed, her voice dripping with desire as her eyes traced the gentle swell of Paxx's breasts, the curve of her hips, and the smoothness of her stomach. Jaylee's gaze physically vibrated through her.

"Your turn," Paxx whispered, her voice husky with desire.

After a brief pause, Jaylee positioned her phone and stepped back to reveal her own naked body, an exquisite display of toned curves and inviting fullness in all the right places. Her breasts were perfect, round, and full, with the silver ring glinting in the soft light as it hung from her dusky pink nipple while the other stood erect with desire, both begging for attention. Paxx's mouth watered at the sight.

"You're absolutely breathtaking," Paxx whispered, her voice quivering with longing as her fingers twitched, eager to touch and caress Jaylee's skin. However, for the moment, she had to settle for watching her through the screen. She observed as Jaylee's hand wandered over her breasts, teasing the nipple ring with her fingertip before sliding down her stomach, her fingertips skimming her skin. The sight caused a warm wetness to gather between Paxx's thighs.

"I wish you were here," Jaylee moaned, her hand sliding lower, teasing the soft curls at the apex of her thighs. Paxx's breath hitched as Jaylee's fingers dipped between her lower lips, parting them. The smooth, wet sound of Jaylee touching herself was almost too much to bear. Instinctively, Paxx moved her hand to explore herself in response.

"Fuck, Jay, you're driving me crazy," Paxx murmured, her breath quickening as she mirrored Jaylee's movements. "I want to feel you everywhere."

"You have no idea what you do to me," Jaylee confessed, watching intently as Paxx explored herself. Her hand worked feverishly now, fingers moving in rhythm with the rising heat shared between them.

In that intense moment, the rooms around them faded until nothing remained but the glow from the phone screens. Every stroke, every caress of their fingertips intensified their fantasy of being together, flesh against flesh, a warmth enveloping them both despite the distance.

They eventually collapsed onto their beds, phones in hand, gazing into each other's eyes through the screens.

"Fuck, that was hot," Paxx panted breathlessly.

"I have never done anything like that before," Jaylee admitted quietly.

"Neither have I," Paxx whispered, shaking her head in amazement.

After a pause, they both turned to one side, letting their heart rates settle. Jaylee whispered. "Can I ask you something?"

"Of course."

"Today, in the bathroom, if this morning hadn't happened, would you have done that?"

"I don't know," Paxx admitted. "I think maybe it made it easier to suggest. Why do you ask?"

"No reason, really," Jaylee replied, though her tone was unconvincing.

"Jay, what's going on? Does it make you uncomfortable? Today in the bathroom, did I push you too far?"

Jaylee shook her head, "No, not at all, that's just it, Paxx. I feel like you are being careful with me; you're not truly being you, sexually anyway."

Paxx smiled as she licked her lips. "Of course, I am being careful with you, Jay. I love you and want you to always feel safe and comfortable with everything we do."

"Paxx, I won't break. I trust you completely. I want to experience everything you enjoy," Jaylee said seductively, a smile creeping into her voice. "All of it."

Jaylee's words went straight to Paxx's lady parts, lighting a new fire between her legs. "Fuck, I want to touch you right now," she slurred, voice thick with arousal.

"Me too," Jaylee agreed. "I have never had sex more than once in a day; if you're not careful, I'm going to crave you more than once a day, every day.

"Jaylee, my love," Paxx murmured, nodding despite her suddenly dry throat. "I already want you more than that every day. And when we get home, I'll show you... Everything."

A comfortable silence settled between them, the air thick with anticipation and unspoken promises. Jaylee's gaze wandered over Paxx's face, drinking in every detail.

"I can't fucking wait," Jaylee whispered, her voice filled with longing.

Paxx nodded, a smile playing on her lips. "Soon, Jay. Very soon."

Paxx locked her eyes on Jaylee's face, glowing on the screen as if their connection could transcend the miles between them. "What are you thinking about?" she murmured, hoping to draw Jaylee out of that dreamy gaze.

Jaylee reached out, tracing her fingers along the edge of the phone screen as if she could bridge the distance just a little more. "I'm thinking about how much has happened in such a short time," she whispered as she leaned closer to the camera, making it seem like she was almost within reach.

"It's pretty amazing."

"I never imagined I would meet someone, fall in love, and see the possibility of having a forever life with them all within a month."

A tender smile appeared on Paxx's lips as she asked, "You see us having a forever life together?"

"I was scared at first when you offered me a key to your house, but now I do."

"I was scared when I offered you the key, too," Paxx confessed, "and honestly, I never thought I would."

Jaylee's eyes narrowed, a mix of surprise and joy dancing across her features. "Really?" she whispered, her voice trembling with emotion.

Paxx nodded, her heart swelling with affection. "Really. Jay, you've changed everything for me. I can't imagine my life without you."

Jaylee let out a contented sigh. "I can't believe how lucky I am to have found you, Paxx. You make me feel so alive, so loved, so cherished."

Paxx smiled, her heart overflowing. "And I feel the same way about you, Jay. You've changed my life in ways I never thought possible."

Glancing over at the clock on the nightstand, Jaylee whispered, "Paxx, it's two o'clock, and you have a long day today."

"I don't want to hang up," Paxx confessed.

"Me neither, but I promise to dream about you and imagine myself exploring every inch of you," Jaylee whispered, a slow lick of her lips punctuating her words.

"I'm not getting any sleep tonight if I imagine you doing that," Paxx laughed.

Jaylee wished Paxx luck before they said, "I love you," and ended the call.

Paxx set her phone aside and closed her eyes, feeling both exhilarated and calm. As she drifted off to sleep, thoughts of Jaylee filled her mind, a promise of forever fueling sweet, seductive dreams that felt closer than ever.

❓ ❓ ❓
TWENTY-THREE

A n urgent knock jolted Paxx out of a deep sleep filled with alluring dreams of Jaylee.

"Just a minute," she called out, sitting up and trying to orient herself. As the hotel room came into focus, she swung her legs over the side of the bed and placed her feet on the floor.

Knock, knock, knock... the pounding resumed.

"Just a damn minute," she called out in frustration, slipping on her robe and heading to the door that connected her room with Paul's. Opening it, she was surprised to find Paul's door closed.

Knock, knock, knock... Turning around, she realized the knocking was coming from the main door to her room. 'What the hell,' she thought as she moved across the room.

Peering through the peephole, she was even more startled to see a man and a woman with badges on their belts standing in the hallway. Opening the door cautiously, Paxx asked, "Can I help you?" as she took in their appearances. The man was tall, around six-two, Paxx guessed, with dark brown hair, a three-day beard, and dull blue eyes. He wore jeans, a navy blue dress shirt, a red tie, and cowboy boots. The woman stood several inches shorter than her partner and wore sleek black slacks, a light blue T-shirt, a black blazer, and black combat-style boots. Her blonde hair was in a neat ponytail, and she wore no makeup, yet her features were distinctly feminine.

"Paul Algatta?" the man inquired, noting Paxx's tired appearance.

"That's my brother," Paxx replied, rubbing sleep from her eyes.

"Is he here?"

"He's actually in the room next door," Paxx answered, just as Paul called from the connecting doorway.

"Paxx, are you awake?"

Stepping back from the door, she glanced at Paul standing in the adjoining doorway and said, "Paul, there are some detectives here for you."

Looking confused, Paul asked, "Detectives, why?"

Inviting the detectives in, Paxx suggested, "Why don't you ask them?"

As they gathered in her room, Paxx tightened her robe, feeling uneasy as the female detective smiled and boldly surveyed her from head to toe.

"Paul Algatta," the man said.

"Yes."

"Good morning, I'm Detective Coleman Brant, and this is my partner, Bailey Rosalba."

"Detective Brant, Rosalba," Paul greeted as he extended his hand. "This is my sister, Detective Paxxton Algatta."

Paxx nodded in greeting but did not offer her hand.

"I'm sorry to wake you up so early," Coleman apologized. "I understand you are in town to interview Clancy Devonshire at the prison."

"We are," Paul confirmed.

"There was an incident last night," Bailey began, still looking at Paxx. "Mr. Devonshire was stabbed multiple times."

"Is he dead?" Paxx asked, shocked.

"No, Detective Algatta," Bailey quickly reassured, placing her hand on Paxx's shoulder. "But he is in the ICU at the local hospital."

Stepping away, Paxx grabbed her bag and pulled out her clothes. "Can we see him?" she asked.

"He got out of surgery a little over an hour ago; he should be in recovery by now," Coleman said.

Meeting Paul's gaze, she urged, "If you all will excuse me, I need to shower, dress, and call my girlfriend before we go."

Paul noticed Bailey's attention towards Paxx and, stepping aside, suggested, "Sure, if you two come into my room, Paxx can call her girlfriend and get ready."

Paxx gave Paul a grateful wink as she shut the door behind them. Leaning against the door, she inhaled, trying to comprehend the unexpected events. Quickly, she gathered her belongings, shed her robe, and showered. After showering, she dressed in jeans and a green button-down shirt, slipped on her boots, and clipped her detective badge to her belt. From the other room, she could hear the muffled, serious voices of Paul and the detectives. Grabbing her phone from the bedside table, she dialed Jaylee's number and put it on speaker to chat while fixing her hair.

"Good morning, gorgeous?" Jaylee's drowsy voice came through.

"Good morning, beautiful. Did I wake you?"

"You can wake me anytime."

"We've had a bit of a situation," Paxx said quietly. "Clancy Devonshire was stabbed last night. He's in the ICU at the local hospital. We're heading to the hospital soon."

There was an audible gasp from Jaylee. "What?"

"Two detectives arrived here this morning; they're waiting in Paul's room while I get ready," Paxx said as she styled her hair. "After last night, I needed a shower."

"Serves you right for getting me all hot and bothered."

"I just wanted to let you know what's going on and that I missed waking up next to you this morning."

"I miss having you here, too," Jaylee responded. "I love you. Tell me how it goes and when you're heading back."

"I will, and I love you too," Paxx said before disconnecting the call.

After styling her hair and applying mascara and eyeliner, Paxx gathered her things and repacked her overnight bag. Opening the door to Paul's room, she avoided Bailey's raised eyebrows and seductive stare as she entered. "Are you ready to go?" she asked.

Paul picked up his bag and opened the door to the hallway. "Ready when you are."

"Let's go," Paxx said as she walked toward the elevator hallway.

After a few steps, Bailey caught up with her. "Are you a homicide Detective?" she asked, pushing the down button on the wall.

"Narcotics," Paxx corrected.

"I know a little, but why are you and your brother here to talk to Mr. Devonshire?" Bailey asked as the doors opened, and they stepped inside.

Leaning against the back wall, Paxx explained. "Clancy Devonshire is responsible for thirteen murders in Chandler County, Nebraska; He is also tied to our father's murder, as well as the incident where I was shot last month."

The two detectives exchanged glances, their faces showing surprise. "Wow," Coleman whispered. "He seems to have it out for your family."

"It would seem that way," Paul replied, not adding further information.

"Was your shooting life-threatening?" Bailey asked, leaning against the wall and meeting Paxx's gaze.

"Four hours in surgery and three weeks in the hospital," Paxx stated.

"So sorry," Bailey replied.

Before Paxx could reply, the doors opened, and they exited the elevator. Walking to their separate vehicles, Paxx was grateful to be away from Bailey and her lustful gaze.

"What the hell is her deal with you?" Paul asked as he started the car.

"Fuck if I know," Paxx shrugged.

Paul laughed as he pulled out onto the street behind the detective's Tahoe.

As they trailed behind the detectives' car through the early morning traffic, Paxx's thoughts whirled with questions. Who would want Clancy Devonshire dead? Was it a random act of violence, or was someone trying to silence him? And why now, just when they were about to interview him?

"What are you thinking?" Paul asked, glancing at his sister's furrowed brow.

Paxx sighed, "I don't know, Paul. This feels off. The timing is too convenient."

Paul nodded, his grip tightening on the steering wheel. "I was thinking the same thing. Do you think someone knew we were coming?"

"It's possible, I guess," Paxx mused. "But who? And why try to kill him instead of just warning him not to talk?"

"I don't know," Paul sighed. "So many questions."

"Yeah, just... a lot to take in," she replied, turning back toward him. "Clancy's not just some guy; he's been a shadow over our lives for too long." She paused, finding the right words in the chaos of her thoughts. "Now we are going to see him, talk to him, and face whatever comes next."

Paul nodded, understanding flickering across his face. "This could finally be it, Paxx, the chance to put an end to all the questions and unknowns."

"Or it could spiral into more trouble," Paxx countered. The thought of Clancy's connections and the web of violence he spun sent a shiver down her spine. "You know how these things go."

"True," Paul admitted. "But if he's alive and can talk..." His voice trailed off as they approached the hospital entrance.

As she exited the car, Paxx felt a surge of determination and dread. "Let's focus on getting answers," she said, taking a deep breath and willing herself to remain composed. She followed

Paul and the Detectives as they walked towards the entrance, their footsteps echoing in the nearly empty parking garage.

Once in the hospital, Coleman and Bailey led them to a secure elevator, which took them up six floors to a floor dedicated to prisoners.

"They have a designated floor for prisoners?" Paxx inquired curiously.

"Some of the state's worst criminals are in this prison; they have a minimal medical facility, so anything more than a minor ailment comes here," Coleman informed.

Stopping outside a locked door where an armed guard stood, Coleman asked. "You ready for this?"

"No," Paxx admitted quietly. But she pushed past that, knowing there wasn't an option to back out now.

Inside, Clancy lay connected to machines that beeped softly, a hollow shell of the infamous criminal he once was. The sight stirred a bitter mix of emotions within her: anger at what he'd done, fear that he might not wake up, and fear of what she might learn if he did.

"Clancy," she said quietly, stepping closer. His face was pale against the stark white sheets, his breathing steady but shallow.

Paul hung back, observing his sister as she leaned over him. So many questions swirled in his mind, and he felt like he was staring into an abyss of uncertainty.

"How did it come to this?" she whispered, more to herself than to him.

Just then, a low groan escaped Clancy's lips, bringing both siblings' attention back to him.

"Mr. Devonshire," Paul said as he approached the bed.

Clancy's eyes fluttered and then opened, his pale blue eyes squinting as he tried to focus.

"Mr. Devonshire," Paul said again, "Can we ask you a few questions?"

Clancy licked his dry, chapped lips. "Water," he said, barely audible.

Looking around, Paxx picked up a cup of ice from a table against the wall. Seeing a box of gloves on the edge of the small sink in the corner of the room, Paxx pulled one out and slipped it on her hand before taking a piece of ice from the cup and dropping it into Clancy's open mouth.

"Don't chew; just suck on it," Paxx said, remembering the instructions she had received in the hospital just a month ago.

As Clancy sucked on the ice, his gaze shifted more intently toward Paxx and Paul. His expression grew suspicious and menacing. "Who are you?" he finally whispered in a raspy, low voice.

"I'm Detective Paxx Algatta with the Ivan Hope Police Department, and this is my brother Paul, a Chandler County Sheriff's Department detective. We want to ask you some questions about James Algatta," she explained slowly.

Clancy closed his eyes as his brows furrowed. "James Algatta, who is that?" he finally asked without opening his eyes.

"James Algatta is the Detective you shot and killed in Ivan Hope two years ago," Paul answered.

Clancy's eyes popped open, confusion on his face. "I never killed no cop."

Exchanging shocked glances, Paul and Paxx pressed on. "Two years ago, after being away from Nebraska for a year and a half, you returned, shot, and killed James before disappearing," Paxx stated firmly.

Clancy shook his head as the monitors surrounding him began beeping loudly, and red lights started flashing. "I have never killed a cop," he spat angrily.

Paxx felt the tension in the air shift, a palpable charge that sent her heart racing. The monitors' beeping intensified, piercing through the room like a warning. She stepped back instinctively, her eyes darting toward the nurse's station visible just outside Clancy's room.

"Hey!" she called out, urgency creeping into her tone.

But before she could raise her voice any higher, a flurry of activity erupted at the door. A nurse rushed in, followed by a doctor. Clancy's eyes darted, panic etched across his gaunt features.

"Mr. Devonshire!" the doctor barked, his voice firm yet calm as he assessed Clancy's condition. "You need to relax."

"Get...away from me," Clancy growled, his voice suddenly gaining strength despite his weakened state.

Paxx exchanged a glance with Paul as they retreated further into the background, watching the medical team swiftly stabilize Clancy. The nurse adjusted the IV lines while the doctor checked monitors and issued commands that reverberated against the sterile walls.

"His heart rate is spiking," one of them said urgently.

"Clancy, you need to breathe," the doctor coached. "Focus on my voice."

It felt surreal, watching someone who had once been a ruthless figure in their lives dissolve into a state of vulnerability. As they worked, Paxx felt an odd sense of pity for him. He was still dangerous, yes, but now he was just a man fighting for his life.

Paxx felt a hand on her arm, pulling her away. It was Bailey, her face a mix of concern and curiosity. "Come on, let's give them space to work."

Reluctantly, she nodded in agreement and backed away. As they exited the room, Paxx's mind whirled. Clancy's words echoed in her head, contradicting everything she thought she knew. She leaned against the wall, trying to process the implications, her pulse still racing from the chaotic scene unfolding just moments ago. She couldn't shake the image of Clancy's gaunt face and the fierce denial in his eyes when he'd rejected the truth about James's death. "I never killed no cop." How could that be possible? Everything they knew, every piece of evidence they had gathered over the past two years, pointed to Clancy as their father's killer.

"You, okay?" Bailey asked, her voice tinged with genuine concern.

Paxx nodded, not trusting her voice at the moment. She glanced at Paul, who looked equally shaken.

"What do you think?" Paul asked, coming to her side. He furrowed his brow, concern etched into his features.

"I don't know what to think," she admitted, pushing her hair back from her face.

Coleman shook his head. "It could be the medication talking. Or he could be lying."

The sterile scent of the hospital hung heavy in the air, mingling with the bitter taste of uncertainty. "But why would he lie now?" Paxx exclaimed. "He has nothing to lose."

Paul shifted, leaning closer as though sharing a secret in the quiet hallway. "Is it possible he didn't pull the trigger? Maybe someone else did? Or maybe there's more to this story than we know."

Paxx bit her lip, weighing her brother's suggestions carefully. It made sense; there were always layers of deception in situations like this. "If that were true..." she trailed off, lost in thought.

"You're thinking too hard about it," Bailey interjected, suddenly beside them again with an air of confident authority that made Paxx bristle.

Paxx nodded, frustration simmering within her at the uncertainty that loomed like a dense fog over them. "I wish we had more answers already."

Just then, the door to Clancy's room opened again, revealing a doctor emerging with a weary look and a hospital chart clutched under one arm.

"Detectives," he called to them as he approached cautiously.

Paul stepped forward while Paxx held back, wary of what might come next.

"Mr. Devonshire is stable now, but still recovering from surgery," the doctor explained solemnly. "We've sedated him again for his safety."

"How long will he be out?" Paxx asked.

"I would guess four to six hours." The doctor replied after looking at the chart in his hand.

"Shit," Paxx spat, "we have to be on a plane in three hours."

"Then I am afraid you won't be able to talk to him again," the doctor replied.

"Understood," Paul replied quickly.

As they stepped aside and allowed space for medical staff to move freely once more, Paxx felt her stomach twist anxiously with thoughts she couldn't shake loose.

"I just really thought we'd get some answers today, some closure," she muttered under her breath.

"No one said this would be easy," Paul reminded her as they began walking away from Clancy's room and further down the sterile corridor.

They rode the elevator down in silence, exiting once the doors opened.

"Do you have time for some breakfast or an early lunch before you go to the airport?" Bailey asked as they exited the building.

Paul and Paxx exchanged glances before Paul said, "We could grab a quick bite."

"Good," Coleman said, pulling his keys from his pocket, "I would like more information on your dad's case. Maybe this afternoon or tomorrow, I can get some more answers from Clancy for you."

Walking to their vehicles, Paul and Paxx followed them to a restaurant, where they spent the next hour and a half discussing their dad's case and all the questions surrounding it, as well as Paxx's shooting.

??? TWENTY-FOUR

As they passed through security and boarded the plane, Paxx and Paul were quiet, each absorbed in their own thoughts.

After the plane took off, Paxx finally spoke up. "I can't tell if this trip was a success," she admitted, perplexed.

Paul nodded in agreement. "I feel the same way, but I don't think he was being dishonest, Paxx; I don't believe he killed Dad."

Paxx sighed and pinched the bridge of her nose. "I agree, but if he didn't do it, then who did?"

The question hung in the air between them, heavy with unspoken fears and suspicions. Paxx leaned back in her seat, her eyes fixed on the clouds outside the small oval window. The gentle hum of the plane's engines filled the silence, a stark contrast to the turmoil in her mind.

"We're missing something," she muttered, more to herself than to Paul. "There has to be a piece of the puzzle we haven't found yet."

"Let's let it rest until we get back home."

"I will try, but you know how my mind works."

"Yes, I do," Paul smiled, "Non-stop."

"Did you talk to Anna this morning? Did she say how Mom was doing?"

"I did, and she said there was no change in her condition."

Paxx looked at the blue sky out the window. "That's good."

"Yeah."

"Paul, Jaylee, and I must leave for home early tomorrow morning. I need to be at the firing range tomorrow to re-qualify, and she needs to get back to work."

Paul squeezed her hand in understanding. "I get it, and so will Mom. Anna and I will stick around until Wednesday, then fly back; the painters are supposed to wrap up by Thursday." He leaned back in his seat. "I really want us to move in by Saturday."

Turning to face him, Paxx proposed, "Why don't you let Embry spend Friday night with Jaylee and me?"

Paul looked confused. "Why?"

After a thoughtful pause and a sigh, Paxx explained, "I don't want this to sound odd coming from your sister, but I think you and Anna need some time alone. Take her out for dinner, then spend the night making love to her."

"Paxx," Paul began to protest, but she raised her hand to silence him.

"Hear me out. You two have been through so much lately. You need space to reconnect and remember what brought you together in the first place."

Paul's expression softened with a mix of gratitude and slight embarrassment. "Thank you, Paxx. You're right. Anna and I haven't spent much quality time together lately."

With a small smile, Paxx added, "I'm just pointing out the obvious and poking around in your love life. Besides, Embry will have a great time with us, and you two can christen the new house."

Paul chuckled, "It's been a while since we connected anywhere but the bedroom."

"Then surprise her, make her feel special and sexy."

Lowering his voice, Paul asked, "Has she mentioned something to you?"

Paxx shook her head. "No, but I sense something is off. I know sex isn't a cure-all, but maybe it could help bridge that gap."

Paul hesitated before speaking. "Can I tell you something? Maybe you can help, I don't know..."

"What is it?"

"Anna is nervous about this pregnancy."

"Why?"

Paul exhaled slowly. "Having Embry was hard on her; she was bedridden for the last month, and the birth was difficult."

"I'm so sorry I wasn't there."

"I know," Paul replied. "But you'll be here this time, and she really needs you, Paxx."

Leaning over to rest her head on Paul's shoulder, Paxx promised, "I'll talk to her, and I won't mention that you said anything."

"Thank you, Paxx," Paul whispered, resting his head against hers.

They sat in a comfortable silence, each wrapped up in their thoughts. Paxx's mind raced, shifting from the unresolved mystery of their father's death to the additional worry over Anna's pregnancy. She felt a sudden surge of determination to support her family in every possible way.

Straightening in her seat as the plane began its descent, Paxx turned to Paul. Her tone grew serious. "I've been thinking. Maybe we should hire a private investigator to investigate Dad's case."

Paul's eyebrows shot up in surprise. "You really think that's necessary?"

Paxx nodded. "I can't shake the feeling that we're missing something vital. An outside perspective might reveal what we've overlooked."

After a moment of thought, Paul nodded. "Alright, we can talk about it. Do you have someone in mind?"

"I do," Paxx said. "I met her about five years ago when she and her husband were on the force."

"Were?" Paul prompted.

"Her husband was killed in the line of duty six months after Renee, and shortly after that, she quit the force and went through a really tough time; we connected because of our grief, and we've had more than a few drinks together since then."

"Were you two involved?"

Paxx shook her head. "No, we're just friends. The last time I saw her, she was dating her husband's former partner, now a homicide detective with the sheriff's department. You'll meet him when you start working there."

As the seatbelt sign went off and passengers began gathering their belongings, Paul asked, "What's his name?"

"Jake Braddock. I'll call Tracie when we get home, and maybe we can all have dinner soon." Paxx smiled, her earlier tension easing.

"Sounds good," Paul replied, standing up to retrieve their bags from the overhead compartment.

Jaylee, Anna, and Embry were waiting when Paxx and Paul came through the causeway.

Paul and Paxx stopped short when they saw them; both women stood dressed in short skirts and button-down blouses, exposing a seductive amount of cleavage.

Embry's excited screams caused several people to turn and look, bringing them out of their trances. Jaylee sat Embry down and smiled as she wobbled quickly into her daddy's arms.

"How's my girl?" Paul laughed as he swept her up into his arms.

Paxx smiled at the scene and the cheerful look on Anna's face.

Giving Anna a quick wink, Paxx stepped into Jaylee's open arms and melted into her embrace.

"Damn, you look sexy. How's my girl?" she whispered against Jaylee's ear as she breathed in her familiar and calming scent.

"So glad you're back," Jaylee purred as she breathed deeply. "I missed you."

"I missed you, too," Paxx replied before capturing her lips and kissing her deeply.

After breaking their kiss, Paxx looked at Paul and Anna, wrapped in one another's arms. Embry giggled as they kissed.

"You'd think we had been gone a week instead of a day," Paxx laughed as she took Embry from Paul.

"What, can we say we missed you," Anna admitted.

"We missed you, too," Paxx said as she hugged her.

After picking up their bags, Paxx and Paul grasped their partners' hands and exited the airport. Once in the van, Paul asked, "How's Mom?"

"Stable," Anna said confidently.

"That's good," Paul nodded.

In the back of the van, Paxx turned to Jaylee and said, "We need to fly home tonight or early in the morning."

Jaylee smiled, "I thought the same thing, so I have us booked on a red eye tonight, and the flight leaves at midnight."

Paxx grinned as she pressed their lips together. "I love you."

"I love you, too," Jaylee murmured against her lips.

"Paul, we are going to fly home tonight," Paxx said, looking up to the front of the van.

Paul nodded. "Okay, what time is your flight?"

"Midnight."

"That gives you enough time to see Mom and return to the hotel to get your luggage."

The van was silent as they rode the rest of the way to the hospital. Once in the parking garage, Paxx removed Embry from her car seat, where she had fallen asleep.

"Want me to take her?" Anna asked as they closed the door.

Paxx shook her head. "No, I've got her."

As they entered the hospital, the sterile smell hit Paxx's nostrils, bringing back memories of her recent stay. She held Embry closer, the little girl's warmth comforting her. Then

Jaylee's hand found hers, their fingers intertwining, and Paxx felt a surge of gratitude for her partner's steady presence.

They rode the elevator up in silence, the tension palpable. When they reached the third floor, Paxx felt Jaylee's grip tighten, giving it a reassuring squeeze.

Outside the room, Paul hesitated with his hand on the door handle. Anna placed a gentle hand on his shoulder. "It's okay," she murmured. "She's doing better."

Paul nodded and pushed the door open. The steady beep of monitors filled the air as they entered. Patsy smiled as they entered, her color better than the last time Paul and Paxx had seen her, just twenty-four hours ago.

"You look much better," Paul said happily, kissing her forehead.

"Thank you," Patsy chirped, "I feel better."

Paxx didn't approach the bed, still unsure how to feel about their relationship.

Patsy's eyes found Paxx lingering on Embry, sleeping in her arms. A flicker of emotion crossed her face.

"Paxx," she whispered. "It's good to see you."

Paxx nodded stiffly, her body tense. Jaylee squeezed her hand, a silent reminder of her support.

"I'm glad to see you feeling better," Paxx managed.

"The doctors say I'm making good progress."

An awkward silence fell over the room. Paul cleared his throat.

"Mom, Paxx, and Jaylee are flying back home tonight. They just wanted to check in before they left."

Patsy's face fell slightly, but she quickly composed herself. "Of course. I understand. Thank you for coming."

Paxx handed Embry to Anna before stepping closer to Patsy's bedside. "Jaylee and I both have to get back to work tomorrow."

Patsy smiled as she grasped Paxx's hand. "It's all right, Paxx. I really do understand. And Paxx," she began, moving her gaze to Jaylee. "Jaylee is a delightful woman. I can see why you are friends with her."

Paxx's eyes filled with tears as she glanced at Jaylee and then back at her mom. "Thank you, Mom. But we are more than friends."

Patsy's smile faltered, just a fraction, before she regained her composure. "Oh. I see." Her voice was gentle, but Paxx could hear the disappointment beneath it.

Paxx's shoulders slumped, her earlier hope dimming. "I know this isn't what you wanted. But it's what I want, it's who I am."

Jaylee stepped closer, placing a reassuring hand on Paxx's back. "Patsy, I care about Paxx very much. I want her to be happy."

Patsy's eyes softened as she looked up at Jaylee, but a hint of reluctance lingered. "I'm sure you do," she said, her tone polite but guarded. "You're both grown women. You'll make your own choices."

"We're good for each other, Mom," Paxx insisted, a plea in her tone.

Patsy nodded, though her eyes stayed guarded. "As long as you're happy, that's what matters."

Paxx swallowed back her frustration, a sense of déjà vu settling over her. How many times has she had this conversation with her mother? Trying to justify her choices, her life?

216

Paul shot Paxx a look of encouragement as she walked to the door. Jaylee stayed by her side, a steady presence.

Paul sat beside the bed, taking Patsy's hand in his.

"You have to understand," he whispered. "Paxx is happy. For the first time since... since, well, ever."

Patsy sighed, a weary sound. "I know. It's just not how I imagined her life." She paused, searching for the right words. "I thought she'd settle down, have a family."

"She still might. Just not the way you expected."

Patsy placed a trembling hand over her eyes, years of worry and hope mingling in her voice. "I just wish I could understand." The two talked as if Paxx and Jaylee were not still in the room listening.

"Believe me, Mom," Paul reassured her, "I've never seen Paxx so... alive."

Patsy managed a small, sad smile. "I'll try, Paul. I will."

Patsy looked at Paxx, the sadness in her eyes palpable. "Paxxton, I will try." She whispered.

"Thank you." Paxx replied, "I hope you can accept Jaylee and me."

Paul watched the door close, concern etched on his face. "She's trying so hard, Mom. You know how much this hurts her."

Patsy sighed again, resigned but determined. "I just need time," she said, more to herself than to Paul. "I love her, but I need time."

"You have had twenty years, and you owe it to her to accept who she is and who she's with."

Patsy removed her hand from her eyes, softening her resolve. "I guess I do," she admitted. "She's waited long enough."

Paul nodded, knowing how difficult this was for her. "She needs you, Mom."

"I'm trying, Paul. I just can't pretend to be something I'm not."

"What she needs is for you to love her, not change who you are or who she is." He paused, letting the words sink in. "She just needs you to try."

Outside the room, Paxx leaned against the wall, eyes closed, trying to calm the maelstrom inside her. Jaylee stood close, silent, letting Paxx absorb the moment.

"Are you okay?"

Paxx opened her eyes and exhaled. "I should have known."

Jaylee brushed her hand against Paxx's cheek. "She'll come around. It's a lot for her to take in right now."

"Will she?" Paxx shook her head. "I feel like I am back in high school, and we're having the same fight all over again."

Anna walked out, Embry cradled in her arms. "Hey, it's not gonna be easy," she said. "But your mom loves you. She'll figure it out."

Paxx gave a half-hearted smile. "Thanks, Anna."

"I mean it," Anna insisted. "Give her some time."

As they stood there, the hushed sounds of the hospital surrounding them, Paul emerged from Patsy's room. "Paxx," Paul said as he approached them, "I am so proud of you."

Paxx nodded. "I know she is trying, and so am I."

"You're doing great," Anna said.

"Thank you, Anna," Paxx smiled, "And thank you for being such a wonderful friend to me."

Paul took Embry, who was now awake, from Anna so she could hug Paxx. "Paxx, I am so happy to be back in your life," Anna murmured through tears.

"Me too," Paxx assured as she tightened her embrace. "I can't wait for us all to start the next chapter of our lives together."

"Me too," Anna replied, pulling Jaylee and Paul into their embrace.

As they broke apart from their group hug, Paxx felt a mix of emotions swirling within her: relief, hope, and lingering uncertainty. She glanced back at her mother's hospital room door and then at the faces of her loved ones surrounding her.

"Let's grab a bite to eat before you two have to be at the airport," Anna chirped.

"That sounds great," Paxx replied, taking Jaylee's hand.

As they made their way down the hospital corridor towards the elevators, Paxx felt a strange lightness in her chest. The weight she'd been carrying for years seemed to have lifted slightly, replaced by cautious optimism.

After dinner, they stopped by the hotel to pick up their belongings before Paul and Anna dropped them off at the airport. After passing through security and checking their bags, Paxx and Jaylee waited to board the plane.

Paxx and Jaylee found a quiet corner in the bustling airport terminal, sinking into uncomfortable plastic seats. The day's events weighed heavily on them, a mix of emotional exhaustion and anticipation for the journey home.

Jaylee reached over, intertwining her fingers with Paxx's. "How are you feeling, love?"

Paxx let out a long breath, her shoulders sagging. "Honestly? I'm not sure. It's all so... complicated."

"I know. But you handled it beautifully. And if your mom wants to be a part of your life, she will come around."

Paxx nodded, her brow furrowed in thought. "Yeah, I know, and she said she will try. I just... I'm not sure if I can trust it yet, you know? After everything..."

"I know, but you took a huge step, and she reciprocated, so that has to be worth something." Jaylee encouraged.

"It does, and thank you, Jaylee; I couldn't have done any of this without you," Paxx assured.

Jaylee pressed her lips to the back of Paxx's hand. "Thank you for letting me be a part of this, for letting me be here with you, and for letting me be here for you."

Before Paxx could respond, the boarding call came over the loudspeaker.

Paxx and Jaylee gathered their carry-on bags and joined the passengers shuffling toward the gate. As they inched forward, Paxx felt a sudden wave of anxiety wash over her. The events of the past few days, confronting her past and reconnecting with her mother, and the realization that Mr. Black had not killed her father, had left her emotionally raw.

Jaylee sensed the shift in Paxx's mood. "Hey, are you okay?"

Paxx nodded, forcing a weak smile. "Yeah, I just... I don't know. It feels strange to leave like this. Like I'm closing a door I have fought to open for twenty years."

"It's not closing, Paxx, honey; I am confident it will never close again." Jaylee smiled.

Paxx looked at Jaylee as questions swirled in her mind. She wanted to believe Jaylee's words, but doubt gnawed at her. "What if she doesn't come around or if she does, what if it all falls apart again? What if my mom and I can't maintain this fragile connection we've built?"

Jaylee's eyes softened, her hand moving to squeeze Paxx's arm reassuringly. "That won't happen."

As they neared the gate, Paxx's phone buzzed. She fumbled to retrieve it, her heart rate quickening when she saw the caller ID. "It's the hospital," she whispered, her voice tight with emotion.

"Answer it," Jaylee urged.

Paxx's thumb hovered over the screen for a moment before she swiped to accept the call. "Hello?"

"Paxx."

"Mom, is everything okay?" Paxx asked, a sudden sense of fear overcoming her.

"Yes, honey, everything is fine." Patsy assured her, "I just wanted to tell you I love you and am so happy you came to see me."

Paxx's throat tightened, tears pricking at the corners of her eyes. She turned away from the line, seeking a moment of privacy as she pressed the phone closer to her ear.

"I love you too, Mom," she whispered, her voice wavering. "I'm glad I came too."

A heavy silence hung, laden with unspoken words from years of separation. Paxx could hear her mother's shaky breath on the other end of the line.

"Honey," Patsy began, her voice soft but determined, "I want you to know this isn't goodbye. I know we have much to work through, but I'm committed to being in your life. If... if you'll let me."

"I would like that, we would like that," Paxx promised, her free hand reaching for Jaylee's, "But I am with Jaylee, and if you want to be in my life, then you have to accept that she is with me."

Patsy's voice came through, full of emotion. "I understand, I do, and I'm sorry if I ever made you feel otherwise. I'm trying to be better, Paxx. I really am."

Paxx swallowed hard. "We'll work through it, Mom. I just need to know you're there."

"I'll be right here, and I hope the offer for me to come visit still stands," Patsy replied, a mix of hope and vulnerability in her words.

"It still stands. Jaylee and I would like you to come and visit. We've got to get on our flight," Paxx said, blinking back tears. "But promise you'll call?"

"I promise, honey. Safe travels."

"I'll talk to you soon."

As she ended the call, Paxx looked up at Jaylee, her eyes shimmering with unshed tears. Jaylee squeezed her hand, a silent gesture of support and understanding.

Paxx couldn't speak as they returned to the line and boarded the plane.

？？？
TWENTY-FIVE

They eased into their seats once they stowed their carry-on bags in the overhead compartments. Paxx clutched Jaylee's hand tightly during takeoff, then relaxed once they reached cruising altitude.

"I didn't say anything on the flight up, but are you afraid of flying?" Jaylee asked.

Paxx smiled, "Not so much of flying as of crashing."

Pulling Paxx's hand into her lap, Jaylee leaned close and whispered, "What can I do to take your mind off everything?"

The plane's engines hummed like a hushed promise, vibrating through Paxx's core as she leaned into Jaylee's space. The cabin was dimly lit, with only the soft glow of emergency lights and the sporadic flashes from a tablet screen. Paxx's breath hitched as she whispered, "Are you a member of the mile-high club?" Her voice was low, sultry, and dripping with intent.

Jaylee's lips curled into a smirk that could've melted steel, her eyes locking onto Paxx's with a hunger that made Paxx's pulse throb in all the right places.

"No," Jaylee purred, her voice a velvet tease. "Are you?"

"No," Paxx admitted, her heart pounding with anticipation.

Jaylee moved, guiding Paxx's hand to rest on her bare thigh. The heat of Jaylee's skin sent tremors through Paxx as her fingers inched higher, sliding under her skirt to find the delicate lace of Jaylee's panties. Jaylee bit her lip, eyes fluttering closed as Paxx's touch sent electric shocks through her body. Paxx's fingers drifted over the damp cloth as she leaned in, her lips brushing against the delicate skin of Jaylee's neck as her fingers slid under the lace of her panties and into her wet heat. "Do you want more?" Paxx whispered, her voice a murmur, as Jaylee's warmth filled her with a desperate desire.

In response, Jaylee's hand shot out to grasp Paxx's knee as a low moan escaped her lips.

Paxx glanced around the cabin, her heart pounding as she scanned for prying eyes. Most passengers were asleep, their heads lolling against seats or lost in their own worlds. The coast was clear. She stood abruptly, her hand clutching Jaylee's, and guided her down the narrow aisle, their steps quick and quiet. The plane jostled, turbulence adding to the thrill, but neither woman cared.

Paxx led Jaylee inside the small bathroom, locking the door with a click. The cramped space pressed their bodies together. Paxx didn't waste a second. She pressed Jaylee against the wall, her mouth crashing onto Jaylee's with a fierceness that left them both gasping. Her hands ravaged as she tugged at Jaylee's blouse, freeing her breasts from their confines, her mouth immediately latching onto a hardened nipple. Jaylee's head fell back with a muffled moan, her fingers threading through Paxx's hair, urging her on.

Paxx dropped to her knees, pushing Jaylee's skirt up around her waist, then slid Jaylee's panties down her legs, removing them. Lifting Jaylee's leg over her shoulder, Paxx buried her face into the warm, inviting, sensitive flesh. Jaylee's thighs tightened around Paxx's head as she came, her cries muffled by the hand she clapped over her mouth. Paxx didn't let up until Jaylee was trembling and spent, slumped against the wall with a dazed smile. Paxx stood, pulling Jaylee's panties up her legs and then readjusting her skirt over her hips before leaning in to capture Jaylee's lips in a deep, hungry kiss.

Jaylee began fumbling with the buttons of Paxx's jeans. "My turn," she whispered in a husky tone. With a soft thud, the denim dropped to the floor as Jaylee knelt, locking her eyes onto Paxx's as she tasted her. A low groan escaped Paxx as her hands tangled in Jaylee's hair while Jaylee worked her skillfully. Paxx muffled her cries with one hand as the other pressed against the wall, and she shuddered through the aftershocks.

Jaylee stood, pulling Paxx's jeans up as she went, then pulled Paxx into a deep kiss. The taste of each other mingled on their tongues, a delicious reminder of their shared release. As they broke apart, her eyes met Paxx's, a mischievous glint sparkling in them. "Well," she whispered, her voice soft, "I guess we can both say we're club members now."

Paxx laughed softly, her cheeks flushed with a mix of exertion and lingering arousal. Tucking a stray strand of hair behind Jaylee's ear, she purred. "I'd say that was one hell of an initiation."

They straightened their clothes as best they could in the cramped space, stifling giggles.

Before leaving the bathroom, Paxx whispered, "I love you."

"I love you, too," Jaylee responded, pressing their lips together.

After a moment, Jaylee pulled back and murmured, "Promise me you'll always want me."

Paxx met her uncertain gaze and assured her, "For the rest of my life, I will want you."

Jaylee's eyes softened at Paxx's words, a look of relief flooding her features. She leaned in, pressing her forehead against Paxx's.

"We should probably get back to our seats," Jaylee whispered, even though her body language suggested she was reluctant to leave their intimate space.

Paxx nodded, stealing one last kiss before reaching for the lock. She opened the door, peering out to ensure the coast was clear. The aisle was empty. They slipped out of the bathroom, trying to appear nonchalant as they returned to their seats.

Once seated, Jaylee leaned in close, her breath hot against Paxx's ear. "I can't believe we just did that," she whispered with a hint of excitement.

Paxx turned, her lips brushing against Jaylee's cheek. "I can't believe how much I want to do it again," she replied, her hand slipping into Jaylee's as their fingers interlaced.

"Do you feel like our relationship is solely based on sex?"

Taken aback, Paxx replied, "Not at all, Jay. Why would you think that?"

Jaylee's cheeks flushed with embarrassment. "Well, I mean, we do have a lot of sex."

"Jay," Paxx said, "We knew each other almost a month before we had sex."

"I know, but we couldn't because you were hurt," Jaylee defended.

Paxx gripped her hand a little tighter. "Jay, believe me, if sex were all I wanted from you, no amount of pain would have stopped me from being with you. I felt something deeper than physical desire from the moment I met you."

Tears welled in Jaylee's eyes.

Paxx gently touched Jaylee's cheek, "Why are you asking this? What's really going on?"

"Monica, my ex, texted me while you were in Pennsylvania." Jaylee said, "She asked me if I was ready to come back to her."

A surge of anger choked Paxx. "Did you tell her to fuck off?"

Jaylee smiled faintly. "I told her I was in a relationship with a wonderful woman who meets all my needs as much as I meet hers."

Paxx exhaled, easing. "Good."

"That's not all," Jaylee continued. "She assured me you would tire of me, and when that happened, she would allow me to return to her."

"Jay, you are never going back to her," Paxx spat. "We are so much more than just sex. I value your friendship and am dedicated to you and only you." Paxx paused, "Jay, I have never wanted to get married, and honestly, I still don't, but I do want to be with you for the rest of our lives."

Jaylee's lips trembled as she fought back tears. Resting her forehead against Paxx's shoulder, she murmured, "I want that too. More than anything."

Paxx wrapped an arm around her, pulling her closer. "Then I make you this promise right here and right now, at thirty thousand feet, that I will love and protect you for the rest of my life."

Jaylee looked up into Paxx's eyes. The sincerity she saw comforted and strengthened her. "And I promise to love and protect you for the rest of my life," she affirmed boldly.

Looking down at Jaylee's hand, where she wore the gold band, Paxx ran her thumb across it. "If I bought you a different ring, would you wear it?"

Sitting up, Jaylee grinned, "Only if you will wear one too."

Paxx only thought for a second before nodding her head in agreement. "Of course, I will."

Jaylee leaned in and captured Paxx's lips in a tender kiss. "I love you."

"I love you, too," Paxx whispered. "And there's one more thing I want to ask."

"Sure, what is it?"

Taking a deep breath, Paxx asked, "Will you move in with me?"

Jaylee grinned as she said, "I wanted to talk to you about that. My lease is up next month, and I was hoping not to renew it."

"So, is that a yes?"

"Yes!"

Paxx felt warmth spread through her chest as she gazed at Jaylee's radiant smile. She leaned in for another kiss, savoring the softness of Jaylee's lips.

As the plane descended, Paxx kissed Jaylee's forehead. "I can't wait to wake up next to you every morning," she breathed.

Jaylee met Paxx's gaze, her eyes shining with tears of happiness. "Me too," she said, her voice steady with the weight of her commitment.

Once the plane was on the ground and Paxx could use her phone, she texted her ranch manager, Jimmy, and asked him to pick them up. After disembarking the plane and collecting their baggage, they only had to wait another five minutes before Jimmy pulled up in the loading zone.

"Sorry to wake you," Paxx apologized, climbing into the truck. "I should have called you yesterday."

"It's okay. Meg and I have been up since one with Daniel. He's all packed and ready for his trip to California," Jimmy said.

"That's right," Paxx exclaimed, "I had forgotten all about that."

Turning to face Jaylee, Paxx explained, "Jimmy's oldest son Daniel has a rock band, and a record company in L.A. has invited them out to do a demo."

"Wow," Jaylee gasped, "How exciting. How old is he?"

"Nineteen," Jimmy smiled.

"That's hard, letting your kid spread their wings and follow their dreams," Paxx said.

"It is," Jimmy agreed, "But his bandmates are a good bunch, and all of their parents are behind them one hundred percent, so I am confident they will make good choices."

"You're a wonderful dad, Jimmy, and tell Meg, if there is anything she needs, just call or come to the house. Jay and I will be there for her," Paxx assured, meeting Jaylee's gaze.

"Absolutely," Jaylee agreed happily.

"Thank you both; I know she will be happy to hear it."

The rest of the ride home was quiet as Paxx considered what had happened over the past three days. After unloading their luggage, Paxx and Jaylee bid Jimmy farewell before entering the house.

"It's good to be home," Paxx sighed as she walked from the living room into the kitchen, where she began brewing a pot of coffee.

Jaylee leaned against the counter and watched Paxx, a bright smile on her face. "It's good to be home."

Once the coffee was on, Paxx removed a keychain from a hook near the back door. Turning toward Jaylee, she handed it over and pulled her into a warm embrace. "This is your house now, Jay. Do whatever you need to make it feel like home; I want you to feel completely free here."

Leaning deeper into Paxx's arms, Jaylee confessed, "Paxx, it felt like home the first night I stayed here."

Paxx's voice quivered with emotion as she replied, "I've lived here for eight years, and in the past month, it has felt more like home than ever. You're a big part of that."

They shared a tender kiss, losing themselves in the moment. When Jaylee eventually broke the kiss, she glanced at the clock above the stove. "It's 4:30, and my first client is meeting me at ten. I need to shower and catch a few hours of sleep."

Paxx kissed her once more before stepping back. "I need a shower, too, but I also have some paperwork to prepare before I return to work after the shooting range this morning."

"Would you like to join me in the shower?" Jaylee teased as she moved a step back.

Paxx shook her head, smiling. "If I join you, you won't get any sleep, and I won't be able to do any work."

With an exaggerated pout, Jaylee turned and slipped out of the kitchen. Once the coffee finished brewing, Paxx poured herself a cup and settled into her office.

Four hours later, Jaylee surprised Paxx by wrapping her arms around her waist.

"Sorry," Jaylee said, stepping back, "I didn't mean to startle you."

Paxx turned around and hugged Jaylee, "It's okay, I was just lost in thought."

Jaylee gazed into Paxx's weary, bloodshot eyes. "You look exhausted."

"I'll be fine. I'll take a cold shower and have another cup or two of coffee."

"Please be careful today."

Paxx pulled Jaylee closer and kissed her. "I will, and you have a great day."

"Thank you, I will," Jaylee promised. "I love you; see you tonight."

"I love you too, and I'll call or text as soon as I know when I'll be home."

After Jaylee left, Paxx showered, dressed, and poured herself a to-go cup of coffee. By eleven o'clock, she had completed her prequalification at the firing range and was heading to the precinct.

? ? ?

Return to duty

Focus on the road ahead, not the path behind.

??? TWENTY-SIX

A s she stepped inside, the precinct was alive with a quiet buzz of conversation and the constant clicking of keyboards. Paxx was familiar with the rhythm, but today it felt off, almost suffocating, like trying to squeeze into a favorite jacket that no longer fit. Her boots echoed across the tiled floor as she made her way to her desk, and the piercing, inquisitive stares that followed her added to her discomfort.

Standing at her desk, Paxx gasped at the stacks of get-well cards, mail, and other correspondence covering it. Her fingers trembled as she reached for the nearest card, its cheerful floral design a stark contrast to the turmoil churning inside her. She flipped it open, scanning the well-wishes from a colleague she barely knew. The words blurred before her eyes, and she set the card down, unable to process the sentiment.

A familiar voice cut through the hum of the precinct. "Welcome back, Detective."

Paxx turned to see Captain Kimble approaching; his usually stern face softened with concern. She straightened, instinctively squaring her shoulders.

"Thank you, sir," she managed, her voice sounding stronger than she felt.

Kimble gestured to the cluttered desk. "Take your time settling in. No need to rush back into things."

"Yes, Sir."

"Have you seen Dr. Flint?"

Paxx shook her head as she handed him her shooting range silhouette. "No, but I passed my requalification this morning."

Taking the paper, he nodded his head. "That's good. Now, all you must do is see Dr. Flint and pass your psych evaluation. Then I will return your service weapon, and you can be back to full duty."

With an exasperated sigh, Paxx reluctantly agreed. "I will call him now."

"Good," Captain Kimble said as he patted her shoulder and walked away.

Picking up the phone, Paxx called the department's shrink and set an appointment for two o'clock that afternoon.

A shadow fell across her desk, and Paxx looked up to see Rowan standing there, his blue eyes unreadable. "Welcome back," he said, his voice low and controlled. "How are you feeling?"

The question hung in the air between them, loaded with unspoken tension. Paxx forced a smile that didn't reach her eyes. "I'm fine," she lied. "Ready to get back to work."

He looked at her hip, where her gun should be, and asked, "Have you been cleared?"

She picked up another envelope and said, "Meeting with Dr. Flint at two."

"Great, then you will be ready to go first thing in the morning," Rowan said confidently.

"Absolutely," Paxx agreed. "Did everyone in the department get me a card?" she asked, a bit overwhelmed.

Rowan laughed as he sat at his desk across from hers. "Every day, the pile has gotten higher and higher."

"Why didn't you bring them to me?" Paxx questioned.

Rowan shrugged. "I thought it would be nice for you to come back and see how much everyone had missed you."

———◇———

For the next two hours, Paxx sorted through cards and mail, separating them into piles and arranging them in order of importance. A constant stream of officers filtered through, welcoming her back. Some stopped to chat, others insisted on hugs, but most said a quick welcome back before they moved on. By the time she left for her appointment, she was mentally and emotionally exhausted.

Paxx's stomach churned as she rode the elevator to the fifth floor and approached Dr. Flint's office. She paused outside the door, her hand hovering over the knob, and took a deep breath to steady herself. Stepping into the waiting area, she approached the secretary's desk. The petite young redhead smiled brightly.

"Are you Detective Algatta?" she asked.

Paxx nodded, "I am."

"Go right in; he is expecting you."

Hesitantly, Paxx opened the door to his office.

"Come in, Detective Algatta," Dr. Flint greeted.

Swallowing hard, she entered the room. Dr. Flint sat behind his desk, his salt-and-pepper hair neatly combed, his kind eyes peering at her through wire-rimmed glasses.

"Please, have a seat." He gestured to the chair across from him.

Paxx lowered herself into the chair, her back rigid, hands clasped tightly in her lap. A thick and uncomfortable silence stretched between them.

Dr. Flint leaned back in his chair, studying Paxx with a practiced eye. "So, Detective, how are you feeling about returning to work?"

Paxx's jaw clenched. She hated these kinds of questions, the probing into her psyche. "Fine," she said curtly. "Ready to get back to work."

Dr. Flint nodded, his pen tapping against his notepad. "And the nightmares? Have they subsided?"

A chill ran down Paxx's spine. How did he know? Jaylee was the only one who knew about the dreams that plagued her, the vivid replays of her shooting that left her drenched in sweat and gasping for air. "I'm fine," she insisted, her nails digging into her palms.

"Detective."

"How?"

"Detective, everyone has flashbacks and nightmares; it's perfectly normal," he assured. "I want to know how you are dealing with yours."

Paxx relaxed as she thought of Jaylee and her comforting words and touch.

"What are you thinking about?"

"Huh?" Paxx said, meeting his gaze.

Leaning forward in his chair, he asked, "Just now, your face softened, and your shoulders relaxed. What were you thinking about?"

Paxx glanced down at her hands in her lap, "I was thinking about my girlfriend, and how she comforts me when I wake up after..." she trailed off.

Dr. Flint's eyebrows rose. "Your girlfriend? How long have you been together?"

"It's... recent," she said carefully. "Since the incident."

"I see," Dr. Flint said, jotting something in his notepad. "And how has this relationship been affecting your recovery?"

Paxx hesitated, weighing her words. "It's been... helpful," she admitted. "Jaylee understands what I'm going through. She's patient with me."

Dr. Flint nodded encouragingly. "That's good. Support systems are crucial in times like these. Can you tell me more about how she helps you?"

Paxx shifted uncomfortably in her seat, unused to discussing her personal life, especially her relationship with Jaylee. But something in Dr. Flint's gentle demeanor made her want to open up, just a little.

"She... she's there," Paxx whispered. "When I wake up in the middle of the night, heart racing, she holds me. Tells me I'm safe and that it's all over."

Dr. Flint leaned back, his eyes kind but probing. "And do you believe her when she says that? That it's over?"

Paxx nodded. "I believe the shooting is over, but until we catch the shooter, it's not fully over."

"Do you believe you are still in danger?" he asked carefully.

Paxx met his gaze, trying to read his intention in asking that question. "Honestly, I don't know. The person whom my shooter claimed to be has been in prison for over a year, so there are questions about who shot me and why. They seem to grow increasingly every day that he is out walking the streets," she confessed.

Dr. Flint carefully selected his next words: "Two years ago, your father was shot and killed, right?"

Paxx felt her chest tighten at the sudden mention of her father. She nodded stiffly, her jaw clenched. "Yes, that's correct."

Dr. Flint's eyes softened with sympathy. "I apologize for bringing up such a painful topic, but I believe it applies to your current situation. How, in your mind, do you see the two incidents as connected?"

Paxx took a deep breath, trying to steady herself. "I... I don't know," she admitted, her voice barely above a whisper. "Sometimes I wonder if those things are connected. If whoever was behind my father's murder is also responsible for my shooting."

Dr. Flint leaned forward, his elbows resting on his desk. "That's a heavy burden to carry, Detective. Have you shared these thoughts with anyone? Your partner? Your girlfriend?"

"My brother," Paxx admitted, "He and his wife are moving back here from Chicago. The County Sheriff's office hired him as a Homicide Detective."

"How long have they lived in Chicago?"

"Ten years."

"And I assume, since you have confided in him about this, that the two of you are close? How about his wife? Do the two of you get along?" he asked while writing in his notebook.

Paxx couldn't help but smile as she told him about Anna and their being best friends since high school, about Paul and how close they had been growing up, and even about Embry and the baby on the way. She also mentioned how eager she and Jaylee were about being aunts.

"It sounds like you have a solid support network, and I must say, you've made remarkable progress since we spoke after your partner's death."

"That was a tough period for me, and I wish I had the support back then that I have now," Paxx admitted. "I think my actions would have been very different."

"Don't dwell on the past, Detective. You seem to be managing everything well, and it's wonderful you have family to rely on."

After another ten minutes of standard questions, Dr. Flint signed off on her release form, allowing her to return to full active duty, and walked her to the door.

"I'm available if you need anything, Detective," he said as he opened the door.

"Thank you," Paxx responded as she exited the room.

While descending in the elevator to the second floor, Paxx sent a text to Jaylee.

'Cleared for duty. I want to take you out for dinner tonight to celebrate.'

'Congratulations! I'll be finished around four.'

'See you at home, love you.'

'See you at home. Love you too.'

———————◦◦◦———————

P axx felt relieved to be cleared, yet an unsettled feeling crept in as she knocked on Captain Kimble's door, entering when he waved her in.

"Yes, sir. She just walked in," he said to someone on the other end before hanging up.

Paxx handed him the clearance paperwork from Dr. Flint.

"Thank you," he said, opening a drawer at his desk and pulling out her service weapon, setting it on the desk in front of her. "Are you ready to hit the ground running?" he asked, motioning for her to sit down.

Paxx sat in a well-worn chair in front of his desk. "Yes, sir, what do you have?"

"There is an abandoned house just outside of town; we have had eyes on it for the past three weeks, and the movements suggest a large drug operation," he said as he handed her several photos showing multiple people entering and exiting the premises, the time stamps showing all hours of the day and night. "There is supposed to be a new shipment arriving late tomorrow afternoon, so we will breach it tomorrow night."

Paxx nodded, a tinge of anxiety pressing against her chest.

"Are you up for this, Paxx?" Kimble asked cautiously.

"Yes, sir," Paxx declared, lifting her chin and squaring her shoulders.

"Okay, Rowan has copies of the building layout and the action plan for you; take them home, get a good night's sleep, and I will see you back here tomorrow at nine a.m.."

Standing, Paxx said, "Yes, sir, see you in the morning."

Back at her desk, Paxx gathered the letters, cards, and mail and placed them in her backpack as she looked around for Rowan.

He appeared moments later. "Hey, partner, I see you are all cleared," he said with a smile that didn't quite reach his eyes as he nodded toward the gun on her waist.

"I am."

"Did Kimble tell you about tomorrow night?"

Paxx nodded, trying to match Rowan's enthusiasm despite the knot in her stomach. "Yeah, I just need those files from you."

Rowan opened a drawer in his desk and handed over a thick manila folder. "It's all in here. I've marked the key entry points and potential trouble spots. You'll want to study this carefully tonight."

"Thank you," Paxx murmured.

Rowan leaned against Paxx's desk, his voice low. "You sure you're ready for this?"

Paxx bristled at the question. "Of course, I am. Why wouldn't I be?"

Rowan shrugged, his gaze intense. "Just checking. It's been a while since you've been in the field. And after what happened..."

"I'm fine."

Holding his hands up in mock surrender, Rowan said, "Okay, I just asked."

Paxx's jaw clenched as she shoved the folder into her backpack. She knew Rowan meant well, but his concern grated on her already frayed nerves. "I appreciate your concern, but

I don't need to be coddled," she said, her tone softening slightly. "I've been cleared for duty, end of story."

Rowan nodded, his expression unreadable. "Alright. Just remember, I've got your back out there."

"Right," Paxx replied, slinging her backpack over her shoulder. "See you tomorrow."

As she walked to her Jeep, Paxx's mind raced. The weight of her gun at her hip felt both familiar and foreign. It had been a month since she'd worn it, since she'd been in the field. Images from that night flashed unbidden through her mind: the impact of the bullet, the searing pain, the metallic taste of blood in her mouth.

Paxx shook her head, trying to dispel the memories. They cleared her for duty. She was ready. She had to be.

? ? ?
TWENTY-SEVEN

When Paxx got home, she emptied her backpack onto the dining table, organizing the items into relevant piles. She grabbed a beer from the fridge before sitting down and opening the manila envelope Rowan had given her. Paxx examined the floor plans and pictures for the next thirty minutes, read through the reports, and took notes. Hearing the front door open, she couldn't help but smile as Jaylee appeared in the kitchen doorway. "Hi, beautiful," Paxx greeted, getting up to wrap Jaylee in a much-needed hug.

"Hey, gorgeous," Jaylee responded, melting into Paxx's arms.

"You look tired."

"So do you," Jaylee replied, leaning back to study Paxx's face.

Paxx cupped Jaylee's face in her hands, brushing a stray hair behind her ear. "Long day?"

Jaylee nodded, her eyes fluttering closed at Paxx's touch. "You have no idea. One of my new clients is... demanding."

"Want to talk about it?"

Jaylee's gaze drifted to the dining table. "What's all that?"

Paxx sighed, running a hand through her short, tousled hair. "It's a case that's... complicated."

Jaylee's brow furrowed with concern. "Anything you can talk about?"

"I will tell you about it later. Right now, I want to hear about your day," Paxx encouraged, leading Jaylee to the couch. "Is this a Physical Therapy client or a Personal Training client?"

Jaylee sank into the couch, kicking off her shoes with a grateful sigh. Paxx settled beside her, pulling Jaylee's feet into her lap, massaging them. Jaylee's eyes closed in bliss.

"So, this demanding client."

"Physical therapy," she sighed, "He's an ex-professional athlete who believes he knows more about his recovery than we do. I took him on from another therapist because he consistently overexerts himself and then gets annoyed when he relapses. My boss assigned him to me to speed up his recovery process."

Paxx's fingers worked on Jaylee's tired feet, eliciting a soft moan of appreciation. "Sounds like a real piece of work. You're not letting him bully you, are you?"

"No way," Jaylee said, a hint of steel in her voice. "I told him if he doesn't follow my instructions, we will drop him as a client. His choice."

Paxx smiled proudly. "That's my girl."

They sat in comfortable silence, the day's tension melting. But Jaylee couldn't shake the nagging curiosity about the papers strung across the table.

"Can you tell me about this case?"

Continuing to massage Jaylee's feet, Paxx said, "It's a drug house; we are serving a warrant tomorrow night."

Jaylee pulled her feet from Paxx's lap, a fearful look in her eyes.

Paxx closed her eyes, waiting for the argument she was sure would come. But Jaylee still hadn't said anything after nearly a minute, so Paxx slowly opened her eyes.

"I know this is what you do," Jaylee said.

Paxx turned to face her, grasping her hands. "Jay, I want to be completely honest with you. I need to be able to confide in you about my job. I can't tell you specifics or discuss ongoing cases, but I need you to support me."

Jaylee leaned in, pressing a gentle kiss to Paxx's forehead. "You're amazing at what you do, Paxx, and I support you a thousand percent. But that doesn't mean I won't worry when you are out there or hold my breath until I know you're safe."

"I will always come home to you, Jay; you give me a reason to come home."

Jaylee brushed away a tear from her cheek and said, "Paxx, we both know you can't guarantee that. Still, I believe you will do all you can to return to me every night."

"I promise I will."

Paxx pulled her closer, their foreheads touching. Her promise hung between them, heavy with unspoken fears and hopes. They breathed together, finding comfort in each other's presence.

"I love you," Paxx whispered, her voice thick with emotion.

"I love you, too," Jaylee replied, her fingers tracing the line of Paxx's jaw. "Now, tell me more about this case. What can you share?"

Paxx hesitated, weighing her words carefully. "It's a high-risk operation. The gang we're targeting is known for violence, and they've got a lot to lose."

Jaylee's grip on Paxx's hand tightened. "And you're leading the team?"

Paxx shook her head. "No, Rowan is. I'll be second in command on the scene."

Jaylee snuggled closer to Paxx, holding back tears. "Do you mind if we stay in tonight?"

Holding her tighter, Paxx replied, "Not at all. It's been a strange day; I should be thrilled about being cleared to return to duty."

"But?"

"I have more to live for now, more reasons to come home than ever. With you, Paul, Anna, Embry, and the new baby on the way, Jaylee, I'm more afraid of dying than I've ever been."

Jaylee pulled back, her eyes searching Paxx's face. She could see the vulnerability there, the raw honesty that Paxx rarely showed to anyone. It made her heart ache with equal measures of love and fear.

"Oh, sweetheart," Jaylee murmured, cupping Paxx's face. "That fear... It's normal. It means you have something precious to protect. But it doesn't make you weak. If anything, it makes you stronger."

Paxx leaned into Jaylee's touch, her eyes closing briefly. When she opened them again, determination and vulnerability filled her eyes. "I know. It's just different now. Before, the job was everything. Now, it's important, but it's not my whole life anymore."

Jaylee nodded with understanding. "And that's okay. It doesn't make you any less dedicated or capable."

They sat silently for a moment, the weight of their conversation settled around them. Then Jaylee stood up, tugging on Paxx's hands. "Let's get something to eat, then take a long, hot bath before we snuggle up in bed."

Paxx smiled as she stood and followed Jaylee into the kitchen. "If you start dinner, I will pull your car into the garage."

Jaylee turned and looked at Paxx in confusion. "There is no room in the garage."

Kissing her on the tip of her nose, Paxx replied, "I had Jimmy take the truck to the barn so you can have the second bay."

New tears formed in Jaylee's eyes. "You didn't have to do that."

"Yes, I did. This is your house now, so one of those garage bays belongs to you."

Jaylee's heart swelled with emotion at Paxx's gesture. It was more than just a parking spot; it was a tangible sign of their commitment. To Paxx, making room for her in every aspect of her life.

"Thank you," Jaylee whispered, pulling Paxx in for a tender kiss.

Paxx smiled, her eyes soft and affectionate. "Anything for you, my love."

As Paxx headed out to move Jaylee's car, Jaylee busied herself in the kitchen, pulling out ingredients for a quick stir-fry. Her mind wandered to the papers on the dining table, worry gnawing at her insides. She tried to push it away, focusing instead on the sizzle of vegetables hitting the hot pan.

When Paxx returned, she wrapped her arms around Jaylee from behind, resting her chin on her shoulder. "Smells amazing."

"It will be ready in about twenty minutes if you want to clean off and set the table."

Paxx nodded, kissing Jaylee's neck before stepping away. As she cleared the dining table of her case files, tucking them back into the manila envelope, she couldn't help but feel a pang of guilt. She knew Jaylee was worried, even if she was trying her best to be supportive. After setting the table, Paxx went to the bathroom to wash up. She splashed cold water on her face and stared at her reflection in the mirror. The woman looking back at her seemed different; she felt older, more tired, and more grounded. She took a deep breath, steeling herself for tomorrow's operation while reminding herself of all she had to come home to. After dinner, they sank into a steaming bath together, Jaylee nestled between Paxx's legs, her back against Paxx's chest. Paxx's fingertips traced lazy patterns on her slick stomach.

"You're so soft," Paxx murmured, her voice low, sending shivers down Jaylee's spine.

Jaylee's heart raced as Paxx's hands wandered lower, skimming over her hips and thighs. She bit back a moan, not wanting to break the spell of quiet that enveloped them. She tilted her head back, exposing her neck, and Paxx took the invitation, pressing open-mouthed kisses along the sensitive skin. A loud crash from downstairs shattered the peaceful moment. Jaylee's eyes snapped open as she sat up. Paxx was out of the tub, pulling on T-shirt and sweatpants over her wet body before Jaylee stood and reached for a towel. Opening the small gun safe on a shelf in the closet, Paxx chambered her pistol. "Wait here!"

Jaylee shook her head as she dried off before pulling on her robe.

Jaylee's heart pounded as she followed Paxx out of the bathroom, her bare feet silent on the hardwood floor. The house was eerily quiet now, the earlier crash echoing in her mind. She watched Paxx move with practiced ease, her gun held low but ready.

"I'll be back in a minute," Paxx assured, kissing Jaylee's cheek.

Paxx crept downstairs, eyes scanning every shadow. Soft voices murmured from the kitchen. As she cautiously approached, Paxx raised her pistol as a familiar squeal broke the silence.

Exhaling in relief, Paxx set her gun on a shelf in the living room before entering the kitchen.

"What the hell?" she gasped when she saw Anna on her knees, picking up broken glass.

"Oh my god, Paxx! I'm so sorry!" Anna exclaimed, her face flushed with embarrassment. "We didn't mean to scare you!"

"Paxx, Paxx," Embry screamed from her daddy's arms.

Paul looked up sheepishly, a broom in one hand and Embry in his arms. "We came home early; we tried to sneak in without bothering you."

Paxx leaned against the doorframe, her heart still racing from the adrenaline. She ran a hand through her wet hair, exhaling. "Jesus, you two. You nearly gave us a heart attack," she exclaimed, pushing off the doorframe and taking Embry from Paul.

Jaylee appeared in the doorway, tying her robe tighter around her waist. Her eyes widened at the scene in the kitchen. "What's going on?"

Anna stood up, clutching a handful of glass shards. "I'm so sorry, Paxx, your mom sent us home with a vase of flowers. Paul set it on the counter, and I knocked it off with my purse."

Jaylee's shoulders relaxed as she took in the scene: broken glass on the floor, Anna looking mortified, and Paul sweeping. She couldn't help but laugh, the absurdity of the situation hitting her all at once.

"Oh, Anna, Paul! Welcome back," she said, stepping into the kitchen. "Are you okay? Did anyone get hurt?"

Paul shook his head, sweeping up the last of the glass. "We're fine."

Embry reached out for Jaylee, who took her from Paxx's arms. "Hey there, little one."

Paxx noticed Paul averting his gaze and Anna stifling a laugh. Looking down, she realized her white shirt was soaking wet, resulting in it now being see-through.

"That's what you get for interrupting our bath," Paxx smirked as she turned and retreated upstairs, picking up her gun as she went.

Jaylee cleared her throat, bouncing Embry in her arms. "So, how was your trip?" she asked, trying to change the subject.

Anna's eyes sparkled with mischief. "Oh, it was lovely. But clearly not as lovely as your evening was shaping up to be."

Paul groaned. "Anna, please. I don't need to think about that."

Jaylee laughed, the tension in the room dissipating. "Why don't you two get settled in? We can catch up properly in the morning."

Embry giggled, squirming in Jaylee's arms. "Down, down!"

"Not yet, sweetie, there might still be some glass on the floor."

Paul nodded, dumping the last of the glass into the trash as Anna took Embry from Jaylee.

"You better go upstairs and finish what we interrupted," Anna winked.

? ? ?
TWENTY-EIGHT

As Jaylee pushed open the bathroom door, she found Paxx stretched out in the tub, warm water rippling around her. Paxx's wet hair was slicked back and her eyes were gently closed. Jaylee couldn't suppress a smile at the peaceful sight.

"Is there room for one more?" Jaylee asked softly, letting her robe fall away.

Paxx's eyes fluttered open and she returned Jaylee's smile. "Always," she said, reaching out to guide Jaylee into the bath.

Jaylee eased herself in and settled against Paxx's chest. The warmth enveloped her, and with it came relief from the day's earlier tension. Paxx wrapped her arms around Jaylee's waist and leaned in close. "Where were we?" she whispered in Jaylee's ear.

Jaylee shivered at the nearness of her voice. Turning her head, she met Paxx's gaze. "Right about here," she murmured, brushing her lips across Paxx's in a slow kiss. Paxx's hands moved tenderly along Jaylee's sides, and Jaylee sighed, pressing herself closer.

They paused only briefly when Jaylee spoke up. "Paxx, remember you promised to show me everything?"

Paxx held her for a moment. "I do."

"I'd like to try tonight," Jaylee said, meeting her eyes steadily. "With you."

Paxx's arms tightened around Jaylee. Her voice was low and warm. "Only if you're sure."

Jaylee nodded. "I am."

When the bath ended, they stepped out, wrapped themselves in towels, and headed to the bedroom.

Paxx paused at her closet, took down a small bag. Jaylee watched, curiosity and excitement flickering in her eyes. Paxx cleaned everything with calm care and fastened the harness around her hips.

Jaylee's breath caught at the sight of Paxx standing there so confidently. Paxx crawled onto the bed and cupped Jaylee's face. "We'll go slow," she said gently. "If you need to stop, just tell me."

Jaylee leaned into Paxx's hand and whispered, "I want this," then drew her in for a kiss that was soft and urgent all at once. Paxx's fingers traced reassuring circles on Jaylee's back as they fell into a quiet rhythm of closeness.

When they both felt ready, Paxx guided the toy with a few careful movements. Jaylee's body responded with a series of gentle tremors, and she wrapped her arms around Paxx's neck. Paxx paused once more, letting Jaylee adjust. Then they continued, hearts pounding in unison, lost in trust and affection rather than heat alone.

Afterward, they lay tangled together, sharing soft words and gentle strokes as they came back down from the shared intimacy. Jaylee rested her head on Paxx's shoulder while Paxx brushed damp hair from Jaylee's face. "Was that... okay?" Paxx asked, voice tender.

Jaylee smiled, eyes bright. "More than okay," she said.

They nestled closer under the covers, feeling a quiet, glowing contentment. Jaylee traced lazy circles on Paxx's arm.

"I love you, Jaylee,"

Jaylee pressed her lips to Paxx's. "I love you, too."

They lay back down together, hearts unclenched, and fell asleep in each other's arms, closer than ever.

? ? ?
TWENTY-NINE

Paxx awoke with sunlight filtering through the window; she lay motionless as the previous night's events played through her mind. Turning over, expecting to see Jaylee lying behind her, she frowned as she sat up and looked at the empty space. Getting out of bed, she padded to the bathroom, only to find it empty. Back in the bedroom, she glanced at the clock beside the bed: six thirty. 'Jaylee didn't say she had to leave early this morning,' Paxx thought.

Sitting on the edge of the bed, Paxx placed her head in her hands. 'Maybe last night was too much; maybe she wasn't ready after all.' Paxx let her mind wander with regret and fear.

She flinched when someone touched her on the shoulder.

"Paxx, honey, what's wrong?" Jaylee asked as she sat two cups of coffee on the nightstand.

Paxx released a heavy sigh, embarrassment filling her. "I thought you left."

Kneeling before her, Jaylee grasped her hands. "Paxx, tell me what's going on. Why are you so scared that I will leave you?"

Paxx shook her head, "Jay, something is not right; it's like something inside of me has been rewired. I feel suffocating fear, something I have always been able to control and push down deep, but now I can't seem to control it. I feel like it's choking me."

"Paxx, honey, it's called PTSD, and it is very normal after going through something traumatic." Jaylee said, "You can talk to me; I am always here for you. But you may need to talk to someone who specializes in this."

Paxx kissed her forehead before standing and pulling her to her feet. "Right now, all I need is you in the shower," she murmured, taking Jaylee by the hand and leading her to the bathroom.

The warm water cascaded over their bodies as Paxx pressed Jaylee against the cool tile wall. Their lips met in a passionate kiss, hands roaming over slick skin. Paxx's fears melted away momentarily, replaced by the intoxicating sensation and the feel of Jaylee's body beneath her hands.

But as steam filled the shower, a sudden flash of memory hit Paxx like a punch to the gut: the oppressive humidity, the feeling of being trapped, unable to breathe. Her heart raced, and panic rose in her chest.

Jaylee sensed the change. "Paxx? What's wrong?"

Paxx tried to shake it off, pressing Jaylee harder against the wall as she pressed her hand between her legs; the need to have her was overwhelming. Jaylee flinched as Paxx's fingers entered her hard and fast. She didn't complain; instead, she wrapped her arms around her shoulders and whispered in Paxx's ear, "Baby, I'm here, slow down."

"I need you," Paxx growled.

"You have me, Paxx."

Paxx stiffened and released Jaylee, backing until her back was against the glass surround, shame and guilt covering her face. "Jay, I'm so sorry."

Jaylee moved towards her, ignoring the hands Paxx held up, trying to stop her. "No! Do not apologize; you have done nothing wrong."

"I hurt you," Paxx said, her voice barely audible above the shower noise.

Jaylee pulled Paxx into her arms. "You did not hurt me, I promise."

Paxx leaned into her embrace, tears streaming down her face.

Jaylee clutched Paxx, letting the warm water wash over them as Paxx's body shook with silent sobs. She caressed Paxx's back. "I've got you," she murmured, her lips brushing against Paxx's ear. "Let it out. It's okay."

After a few minutes, Paxx's breathing slowed, and she lifted her head from Jaylee's shoulder. "I'm sorry," Paxx whispered again, her eyes red-rimmed and vulnerable.

Jaylee cupped Paxx's face in her hands, her gaze intense. "Listen to me. You have nothing to be sorry for. What you're going through is real and scary, but we'll face it together. Okay?"

Paxx nodded, leaning into Jaylee's touch. "I don't know what's happening to me, Jay. One minute I'm fine, and the next I feel like I'm losing control."

"Maybe you should take a few more days before you return to the field," Jaylee suggested carefully.

Paxx closed her eyes and shook her head. "I need to get back out there, even if I'm scared," she admitted, pausing as the words slipped out. "Jay, I'm afraid that if I don't confront my fear and return to my duties, I might never be able to."

Jaylee leaned back, meeting Paxx's wide, fear-filled eyes. "It's okay to be scared, Paxx. You were shot and almost died thirty-eight days ago. You have every right to be scared of returning to the streets and into the same situation."

"Thirty-two days," Paxx sighed. "You know how many days it's been?"

"Yes, I know how many days it's been," Jaylee confirmed. "It has been thirty-three days since we met," she replied, tracing the scar on Paxx's side.

Paxx closed her eyes, letting Jaylee's words wash over her. The fear was still there, lurking beneath the surface. Paxx took a deep breath, trying to steady herself. "Thirty-three days," she repeated, a hint of wonder in her voice. "It feels like I've known you forever."

Jaylee smiled, her fingers still tracing the raised scar on Paxx's side. "Me too, and we still have so much more to learn about each other."

The water started cooling, and Paxx reached behind Jaylee to turn it off. They stood there for a moment, dripping and vulnerable, before Jaylee grabbed a towel and wrapped it around Paxx's shoulders.

"Come on. Let's get dressed and drink our coffee. We can talk more about what's going on."

As they dried off and dressed, Paxx felt the weight of her impending return to work settle heavily within her.

"I don't know what time I will be home tonight," Paxx said as they sat on the loveseat in their bedroom and drank lukewarm coffee.

"Please call me once you finish the raid and are safe."

"I will call as soon as possible, I promise."

They sat silently for the next twenty minutes, Jaylee leaning against Paxx as they finished their coffee and thought about the day ahead.

When Jaylee left for work at seven-thirty, Paxx sat in her office, reviewing the files Rowan had given her the day before.

"Paxx," Anna's voice broke her concentration.

"Yeah," Paxx sighed, not making eye contact.

"Is everything alright?"

"Yes, I just have a big case right now, and it's going to be a long day and night."

"Are you and Jaylee okay?"

Paxx looked up from her paperwork, confused. "Yeah, why do you ask?"

Anna sat in the chair in the corner of the room. "After the enjoyment we heard last night coming from your room, I expected the two of you to be on cloud nine this morning."

Heat spread up Paxx's cheeks. "I'm sorry. I forget you were in the room below ours."

Anna waved her hand, dismissing her apology. "Don't worry about it; we made enough noise of our own to cover yours up."

Paxx chuckled at the look on Anna's face. "You two make as much noise as you want; I will never complain."

Anna's smile faded as she studied Paxx's face. "But seriously, you seem... off this morning. Is everything okay with you and Jaylee?"

Paxx hesitated, debating how much to share. She trusted Anna, but discussing her fears felt like admitting weakness.

Finally, she sighed. "We're good. Great, actually. It's just... I'm heading back into the field today. First big operation since..." she trailed off, her hand unconsciously moving to her side.

Anna leaned forward, concern etched on her face. "No one would think less of you if you needed more time. You've been through hell."

"I appreciate the concern, but I need to do this. I need to prove to myself that I can." Paxx said firmly, more to convince herself than Anna. "The team needs me. I can't let them down."

Anna nodded, recognizing the stubborn determination in Paxx's eyes. "Just... be careful out there, okay?"

"I will," Paxx assured, pausing a moment before continuing. "Will you do me a favor?"

"Of course."

"Anna, we are raiding a drug house tonight. I have been honest with Jaylee, but she is scared." Paxx swallowed hard before she admitted, "Hell, I'm scared, but I need you to keep her busy. Don't let her sit around and worry; can you do that?"

Anna stood and closed the distance between them. "I will make sure we keep her busy, but Paxx, I can't keep her from worrying about you. Every time Paul leaves for work, I worry," Anna admitted. "It has gotten better over the years, but there are days when I know he is working on a big case, and I wonder if that is the day someone will knock on my door...."

Paxx and Anna embraced, each comforting the other. "You understand what she is going through more than I do," Paxx admitted. "I have had no one to worry about me, and I have never had someone to come home to, so this is unfamiliar territory for me."

"And for her," Anna replied. "I will help as much as I can."

"Thank you," Paxx said, releasing her hold. "Also, she is moving in." Paxx grinned.

Anna smiled and hugged Paxx again. "I was wondering when that would happen."

"You don't think it's too fast?"

"Not if this is what you both want."

Paxx nodded happily. "It is."

"Then congratulations."

"I have one more favor to ask."

"Okay," Anna replied curiously.

"I want to get her a ring," Paxx began, raising her hand to stop Anna from interrupting. "It's not an engagement ring," she clarified. "Have you noticed the wedding band she wears?"

Anna nodded.

"She wears it to deter guys from asking her out. We've talked and want to commit to each other. Neither of us wants to get married, but we want to exchange rings."

"You seem surprised," Anna said, taking her hands.

Paxx met her eyes, a new awareness dawning. "Anna, she's the woman I want to spend the rest of my life with."

"I can see that," Anna whispered, holding back joyful tears. "And, of course, I'll help you find a ring. Do you want something simple or elaborate?"

Paxx thought momentarily before responding, "I want something that reflects Jaylee; she's tough and sexy, sweet and empathetic, bold yet shy."

Anna nodded, agreeing with Paxx's description. "I'll do some research and see what I can find."

"Thank you," Paxx said, glancing at her watch. "Oh shit, I'm going to be late," she exclaimed, quickly gathering papers and stuffing them into her backpack. She kissed Anna's cheek and hurried out of the office, calling back, "I love you. Thanks again."

"Paxx," Anna called after her.

Paxx halted and turned.

"Be careful, you have more than Jaylee to come home to."

Paxx dropped her backpack and rushed back to embrace Anna. "I will be careful, and I'm so grateful to have you all to come home to."

"I love you, sweetie," Anna said as Paxx let go.

Paxx hurried out of the house, her mind racing with thoughts of the upcoming raid and the conversation with Anna. As she climbed into her Jeep, she felt a mix of anticipation and dread settling in her stomach.

? ? ?

Unexpected Betrayals

Sometimes the person you would take a bullet for, is the person holding the gun.

THIRTY

As she drove to the precinct, Paxx tried to focus on the upcoming operation, pushing aside her lingering fears. She needed to be sharp and alert; lives depended on it.

The briefing room was buzzing with activity when she arrived. Rowan nodded at her from across the room, his face etched with concern. Paxx gave him a reassuring smile, trying to project confidence she didn't feel.

"Alright, pay attention," Captain Kimble announced. "We have reliable information on a significant drug operation being conducted out of an abandoned house on the outskirts of the east side of town. This is a big deal, folks. If we succeed, we could dismantle a key distributor. I trust everyone is familiar with the house's layout and the intelligence gathered." Kimble caught Paxx's eye. "We're fortunate Detective Algatta is back with us to help bring these criminals down."

"Rowan will take the lead at the site, with Paxx as second in command; Lieutenant Rankin will be in the mobile unit," Kimble announced, glancing at his watch. "We have secured the warrants for the property and all involved suspects; I expect everything to proceed without a hitch," he insisted. "You have five hours to ask questions, gather information, and memorize all breach and potential trouble points. Let's get moving; I want everyone on-site and prepared for entry by six o'clock."

Paxx nodded and scanned the room, meeting each inquisitive and critical gaze with confidence.

As the briefing room emptied, Paxx felt a hand on her shoulder. She turned to find Rowan staring at her.

"You sure you're ready for this?" he asked in a low voice.

Paxx squared her shoulders. "I'm fine, Rowan. I need to be here."

He studied her face for a moment, then nodded. "Alright. But no heroics."

"Wouldn't dream of it," Paxx said wryly.

They spent the next few hours poring over blueprints, surveillance photos, and intelligence reports. Paxx immersed herself in the details, grateful for the distraction from her nerves as she pushed aside her lingering anxiety. As the team geared up, she felt the familiar rush of adrenaline building.

"Algatta," she heard Captain Kimble call from his office.

"Sir," she responded, meeting his gaze as he motioned for her to join him in his office.

"How are you doing?" he asked with a tinge of concern.

Paxx pushed down the anger that threatened to explode. "Honestly, Cap., I would be better off if everyone stopped asking how I'm doing."

Kimble nodded, his eyes softening. "We just want to be sure you're ready for this."

"I'm ready," Paxx assured, her stomach churning with nerves.

Reaching into a bag, he pulled out a vest and handed it to her. Paxx took it, and another wave of fear washed over her as she looked at the bulletproof vest.

"Thanks."

"Be safe out there."

"Yes, sir," Paxx nodded before leaving his office.

As Paxx left Kimble's office, she felt the weight of the new vest in her hands. It was a stark reminder of the danger she was about to face. She took a deep breath, stealing herself as she walked to the locker room to change.

The Kevlar felt stiff and suffocating against her as she secured the straps. Paxx caught her reflection in the mirror, noting the determined set of her jaw. She wouldn't let fear hold her back.

"Ready?" Rowan's voice came from behind her.

Paxx turned, nodding. "Let's do this."

They made their way to the parking garage, where the rest of the team was assembling. Tension filled the air as the team made final equipment checks and tested radios. Paxx climbed into the lead vehicle with Rowan, her heart pounding.

The drive to the east side was tense, filled with a heavy silence broken only by occasional radio chatter. Paxx's mind raced, cycling through the details of the operation, potential scenarios, and escape routes. She couldn't shake the image of Jaylee's face, worry etched on her beautiful features.

Rowan's voice crackled over the radio as they approached the target building. "All units, get into position. Remember, we're looking for Davis Mendoza and his crew."

Paxx pulled out her phone, turning off the ringer. Before securing it back in her pocket, she quickly texted Jaylee: 'I love you. Never forget or doubt that. Talk to you soon.'

Three dots appeared: 'I love you too. Please be safe and talk soon.'

They set up base operations a quarter mile away, then walked through the dense woods to the house.

Paxx's heart rate quickened as she positioned herself near the rear entrance. From the earpiece in her ear, she could hear Rowan coordinating the teams. "Paxx, we are ready in the front," Rowan whispered in her ear.

"All set here," Paxx relayed softly into her mic.

"Copy that. On my mark, we breach," Rowan replied, his voice steady despite the tension in the air.

Paxx focused on her breathing, counting down from five in her head. She felt the energy of the team around her, a palpable mix of nerves and determination. It was now or never.

"Three... two... one... breech!" Rowan demanded.

As Paxx crossed the threshold, her focus narrowed to the back of the officer in front of her, her hand tapping his shoulder to continue forward. Memories of the night she was shot flooded her mind as she moved deeper into the house. Holding her hand in a fist, she brought the line of officers to a stop as she heard heavy footsteps above her.

"Rowan, we have movement upstairs," she conveyed into the mic on her collar.

Motioning to three officers behind her, Paxx silently instructed them to branch off and clear the downstairs rooms. Once their heads nodded in understanding, Paxx again tapped the shoulder in front of her and motioned above them with her hand. "Team two approaching the stairs," she relayed across the coms.

"Team one has located the stairs to the basement. Descending now," Rowan's voice filled her ear.

After only four steps up, gunfire erupted from the landing above them, wood from the banister shredding as the bullets made contact; the next few minutes were a blur of gunfire, loud voices, and chaos.

Paxx instinctively dropped to a crouch, her heart pounding in her ears as bullets whizzed overhead. The acrid smell of gunpowder filled the air, mingling with shouts and the thunderous echo of gunfire. She could feel the vibrations of each shot thumping in her chest.

"Officer down!" a voice crackled through her earpiece. Paxx's stomach lurched, but she forced herself to focus.

"Team two, hold position!" she barked into her mic, assessing the situation. The stairs offered little cover, leaving them exposed to the assailants above. Paxx's mind raced, weighing their options.

A flash of movement caught her eye. Through the haze of gun smoke, she spotted two figures darting between rooms on the upper floor.

Paxx pressed forward, returning fire as she and the three officers continued up the stairs. A sudden jolt knocked her back against the wall of the staircase. "Algatta's hit," she heard a voice call out. Pressing her hand to her chest where an almost debilitating pain now thrummed, Paxx shook her head.

"My vest caught it," she replied as tears clouded her eyes. "Fuck, keep going." She urged, fighting through the pain as she continued to return fire.

Once they were on the landing, the remaining suspects retreated into rooms. "Monty, High, clear that room," she demanded, pointing to the door beside them.

The two officers entered the room a moment later and called out the all-clear. Paxx leaned against the wall, catching her breath as she assessed the situation. The pain in her chest was intense, but she pushed it aside, focusing on the task at hand. She could hear shouts and gunfire echoing from other parts of the house.

"Rowan, what's your status?" she whispered into her mic.

"We've secured the basement," his voice crackled back. "Two suspects in custody. How are things upstairs?"

"We've got at least two more up here," Paxx replied. "We're clearing rooms now."

She motioned to the remaining officer. "Cover me," she mouthed, then moved swiftly to the next door. With a deep breath, she kicked it open, gun raised. She was met with gunfire, and without hesitating, she squeezed the trigger of her pistol, firing two shots.

"Suspect down," she relayed as she stepped deeper into the room. As Paxx opened the closet door, a strong repulsive odor hit her. "Shit," she gasped as she stepped back.

On the floor of the closet, the bloated body of a woman lay in an unnatural position, as if someone had tossed her aside like a rag doll. "We've got the body of a woman, been dead several days," she reported.

Turning away from the closet, Paxx met the gaze of Henry Garst, the man she had been following since entry. "The house is clear," he informed, concern etched on his face. "No offense, Algatta, but you look like shit."

As silence crept over the house and Paxx's adrenaline eased, she reached out a hand to Garst, nearly collapsing in his arms. "Fuck you," she smirked.

"Let's get you downstairs."

"Henry, I need to walk; just give me a minute," Paxx breathed heavily.

"Understood," he replied, blocking the doorway, giving her a private moment to regain her composure.

Leaning against the wall, Paxx took ragged breaths, the pain in her chest excruciating. As she looked around the room, her eyes fell on the suspect she had shot just a moment before. Pushing herself off the wall, she walked to the crumpled figure.

"Paxx don't," Henry said, catching her arm, halting her advance.

Looking back at him, Paxx saw sadness in his eyes. Pulling away, Paxx knelt and turned the figure over onto his back. The blank blue eyes of the boy who looked up at her caused her heart to ache worse than anything she had ever felt.

"Fuck, he's just a kid," she sighed.

"A kid who tried to kill you," Henry said.

Knowing there was no chance he was alive, Paxx still pressed two fingers against the side of his neck, praying for a pulse.

Slowly, Paxx made her way downstairs and outside. Floodlights and a canopy tent had been set up, and a flurry of activity buzzed around her. Henry helped her to a picnic table away from the chaos, where she sat down and lay back on the bench.

Paxx lost track of time as she lay there, every movement she had made replaying in her mind. Hearing someone calling her name, Paxx opened her eyes, making eye contact with Sergeant Molly Rankin, who stood over her, calling out her name.

"I hear you," Paxx murmured as she sat up, pressing her hand against her chest.

Molly moved her hands around Paxx's torso as if searching for something.

"What are you looking for?" Paxx asked in confusion.

"I'm looking for the Please shoot me sign you must have attached to you somewhere." Molly chuckled.

"Very funny," Paxx responded as she looked around at the scene. The officers' faces were grim, some bloody, and some limping as they walked.

"Did we lose anyone?" Paxx asked.

"No," Rowan said as he approached her, "Two, make that three, were shot." he sighed, pointing at the bullet lodged in her vest. "One in the leg, the other the shoulder."

Paxx nodded, relief washing over her despite the pain. She watched as paramedics tended to the injured officers, their faces etched with a mix of pain and determination. The adrenaline continued to wear off, leaving her feeling drained and shaky.

"You need to get yourself checked out, too," Rowan said, his brow furrowed with concern.

"I'm fine," Paxx insisted, wincing as she tried to stand. "Just bruised."

Rowan raised an eyebrow. "Humor me, Algatta. Let the medics take a look."

Before she could protest further, a paramedic approached with a medical bag in hand. Paxx reluctantly pulled her vest off and then allowed herself to be examined, hissing in pain as gentle hands probed her ribs and sternum.

"Doesn't feel like anything's broken," the paramedic said. "But you'll need X-rays to confirm, and that cut above your eye will need stitches."

Shocked, Paxx lifted her hand to her left eye, wincing as she touched the gash above it.

As she rode to the hospital in the back of an ambulance, she texted Jaylee.

'Raid is over. Lots of paperwork to do. Be home as soon as possible.'

A few moments later, Jaylee responded, 'I'm glad it's over and you're safe. See you when you get home. I love you.'

'I love you too.' Paxx responded before leaning back against the gurney. The paramedic retook her pulse and blood pressure.

The hospital released Paxx three hours later after she received ten stitches above her eye, and X-rays showed no broken bones, only a severely bruised sternum. Back at the precinct, Paxx sat at her desk, filling out reports and recounting every detail from posting up at the back entrance of the house to finding the body in the closet. Leaning back in her chair, Paxx glanced at her watch, grimacing at the time.

"It's three a.m., and I'm heading home," she said to Rowan, who sat at his desk across from her.

Rowan glanced up at her. "Shit, I didn't realize it was so late."

"I will see you Sunday," Paxx said as she pulled on her jacket, closing her eyes against the pain.

Paxx ambled to her Jeep, every movement sending sharp pains through her chest. She slid into the driver's seat and took a long, shaky breath. The events of the night replayed in her mind: gunfire, the chaos, the young boy's lifeless eyes staring up at her, and the woman's body crumpled on the closet floor. She gripped the steering wheel tightly, pushing away the flood of emotions threatening to overwhelm her.

The drive home was a blur, and Paxx found herself parked in her driveway, not remembering how she got there. Pushing the button on her garage remote, Paxx parked the Jeep, then sat, gathering the energy to move. With a deep, painful breath, Paxx exited the Jeep and quietly entered the dark house.

Pulling a beer from the fridge, she sat at the dining table, removed her boots, and tried to calm her nerves before going upstairs. Once the bottle was empty, Paxx stood up and headed for the staircase, quietly ascending the steps. She opened the bedroom door; Jaylee was peacefully asleep in bed, soft breaths filling the room. Paxx carefully closed the door and tiptoed to the bathroom, where she shut the door before turning on the light.

Stripping off her clothes, Paxx stepped into the shower, turning the water as hot as she could stand it. With her hands against the tile wall, she let the water cascade over her body, relaxing her frayed nerves with every passing minute. After washing her hair and body twice, she stepped out of the shower, wrapping a towel around her as she stepped to the sink. Looking in the mirror as she brushed her teeth, Paxx shook her head at the bruises forming around her eye. Removing the towel, she sighed at the large red spot between her breasts, aware that a deep bruise would soon appear.

Entering the closet, she selected a T-shirt and boxer shorts from a shelf and dressed. She switched off the light, opened the door, and climbed into bed, taking care not to disturb Jaylee. But as soon as their bodies made contact, Jaylee instinctively turned towards her, snuggling closer.

Paxx tensed, afraid the movement would wake her, but she sighed contentedly in her sleep. Slowly, Paxx relaxed, allowing herself to sink into Jaylee's warmth. The soft rhythm of her breathing began to soothe Paxx's frayed nerves.

As Paxx lay there, staring at the ceiling, her mind raced with images from the night. The boy's lifeless eyes. The woman's crumpled body. The chaos and gunfire. Paxx's chest tightened, her breath coming in short, painful gasps.

Jaylee stirred, lifting her head. "Paxx?" she murmured, her voice thick with sleep. "You okay?"

Paxx swallowed hard, not trusting her voice. "I'm good. Go back to sleep," Paxx whispered.

Paxx fought to sleep, closing her eyes only for a few minutes before stark images invaded her mind. As faint light streamed through the window, Paxx gave up and slipped out of bed, quietly making her way downstairs, where she made coffee. Leaning against the counter as the coffee brewed, Paxx dreaded the conversation she knew she would have to have once everyone was awake.

Pouring a cup of coffee, she grabbed a throw blanket off the back of the couch and stepped onto the front porch. She settled on the porch swing, covering her legs with the blanket, and watched the sun rise as she drank her coffee.

??? THIRTY-ONE

T he creak of the front door startled Paxx from her thoughts. She turned to see Anna stepping onto the porch, her hair tousled from sleep, concern etched across her face.

"Hey, you're up early. Are you alright?"

Paxx managed a weak smile. "Just couldn't sleep," she replied, her voice hoarse.

Paxx pulled her knees up, giving Anna room to sit beside her. Her eyes widened as she noticed the swelling and bruising around Paxx's eye and the bandage above it. "Oh my god, Paxx. What happened?"

"The raid didn't go as smoothly as we hoped."

"Want to talk about it?"

Paxx sighed as she recounted vague details about the night before, leaving out the gruesome and heart-wrenching details of the young man and the woman.

Anna sat and listened intently, her expression staying calm as she took in every word. Pressing a hand to her chest, she asked, "Are you okay?"

"Just sore," Paxx replied.

Anna took Paxx's cup from her hand and stood. "Want a refill?" she asked as she stepped away.

"Yes, please."

Anna disappeared into the house, leaving Paxx with her thoughts again. The early morning air was crisp, carrying the scent of dew-dampened grass and distant wood smoke. Paxx closed her eyes, trying to focus on these peaceful sensations rather than the haunting memories of the previous night.

A few moments later, Anna returned with two steaming cups. She gave one to Paxx and sat back on the swing. "How is Jaylee dealing with this?" Anna asked, gesturing above her left eye.

Paxx looked away. "She doesn't know; she was asleep when I got home this morning."

"This morning?" Anna exclaimed, "Paxx, you haven't slept since yesterday?"

Paxx shook her head. "I don't have to be back until Sunday, so I will rest today and help you unpack tomorrow."

"Yes, you will rest today, but we will see about you helping us tomorrow," she said sternly.

Paxx didn't argue, knowing it wouldn't do any good anyway. "Is the painting all finished?"

"Yes, and all the appliances have been delivered. Paul is going over today to set up the beds."

"What do you and Embry have planned for the day?"

"We are going to pack up our things and get your house back in order."

"Are you staying at your house tonight?" Paxx asked, hoping Paul had taken her advice and scheduled a special night for them.

Anna nodded. "Yes, Paul wants to go out to eat and celebrate; you and Jaylee should come along."

"I have a better idea," Paxx grinned, "Why don't Jaylee and I keep Embry, and you and Paul go have a nice evening out?"

"That sounds like a wonderful idea," Paul said from the doorway.

"Are you sure you're up for it?" Anna asked.

"Why wouldn't she be, shit Paxx, what happened?" Paul gasped as he got closer and saw her eye.

"Rough night at the office," Paxx smirked, trying to keep the mood light. "Speaking of, I had better get upstairs before Jaylee wakes up."

"I heard the shower turn off several minutes ago; I'd say she's up," Paul said, grimacing at the swelling and bruising on Paxx's face.

"Is it that bad?" she asked, wincing as she stood up.

Paul nodded. "Prizefighters have nothing on that mug," he chuckled.

Paxx laughed and punched him in the arm just as the door opened, and Jaylee stepped out, dressed in dark blue scrubs, her damp hair pulled up in a messy bun, and slippers on her feet.

"Is this where the party's at?" she chirped, then froze as Paxx turned to face her.

The smile slipped from Jaylee's face as she took in the swelling and bruising on Paxx's face. Her eyes widened, filling with concern and a hint of anger. "What the hell happened?" she demanded, rushing to Paxx's side.

Paxx winced, both from the pain and the intensity of Jaylee's reaction. "It's not as bad as it looks."

"Like hell it isn't," Jaylee's voice rose an octave. "Your face looks like you went ten rounds with a brick wall!" She gently cupped Paxx's chin, tilting her face to examine the bruising more closely.

"We'll, uh, go start on breakfast," Anna said, ushering Paul back into the house.

"I'm fine, Jay. Really," Paxx insisted, pulling her into an embrace. "It was just a rough night."

Jaylee leaned into the embrace, causing Paxx to flinch at the pain in her chest. Jaylee pulled back, "What else? Paxx, what else happened?"

Paxx hesitantly pulled her shirt up, keeping her breasts covered in case Paul and Anna were watching.

Jaylee's eyes glistened with tears as she gently touched the deep bruise between Paxx's breasts. "What happened?"

Pulling her shirt down, Paxx looked Jaylee in the eyes as she gripped her hands. "I took a bullet in the vest."

Jaylee sat on the swing, her hands still in Paxx's grip.

"Jay, I'm fine, just bruised and a little sore."

Jaylee's face paled, her voice barely above a whisper. "A bullet? Paxx, you could have..." she trailed off, unable to finish the thought.

Paxx knelt before her, ignoring the protest of her sore muscles. "But I didn't. The vest did its job. I'm here, I'm okay." She squeezed Jaylee's hands reassuringly.

Jaylee took a shaky breath, trying to calm herself. "You promised me you'd be careful. You promised me you'd come home safe."

"And I did," Paxx said, kissing Jaylee's cheek. "I came home to you, just like I always will, I promise."

Jaylee leaned down into Paxx's arms. "Hold me," she whispered, "Please just hold me."

Paxx stood and sat beside her, not releasing her embrace. "Baby, I'm here, I'm alright."

For the next several minutes, Paxx held Jaylee, the physical pain in her chest replaced by the fear and hurt she was causing her.

"Let me see if I can rearrange my clients for today," Jaylee said as she sat up, determined to control her crumbling emotions.

Paxx shook her head. "Jaylee, I'm fine; you cannot take off work every time something happens."

Jaylee nodded in agreement as she stood. "I need to finish getting ready."

Paxx watched her disappear into the house. She sat for a moment longer before following her inside. Paxx climbed the stairs and entered the bedroom, where she heard soft crying from the bathroom. She crossed the room and pushed open the bathroom door. Jaylee stood in front of the sink, her hands on the countertop, as she wept, her shoulders shaking with each sob.

Paxx's heart clenched at the sight. She stepped forward, wrapping her arms around Jaylee from behind and resting her chin on her shoulder. "I'm sorry," she whispered, her voice thick with emotion. "I'm so sorry I scared you."

"I just can't bear the thought of losing you," she choked out between sobs. "Every time you go out there...."

"I know, Jay. I know it's hard. But this is who I am, what I do. I can't change that."

Jaylee turned in her arms, her face streaked with tears, her lips trembling. Without a word, she crashed her mouth against Paxx's, kissing her with a ferocity that left them both gasping. Her hands clawed at Paxx's shirt, yanking it up and over her head, her fingers skimming over the angry bruise between her breasts. Paxx hissed at the contact, but Jaylee didn't stop. She couldn't stop. Her lips found the wound, kissing it before moving up to capture Paxx's mouth again.

"I need you," Jaylee breathed against her lips, her voice ragged with need. "I need to feel you, to know you're really here."

Paxx didn't hesitate. Her hands moved to the waistband of Jaylee's scrub bottoms, pushing them down. Jaylee stepped out of them, kicking them aside. Paxx pulled her top over her head and released her bra, dropping it to the floor. She groaned as her hands slid up Jaylee's sides, cupping her breasts, thumbs brushing over hardened nipples. Jaylee arched into the touch, a low moan escaping her lips.

"I need you, Paxx," Jaylee whispered, her voice breaking.

Paxx gripped Jaylee's ass, picking her up and setting her on the counter. Her hands slid between Jaylee's legs, fingers parting her folds to find her already wet, already aching. She teased her entrance, her touch light but deliberate, before sinking two fingers deep inside. Jaylee cried out, her nails digging into Paxx's shoulders as she rocked against her hand.

"Harder," Jaylee begged, her voice a desperate whine. "Please, harder."

Paxx obliged, her fingers thrusting in and out of Jaylee with a rhythm that had her trembling. She curled her fingers, brushing against that spot that made Jaylee's back arch and her legs twitch. Jaylee's moans turned into cries, her hips grinding against Paxx's hand as she wrapped her legs around Paxx's waist and her arms around her shoulders.

Paxx slowed her movements, wrapping her free arm around Jaylee's waist.

"Don't stop," Jaylee begged, her body now racked with sobs.

But she did stop. Pressing her forehead against Jaylee's, their breaths mingling, she whispered, "I'm here, I'm right here with you. Look at me."

Jaylee's eyes fluttered open, locking onto Paxx's. The vulnerability in her gaze made Paxx's heart clench. Paxx wrapped both arms around her and pulled her close, peppering soft kisses along her neck and shoulder.

Paxx held her as Jaylee sobbed against her shoulder, whispering soft words of comfort and love into her ear. "It's alright, Jay, I'm here. I promise I won't leave you."

Jaylee shook her head against Paxx's shoulder. "You can't promise me that."

Paxx held her tighter, knowing her words were valid. "I love you so much," she vowed instead of arguing.

"Forever," Jaylee whispered.

"Forever."

Paxx lifted Jaylee off the counter, setting her down. They stood there for a long moment, their bodies pressed together. Leaning back, Jaylee's fingers traced the outline of the bruise on Paxx's chest, her touch feather-light.

"I'm sorry," Jaylee murmured. "I shouldn't have reacted like that. I know how important your job is to you."

Paxx pulled back, cupping Jaylee's face in her hands. "Don't apologize. Your feelings are valid, Jay. I know it's not easy, loving someone in this line of work."

Jaylee nodded, her eyes still glistening with unshed tears. "Will it ever get easier?"

"I don't know," Paxx admitted. "You should talk to Anna and ask her how she has dealt with Paul being a cop for the past ten years."

"We talked last night. I know she was trying to keep me occupied and my mind off where you were and what was happening," Jaylee grinned. "She would have been convincing had she not been as worried as I was."

"The two of you can lean on each other," Paxx replied. "Confide in her; she understands."

"I know she does, and we are becoming good friends; she really loves you and has some great stories about the two of you in high school," Jaylee giggled.

"I hope you still love me after she tells all my dirty secrets," Paxx teased.

"I love you more after every story." Jaylee smiled. "Now I need a quick shower so I can get to work before I'm late."

"You don't want to go to work smelling so delicious?" Paxx chuckled, teasing Jaylee's inner thigh.

"No, I would rather not."

While Jaylee showered, Paxx dressed.

"Are you okay babysitting Embry tonight so Paul and Anna can have a night out?" Paxx asked Jaylee when she entered the bedroom, dressed in a clean pair of purple scrubs.

"Sure," she grinned, pulling her hair up high on her head and fastening a barrette into it.

"Good, they need to break in the new house," Paxx said slyly, raising her eyebrows.

"Agreed," Jaylee replied, tying her shoes.

Before they left the bedroom, they shared one more passionate kiss. "What do you think about getting tattoos instead of rings?" Jaylee asked Paxx as they descended the stairs.

A broad smile covered Paxx's face. "I think that's perfect."

"I'll call and make an appointment at the tattoo parlor I go to unless you have one you prefer."

"Which one do you go to?"

"Prestigious Art, over on Thaft Street."

Paxx paused, her eyes bright with a smile. "That is where I have gotten all my work done. How is it we never met before I was in the hospital?"

"Monica, is that the tattoo artist you dated?"

"Not Monica, Lacy."

Jaylee thought as she retrieved her bag from the entry closet. "Lacy hasn't worked there for about a year; she moved to St. Paul."

"I haven't been there in about two years since she finished my dragon tattoo."

"So, are you okay with getting them done there?"

"Absolutely. Monica is a great artist."

"Great, then I will make the appointments." Jaylee kissed her on the cheek as she said goodbye to Paul and Anna before leaving.

"Appointments for what?" Anna asked.

Paxx held up her left hand. "Our rings," she smiled. "We are going to get tattoos."

"Wow," Paul murmured, "you two really are serious."

"I told you they were," Anna smiled.

"Where's Embry?" Paxx asked, noticing her absence.

"It's only seven-fifteen; she should be up in another thirty minutes or so," Anna replied, handing Paxx a hot cup of coffee and setting a plate of pancakes on the table.

"Thank you," Paxx nodded, sitting down and taking a bite, moaning at the taste. "These are delicious."

"Thank you," Anna smiled at the compliment.

"What are you doing today, Paxx?" Paul asked, joining her at the table.

"After I eat, I am going to get some sleep; I want to be rested and ready this evening," Paxx replied as she took another bite.

"Are you sure you're up for keeping a rambunctious two-year-old?" Anna asked.

"Sure, Jaylee is excited; we will be fine," she assured.

"Okay, then it's all set," Paul said as he stood and kissed Anna. "I will go get the house in as much order as possible, and I will be back by five, so we can enjoy an evening out."

"Be careful, my dear man," Anna whispered, pressing her lips against his.

Paxx smiled at their intimacy, then averted her gaze.

Once Paul left, Anna retreated to the bedroom, where Embry called out for her. When Anna returned with the sleepy-eyed, wild-haired toddler in her arms, Paxx smiled at her.

"Good morning, beautiful," Paxx greeted.

"Morning," Embry said softly.

After cleaning up her dishes, Paxx kissed Embry and Anna on the cheeks. Then she retreated upstairs, took two pain pills, crawled into bed, and drifted off into a deep sleep.

???
THIRTY-TWO

Paxx awoke to laughter, and Embry's excited squeals coming from downstairs. She blinked, her vision blurry as she looked around, disoriented, before realizing where she was. The clock on the nightstand read 4:30 PM. She'd slept for nearly eight hours.

Groaning, she sat up, wincing as her bruised sternum protested the movement. The pain in her chest and head had dulled to a persistent ache, but it was still there, a constant reminder of how close she'd come to... She shook her head, dispelling the thought. There is no use dwelling on what could have been. She was alive, and that's what mattered.

Sliding out of bed, she padded to the bathroom, relieved her screaming bladder, and brushed her teeth. She looked into the mirror at her swollen and bruised eye, the swelling worse now than when she went to bed.

Making her way downstairs, she grinned at Jaylee and Embry, sitting on the floor in the living room, building a tower with blocks. When Embry saw her, the stack of blocks tumbled over, and she raced across the room. "Paxx, Paxx," she screamed.

Kneeling on one knee, Paxx scooped Embry into her arms, ignoring the sudden jolt of pain in her chest when Embry ran into her. "There's my sweet girl," Paxx chirped.

"Owie," Embry said softly as she gently touched Paxx's eye.

"Yeah, Aunt Paxx has an owie," Paxx sighed.

Jaylee grimaced at Paxx's swollen eye as she picked up the blocks and dropped them in a canvas bag.

"JJ, Paxx, owie," Embry murmured as Jaylee approached them.

"I see," Jaylee replied, kissing Paxx's cheek. "You need to get some ice on that," she urged.

"Do you want to help Aunt Paxx get some ice?" Paxx chirped at Embry as she carried her to the kitchen.

Anna stood at the sink, cleaning vegetables. "Anna, what are you doing?" Paxx asked.

"Putting a vegetable soup on for tonight's dinner." She replied, frowning at Paxx's eye.

"You don't have to do that; Jaylee and I are more than capable of cooking," Paxx replied as she opened the freezer door, took out a frozen bag of corn, placed it over the left side of her face, and closed the door with her hip.

Anna raised an eyebrow at the effortless way Paxx maneuvered while holding Embry. "You are a natural with a baby on your hip, Paxx," she chuckled.

"Don't start," Paxx replied, smiling at Jaylee as she entered the room.

"Don't start what?" Jaylee asked.

"I was just admiring how Paxx navigated while holding Embry," Anna said. "She's a natural."

Jaylee smiled, "Yes, she is a natural aunt, just like me."

Anna paused at the sink, glancing between the two of them. "Neither one of you wants kids?" she asked in disbelief.

Paxx and Jaylee exchanged looks before they said in unison, "No."

Anna's brow furrowed as she turned back to the sink. "Well, that's a shame. You'd both make wonderful mothers."

"Down," Embry said, wiggling in Paxx's arms.

Grateful for the distraction, Paxx set Embry down, wincing as she straightened up. The bag of frozen corn was dripping condensation down her arm.

"We have talked about kids and decided we're happy being aunts," Paxx said, pulling a towel off the counter and drying her arm.

Jaylee cleared her throat. "Neither of us feels that maternal pull?"

Paxx nodded in agreement, shifting the bag of frozen corn on her face. "Plus, our jobs aren't exactly conducive to raising kids."

Anna nodded, her features relaxing. "I understand that. And your relationship is still new, but Jaylee, you're young; you don't think you'll change your mind?" she asked, not letting the subject drop.

"I don't think so," Jaylee replied hesitantly, "but I guess anything could happen."

Paxx looked at her, a thin smile crossing her lips.

Anna smiled. "There's always a chance."

"Daddy," Embry cried from the living room.

Paxx looked at Anna, a sly smile on her face. "You better get ready for your date; I will finish putting the soup on," Paxx said, taking the knife from Anna's hand.

Anna hesitated for a moment, then nodded. "Thank you, Paxx. I suppose I should freshen up a bit." She wiped her hands on a dishtowel and headed to the bedroom, leaving Paxx and Jaylee alone in the kitchen.

Paxx set the knife and corn down and turned to face Jaylee, her expression mixed with amusement and concern. "So, 'anything could happen,' huh?"

Jaylee's cheeks flushed as she averted her gaze. "I was just trying to be polite."

"Jay, please don't say you don't want kids if you do," Paxx said, pulling Jaylee into her arms. "I want you to be happy, and I want you to be honest with me."

"Can we table it for now? Not say yes or no?" Jaylee urged, cupping Paxx's cheek.

"Of course, we have plenty of time to decide." Paxx smiled, pressing their lips together.

Their kiss deepened, and Paxx felt a familiar warmth spreading through her body. She pulled Jaylee closer, savoring the softness of her lips and the comforting weight of her body pressed against her own. The pain in her chest and face faded momentarily, replaced by a rush of desire and affection.

A loud crash from the living room startled them apart. "I'll check on her," Jaylee said, giving Paxx a quick peck before hurrying to the living room. Paxx nodded, picking up the bag of corn and pressing it to her eye again as she followed Jaylee to the living room, where Embry had upended the toy box, scattering toys across the floor. She sat amid the chaos, happily banging two action figures together.

Paxx chuckled as Jaylee moved toys around, giving her room to sit in the middle of the mess with Embry. Paxx returned to the kitchen, where she put the corn back in the freezer, finished cutting the vegetables, and added them to the soup pot.

At 5:30 p.m., Paul and Anna left for their date night. Paxx and Jaylee sat on the living room floor with Embry until 6 p.m., when Jaylee retreated to the kitchen to finish dinner.

"Embry wants to make some cookies." Paxx smiled as she entered the kitchen with Embry on her hip.

Jaylee smiled at them, and an unsettling yet happy flash of Paxx holding their child took her off guard. "That sounds like fun," she replied, not as enthusiastic as she intended.

Paxx caught her gaze with a questioning look. "You okay?"

Jaylee nodded, a slim smile on her lips. "I'm fine. Let's eat and then make cookies."

After dinner, Embry stood on a chair next to the counter where Paxx rolled out sugar cookie dough, and Jaylee helped her cut out shapes of her favorite farm animals: horses, pigs, and sheep. Once the cookies were in the oven, Paxx bathed Embry, spending thirty minutes playing in the water as she washed her. After the bath, Paxx put purple pajamas on Embry and returned to the living room. Jaylee had a plate of cookies waiting on the coffee table, a sippy cup of milk for Embry, and a cup of steaming coffee for herself and Paxx.

"Cookies," Embry squealed as she ran to Jaylee.

After Embry made sounds for each animal's shape, they ate some cookies, and then the three of them sat on the couch and watched a movie about pets. By eight o'clock, Embry was asleep, stretched out with her head on Paxx's lap and her feet in Jaylee's lap. Carefully, Jaylee slid off the couch and picked her up, Paxx leading the way as she carried her to the downstairs bedroom. Once Paxx tucked Embry into her big girl's bed, she picked up the monitor, and then she and Jaylee poured a fresh cup of coffee and retreated to the front porch.

Leaving the front door open, Paxx settled onto the porch swing, careful not to spill her coffee as she placed the baby monitor on the small table beside them. The wood creaked beneath them as Jaylee nestled against her side. Crickets chirped in the distance, and the soft creak of the swing's chains provided a gentle rhythm to their silence.

Paxx glanced at Jaylee, noticing the distant look in her eyes. "Penny, for your thoughts?" she whispered, reaching out to tuck a stray strand of hair behind Jaylee's ear.

Jaylee leaned into the touch, a small smile playing on her lips. "Just thinking about today. About us. About..." she trailed off, her gaze dropping to her coffee cup.

"About kids?" Paxx finished for her.

"I just..." Jaylee paused, searching for the right words. "I've always been so sure I didn't want children. But today, watching you with Embry and spending time with her, I feel like something has shifted. And it scares me."

Paxx felt a warmth spread through her at Jaylee's earnestness. "We're still figuring things out, and that's okay. There's no rush,"

They fell into a peaceful silence again, comfortable with each other's presence as they finished their coffee and enjoyed the peaceful evening.

"Do you think we should check on Embry?" Paxx asked reluctantly after another long pause.

"Probably," Jaylee conceded with a small sigh as she glanced toward the living room.

They stood together, Paxx wincing as she rose from the swing.

"You need to take something. A hot bath probably wouldn't hurt," Jaylee encouraged.

"I will take the pain meds before bed. They knocked me on my ass this morning."

They returned inside, the screen door closing with a gentle thud behind them. Paxx set their empty mugs in the kitchen sink while Jaylee crept to Embry's room. The door creaked as she pushed it open, revealing the small figure bundled beneath a princess pony-printed comforter. The horse nightlight beside her bed, casting a soft glow across Embry's peaceful face.

Paxx appeared behind Jaylee, wrapping her arms around her waist. "Still out like a light," she whispered, her breath tickling Jaylee's ear.

"She's exhausted from all that cookie-making," Jaylee replied, leaning back against Paxx's chest.

"I'm going to go shower and get ready for bed," Jaylee said as they returned to the living room.

"I'm going to sleep down here so I can be close to Embry," Paxx replied.

"Then I will be down in a bit," Jaylee smiled, pressing a kiss to Paxx's lips, "I'm not really tired, and I would like to snuggle on the couch with you for a while."

Paxx kissed her back, caressing her arms. "Snuggling sounds good to me," she murmured against her lips.

While Jaylee showered, Paxx scrolled through TV channels, finally settling on an episode of an FBI show.

The sound of running water upstairs faded into the background as Paxx settled deeper into the couch, her body aching with exhaustion despite her long sleep earlier. On-screen, agents pursued a suspect through an abandoned warehouse, but her mind drifted to Jaylee's hesitation about children. The conversation had awakened something in Paxx, too, feelings and questions she'd buried beneath years of career ambition and independence.

A soft creak from Embry's room caught her attention. Paxx muted the TV, straining to listen. Another creak, followed by rustling sheets. She rose, wincing as her bruised chest protested, and made her way to the bedroom door.

Pushing it open, she found Embry sitting up in bed, clutching her stuffed rabbit, eyes wide in the dim glow of her nightlight. "Hey, sweet pea," Paxx whispered.

"Mommy," Embry sniffled.

"Mommy and Daddy will be back tomorrow," Paxx assured as she picked her up, cuddling her close as she swayed back and forth. Moments later, the soft sounds of sleep escaped Embry's lips, and her body relaxed in Paxx's arms. Carefully, Paxx lay her back in bed, snuggling the blankets around her.

Paxx lingered by Embry's bedside for a moment, watching her chest's gentle rise and fall. A wave of protectiveness washed over her, surprising her with its intensity. She brushed a stray red curl from Embry's forehead before slipping out of the room.

As she settled back onto the couch, Paxx heard Jaylee's soft footsteps on the stairs. She looked up to see her padding into the living room, hair damp and skin flushed from the shower.

Jaylee wore one of Paxx's oversized t-shirts, the hem barely skimming the tops of her bare thighs.

"Everything okay?" Jaylee asked, noticing Paxx's pensive expression.

Paxx nodded, opening her arms in invitation. "Embry woke up for a moment, but she's back asleep now."

Jaylee curled into Paxx's embrace. "Want to watch a movie?" she asked, looking at the television.

Sliding her hand under Jaylee's shirt, Paxx slurred, "I'd rather make out."

Jaylee's breath caught at Paxx's touch, a shiver running through her body. She turned and slid onto Paxx's lap, their lips meeting in a slow, sensual kiss. The kiss deepened, growing more urgent as Paxx's hands roamed beneath Jaylee's shirt, tracing the curves of her waist and hips.

Jaylee moaned softly into the kiss, her fingers tangling in Paxx's hair. The tension of the day melted away as they explored each other with gentle caresses and passionate kisses.

A muffled cry from Embry's room broke through their haze of desire. They froze, listening. When no further sounds came, Jaylee relaxed against Paxx's chest with a sigh.

"We should probably keep this G-rated," Paxx whispered with a giggle, removing her hands from under Jaylee's shirt.

Jaylee pressed their foreheads together, releasing a soft sigh. "Probably a good idea," she regretfully agreed, without moving off Paxx's lap. "Will you hold me for a while?"

"Always," Paxx whispered, wrapping her arms around her and caressing her back. "Do you want to talk about this morning?"

Jaylee tensed in Paxx's arms, then relaxed as she let out a long breath. "I'm sorry I fell apart like that."

"Don't apologize," Paxx said firmly, her fingers tracing soothing patterns along Jaylee's back. "I'm sorry I put you through that," she whispered into Jaylee's hair, tightening her arms around her, ignoring the dull ache in her chest.

"But that's just it," Jaylee said, pulling back slightly to meet Paxx's gaze. "I don't want you to be sorry for doing your job. I don't want to be the person who makes you feel guilty for who you are." Her eyes glistened with unshed tears. "I fell in love with you, all of you, including the part of you that wears a badge."

"I need you to know that what has happened over the past month is not normal. In seventeen years, I've been shot three times, I've discharged my weapon only four times, and only two of those shootings resulted in a fatality."

Jaylee stiffened in Paxx's embrace. "You have killed someone?"

"It was me or them."

"How long ago?"

Paxx grimaced, realizing she had not told her about last night's encounter. When Paxx didn't reply, Jaylee leaned back, her brow furrowing at Paxx's expression.

"Paxx."

"Six years ago, and last night."

Jaylee's eyes widened, her body rigid. "Last night?" she echoed, voice barely above a whisper. "When you were...." She slid off Paxx's lap, creating a small space between them on the couch. "You killed someone last night and didn't tell me?"

The distance between them felt like miles to Paxx. She reached for Jaylee's hand, relief washing through her when Jaylee didn't pull away.

"It happened during the raid," Paxx explained, her voice steady despite the storm of emotions inside her. "We were clearing rooms. In one room, there was a kid. He shot at me. I didn't have a choice." She swallowed hard, the memory of the moment flashing through her mind, the split-second decision, the recoil of her weapon, the sound that would never quite leave her.

Jaylee's face went pale as she replied, "A kid?"

Paxx sighed heavily. "Late teens, early twenties."

Jaylee moved closer; this time, she wrapped her arms around Paxx, pulling her close. "Paxx, I'm so sorry. The fact that you would have to defend yourself and take a life never occurred to me."

Paxx pressed into Jaylee's embrace, grateful for the comfort yet still feeling the weight of her confession hanging between them. Her throat tightened as she struggled to find the right words.

"It's not something I talk about easily," she admitted, her voice low. "There's a protocol after a shooting, administrative leave, psychological evaluation, the works. My superiors cleared me to work the investigation due to its urgency, but..." Paxx looked out the window where rain had begun to patter against the glass, mirroring the heaviness in her chest. "I wanted to protect you from this part of my life."

Jaylee cupped Paxx's face between her palms, her touch gentle. "You can't protect me by keeping parts of yourself hidden."

Paxx nodded. "Okay."

"Are you ready to go to bed?"

"Yes," Paxx replied, standing when Jaylee offered her a hand up.

❓ ❓ ❓
THIRTY-THREE

Paxx slept, but visions of lifeless bodies and sharp, searing pain in her side and chest haunted her dreams. She jolted awake at four thirty the following day, feeling Jaylee's body nestled against her. Smiling, Paxx draped an arm over Jaylee and delighted in the small figure beside her. Taking care not to disturb them, Paxx slipped out of bed and tiptoed around to their side. She gazed at the two sleeping redheads. Returning to her side of the bed, Paxx picked up her phone. Circling the bed again, she snapped a picture of them, cringing as the flash illuminated the room.

Paxx then retreated to the kitchen to make coffee, staring at the photo while waiting for the brew to finish. 'They could easily be mistaken for mother and daughter,' Paxx thought. She poured herself a cup of coffee and headed to the front porch to sit on the swing. She sipped her coffee, watching the first light of dawn pierce the darkness. The swing creaked beneath her as she rocked, each sound echoing in the stillness of the early morning. She couldn't shake the images from her dreams: blood seeping through fabric, vacant, cold eyes staring back at her. Her hand moved to her side.

Hearing a vehicle, Paxx glanced down at the barn where Jimmy parked his truck and stretched as he stepped out. Paxx returned to the house, leaving her cup on the kitchen counter; she climbed the stairs, dressed in jeans and a T-shirt, and carried her boots and jacket downstairs. After checking on Jaylee and Embry, who were still sleeping, Paxx sat on the couch to pull on her boots. She scribbled a note for Jaylee and placed it next to the coffeepot before putting on her jacket, pulling on a ball cap, and heading to the barn.

"Morning, Paxx," Jimmy greeted her.

"Morning, Jimmy," Paxx replied. "How's everything going?"

Jimmy was busy filling a horse's feed bucket with grain. "Going well. Are you riding this morning?" he asked.

Paxx approached the third stall, where Mystic, her black-and-white paint gelding, waited with his head resting over the half door. She patted his nose as he nudged her affectionately. "Yeah, it's been a while, hasn't it, boy? Has he eaten yet?"

Jimmy chuckled. "He's always the first to eat."

"He doesn't have much patience," Paxx remarked, opening the stall door.

Jimmy laughed as he headed to the tack room. "Definitely not. I'll fetch his saddle." Once Mystic was saddled, Paxx led him out of the barn. Mystic pranced beneath her, eager and lively after a month of rest. Paxx felt their familiar bond as she settled into the saddle. She guided him across the pasture toward the trail that snaked through her property's eastern woods, seeking the solitude she needed to untangle her thoughts.

"Easy, boy," she murmured, letting him pick up a slow trot once they cleared the gate.

Mystic's rhythmic movement soothed her frayed nerves. With only the sound of hoofbeats and birds chirping, Paxx could almost forget the nightmares. Almost.

Paxx inhaled deeply, letting the earthy scent of pine and wet soil replace the lingering unease from her dreams. Winding their way through the trees, Paxx urged the horse into a lope, then eventually into a full run as they crossed the open hay field.

Slowing as they approached a rise, Paxx smiled at the sun cresting the horizon. She sat on Mystic's back for the next hour and watched the sunrise. The vibrant colors painted across the sky gradually faded into the soft blue of morning. Paxx let the quiet calmness of the morning settle into her. Mystic shifted beneath her, pawing at the ground or swishing his tail.

"What do you think, boy?" she whispered, running her hand along his neck. "Am I crazy for getting involved in all of this?"

The horse snorted, tossing his head as if answering her, causing Paxx to chuckle.

"Yeah, that's what I thought, too."

Her side twinged, a stark reminder of wounds that had healed on the outside but still lingered within. Paxx winced as she straightened in the saddle. "Let's head back," she told the horse, pulling the reins to the left and tapping her heels against his flanks. The ride back was fast through the field, then slow as they made their way through the trees; as she approached the barn, Paxx noticed Paul and Anna's van at the house. Riding past the barn, she smiled with a new sense of calm and happiness when she saw Paul, Anna, Jaylee, and Embry gathered on the front porch.

"Morning," she greeted as she approached the porch.

"Mommy, horsey," Embry cried as she bolted toward the steps.

"Not so fast," Paul gasped as he swooped her up.

Paxx dismounted Mystic and walked him closer, motioning Paul to bring Embry. "Bring her here; she needs to learn how to act around them."

Paul carried Embry to Paxx, who took her and handed him the reins. Paxx showed Embry how to pet gently, where to stand, and where not to.

"You know she's only two, right?" Paul said sarcastically.

Paxx smiled. "Yes, I do. She may have to be told several times, but it's never too early to start."

Looking over at Jaylee and Anna sitting on the swing, Paxx said to Paul, "Why don't you take her for a ride around the yard?"

Paul hesitated, glancing between Paxx and the horse.

"He's gentle, I promise," Paxx assured.

"Okay," Paul said as he placed his foot in the stirrup and swung up on Mystic's back. Paxx raised Embry and put her on the saddle in front of him. Stepping back, Paxx watched as Paul nudged the horse, a proud feeling spreading when Mystic walked away.

Stepping onto the porch, Paxx leaned against a post, joining Anna and Jaylee.

"You were up early," Jaylee said, a bit of concern in her voice.

Paxx shrugged. "I couldn't get back to sleep once I woke up."

Jaylee nodded, then looked down into her coffee cup. "I need more coffee, Paxx? Anna?"

"Yes, please," Anna smiled, handing her the cup.

"That would be great," Paxx said, stepping in front of Jaylee and kissing her before whispering, "Morning, beautiful."

Jaylee smiled, kissing her back. "Morning," she whispered, then retreated into the house.

Paxx watched her, then paused a moment before turning to face Anna. "So, how was your evening?"

Anna's face flushed red. "Was that your idea?"

Paxx shrugged.

"Well, thank you, Paul hasn't been that...." she paused, trying to find the right word, "Attentive since before Embry was born."

"I'm glad you two could enjoy yourselves, and we are here anytime you need another one of those nights."

"We sure are," Jaylee added, pushing the screen door open with her hip and stepping out, holding three steaming cups of coffee.

Paxx hurried to help her, holding open the door and taking one cup.

"We had so much fun," Jaylee continued, handing Anna her coffee.

"She didn't fuss?" Anna asked.

Paxx shook her head. "She woke up once and asked for you, but after a few minutes of me holding her, she went back to sleep."

"She woke up around two this morning and crawled into bed with us," Jaylee interjected. "But she nestled close to me and went right back to sleep."

Paxx set her cup on the railing and took out her phone. She pulled up the picture of Jaylee and Embry she had taken and showed it to Anna and Jaylee.

"Please send that to me," Anna and Jaylee both asked.

"Sure," Paxx agreed.

"Last night was the first night she has ever spent away from us," Anna admitted.

"She did fine," Paxx reassured.

The three of them watched as Paul guided Mystic in a gentle circle, Embry's delighted giggles carrying across the yard.

Jaylee leaned against the porch railing, her shoulder brushing against Paxx's. "Did you sleep okay?" Jaylee whispered, her eyes studying Paxx's face with concern. "Besides waking up early?"

Placing her hand over Jaylee's, Paxx leaned against her. "I didn't feel Embry get into bed with us."

"Yes, but you seemed restless," Jaylee murmured, meeting Paxx's gaze.

"I had some unsettling dreams, but I'm alright."

"I need to go get some things from my apartment today. What are your plans?" Jaylee asked, shifting the subject away from what she could tell Paxx didn't want to discuss.

"I want to go through Dad's things." Paxx replied, "They're stored in the barn loft, and I hope I can find the journals and notebooks he kept on his cases."

"I can help you at your apartment if you like," Anna said from the swing. "My van has more room than your car."

"You can take the truck, or once you have several boxes ready, you can call. Then Jimmy and I will bring the truck and load it." Paxx offered.

"I'll help," Paul said from atop Mystic.

Jaylee nodded, and Paxx noticed a sadness in her eyes. "Can I talk to you a minute?" she asked Jaylee as she intertwined their fingers.

"Sure," Jaylee agreed, following Paxx into the house.

Once in the house, Paxx turned to face her. "Are you alright? Are you having second thoughts about moving in?"

"No," Jaylee said sadly. "I thought this would be something we would do together. "

Wrapping her arms around Jaylee's waist, Paxx kissed her forehead. "We can do it together. I can go through Dad's things this evening, or maybe Paul and Anna will go through them."

"Are you sure?"

"Of course, I am. If you want me there, I will be there."

When they returned to the porch, Paxx smiled at Jimmy, who had come up from the barn and was now leading Mystic back. "Thank you, Jimmy," Paxx called out.

"Sure thing," he replied. "And if you need help moving anything, let me know. I'm free all day."

Paxx glanced at Paul, puzzled.

"I may have asked if he was free today," Paul grinned.

"Thank you," Jaylee nodded.

"Okay, so let's make a plan," Paxx began. "I am going to go with Jaylee to her apartment. Paul and Anna, would you mind going to the barn? Dad's things are up in the loft. I'm hoping we can get some answers if we can find his notebooks and journals."

Paul and Anna nodded in agreement. "Paul, can you get the play panels from the garage? Maybe Embry will play or nap."

"The loft is not a hayloft." Paxx chuckled, "It has been completely renovated. I thought about renting it out for extra cash, but I never have. It might be dusty, but it has a TV, some furniture, a fridge, a full bathroom, basically everything you need."

"That sounds more like an apartment than a loft." Paul replied, "Here, I imagined us digging through cobweb-covered boxes."

"Jimmy can show you up there." Paxx smiled.

Jaylee squeezed Paxx's hand. "We should head out soon? I want to get an early start before the day escapes us."

"Let me grab a quick shower first," Paxx replied. "Give me fifteen minutes."

Jaylee nodded as she gathered empty coffee cups and took them to the kitchen.

The shower's hot water washed away the lingering scent of the horse from Paxx's skin, but did little to clear the feeling of unease that had settled in her mind since waking. She leaned against the cool tile, letting the steam envelop her as she traced the jagged scar along her ribs, a permanent reminder of how quickly life could change.

Twenty minutes later, dressed in clean jeans and a T-shirt, Paxx descended the stairs to find Jaylee sitting at the kitchen island, making a list.

"Ready?" Paxx asked, grabbing her keys from the hook by the door.

Jaylee looked up, her green eyes brightening. "Almost. Just making a list of what to pack first." She folded the paper and tucked it into her pocket. "I keep thinking I will forget something important."

"You know you can bring everything."

"I know, and I will. But in case we don't finish today, there are a few things I don't want to forget."

Paxx kissed her forehead, "I love you so much," she smiled.

The drive to Jaylee's apartment was quiet; Paxx glanced at Jaylee, watching her profile as she stared out the window, her fingers drumming nervously against her thigh. "What's on your mind?" Paxx finally asked.

Jaylee looked over at her, a soft sadness in her eyes. Paxx reached over and grasped her hand, bringing it to her lips. "Jay, talk to me."

"Honestly?"

"Total honesty."

"I am so happy; and I feel safer than I have ever felt. I feel like I have friends I can count on with Anna and Paul. I am totally infatuated with little Embry, and I have found the love of my life," she said, her voice shaky. "I keep expecting to wake up from this fantasy or for it all to fall apart," she admitted.

Paxx squeezed Jaylee's hand, her throat tight with emotion. "This isn't a dream, Jay. I'm real, we are real." Stopping at a red light, Paxx continued, "And I'm not going anywhere."

The vulnerability in Jaylee's eyes made Paxx's chest ache. How many times had others disappointed, abandoned, or hurt her?

"I know it seems fast," Paxx continued as the light changed, and she accelerated through the intersection. "And maybe it is. But sometimes... sometimes you just know. I've never been more certain of anything."

Jaylee nodded, wiping at the corner of her eye. "Neither have I."

Once parked, they stepped out of the Jeep, and Paxx intertwined their fingers as they walked to the building. Once in the apartment, Jaylee locked the door and began undressing. Paxx raised an eyebrow as she watched Jaylee's slow, seductive movements.

"You know, I have never had sex in this apartment," Jaylee purred.

"Oh, we must fix that," Paxx growled, picking Jaylee up and carrying her to the bedroom.

Paxx laid Jaylee on the bed, covering her until their bodies pressed together.

Jaylee's fingers tangled in Paxx's hair. "I want to leave this place with at least one good memory," she whispered, her voice thick with emotion. "Something to replace all the nights I spent here alone, wondering if I'd ever find someone who...."

"Tell me what you want," Paxx whispered against Jaylee's lips.

Jaylee pulled Paxx's shirt and bra off, then unfastened Paxx's jeans. "I want you," Jaylee breathed, her hands exploring every inch of Paxx's exposed skin. "All of you."

The morning light filtered through the curtains, casting a soft glow across their bodies as they moved together. Paxx took her time, caressing Jaylee's body with gentle touches, determined to create a memory that would replace all the loneliness this apartment had witnessed.

Afterward, they lay tangled in sheets, Jaylee's head resting on Paxx's chest, listening to her heartbeat slow.

"Well," Paxx said, tracing her fingers along Jaylee's spine, "that's one way to start packing."

? ? ?
THIRTY-FOUR

Paxx slipped out of bed and began searching for her clothes, grinning at Jaylee, who was already dressed and sifting through boxes stacked by the wall.

"How should we label these?" Paxx inquired, picking up an empty box.

Jaylee thought, then suggested. "Maybe by room? That could help us decide what to take back first."

"Sounds good." Paxx agreed, picking up two markers from the dresser and handing one to Jaylee.

As they started labeling boxes, some for kitchen items, others for books and clothes, Jaylee opened her phone's music app, filling the air with a mix of country and pop tunes. While going through drawers, they talked and laughed when they found old photos that sparked stories from Jaylee's past. Occasionally, when a slow song played, Paxx would pull Jaylee into her arms and sway with the music. These interruptions often led to more than dancing, lasting from a few minutes to half an hour or more.

The late afternoon sunlight streamed through the apartment, casting long shadows over the labeled boxes.

"At this pace, we'll never be done," Jaylee said with a laugh, her cheeks still rosy. She tucked a loose strand of hair behind her ear and returned to a box marked 'Bedroom.'

"Let's call Paul and see if they can come over to load up," Paxx suggested. "Maybe we won't get distracted so much with them here." She chuckled.

Jaylee laughed and agreed.

Paul, Anna, Jimmy, and his wife Megan arrived thirty minutes later. While the men took apart the bed and carried the heavier furniture to the waiting truck and trailer, the women carried boxes out while taking turns entertaining Embry.

"You know we can help carry some of the furniture," Paxx commented to Paul and Jimmy as she passed them in the hallway.

"You could, but the boxes need to go, and Jimmy and I want to show off our muscles to our ladies," Paul said, smiling broadly at Anna.

"And if I want to show off for my lady?" Paxx smirked, winking at Jaylee.

Jaylee slipped her hand into Paxx's and said loud enough that she thought only Paxx could hear. "You have already shone off the only muscles I care about today."

Paul and Jimmy stumbled, nearly falling down the stairs. Jaylee's cheeks reddened, realizing she had talked louder than she had intended.

Paxx burst out laughing, "You guys alright?"

"We're fine," Jimmy stammered as he regained his footing. Paul cleared his throat, failing to hide his amusement. "Just... just watch those stairs. They're tricky."

The men disappeared down the stairwell with the head-board between them, leaving Jaylee mortified against Paxx's shoulder.

"I can't believe I said that out loud," Jaylee whispered, her face burning.

Paxx wrapped an arm around her waist. "If they are going to be around us, they need to get used to it," she said pressing Jaylee against the hallway wall and kissing her passionately.

As the afternoon wore on, shadows lengthened across the bare floors, casting the near-empty rooms in an eerie glow that made Jaylee pause.

"You okay?" Paxx's voice came from behind her, soft and concerned.

Jaylee nodded, not trusting her voice. "Just... saying good-bye, I guess."

Paxx wrapped her arms around Jaylee's waist from behind, resting her chin on her shoulder. "Having second thoughts?"

"No," Jaylee said, turning in Paxx's arms. "Not about us. Never about us. It's just... I've been here for three years."

"I know it's hard, but I hope you make our house your own," Paxx whispered, kissing her cheek.

"I already feel like it's mine, ours."

"And it always will be."

The last box was packed and loaded by eight o'clock. Upon arriving at the house, Paxx parked her Jeep in the driveway to allow room for the trailer to be backed into the garage.

Jaylee and Anna arrived a few minutes later after stopping to pick up pizza.

"Anyone want a beer?" Paxx offered as they all gathered on the porch.

All but Anna raised their hand in acceptance. Paxx disappeared into the house, returning moments later with five bottles of beer and a can of Pepsi Zero.

As the group ate, they laughed and talked. Jimmy and Megan shared stories about growing up in Kentucky before moving to Nebraska, where they both attended college. The six of them fell into a comfortable rhythm of conversation.

"Paxx, have you talked to Tracie lately?" Megan asked.

"Shit," Paxx cursed, "I meant to call her when we got back from Chicago." Paxx pulled out her phone and sent Tracie a text message. A moment later, her phone chimed with a response.

"Paul, are you busy tomorrow evening?" Paxx asked after reading the text.

Paul shook his head. "No, what's up?"

"Tracie is the detective I told you about; I'm asking if she is free tomorrow evening," Paxx responded as she typed.

Anna and Jaylee looked at one another in confusion. "Paxx wants to hire a Private Investigator to look into Dad's case," Paul explained.

"Tracie is excellent," Megan assured.

Slipping her phone back into her pocket, she said, "Tracie and Jake are coming over tomorrow evening around six."

"I'll make lasagna for dinner," Jaylee chirped.

Paul looked at Anna, who smiled. "Okay, that sounds good," he replied.

"Jimmy and Megan, will you come too?" Paxx asked.

After exchanging glances, Jimmy agreed.

By the time everyone left, the night air had grown cool, leaving Paxx and Jaylee alone on the porch.

"So, this detective," Jaylee began, her voice careful. "You've known her a long time?"

Paxx nodded. "I met Tracie a little over five years ago after her husband died. She was still with the police department before she went private." Paxx paused, studying Jaylee's expression. "She's good, Jay. If anyone can find something the police missed in Dad's case, it's her."

"What happened to her husband?"

Paxx paused, afraid of Jaylee's reaction to yet another cop being killed in the line of duty. Leading her into the house, Paxx locked the door before joining Jaylee, who had sat on the couch.

"He was shot and killed during a robbery." Paxx sighed, "And I haven't told you this, not because I'm trying to hide it, but in case she brings it up tomorrow night." Paxx paused, gripping Jaylee's hands. "Almost five years ago, my work partner Renee was also killed in the line of duty."

Jaylee met Paxx's gaze with a mix of sorrow and relief. "Oh, Paxx, I'm so sorry."

Paxx tilted her head, questioning Jaylee's response.

"I thought you were going to tell me you and Tracie had been in a relationship, and you were afraid she would say something."

"No, we met at the absolute worst times in our lives, and we leaned on one another for support and alcohol, but never that."

A flicker of guilt crossed Jaylee's face. "I feel ridiculous now."

"Don't," Paxx said, tucking a strand of hair behind Jaylee's ear. "It's a natural question."

Jaylee leaned into Paxx's touch. The tension in her shoulders dissolved. "Tell me about Renee."

Paxx's expression shifted, a familiar shadow clutching her chest, but not as dark as it once had been. She took a deep breath. "She was my partner for three years before... before it happened. After Anna left, she was the closest I came to having a trusted friend. We were making a drug bust, as routine as one could be, or so we thought." Paxx's gaze drifted to the window, where darkness had settled outside. "She was shot in the neck. I killed the perp, but I couldn't save her."

Jaylee squeezed Paxx's hand, her touch grounding, steady. "I'm so sorry, Paxx."

"For a long time, I blamed myself for her death, for leaving her husband without a wife and her kids without a mother," Paxx continued, her voice barely above a whisper. "Maybe if I'd been faster, or if I'd noticed something was off..." She shook her head. "I lost myself in alcohol and women, trying to numb the pain." Paxx's fingers tightened around Jaylee's. "The department shrink said it was survivor's guilt. Whatever label they gave it, it didn't change how I felt. After a while, Tracie helped me see that I couldn't have known. That sometimes, no matter how prepared you are, things just..." Her voice trailed off.

"Happen," Jaylee finished for her.

Paxx nodded. "She was grieving, and I was grieving. Dad is the one who introduced us. He knew her husband, Lance. That may be the only selfless thing he ever did for me."

"I am looking forward to meeting her," Jaylee said as she stood, pulling Paxx to her feet. "What time do you have to be at work in the morning?"

"Nine," Paxx replied, following Jaylee upstairs.

After a quick shower, they slipped into bed, then, wrapped in each other's arms, they drifted off to sleep.

Paxx woke before dawn. Across from her, Jaylee slept, one arm flung across the space next to her. For a moment, Paxx watched her: the gentle rise and fall of her chest, the way her hair spilled across the pillow like liquid fire in the dim light filtering through the curtains.

This was real. After years of emptiness, of filling the void with meaningless encounters, she had someone who made her want to come home at night.

Careful not to wake her, Paxx slipped out of bed and went downstairs. She made coffee and leaned against the counter as she waited.

"What are you thinking about?" Jaylee interrupted Paxx's thoughts as she entered the kitchen.

"Nothing," Paxx replied as she poured coffee into Jaylee's mug. "Morning."

"Morning, and that was not a nothing face," Jaylee replied, leaning against the island and meeting Paxx's gaze.

"I want, no, I need, to go back to the warehouse."

Jaylee stiffened, unable to hide the sudden fear that filled her. "The warehouse where you were shot?"

Paxx nodded but didn't move. "I have to, Jay. The other night, when we raided the house, I was so scared, I nearly got one of my men killed; hell, I nearly got myself killed." Pushing off the counter, Paxx set her cup down and stepped in front of her. "I have to face that place if I have any chance of moving on and regaining my confidence."

Jaylee nodded in understanding. "You won't go alone, though, will you?"

"No, I won't go alone."

The tension in Jaylee's shoulders eased, but her eyes remained troubled. "When?"

"After work today," Paxx said, running her thumb over Jaylee's knuckles.

Jaylee nodded, her expression filled with worry. "Promise me you'll be careful." She pressed her palm against Paxx's chest.

"I promise," Paxx whispered, covering Jaylee's hand.

Jaylee set her mug down and wrapped her arms around Paxx's waist, her cheek resting against Paxx's shoulder. "What time should I expect you home, then?"

"I'll be back before Tracie and Jake arrive," Paxx promised, kissing the top of Jaylee's head. "Hopefully before five? That should give us time to set up for dinner."

As Paxx prepared to leave, Jaylee stopped her at the door, pulling her into a fierce kiss that had them gasping for air.

"Are you sure you can't go in a little bit later?" Jaylee breathed, pressing her up against the door.

Paxx glanced at her watch, ready to agree to another half hour, when her phone rang. Pulling it from her pocket, she frowned at Rowan's name on the screen. With her arm around Jaylee's waist, she answered the call.

"Algatta," she greeted.

"Paxx, meet me at the coroner's office in thirty minutes," Rowan demanded. Not waiting for a response, he ended the call.

Paxx looked at her phone in confusion before slipping it back into her pocket. "Sorry, I gotta go," she murmured against Jaylee's lips as she kissed her.

"Be careful." Jaylee once again urged.

"I promise I will." Paxx replied, "I love you. See you this evening."

"I love you, too," Jaylee responded as she opened the door. She stepped onto the porch and watched Paxx climb into her Jeep, waving as she drove away.

? ? ?
Thirty-Five

Paxx arrived with five minutes to spare. The coroner's office is a building next to the precinct, and no matter how much air freshener the staff uses, it always smells of chemicals and death.

She found Rowan pacing outside the autopsy suite, his expression grim.

"What's going on?" she asked, immediately sensing something was wrong.

Rowan's jaw tightened. "We've got a problem."

Before he could elaborate, the heavy steel door swung open with a soft creak, and Dr. Elizabeth Margon, the Chief Medical Examiner, appeared. A tight bun accentuated her high cheekbones and sharp jawline. Her youthful features hide her actual age of sixty-three. Dark blue scrubs hugged her slim, athletic figure. The soles of her white athletic shoes squeaked softly against the polished linoleum floor as she walked. Her expression remained neutral, her lips a thin line, and her brow smooth, but Paxx noticed the flicker of concern in her dark eyes.

"Paxx, good morning," she greeted.

"Good morning, Elizabeth," Paxx responded with a nod.

Rowan ran his fingers through his hair. "The unidentified woman from the raid," he started. "She died from a gunshot wound."

"Alright," Paxx said, puzzled, glancing from Rowan to Elizabeth.

"The bullet matches the gun that shot you," he replied.

Paxx felt the blood drain from her face. Her hand moved to her side where the bullet had torn through her flesh over six weeks ago, the scar now a slight ridge beneath her shirt. The sterile hallway seemed to close in on her, the chemical smell suddenly overwhelming.

"Are you sure?"

"Georgetta ran the ballistics twice. The striations match perfectly." Elizabeth gestured toward the autopsy suite. "Would you like to see the findings?"

Paxx nodded, following Elizabeth through the swinging doors. Under the harsh fluorescent lights, the body lay covered by a thin sheet, only the woman's pale face visible. Paxx approached, studying the features of their Jane Doe, mid-twenties, with a delicate jawline and dirty red hair that reminded Paxx of Jaylee for a moment. Averting her gaze, Paxx shook her head. When she looked back, the young woman looked nothing like Jaylee; the dark roots of her hair and the golden-tanned skin made it obvious that she was not a natural redhead.

Paxx flinched when Rowan touched her arm. "Paxx, you okay?"

She cleared her throat as she stepped away from the autopsy table, crossed the room, and entered the ballistics lab. Georgetta met her at the door, wrapping her in a friendly embrace.

"Hey, sweetie, how are you doing?"

Paxx returned the embrace with a smile. "Hey, George, I'm okay. It's good to see you."

"You too," Georgetta replied, her warm smile softening into a more somber tone. "I wish it were under better circumstances."

She guided Paxx to her workstation, where two computer monitors displayed magnified images of bullet striations, the distinctive patterns of grooves, and lands as unique as fingerprints. Beside the monitors sat two evidence bags, one labeled with Paxx's name, case number, and date of her shooting, the other with Jane Doe, a case number, and Thursday's date.

"See these markings?" Georgetta pointed to the matching patterns highlighted in red on both screens. "Same weapon, no question. A Glock 19, standard issue for..."

"Half the police force," Paxx finished, her throat tightening. The implications hung heavily in the air.

Rowan joined them; his presence made Paxx uneasy. "The question is, why would someone who shot a cop six weeks ago show up at a drug operation?"

"And who tipped them off about the raid? And are we just dealing with drugs?" Paxx asked, her mind racing through possibilities.

"I'm afraid I have more bad news," Elizabeth said from behind them.

Turning, Paxx met her gaze.

"Evidence shows she has suffered extensive sexual trauma." She replied. Her eyes never left Paxx.

Paxx's stomach twisted. The fluorescent lights felt too bright, too exposing. She swallowed hard against the rising bile in her throat. "Human trafficking."

Elizabeth nodded, her professional composure momentarily cracking. "The scarring patterns suggest long-term abuse. And there's something else." She gestured for them to follow her back to the autopsy table.

Elisabeth pulled back the sheet just enough to reveal the victim's right shoulder blade. A tattoo of a black rose, blood-red at the tips, adorned the victim's shoulder blade.

"Christ," Rowan muttered under his breath.

Paxx stepped closer to Elizabeth and gripped the table to stabilize herself. Feeling Paxx brush against her, Elizabeth wrapped an arm around Paxx's waist, trying not to draw Rowan's attention. The gentle pressure of Elisabeth's arm steadied Paxx as the room threatened to tilt.

"Black Rose dipped in blood," Paxx murmured, forcing herself to focus on the crude tattoo. "Mr. Black."

Elisabeth nodded, her arm still firm around Paxx's waist. "The tissue trauma suggests someone inflicted it within the last year. The work is amateur and not done with professional equipment, but done with a makeshift tattoo gun."

Elisabeth's subtle support went unnoticed by Rowan. "Property tags," he said, his voice tight with disgust.

Paxx extricated herself from Elisabeth's hold, though her body protested the loss of contact. Elisabeth covered the body again, her movements reverent as she pulled the sheet over the young woman.

"Did you take pictures of the tattoo?" Paxx asked as she moved away from the table.

"Yes, I have copies of them and the autopsy findings on my desk for you," she replied, disappearing into her office. When she didn't return, Paxx crossed the room, entered her office, and closed the door behind her.

"Paxx, are you alright?" Elizabeth asked as she stood on the far side of her desk.

Paxx nodded. "Thank you for not making a big deal out of that."

"Paxx, sweetie, I have known you a long time," Elizabeth replied, stepping around the desk. "Like I was through Renee's and your father's deaths, I am here if you need to talk."

Paxx sighed, remembering the days she had spent here in Elizabeth's office, waiting for her and her staff to complete the autopsies on Renee and her dad. The hours she had cried against her shoulder and the sleepless nights spent on her couch, she had become like a mother to her in those dark days following both shootings. "I know, and I really appreciate the offer. But I'm okay, and I have..." she trailed off.

"Georgetta told me you are seeing someone, and I'm thrilled for you."

"I'm sorry I didn't come to see you, and I'm sorry it's been so long since we have talked," Paxx confessed, avoiding eye contact.

Elizabeth's expression softened as she moved closer to Paxx, her professional demeanor giving way to the maternal warmth that had sustained Paxx through some of her darkest days. "Don't apologize. You needed space to heal, and I understood that." She reached out, squeezing Paxx's arm. "Besides, I've been keeping tabs on you through Georgetta. I know you've been doing better."

Paxx felt a twinge of guilt. Over the past year, she had pulled away from everyone, including Elizabeth, who had been nothing but supportive. "Still, I should have called."

"Grief takes different paths for all of us," she replied. "You look better than you did the last time I saw you."

"Better," Paxx replied, placing her hand on her side.

Elizabeth noticed the gesture. "How is it healing?"

"Better. Still pulls when I move in certain ways." Paxx hesitated, then added, "Without Jaylee, I would never have survived."

A smile crossed Elizabeth's face. "Ah, so Jaylee is the someone. You deserve happiness, Paxx," she said as she gathered file folders from her desk.

A sharp knock interrupted the moment. Rowan's voice came through the door. "Paxx? We need to get going."

"Be right there," Paxx responded, accepting the folders from her.

"Don't be a stranger," Elisabeth urged as she hugged Paxx.

"I won't, and I would like you to meet Jaylee. She has totally changed my life," Paxx smiled.

"I can see that," Elisabeth grinned. "Mark is going out of town for business in two weeks. Why don't you and Jaylee come over for dinner? I'm sure I can get Grant and Margot to stay with some friends for the evening," she said, concerning her husband and kids.

"That sounds great. Text me the date and time, and we will be there," Paxx assured as she opened the door and joined Rowan in the autopsy suite.

As the elevator ascended to the third floor, Paxx flipped through the autopsy folder, her eyes catching on the details.

"Christ, she is only sixteen years old," she muttered, a mix of anger and despair twisting in her gut. "Says here she's got dental work consistent with South American origins. Multiple healed fractures. Signs of long-term malnutrition." Paxx's voice remained clinical, but her knuckles whitened around the folder's edge. "And track marks. Recent ones."

Rowan leaned against the elevator wall, scrubbing a hand over his face. "Sixteen?"

Paxx continued scanning the report. The photos showed bruising in various stages of healing, evidence of prolonged abuse. Her stomach clenched. "She was just a kid."

The elevator doors slid open with a soft ding. The third floor housed the department's main offices, bustling with activity. Detectives hunched over computers, phones blared, and the air smelled of stale coffee and desperation.

Captain Kimble waved them into his office. His composed demeanor had given way to something tense, more urgent.

"Close the door."

Paxx complied and then took the seat across from his desk.

"Thursday's raid was a fiasco," he began. "This case requires homicide detectives, and I expect a call from the FBI." Kimble continued as he paced behind his desk.

"I have a copy of the autopsy report on our Jane Doe," Paxx sighed.

Kimble sat hard in his seat, a heavy breath existing his mouth. "Give it to me," he gestured with a wave.

Opening the file, Paxx read the disturbing information on the young woman's condition and cause of death. "The worst part..."

"It gets worse?" Kimble interrupted.

Paxx nodded. "She has a tattoo of a black rose with blood-red tips on her right shoulder blade."

"Black Rose," he whispered, the words heavy with recognition.

"Yes, sir. And the bullet that killed her matches the one that hit me six weeks ago," Paxx added, her voice steady despite the churning in her stomach.

The captain's eyes widened, then narrowed as he processed this information. He pushed back from his desk and stood, turning to stare out the window overlooking the city. "So, what we have," he said slowly, "is a teenage trafficking victim killed by the same weapon that shot one of my detectives. What we thought was a drug ring is now a sex trafficking ring with possible ties to Mr. Black." He turned back to face them. "This just went from bad to catastrophic."

"Looks like it," Paxx agreed, leaning forward in her chair. "And the timing can't be coincidental."

Rowan paced the small office, his shoes making soft thuds against the worn carpet. "Someone knew we were coming. We need to consider that someone with connections to both the trafficking ring and the department compromised the raid from the inside."

Kimble's jaw clenched. "I'm aware of the implications, Detective."

Paxx leaned forward, placing the autopsy file on the desk. "The girl was sixteen, South American. Long-term abuse, malnutrition. She wasn't just passing through; someone kept her for a while."

"Rowan, can you give Detective Algatta and me a few minutes, please?" Kimble asked.

Rowan paused, frustration and anger narrowing his eyes. He left the room without responding, shutting the door harder than needed.

"Paxx, what are your thoughts?" Kimble asked once Rowan was gone.

Paxx met his eyes, taking a deep breath before she answered. "I think this is all connected to my dad's death. I don't know if he stumbled upon something he should not have, but I don't think any of this is coincidental. And I also believe one or more cops are involved," she answered. "My brother Paul and I went to Pennsylvania and talked to Clancy Devonshire, AKA Mr. Black; he vehemently denies killing our dad."

"You what?" Kimble asked, shocked. "How did you even get in to see him?"

"My brother was with the Chicago PD; he is now a homicide detective with Chandler County. He called in a favor and got us a face-to-face meeting." Paxx told him the details of Clancy's stabbing and the specifics of their visit.

"I'm sorry, Paxx, and I regret that I wasn't in this department when your father was murdered. I will lean on the higher-ups to look into his shooting. I can't believe investigators didn't do more to find his killer." Kimble said.

"What about the person who shot me?" Paxx questioned. "Where are we with that?"

Kimble looked at her in confusion. "Rowan is supposed to keep you informed."

Paxx glanced out to the bullpen through the windows of the Kimble's office, anger flaring in her chest. "Rowan told me you pulled him off the case and handed it over to special crimes. He said you told him to stay out of it."

Kimble's face darkened, his eyebrows drawing together in a deep frown. "I did no such thing. Rowan has been the lead on your shooting investigation since day one. Special Crimes is strictly there for backup; they are not the lead."

A cold sensation spread through Paxx's chest. She turned to look out the window at Rowan, who was now hunched over his desk, phone pressed to his ear. Her instincts, honed through years on the force, screamed danger.

"Captain," she said quietly, "I think we may have a bigger problem than we realized."

Kimble followed her gaze to Rowan, then back to her. "You think he's involved?"

"I don't know what to think anymore." Paxx kept her voice low. "But he lied to me about the investigation, and now we have a trafficking victim killed with the same weapon that shot me. The coincidences and inconsistencies are stacking up."

"Do you want me to assign you a different partner?"

Paxx shook her head. "No, but I would like you to ask him for all the information he has on my case. I know he won't give me anything, but he has no choice but to give it to you," she said as she stood. "Let's keep our suspicions to ourselves for now, but I would like permission to talk to Thompson and Darby in Special Crimes."

"Do it discreetly."

"I understand," Paxx said, collecting the files from his desk. "I'll keep you updated."

Stepping out of Kimble's office, Paxx felt the weight of suspicion pressing down on her shoulders. She kept her expression neutral as Rowan glanced up from his desk, ending his call.

"Everything okay?" he asked, eyebrows raised.

"Fine," Paxx replied, forcing casualness into her voice. "Kimble wants us to coordinate with Homicide on the Jane Doe case." She settled at her desk, avoiding direct eye contact with him. "I'm going to head down to Special Crimes first, see what Thompson and Darby might have on similar trafficking cases."

Rowan's posture stiffened. "I can handle that. "

"I'm fine," Paxx interrupted, more sharply than intended. She softened her tone. "Really. Besides, Darby has been on me to come see her."

Pulling out her phone, Paxx sent Paul a text.

Did you and Anna find anything useful in Dad's things?

After a few minutes, Paul replied. *I haven't had time to go through everything, but all of his files are stacked beside the door in the loft. I will bring them to the house this evening.*

Great, thank you.

Checking her watch, Paxx was surprised to find it was already one o'clock. Standing, she gathered some papers and files, placing them in her shoulder bag. "I am going to see Darby, then I have a couple of things to take care of before I call it a day. I will see you in the morning." Paxx spoke to Rowan without making eye contact.

"Paxx," he said, "Tell me what's going on."

Looking up, she met his gaze; his eyes were full of anger and questions.

"I have to see HR about the hospital stay and my release," she lied.

"Why didn't you just say so?"
"It's my business," she replied gruffly as she walked away.

THIRTY-SIX

The Special Crimes Unit occupied the east wing of the third floor, set apart from the rest of the department by a set of heavy glass doors. Unlike Narcotics' open bullpen layout, SCU's smaller offices and interview rooms offered more privacy for sensitive cases.

Paxx found Shannon Darby hunched over her desk, surrounded by stacks of files. She had pulled her dark curls back in a tight ponytail, a few strands escaping to frame her face. When she saw Paxx, her tired, deep blue eyes brightened.

"Well, well. Look what the cat dragged in," Darby said, pushing back from her desk. "You look like hell warmed over."

"Good to see you too," Paxx replied, attempting a smile that didn't quite reach her eyes. "Got a minute?"

Darby nodded, gesturing toward an empty chair. "For you? I've got several."

Paxx shut the door and then sat. "Shannon, we've known each other for a long time." Paxx began.

"Since right after the academy."

"I hope I have done nothing to upset or offend you."

Shannon leaned back in her chair, confusion covering her face. "Except for declining each time I have asked you out, you have always been a good friend and colleague," she confessed with a smile. "Paxx, what's this all about?"

"You and Thompson are working on my shooting. Can you tell me what you've found?"

Shannon's dark eyes studied Paxx, the playful glint fading to professional concern. She glanced toward the hallway before leaning forward, lowering her voice.

"I shouldn't tell you anything. You know the protocol; officers involved in shootings are kept out of the loop until the investigation concludes."

"Officially, I am here about Jane Doe from Thursday's raid."

Shannon sighed. "Paxx, it's... complicated. The scene doesn't quite add up. We found the estimated location of the shooter consistent with your statement, but the angle of entry is different." She trailed off, a crease forming between her brows. "Thompson thinks you're holding something back."

"What the hell does he think I am not telling? Rowan was there, except for seeing the person who shot me. He knows as much as I do."

Shannon pulled a folder from beneath a stack of papers, sliding it across the desk. "Thompson and Rowan have had conversations I have not been privy to. I don't know what they have discussed, but they sure as hell don't want me to be part of it. I can tell you there are inconsistencies between your statement and Rowan's."

Paxx leaned forward. "What inconsistencies?"

Shannon hesitated, her fingers drumming on the desk.

"The bullet recovered from your vest?" Shannon slid another document across the desk. "As far as we can tell from the striations on the bullet, the gun is a department issue."

Paxx felt a chill creep up her spine.

Shannon ran her tongue over her teeth, her expression guarded. "Rowan claims he heard the shot, then found you three minutes later. You stated his arrival was at least six to ten minutes after you were hit. She tapped a finger against the folder. "The entry wound's angle suggests the shooter was positioned above you, maybe twelve to fourteen feet."

"So, the floor above me," Paxx murmured.

"Paxx, are you sure about the time between when you were shot and when Rowan arrived?"

"I didn't look at my watch," Paxx smirked, "But I lay there a few minutes before whoever claimed he shot me arrived; he was there another minute or two at least. I heard footsteps from somewhere in the building, but not close. Then, after several more minutes, I heard Rowan call out my name; again, he was not very close."

"I know this may not be something you want to do, but have you been back to the warehouse?"

Paxx shook her head. "I am going over there after I leave here."

"Want some company?"

"I would love some," Paxx smiled as she stood and reached for the doorknob.

Shannon retrieved her service weapon from the top drawer of her desk. After securing it on her hip, she pulled her bulletproof vest and department windbreaker from the coat rack in the corner.

Together, they walked to the elevators, riding one down to the first floor.

Silence hung between them as they exited the precinct, the late afternoon sun casting long shadows across the parking lot.

"I'll drive," Paxx said, unlocking the doors to her Jeep.

Shannon slid into the passenger seat, buckling her seatbelt. "Thompson's going to have my ass if he finds out I'm doing this with you."

"Then let's make sure he doesn't find out." Paxx started the engine, her fingers tight around the steering wheel. "Besides, this is about Jane Doe, remember? Officially."

A hint of Shannon's earlier smile returned. "Right."

"Or we can have a late lunch together," Paxx replied. "I will cover it however you want me to."

"Late lunch it is then," Shannon nodded.

As Paxx pulled into the parking lot, she shivered at the warehouse looming vacant and desolate against the late afternoon sky. Its windows were dark and unforgiving. The yellow police tape that had cordoned off the scene over a month earlier now fluttered in tatters, dancing in the breeze like ghostly fingers.

"You okay?" Shannon asked, studying Paxx's profile as they put on their vests.

Paxx nodded, though the tightness in her jaw betrayed her. "Let's just get this over with."

The heavy metal door groaned as they pushed it open, revealing the cavernous interior. Dust motes swirled in the shafts of sunlight that broke through the high, dirty windows. The space smelled of rust and abandonment, with undertones of something chemical that Paxx couldn't quite place.

"Where were you standing when it happened?" Shannon asked.

"I will walk you through everywhere I went that day, from top to bottom," Paxx replied, pointing to the far side of the warehouse.

Paxx led her through the first floor to a set of stairs at the back of the building. Slowly, they climbed the stairs, both stopping when they heard voices from somewhere above them.

Pulling their weapons from their holsters, they continued up the stairs. On the second floor, they stepped through the doorway into the corridor. They listened, trying to determine where the voices were coming from.

The voices grew louder as they moved cautiously down the dimly lit corridor. Paxx held up her hand, signaling Shannon to stop. They pressed themselves against the wall, weapons ready but lowered.

"I don't care what you must do. Just make sure it's clean this time." A man's voice, low and controlled, carried through the space.

Paxx's breath caught in her throat. She recognized that voice but couldn't place it. A voice responded, too muffled to make out the words.

Shannon leaned in, her breath warm against Paxx's ear. "Two, maybe three people," she murmured. "I think they're on the third floor."

Paxx nodded, then lifted her chin upward. Shannon understood, tightening her hold on her weapon. The two moved together, their years of training clear in their wordless coordination. Paxx led the way, staying close to the wall as they made their way up to the third floor. Each step was deliberate, avoiding any debris that could betray their presence. Suddenly, there was silence, followed by the faint sound of footsteps retreating. Paxx glanced around the third-floor entrance, frowning at the empty corridor. She looked back at Shannon, shook her head, and proceeded through the doorway.

They crept down the third-floor hallway, passing rooms with doors hanging off hinges or missing entirely. The voices had gone silent, but the tension in the air remained thick and oppressive. Paxx signaled for Shannon to check the right side while she took the left, clearing each space.

A sudden scraping sound from the end of the corridor made them both freeze. Paxx gestured toward an open door about twenty feet ahead. They positioned themselves on either side, exchanging a quick nod before Paxx kicked it open, weapon raised.

The room was empty. A single window overlooked the alley below, and the fresh scuff marks on the dusty floor told the story of a hasty exit.

"Fire escape," Shannon muttered, holstering her weapon and moving to the window. She leaned out, scanning the metal structure that zigzagged down the building's exterior.

The area below was empty, and there was no sign of anyone in the parking lot or on the street. "Fuck," Paxx spat as she paced around the empty room. "My Jeep is out there; they know I'm here."

"Did you recognize the voices?"

"Only one of them sounded familiar." Paxx replied, "I don't recognize him."

"Me neither," Shannon agreed. "Let's go back downstairs; I want to see where you were shot."

Paxx led the way back to the main floor of the building, her steps slow and careful as she listened for any sign that someone else was still there.

"You okay?" Shannon asked when Paxx stopped suddenly.

Paxx nodded, her heart hammering in her chest. This was where she'd been shot. The memory flashed through her mind: the impact, the crushing pain, the certainty she was dying. Crime tape and a dark stain of her blood still marked the location on the concrete floor.

"This is it," Paxx said, her voice hollow as she stared at the bloodstain. "I was standing right here when I got hit."

Shannon knelt beside the dark smear, her eyes tracing an invisible line from the stain to the second floor. "The trajectory would put your shooter..." She stood, pointing to a walkway above them. "Up there."

Paxx followed her gaze to a section of the second-floor mezzanine that overlooked the main warehouse floor. "That matches what I remember. The shot came from above, but not too high."

"Let's check it out," Shannon said, already moving toward the stairs.

The floor creaked under their weight as they moved along its length. Halfway around, Shannon stopped and crouched, pulling a small flashlight from her vest pocket.

"I thought CSU had already cleared all of this," Paxx murmured as she looked down both sides of their location.

Shannon walked twenty feet in both directions, her flashlight illuminating the dirty, worn carpet as she went. "CSU said they didn't find any shell casings or any other evidence."

Paxx looked over the railing to the bloodstain on the floor. "Whoever did this was a good shot," Paxx said, "to hit me in the side, between the vest enclosure."

"Too good," Shannon agreed, her voice tight. "That's what's been bothering me. This wasn't some random punk with a stolen gun. This was someone who knew exactly what they were doing."

She ran her flashlight along the railing, stopping at a small nick in the metal. "Paxx, look at this."

Paxx leaned in, studying the mark, a tiny scratch where the paint had been scraped away, revealing the bare metal beneath.

"Could be a rest mark," Paxx said. "For stabilizing the gun."

Shannon nodded, her expression grim. "That would explain the precision. But it also means..."

"Premeditation," Paxx finished. "Someone planned this. They knew I'd be here."

"Why were you here?"

"Rowan got intel from one of his informants that a large quantity of Fentanyl was being distributed from here," Paxx growled. "He told me the two of us could handle it, so we didn't call in SWAT."

"I don't trust that guy," Shannon confessed as she took a picture of the railing with her phone.

"I certainly have my reservations about him," Paxx agreed.

Paxx glanced at her watch, took out her phone, and checked her messages. Jaylee had requested that she pick up beer on her way home.

"Are you ready to head back to the station?" Paxx asked as she responded to Jaylee.

"Yeah, I don't think we will find anything else here."

On the way back to the station, Paxx went through a fast-food drive-through and ordered Shannon a burger, fries, and a drink. Once back at the precinct, Shannon ate while Paxx read through the evidence folder she had given her.

"So, who else knew you would be there that day?" Shannon asked between bites of her burger.

Paxx leaned back against the driver's seat, the file open against the steering wheel. "Rowan and Captain Kimble. But you know how it is, people talk."

Shannon nodded, wiping a smear of ketchup from the corner of her mouth. "And you're sure about that timing discrepancy?"

"Positive," Paxx said, her finger tapping on the timeline in the report. "I remember every excruciating second I spent lying there, wondering if I was going to bleed out before someone found me."

A heavy silence settled between them as Shannon finished her meal, crumpling the wrapper and stuffing it back into the bag. "Look, I need to ask, and don't take this the wrong way, but is there any reason Rowan would want you hurt or dead?"

Paxx shook her head. "I have asked myself that question several times. He could have let me die that day, but he didn't." Paxx sighed. "He seemed truly concerned, but something's not adding up," Paxx said, tapping the ballistics report. "The angle of entry in this report doesn't match what we just saw at the warehouse."

Shannon wiped her fingers on a napkin and leaned over. "This shows a steeper trajectory," she murmured. "It's almost as if..."

"As if someone altered the report to suggest the shooter was on the third floor, not the second," Paxx finished as she flipped through the folder, her brow furrowing deeper with each page.

"I'd better go in," Shannon said reluctantly. "Call me if you think of anything, day or night, no matter what time it is."

"Thank you for having my back on this, Shannon," Paxx replied as she gripped her hand.

"I will always have your back, Paxx."

Exiting the Jeep, she waved as she entered the building.

Paxx pulled out of the parking lot, stopping at the liquor store before continuing home.

? ? ?
THIRTY-SEVEN

A s Paxx arrived home, she was relieved that no one
else was there. She parked her Jeep beside the garage,
where a trailer half-filled with boxes remained. Upon entering the house, she noticed upbeat music drifting down
from upstairs. After placing her bag in the office and taking
off her boots, Paxx headed upstairs. The music became
more audible with each step. She opened the door to the
workout room. She smiled at Jaylee, who was jogging on
the treadmill, singing along with Alanis Morissette as she
sang about being a goddess on her knees.

Jaylee wore faded pink running shorts and a black tank
top. Her red hair was pulled back in a ponytail, wisps
clinging to her neck. When she spotted Paxx, her pace
faltered, but she recovered quickly; as she quit singing, a
bright smile lit up her face.

"Hey! Didn't hear you come in," she called over the
music. Reaching for her phone to lower the volume, she
asked, "How was your day?"

Paxx leaned against the doorframe, crossing her arms.
"Better now," she smiled. She watched Jaylee's stride
slowed to a walk as she pressed a button on the control
panel.

Jaylee pressed a button on her phone to end the music as she stepped off the treadmill. "I'm glad you are home; I missed you." She smiled as she strolled up to Paxx, leaning in and kissing her.

Paxx closed her eyes, savoring the warmth of Jaylee's lips. "I missed you, too," Paxx admitted when they broke apart.

"You look exhausted," Jaylee said, her concerned eyes scanning Paxx's posture. "Something happened today."

It wasn't a question. Paxx straightened up from the doorframe, rolling her shoulders to ease the tension that had settled there. "I will fill you in when everyone gets here. Right now, I want to hold you and tell you how happy I am that you are here," she said, pulling Jaylee into her arms.

Leaning into Paxx's embrace, Jaylee muttered, "I'm happy I'm here, too."

After several minutes, Jaylee leaned back. "I need to shower. Do you want to join me?"

Paxx nodded. "I would love to."

The hot shower melted away more of Paxx's tension that had built up throughout the day.

"Are you alright?"

Paxx hesitated, watching the water cascade down Jaylee's shoulders, following the curves of her body.

"I'm..." Paxx started, then stopped. The practiced lie wouldn't come. "No. Not really."

Jaylee turned off the water and stepped out of the shower, wrapping a towel around herself. When Paxx followed her, she handed her a towel. Leaning against the double sink, Jaylee faced Paxx. "Can you talk to me about what's happening?"

Paxx continued drying her body as she spoke. "There are things concerning my shooting that don't add up." She sighed. "I will explain everything in detail once Tracie and Paul are here. Right now, I want to be here with you. I want my thoughts here with you."

"I'm right here," Jaylee assured. "How can I help you focus on me?" she smiled, dropping her towel to the floor.

Paxx stood and gazed at Jaylee standing naked before her. She dropped her towel on the floor and closed the distance between them, her hands gripping Jaylee's waist as she pressed her against the cool marble of the sink. Their lips met in a hungry kiss, Paxx breathing in the clean scent of Jaylee's skin and the lingering warmth from the shower.

"You're already doing quite well," Paxx murmured.

"Leave everything but us outside," Jaylee whispered, turning Paxx so she faced the sink. Their eyes met in the mirror as Jaylee pressed her lips against Paxx's neck.

Paxx's phone rang from the bedroom. "That's Paul's ringtone," Paxx sighed. "I should answer it."

Jaylee stepped into the bedroom, returning with Paxx's phone. "Hello," Paxx said, holding Jaylee's hand as she moved away, pulling her back and wrapping an arm around her waist.

"Are you home?" Paul asked.

"Yes, what's up?"

"Jimmy is here at the barn with me," Paul began. "What do you think about using the loft as a makeshift war room instead of moving everything to the house?"

Paxx stood up straighter, a fresh determination washing over her. "That's an excellent idea! Let me get dressed, and I'll be right out to help set it up."

Jaylee stepped away from Paxx; disappointment filled her eyes.

"Jay, I'm sorry."

"Don't be," Jaylee replied, "Go help them. I will get everything ready for dinner."

"I will make it up to you tonight, I promise."

Giving Paxx a sly grin, Jaylee purred, "Yes, you will."

Paxx dressed in worn jeans and a gray T-shirt. She slipped her feet into work boots, kissed Jaylee again, and headed to the barn. The barn had once been a derelict structure, but Paxx had spent months renovating it after moving to the farmhouse. Six horse stalls, a tack room, a feed storage room, and a small office were located downstairs. The renovation of the loft above created a comfortable space featuring weathered wooden floors, exposed beams, and large windows that flooded the area with natural light. Most people would call it a barn dominium, but Paxx considered it a future income once she found the right person to rent it.

As Paxx approached, she could hear Paul and Jimmy's voices drifting down from above. She climbed the sturdy staircase, her muscles still relaxed from the shower, but her mind shifted into work mode.

"Hey," she called out as she reached the top. "This is a good idea."

Paul looked up from arranging files on the dining table. He had rolled up his sleeves, revealing forearms marked with the same genetic tendency toward muscularity and tattoos that Paxx had inherited.

"Where's Anna?" Paxx inquired, looking around the open space.

"She will be here shortly," Paul replied as he unpacked the boxes. "She made an apple pie for dessert, so she should arrive in about ten minutes."

Paxx helped Paul unpack years of their father's files, separating them into piles containing tax papers, credit card statements, personal, and his police files.

Jimmy whistled as he surveyed the growing collection of documents. "Your dad was nothing if not thorough. It looks like he kept records of every case he ever touched."

"That's why he was so good," Paul said, his fingers lingering on a folder labeled "Black Rose - 2013." He glanced up at Paxx. "Remember how he used to say..."

"...the devils in the details," they finished in unison, sharing a brief laugh.

Paxx picked up a stack of file folders. "We need to focus on anything related to the Mr. Black cases and the months leading up to Dad's murder."

The barn's large windows caught the late afternoon sun, casting long golden rectangles across the wooden floor. Outside, a truck engine rumbled up the driveway.

Stepping to the window facing the house, Paxx smiled. "That's Tracie and Jake," she chirped, then disappeared down the stairs.

Jogging to the house, Paxx embraced Tracie. "It's so good to see you."

Tracie melted into the embrace. "It's good to see you too; I have missed you."

"Hi, Jake," Paxx said, quickly hugging him. "My brother is in the barn loft. We are going to set up everything in there."

"I will go help them," Jake nodded. "Let you two catch up."

Paxx led Tracie into the house, where she introduced her to Jaylee.

"It's great to meet you finally," Jaylee said, wiping her hands on a dish towel before extending one to Tracie. "Paxx has told me so much about you."

Tracie's sharp detective eyes took in Jaylee's still-damp hair and the easy way she moved around Paxx's kitchen. Her eyebrow raised as she shook Jaylee's hand. "Likewise. Though I suspect Paxx has been keeping some details to herself." She shot Paxx a knowing look.

Heat crept up Paxx's neck. "I was getting around to it."

"I'm sure you were," Tracie smirked, then turned back to Jaylee. "How long have you two been...?"

"We met in the hospital after I got shot," Paxx began, then continued with the events of the past month and a half. "And she's now moved in." She finished with a broad smile.

"I never thought I would see the day when Paxx would settle down," Tracie admitted. "I am so happy the two of you found each other."

The front door opened again, and Anna's voice called, "Where's my favorite sister-in-law?"

"In the kitchen," Paxx called back.

Anna appeared, balancing a pie in one hand and Embry on the opposite hip. Jaylee took the pie, and Paxx took Embry before introducing Tracie and Anna to one another.

"Pleasure to meet you," Anna said, extending her hand to Tracie with a warm smile.

Embry squirmed in Paxx's arms, reaching chubby fingers toward Jaylee. "Jay! Jay!"

"Come here, munchkin," Jaylee said, setting the pie down. She settled Embry on her hip with practiced ease.

Paxx watched the easy interaction, a sense of contentment settling over her that still felt foreign. Family dinners and domestic bliss hadn't been part of her vocabulary months ago, before the shooting, before everything changed.

"Your niece is precious," Tracie said, watching Jaylee bounce Embry on her hip.

"And completely obsessed with Jaylee," Paxx added with a fond smile. "It was love at first sight."

"I have that effect on the Algatta women," Jaylee quipped, kissing Embry's forehead.

The kitchen filled with laughter. Paxx savored the sound, knowing it would be in short supply once they delved into her father's files.

"Dinner should be ready in about thirty minutes," Jaylee announced, shifting Embry to her other hip. "I made lasagna. I hope that works for everyone?"

Tracie nodded. "Can I help with anything?"

"No," Anna chirped, "You two go catch up. I will help Jaylee finish."

"Thank you," Paxx smiled, kissing Anna's cheek.

"Let's go get the guys," Paxx told Tracie. "Embry, do you want to walk down to the barn?"

Embry nodded, giggling when Jaylee placed her on the floor. "We will be back up in a little bit," Paxx whispered against Jaylee's lips before she kissed her.

"Take your time."

Paxx took Embry's tiny hand in hers as they stepped onto the porch, Tracie following close behind.

"So," Tracie began, a sly smile playing at her lips, "you and Jaylee seem pretty serious."

"It happened fast," Paxx replied. "It's different with her, Trace. I can't explain it."

"You don't have to," Tracie assured. "It's written all over your face when you look at her."

Embry tugged at Paxx's hand, pointing excitedly at a butterfly. "Bu-fly!" she squealed.

"That's right, sweetie," Paxx said as she knelt beside her. "Look at it go! Isn't it pretty?"

The little girl giggled, her chubby fingers reaching out as if she could catch the delicate creature flitting just out of reach.

Paxx carried Embry upstairs, set her down, and let her run to Paul. "Dinner is about ready," Paxx said as she watched the three men, each lost in their task.

"Great, I'm starved," Paul replied, bouncing Embry on his hip as he galloped to the stairs.

"Jimmy, is Megan coming over for dinner?" Paxx questioned.

"No, her sister and brother–in–law are having a crisis, so they are at our house. I need to go," he responded, saying his goodbyes and retreating downstairs.

Jake followed Paxx and Tracie down the stairs, the three of them walking side by side to the house.

"So, what have you found so far?" Tracie asked, her voice low enough that it wouldn't carry ahead to Paul and Embry.

"Not much yet," Paxx admitted, her steps slowing. "But something doesn't feel right. Dad was too meticulous, too careful to miss something that would've gotten him killed."

Jake nodded. "I've been going through the call logs from the days before his murder. Nothing unusual stands out."

Paxx inhaled. "After dinner, I want to lay everything out. Something's there, I know it."

The aroma of lasagna and garlic bread greeted them as they entered the house. Paxx took a deep breath, savoring the moment of normalcy before the impending storm. The table in the dining room was set for six adults, with Embry's highchair placed between Paul and Anna.

"This looks amazing," Tracie commented as they entered the dining room. Jaylee placed a basket of bread in the center of the table. "It's nothing fancy," she replied with a shrug.

Paxx crossed to her, placing a hand on her back. "It's perfect," she murmured against Jaylee's ear before pressing a kiss to her cheek.

It wasn't until they were halfway through the meal that Paxx felt ready to unburden herself about what happened at the warehouse. "So... things got complicated today." She glanced at Tracie and Paul, gauging their reactions.

"Complicated how?" Paul asked, taking a long drink of his beer.

Paxx hesitated as she debated how much to say without alarming them. "Detective Darby and I found some inconsistencies in reports related to my shooting."

Tracie set her fork full of salad down. "Inconsistencies? Like what?"

Paxx took a sip of wine before answering. "I think someone is lying about what happened that day. There are discrepancies between my statement and Rowan's."

Paul's brow furrowed. "Rowan?"

"Yeah." Paxx leaned forward, lowering her voice even though they were in the safety of their home. "Rowan claims he came to me immediately after he heard the shots fired and found me lying on that floor, but I know it was longer than he says."

Tracie's eyes widened with concern. "What do you think he's covering up? Or worse..."

"I don't know," Paxx admitted, frustration pooling within her as she recalled Shannon's warnings about Rowan's behavior. "But there's something off about how he acted after I got shot, like he cared but also knew too much."

Paul glanced at Tracie before speaking up again. "You need to be careful, then. If things don't add up..." he trailed off ominously.

"I know," Paxx said. "But I refuse to be intimidated by this mess."

Her determination steeled Paul, and Tracie's resolve, and they nodded in agreement.

As dinner wound down, they moved onto the porch, taking time to visit with Jaylee and Anna before tackling the looming task that awaited them in the loft.

"Thanks for being here," she murmured as silence enveloped them momentarily.

Tracie smiled, reaching for Paxx's hand across the space between them. "Always."

As darkness settled over the farmhouse, Paxx felt the familiar weight of anticipation building. Standing, she suggested they go to the barn and get started.

"I'll bring coffee up in a bit," Jaylee assured Paxx, squeezing her hand before letting her go. The simple gesture anchored Paxx and gave her strength for what lay ahead.

? ? ?
THIRTY-EIGHT

S tanding in the loft with Paul, Tracie, and Jake, Paxx surveyed the organized chaos they'd created. Several piles of files stood stacked, photos pinned to a large cork-board, and a timeline took shape on the whiteboard Paul had found amongst the boxes.

"I've separated everything related to the Mr. Black cases," Paul explained, gesturing to a formidable stack on the right. "Dad kept detailed notes on each one, more than what made it into the official reports."

Paxx moved to the table and looked over the folders. "Are there any mentions of connections between the victims?" she asked.

"Nothing yet," Jake replied, looking up from his laptop. "I've been cross-referencing the names with various data-bases. Two of the victims attended the same church, but were years apart. Might be nothing."

Tracie and Paxx each took a stack of papers, scanning each page for connecting information. Paxx noticed Tra-cie's brow furrow as she looked from one piece of paper to another.

"What did you find?" Paxx asked.

"Notes on three unsolved homicides," Tracie replied, using a highlighter to mark information. "Ebony Moss, Jordan Blackstone, and Mallery Hanks."

Paxx stood and walked up behind Tracie, reading over her shoulder. "The same gun that shot me also killed three of the five women. Why would Dad have notes on them?" Paxx asked, no one in particular.

After scanning several pages of papers, Paul said, "Those weren't his cases."

Tracie's eyes met Paxx's, confusion passing between them. "If they weren't his cases, why was he investigating them?"

"Dad always had a thing for patterns," Paul said, running his fingers through his hair, a gesture so like their father's that Paxx felt a pang in her chest. "He couldn't let things go, especially if he thought someone else had missed something."

Paxx took the papers from Tracie, scanning the neat handwriting she knew so well. Her father's notes were methodical and precise, with each observation followed by a question mark or an arrow connecting to another thought. She moved to the corkboard where Tracie arranged photos of the victims chronologically. Thirteen women with dark hair were found posed with a black rose dipped in their blood.

"Look at this," she said quietly, pointing to the timeline. "The Mr. Black killings stopped abruptly three years ago. No more black roses, no more ritualistic positioning."

Jake looked up from his laptop. "But according to these files, your dad never stopped investigating."

"And then these new shootings started," Tracie added, spreading the papers about.

"There are two more women to add to that list," Paxx said, pulling out her phone and calling Jaylee to ask her to bring her bag, which she had left in her office at the house after work.

Five minutes later, Jaylee arrived with the bag slung over her shoulder and a carafe of fresh coffee. She handed the bag to Paxx and asked, "Are their coffee cups out here?"

Paul stood and crossed to the kitchenette, opening cabinet doors until he found coffee cups. He pulled five from the cabinet, set them on the counter, and opened the fridge door to retrieve a container of creamer Anna had brought earlier.

Jaylee poured everyone coffee, then stood back and looked at the pictures on the board as she listened to the conversation.

"He was building a new case," Paxx whispered. She pulled the files from her bag and spread them on the table beside the others. "Dad thought the shooter and Mr. Black were somehow connected."

"The MO is completely different," Jake said, sipping his coffee. "Mr. Black was methodical. These shootings are quick and messy. No posing, no black roses left at the scenes."

"But look at the victims," Paxx said, arranging the photos side by side. "All these women are around the same age and have similar features." Her fingers trembled as she traced the outline of one victim's face. "Trace, add me and Jane Doe to that list," Paxx urged.

"The timeline," Tracie murmured, reaching for a red marker. She added the new names to the whiteboard: Tressa Nguyen, Fiona Reed, Paxx, and Jane Doe.

Paxx rested her hands on the table and breathed deeply to calm her nerves. "Jake, can you find out when the first victim with a tattoo of a black rose with red tips on their right shoulder appeared?"

Jake typed more on his computer, his frown deepening. "I can't access those files; they are locked."

"I can find out tomorrow," Paxx sighed, the day's events and stress beginning to catch up with her.

Jaylee noticed Paxx's change in demeanor, as did Tracie and Paul.

"Let's call it a night," Tracie said as she gathered papers and files and placed them in her backpack. "I will take some of this home and work on it tomorrow."

Jake stood and gathered his computer and a few files, slipping them into his computer bag. "And I will do some more digging tomorrow at work," he assured.

"Jake, it was nice to meet you," Paul said as he shook Jake's hand. "I will see you tomorrow morning."

Paxx looked at Paul, a realization crossing her face. "Tomorrow is your first day at work."

Paul nodded. "Yes," he confirmed. "I'll be shadowing Jake," Paul added, his eyes bright with determination. "Captain Reed approved it yesterday."

"That's great," Paxx said with a smile that didn't quite reach her eyes.

Jaylee began collecting the empty coffee cups as Jake and Paul headed downstairs. Tracie lingered near the corkboard, her eyes fixed on the victims' photos.

"You should get some rest," Tracie said without turning around, sensing Paxx's exhaustion.

Paxx washed the coffee cups, setting them on a towel after cleaning them. After draining the water from the sink, she assured them, "I am going to the house right now. "

Hand in hand, Jaylee and Paxx walked with Tracie back to the house, where they said their goodbyes.

Once they were alone and the house locked up, Paxx pulled Jaylee into her arms. "I believe I have some making up to do."

Jaylee slid her fingers through Paxx's hair. "You look exhausted."

"I am," Paxx admitted.

Paxx shed her clothes in the bedroom, leaving them scattered on the floor.

"Come here," Jaylee invited, settling into bed.

Paxx crawled into bed, lying next to Jaylee as if they'd been together for years instead of just over a month.

"Jaylee."

"Yes."

"I don't ever again want to be the person I was before I met you," Paxx murmured before drifting off to sleep.

Jaylee slid down further into the bed, holding Paxx close. Even though she knew Paxx was asleep, she whispered, "Neither do I, Paxx, neither do I."

———◆———

Paxx's sleep that night was restless, the voice from the warehouse haunting her dreams. There was something about it, a cadence, a particular way of clipping certain words, that connected with the memory of the man who'd claimed to be Mr. Black after she was shot. Could it be the same man?

Paxx woke before dawn, her body wet with sweat despite the chill in the room. Beside her, Jaylee slept peacefully, her soft features bringing a smile to Paxx's lips.

Careful not to wake her, Paxx slipped out of bed and padded downstairs to the kitchen. As she made coffee, her mind raced through different possibilities. A gun decommissioned from the department. A well-aimed shot. A falsified report. And now, the man who had possibly shot her was meeting with one or two people at the warehouse.

Paxx picked up her phone, her fingers hovered over Shannon's contact information. It was too early to call, but this couldn't wait until she got to the office. She typed a quick text: *'The man at the warehouse, I think he is the one who shot me. Need to talk ASAP. Somewhere private.'*

Three dots appeared almost immediately. Shannon was awake. *'Meet me at the coffee shop on the corner of Thalm and Dyer in an hour.'*

Paxx stared at the phone, her mind already several steps ahead. She poured her coffee and moved to the window, looking at the pre-dawn darkness shrouding the fields as she drank.

Upstairs, she showered and dressed in dark jeans and a navy button-up shirt.

"You're leaving already?" Jaylee's soft voice asked from the doorway.

Paxx turned as she holstered her weapon. "I need to meet Shannon. Something..." she paused. "Something clicked last night."

Jaylee crossed the bathroom, standing before Paxx. "Please be careful."

She pulled Jaylee into her arms. "I promise I will."

"I love you," Jaylee murmured.

"I love you, too," Paxx replied, pressing her lips to Jaylee's left ring finger.

Pressing their bodies together, Jaylee whispered, "I am ready to start forever with you."

"Me too."

With one last kiss, Paxx left Jaylee in the bedroom, a tinge of guilt in her chest for leaving so early.

———◆———

At this time of morning, the town's streets were almost empty except for the occasional delivery truck or early commuter. Paxx drove with her windows open, breathing in the fresh air.

When Paxx entered the small coffee shop, Shannon was already seated at a table in the back. Paxx sat across from her, thanked the waitress who came over, and asked if she wanted coffee. "Black with two creamers, thanks," Paxx told the waitress, then turned to Shannon. "I appreciate you meeting me so early."

Shannon looked as if she hadn't slept much, either. Dark circles under her eyes, and her dark curly hair pulled back in a ponytail, proved her exhaustion. She drummed her fingers against her coffee mug, her deep blue eyes alert despite the hour. "Your text seemed urgent. What makes you think the warehouse guy is the same person who shot you?" she questioned.

Paxx leaned forward. "His voice. There was something in the cadence, the way he said certain words."

Shannon's expression remained neutral, but her posture stiffened. "There are so many variables that are not adding up."

"And I have a few more after going through some of my dad's old case files last night," Paxx replied, pausing as the waitress set her coffee down. She waited until they were alone again before continuing. "So, you know that Jane Doe from the other night was shot with the same gun as me?" Paxx paused as Shannon nodded her head in agreement. "Well, there are five other victims within the last five years linked to that gun. My dad had information about three of them in his files; the first victim was after Mr. Black's last known murder."

Shannon's eyes widened. "Your father was tracking these shootings?"

"It seems that way," Paxx nodded, wrapping her hands around her coffee mug. "But they weren't his cases; he was working them on his own time."

Shannon took a sip of her coffee. "So, we have Mr. Black's murders stopping abruptly, followed by these new shootings with a completely different MO but similar victim profiles. With a decommissioned department-issued gun being used."

"There's something else," Paxx continued. "Jane Doe had a tattoo."

"A black rose with red tips," Shannon finished. "I saw the Medical Examiner's report."

"I find it hard to believe that Mr. Black suddenly changed his MO," Paxx said, frustrated.

"It's more like someone took over," Shannon suggested.

"Do you have open cases with women who have rose tattoos on their shoulders?" Paxx asked as she took another sip of her coffee.

Shannon took a moment, thinking about old cases. "Yes, three that I can think of off the top of my head, but there may be more."

Paxx let out a heavy breath. "Please send me the victims' names when you get to the precinct? I will call Dr. Margon on my way to work and see if she can give me information on others who may have crossed her table."

"That is a good idea; this may be just the break we need," Shannon replied as she finished her coffee.

Paxx nodded, adding, "We're looking at two separate but connected operations. The original Mr. Black killings and now these shootings, plus the trafficking victims with the rose tattoos."

Shannon pulled out her phone and typed a note: "Do you realize what you're suggesting? If these are connected, and especially if a department-issued gun is involved..."

"I know," Paxx said grimly. "Someone in the department is dirty. Maybe several someone's."

"Which means we need to be extremely careful who we trust with this information," Shannon said, her voice dropping even lower. "And you think your dad found a connection between Mr. Black and the shootings."

The waitress passed by their table, setting their bill on the edge, and both women fell silent until she was out of earshot.

"I think he found more than that," Paxx said, her voice dropping even lower. "I think he stumbled onto something that got him killed."

Picking up the ticket, Paxx slid out of the seat. "I need to get to the office."

"Me, too," Shannon agreed as she stood, dropping a five-dollar bill on the table for the tip.

Paxx stopped by the register and paid the bill before following Shannon outside. "Talk to you later," Paxx said as they walked to the parking lot. "And thank you again for your help."

"I should thank you," Shannon replied. "With this new information, maybe we can close several open cases."

"Fingers crossed."

? ? ?

THIRTY-NINE

O n the drive to the precinct, Paxx called Dr. Margon and inquired about the tattoo.

"Let me do some digging," she replied. "I will send you what I find as soon as possible."

"Thank you," Paxx said before disconnecting the call.

By seven, Paxx was sitting at her desk, deep in thought and engrossed in the information Shannon had emailed her moments earlier. The precinct buzzed with its usual morning chaos, but Paxx ignored the ringing phones and hurried conversations around her. The fluorescent lights cast harsh shadows across the crime scene photos Shannon had sent.

"You're here early," Rowan's voice broke into her concentration.

"Catching up on paperwork," she responded, clicking out of the open file on her computer.

"Paperwork, huh?" Rowan asked, leaning against her desk, coffee in hand. His eyes narrowed, like they always did when he suspected something. "You sure that's all it is?"

Paxx kept her expression neutral. "Just trying to stay on top of things."

"Since when does Paxxton Algatta voluntarily do paperwork at seven in the morning?" He took a sip of his coffee, studying her over the rim of his cup. "Does this have anything to do with the Eastside raid?"

"Just dotting i's and crossing t's," she replied with a shrug. "The Captain's been on everyone about documentation."

Rowan pushed away from her desk, tossed his empty cup into the trash, and settled into his chair. "Did you discover anything new at the warehouse yesterday?" he asked, his gaze averted. Paxx tried not to show her surprise as she considered her reply. "No, I needed to confront the place where I nearly lost my life."

"Did you confront your demons?"

Paxx pulled a flash drive from her bag, transferred Shannon's files onto it, and then erased them along with the email exchange from her computer. "I did."

"Good, so you're ready to work on this drug bust debacle from Thursday."

Paxx felt her mouth go dry and bitter as she tried to suppress a sigh. She could already feel the frustration and pressure building in the back of her throat. "Dr. Margon mentioned the tox screen results for our Jane Doe and John Doe from the raid will be ready by noon today," Paxx responded, finishing her now cold coffee.

"He's not a John Doe any longer," Rowan corrected, handing her a file. "His name is Kyle Fronthem; he was twenty-two and was from Tupelo, Mississippi. He's been arrested multiple times for drug possession and assault. And that's just the record from after he turned eighteen." Rowan shook his head in disapproval.

"What's he doing in Nebraska?" Paxx asked as she flipped through the file.

"Probably trying to dodge the two outstanding warrants against him," Rowan replied, moving around to look over Paxx's shoulder.

Paxx tensed, feeling uneasy at his proximity. "He's wanted in Ohio for assault with a deadly weapon and in Missouri for possession with intent to distribute," Paxx read aloud. "Damn, he got caught in Missouri with about half a million dollars' worth of fentanyl; why isn't he in jail?" she exclaimed.

Rowan glanced over her shoulder at a name in the file. "It looks like Henry Gross posted his bail."

Paxx pushed the file aside and typed Henry Gross into her computer, hitting enter to begin a search.

The search results populated, and Paxx leaned forward. "Henry Gross, fifty-seven, is a real estate developer with holdings across three states and no criminal record," she read aloud, looking at his company photo that showed a silver-haired man with a practiced smile that didn't reach his eyes. "Interesting," she continued, scrolling through his information. "Spotless record, major political donor, sits on charity boards. Doesn't seem like the type to bail out a small-time dealer from another state."

"He probably buys their loyalty, then uses them as fall guys when things go south." Rowan straightened up and returned to his desk.

Paxx exhaled, her breath catching as the memory of Kyle Fronthem's shooting hit her. A heavy weight pressed down on her chest, and she struggled between reliving every detail and pushing it away. As she got up to pour more coffee, another email alert chimed on her computer; from Dr. Margon.

Paxx forgot about the coffee and sat back down to read the message.

Twelve women with tattoos have come through in the past three years. The causes of death range from OD, suicide, homicide, and suspicious circumstances.

Paxx clicked on the attachment, which displayed images of the deceased women. She leaned back in her chair, examining each woman's lifeless eyes. Five of these women were the same ones who had been shot with the gun linked to her own shooting. "What the fuck?" she murmured. Three more were victims of Mr. Black; retrieving a file from her bag, Paxx found the list of women in the order they were killed. The three women with tattoos were Mr. Black's last three victims in Nebraska.

Paxx forwarded the email to Paul, Tracie, and Shannon, adding a quick note, 'It's bigger than we thought,' to the subject line. Once the email was sent, Paxx copied the pictures and email content to the flash drive before deleting it from her computer.

Paxx pocketed the flash drive and locked her screen. She needed to appear relaxed, especially with Rowan watching her like a hawk. She grabbed her empty coffee mug and headed for the break room.

"Going somewhere?" Rowan asked without looking up from his computer.

"Getting coffee," she replied, holding up her mug as evidence. "Want some?"

"I'm good."

Paxx poured herself coffee she no longer wanted in the break room and leaned against the counter, mind racing. The connections were becoming undeniable. Women with identical tattoos turning up dead across multiple investigations, Mr. Black's victims, the warehouse shooting, and now this drug raid. Something systematic was happening, something that reached beyond random violence. She can't be the only one putting all this together, she thought as she sipped the strong, bitter coffee. Feeling her phone vibrate in her pocket, she set her cup down.

There was a text from Tracie *'Holy shit, what time will you be done today? Can you come by the house?'*

'Should be by five, I will swing by on my way home.'

'See you when you get here.'

"Captain wants us in his office at nine. Something about the raid report." Rowan said from the doorway.

Paxx nodded, pouring out her coffee in the sink. Looking at her watch, she said, "I'll be there, but right now, I'm going to take a walk and get a decent cup of coffee."

Paxx stepped out into the fresh morning air, grateful for the momentary escape. Lately, the precinct felt like it was closing in on her, becoming almost suffocating at times. She headed toward the coffee shop two blocks away, trying to wrap her head around the recent connections.

The same gun that almost killed her also killed five women with identical tattoos. Three more victims of Mr. Black. The drug raid that had gone sideways. Kyle Fronthem, a small-time dealer with connections to a squeaky-clean real estate developer. None of it made sense individually, but together, it was beginning to form a pattern she couldn't ignore.

Her phone vibrated again. Paul.

'Jesus Christ, Paxx. What the hell have you stumbled into?'

'I don't know yet,' she replied, stepping over a puddle and onto the sidewalk in front of the coffee shop.

"The usual, Detective?" asked Milly, the barista who'd been serving Paxx her morning coffee for years.

"Please," Paxx replied, forcing a smile.

'How's your first day going?' she texted Paul.

'Busy; this place is really understaffed; the unsolved cases are overwhelming.'

'Good luck.'

Paxx thought as she thanked Milly and left with her double-shot, sugar-free hazelnut, with heavy cream Americano. Stopping at the edge of the street to take a large sip, she sighed at the delicious flavor, not caring about the burn on her tongue. Glancing at her watch, seeing she still had thirty minutes before the meeting, she texted Jaylee.

'Are you busy? Can you talk?'

Almost immediately, her phone rang, and Jaylee's smiling face lit up the screen. "Hey, beautiful," Paxx answered.

"Is everything alright?" Jaylee asked, her voice frantic.

"Everything is fine; I just wanted to hear your voice, that's all."

"You scared me." Jaylee exhaled. "I thought something had happened."

"Nothing's happened," Paxx said, though the words felt hollow as she crossed the street back toward the precinct. "Just a complicated morning."

"Complicated how?"

Paxx hesitated, weighing how much to share. "Just work stuff. Connections that make little sense." She took another sip of her coffee. "I might be late tonight. I need to go by Tracie's after work and review some new information."

"How late?"

"Hopefully, it won't be too late, but it'll probably be later than dinner," she replied, opening the door to the precinct.

"Okay," Jaylee murmured, "I will get some more boxes unpacked. I know you want the trailer out of the garage."

"We can do that this weekend. You don't have to work all day, then go home and work more."

"I'd just as soon stay busy." Jaylee sighed, "I've gotta go; my next client is here."

Paxx looked at her phone, frowning at Jaylee's sudden disconnect. She tucked her phone away, the knot in her stomach tightening. She couldn't let all this come between her and Jaylee, but she had to get to the bottom and find the connection.

Eight forty-five. She still had a few minutes before the meeting with the Captain, Paxx thought. As she approached her desk, she noticed Rowan was gone, his computer screen dark. A small blessing. She sat down, took another sip of her coffee, and pulled out her notepad to organize her thoughts before the meeting.

"Detective Algatta."

Paxx looked up to see Captain Kimble standing by her desk, his face unreadable.

"I'd like to speak with you before the meeting."

"Of course," Paxx replied, rising from her chair and following him. Although cluttered, the captain organized his office in a way only he understood. Awards and commendations lined one wall, while case files dominated the rest of the space.

"Close the door," he instructed, settling into his chair.

Closing the door, Paxx then sat across from his desk.

"There is talk that you have been investigating on your own," he said, his brow furrowed as he glanced out his office windows.

"There are things not adding up," Paxx began, stopping when he raised his hand.

Meeting her eyes, Kimble leaned in. "This is not a reprimand, Paxx, but it is a warning that people are talking. You have my support to do whatever it takes to get to the bottom of all this, but you need to be more careful, more discreet with who you talk to and where."

Paxx felt a chill creep up her spine. "With all due respect, sir, who exactly is talking?"

Kimble's weathered face revealed nothing as he leaned back in his chair, the leather creaking beneath his weight. "Ever since your shooting, things have felt... off in this department. People are watching other people. Conversations stop when certain officers walk by."

"I need names, sir. I have an idea of whom to avoid, but it would help if I had some names."

Kimble's expression remained unchanged, but his voice dropped even lower. "I've been a cop for twenty-seven years, Detective. This digging might unearth something dangerous." He pulled a folder from his desk drawer and slid it across to her. "This doesn't exist. You never saw it. But you should know that your father was looking into similar connections before he died."

"I know," Paxx replied, taking the file and setting it in her lap before she opened it. "We found my father's notebooks and files; he has information on several unsolved homicides, including three of the women shot with the mysterious decommissioned gun."

Kimble's eyes widened, the only sign of his surprise. "And you've kept this to yourself?"

"For the most part, yes," Paxx admitted. "Shannon Darby, Tracie McDown, and my brother are helping me piece things together."

"Tracie McDown?"

"She is a friend of mine. She was a homicide detective here for several years, but now has a detective agency. Trace 'em down investigations."

"A small circle. Keep it that way." He gestured to the file in her lap. "That's a confidential Internal Affairs preliminary investigation your father started three months before his death."

Paxx flipped through the pages, her heart racing as she recognized her father's handwriting in the margins. "He suspected officers were involved in protecting trafficking operations?"

"He couldn't prove it, but yes. Paxx, James, was a great cop. One of the best I've ever known." Kimble's eyes drifted to a photo on his wall, showing a younger version of himself next to her father, both in shorts and department T-shirts, holding softball gloves.

Paxx followed his gaze, smiling at the picture. "My father and I had our differences, but I know he was an honest cop."

"I do not doubt his honesty," Kimble confirmed. "And I know you're like him in that you won't stop until you find answers. But Paxx, I don't want you to end up like your father."

Paxx flipped through pages documenting suspected safe houses, shell companies, and partial financial records. "How deep did he get?"

"Deep enough that someone wanted him silenced," Kimble replied, his eyes darting to the windows again. "The inquest into your father's murder was deliberately mishandled. Evidence went missing. Witnesses changed statements."

"It seems my shooting is meeting the same fate," Paxx replied, telling him about what she and Shannon discovered at the warehouse and the discrepancies between her and Rowan's statements.

Kimble leaned forward, his chair creaking with the weight shift. "Rowan Taylor was assigned to you for a reason, Paxx. Keep that in mind."

"By whom?"

"That's what you need to figure out." Kimble checked his watch. "Our meeting with Rowan starts in three minutes. You need to decide right now how much of what you know you're willing to show."

Paxx closed the file and slipped it under her shirt, then tucked her shirt back into her pants. "I've gotten pretty good at keeping my cards close to my chest," she winked.

"Good." Kimble stood, straightening his tie. "One more thing, Jane Doe from the raid? Facial recognition got a hit in the system. Her name is Eliza Monterben, reported missing from Chicago eighteen months ago."

"Chicago," Paxx muttered, pulling out her phone. She sent Paul a quick text with the woman's name, asking him to reach out to his Chicago contacts.

"We should go," Kimble said, moving toward the door. "Remember, in that meeting, Rowan Taylor is your partner investigating a drug raid gone wrong. Nothing more."

Paxx nodded, following him out. The file pressed against her skin as she walked to her desk, transferring the file from under her shirt to her bag. Picking up her bag, she continued to the conference room. She couldn't shake the feeling that she was being watched, cataloged, and assessed by unseen eyes.

Rowan was already seated when they entered. His posture relaxed, but his eyes were sharp. "Captain. Detective," he acknowledged with a slight nod.

"Let's get started," Kimble said, closing the door. "I've got the Chief breathing down my neck about this raid. Two dead, one of them with possible connections to something bigger. I need to know what we're dealing with."

???

FORTY

After an hour and a half of reviewing statements and theories, Paxx was relieved to be back at her desk. Looking at her watch, the growl of her stomach made sense.

"I'm going to lunch," Rowan stated as he walked away.

Pulling her phone from her pocket, Paxx texted Jaylee. *'Can you take lunch now?'*

Several minutes passed before Jaylee replied. *'I need to go to my apartment, make sure everything is clean, and turn in my keys.'*

'Meet you there in ten,' Paxx responded.

Gathering her things, Paxx left a brief note on Rowan's desk: *'Taking a long lunch, be back in a couple of hours.'*

Hurrying to her Jeep, Paxx drove to the flower shop a few blocks away before going to Jaylee's apartment. Pulling into the Apartment parking lot, Paxx saw Jaylee's Camaro parked. Gathering the flowers, Paxx hurried into the building, riding the elevator to Jaylee's floor. The elevator doors slid open with a soft chime. Paxx stepped into the hallway, cradling the pink and white lilies bouquet against her chest.

Paxx hesitated outside Jaylee's door, feeling foolish. Flowers seemed inadequate, too small a gesture for someone who had transformed Paxx's life. She raised her hand to knock.

The door opened before her knuckles made contact. Jaylee stood there, her red hair pulled back in a ponytail, with dark eyeliner and mascara highlighting her green eyes. She wore light green scrubs, looking sexier than anyone Paxx had ever seen. Her eyes widened at the flowers. "What's this?" she asked, shocked.

Stepping through the doorway, Paxx stooped to one knee. "I'm sorry,"

"Sorry for what?"

"I'm sorry for leaving you early this morning and for scaring you when I texted you earlier today. I'm sorry for every mistake I have made so far and for every mistake I will make going forward."

Jaylee joined her on her knees, cupping Paxx's cheek. "Sweetie, you don't need to apologize."

"I do," Paxx said, her voice steadier than she felt. "Because I want to do this right. You deserve that."

The lilies trembled in her grip as she held them out. Jaylee took them, burying her nose in the blooms, her eyes never leaving Paxx's.

"They're beautiful," she murmured, a smile spreading across her face.

Paxx felt the tightness in her chest unravel as the emptiness of Jaylee's apartment surrounded them.

"Come on," Jaylee said, rising to her feet and offering her hand to Paxx. "Let's not have this conversation on our knees."

Grasping her hand, Jaylee pulled Paxx to her feet before wrapping her arms around her waist. "I'm sorry I was less than kind this morning on the phone; I let my fear get the best of me."

"I think we're both learning as we go," Paxx murmured against Jaylee's lips. "I'm not used to anyone worrying about me."

"Well, get used to it, Detective." The empty apartment amplified their voices, the barren walls creating a strange echo.

"How much time do you have?" Paxx asked, a slow, seductive smile crossing her lips.

"Depends, am I going to need a shower after what you have in mind?"

"Only if you don't want to go back to work smelling like you've just been ravished," Paxx whispered while she began removing her clothes.

Jaylee's laughter echoed through the empty apartment as she set the lilies on the kitchen counter, the only surface still available.

"I should be turning in my keys," she said, even as her fingers found the drawstring of her scrub pants.

Paxx stepped closer, her badge and gun already set aside on the counter. "Consider it a proper goodbye to this place. We can be quick."

The kiss that followed was anything but quick; it was deep and consuming as their hands tangled in hair and their bodies pressed closer. They staggered backward, shedding each other's clothes until Jaylee's back met the wall. Once unclothed, they stood facing each other as if witnessing each other's nakedness for the first time. Jaylee's hands glided over Paxx's warm skin, tracing the scar along her side. Paxx shivered, not from pain but from the gentle way Jaylee touched her.

"Let's go slow," Jaylee whispered. "I have plenty of time."

Not fighting the tears that filled her eyes, Paxx said, "I know we say it a lot, but I never want to end a phone conversation again without telling you how much I love you."

Jaylee caught one of Paxx's tears with her thumb, her own eyes glistening. "Me neither."

They moved together against the wall as Paxx's lips traced a path down Jaylee's neck, lingering at the pulse point where her heartbeat raced beneath the skin.

"Feel that?" Jaylee said as Paxx's lips paused on her neck. "That's what you do to me. That's love, fear, and hope, all tangled together."

Paxx moved Jaylee's hand to her chest, pressing it against her heart. The rapid beat pulsed against Jaylee's palm, a rhythm that matched her own. "Feel that? That's what you do to me. That's love, fear, and hope," Paxx replied as she guided them to the floor, where a patch of sunlight streamed through the bare windows. Paxx ignored the warm hardwood, lost in the heat of Jaylee's skin against hers.

Jaylee rested her head on Paxx's chest, her fingers tracing patterns on Paxx's stomach.

"Maybe we should keep this place," Jaylee murmured against Paxx's breast.

Paxx laughed. "A hotel room now and then would be cheaper."

Jaylee propped herself up on her elbow, her gaze serious as she looked at Paxx. "I would like that."

Paxx brushed her thumb over Jaylee's cheek and whispered, "I promised to fulfill all your desires, needs, and fantasies. If you want a mid-day rendezvous in a hotel, I'll make it happen."

Jaylee's smile turned mischievous as she leaned in to kiss Paxx. "I'll hold you to that, Detective."

The sunlight shifted across the floor as they reluctantly began gathering their clothes. Paxx watched Jaylee move through the empty room, memorizing how the light played across her skin. There was something intimate about being here, in this transitional space, a place Jaylee was leaving behind, but that would forever hold this memory.

"What?" Jaylee asked, catching Paxx's gaze.

"Nothing. Everything," Paxx replied, pulling her into her arms. "I love you, Jaylee Pittmore."

"And I love you too, Paxxton Algatta. Now, I need to drop these keys off at the management office. Then I have to get back to work. I have a patient at two."

Paxx nodded, buttoning her shirt. "And I should get back to the station. Rowan's probably wondering where I disappeared to."

Hand in hand, they walked to and rode the elevator down to the main floor; Paxx held the flowers while Jaylee handed in the keys and signed the apartment release form. Outside, they shared another heated kiss before saying goodbye, each returning to the tasks that awaited them. As Paxx drove back to the station, her mind lingered on the warmth of Jaylee's skin; the memory of Jaylee's fingers tracing her scar sent a pleasant shiver through her body, causing her heart to race. As she entered the precinct, she hoped it wasn't obvious what she'd been doing during her extended lunch break, but she didn't regret a single moment of it. The bullpen was quiet when she arrived; most detectives were either in the field or at lunch. Rowan's desk was empty, his computer screen dark.

Paxx slid into her chair, grateful for the momentary solitude to collect her thoughts. A file folder caught her eye as she logged into her computer, one she hadn't left there. Opening it revealed crime scene photos from the warehouse raid where she'd been shot, along with a sticky note in Rowan's neat handwriting: "Thought you might want to review."

Paxx's contentment evaporated as she studied the stark images along with blood spatter analysis, ballistic reports, and speculation on the shooter's position. As she read Rowan's statement, she noticed it differed from the one she had read in Shannon's office yesterday. This account was closer to the statement she had submitted. Paxx frowned, flipping through the pages. The differences were subtle but significant: angles were adjusted by mere degrees, and timing was altered. She pulled a copy of Shannon's report from her bag and compared them. Her brow furrowed as she compared the details. Rowan's statement now described a shooter positioned on the catwalk directly above the main floor, precisely where Paxx remembered seeing movement before the shot rang out. But the report Shannon had given her placed the shooter one floor higher, creating a different trajectory. She glanced around the empty bullpen, heart racing for entirely different reasons now. The elevator doors dinged, and Paxx closed the folder, sliding it to the corner of her desk as Rowan approached, carrying two coffee cups.

"Thought you might need this," he remarked, placing one in front of her. "Long lunch?" he teased, rubbing his neck with a finger. Paxx picked up her phone, launched the camera app, and looked at her neck. A dark red hickey was visible at the opening of her shirt, just above her collarbone. She grinned as she snapped a picture and texted it to Jaylee with the caption, *'I got busted.'*

"You changed your statement," Paxx noted, ignoring the flush in her cheeks. She pointed at the discrepancy. "This isn't what you originally submitted."

Rowan settled into his chair. "I went over the ballistics again and made some adjustments." Though his tone was laid back, his eyes stayed locked on her face, scrutinizing.

"Why the change now?"

"Well, it seems Darby has been looking into your shooting and had all the evidence reexamined. I was upset when I first wrote my report; I've had time to reflect on what happened. My thoughts are clearer now that you're healed and back at work." He tried to sound earnest, but to Paxx, he appeared condescending and insincere.

Paxx nodded, not trusting herself to speak. Something about Rowan's explanation felt rehearsed, as if he'd expected her question. She took a sip of coffee, using the moment to study him over the rim of her cup. "Clearer thoughts that happen to align perfectly with what I've been saying all along."

Rowan shrugged, leaning back in his chair. "The evidence speaks for itself. I'm just following where it leads."

"And where exactly is it leading, Rowan?" Paxx kept her voice low, aware of officers filtering back into the bullpen. "Because yesterday Shannon showed me reports that contradict this."

A flicker of something, maybe concern or deliberate calculation, crossed Rowan's features before his professional mask slipped back into place. "Maybe you should ask Shannon about that."

Paxx's phone vibrated with Jaylee's response: *'Worth it. Wear it proudly, Detective.'*

Despite the tension of the moment, Paxx grinned.

"So, Darby prompted this revelation?" she finally asked, keeping her voice neutral despite the suspicion coiling inside her.

Rowan shrugged, leaning back in his chair. "Not directly. But her persistence got me thinking. And the last I heard, she had a lead on the gun." Rowan's gaze flicked to his computer screen, breaking eye contact just long enough for Paxx to register his discomfort.

Paxx texted Shannon about the new lead on the gun.

The weight of Rowan's inconsistencies settled in Paxx's stomach like a stone. She maintained her expression, careful not to reveal her growing suspicion as she typed the message to Shannon.

"A lead on the gun?" Paxx echoed, keeping her tone casual. "That's interesting. We already know the gun was scheduled to be destroyed years ago. What kind of lead would require revisiting your statement?"

Before he could answer, her phone vibrated with Shannon's response: *'No new leads on the gun. I haven't spoken to Rowan in days. What's he telling you?'*

Glancing at her watch, Paxx said, "I need to follow up on something," as she gathered her things. "I'll see you tomorrow."

Rowan looked up, his expression neutral. "Anything I can help with?"

"Just some loose ends from before my leave," she replied quickly. "Nothing that needs both of us."

Paxx felt Rowan's eyes tracking her as she walked toward the elevator. The weight of his gaze remained heavy until the elevator doors closed. Once the doors closed, she called Tracie.

"Hey, I'm done for the day. Are you free now?" she asked when Tracie answered the phone.

"Sure, you want to come to the office, or I can finish up and be home in about thirty minutes."

"I think it's better at your house or mine; I'm not sure it's a good idea for me to be at your office in town right now."

"Okay," Tracie said, her voice laced with concern. "Paxx, are you alright?"

"I may be reading more into the information someone gave me today, but in case I'm not, I don't want to put you in danger."

"I'll meet you at your place in thirty, do you want me to call Jake?"

"No," Paxx replied, stepping out of the elevator and scanning the lobby before heading toward the exit. "I need to sort through what I know first."

Outside, Paxx took a circuitous route to her Jeep, constantly checking her surroundings. The paranoia felt both ridiculous and necessary. She started the engine but didn't immediately pull away. Instead, she texted Jaylee: *I am on my way home. Everything is fine, but let me know when you are on your way. Love you.*

As Paxx drove to her farmhouse, her mind was in overdrive. Rowan's altered statement, the conflicting reports, and his false claim regarding Shannon's investigation didn't add up unless he had tampered with the evidence. But for what reason? And why now, when she was back at work with access to the files and the ability to challenge him on it? What about Captain Kimble's caution that delving too deep into these matters led to her father's death?

The vibration of her phone interrupted her train of thought. Jaylee was on the line, and Paxx tapped the answer button on the steering wheel.

"Hey, babe," Paxx answered, trying to keep her voice light. "What's up?"

"Tracie is coming to our house instead of me going to hers."

"Okay, I have one more client before I'm finished. Would you like me to pick up something for dinner?"

"We have the soup Anna fixed the other day; we really should eat it."

"That sounds good. If you put it on the stove when you get home, I will make cornbread."

"I can do that."

"Then I will see you in about an hour and a half."

"Okay, and Jay..."

"What is it, Paxx?"

"I love you,"

"I love you, too. Are you sure everything is alright?"

"Just be safe, and I will see you when you get home," Paxx said before disconnecting the call.

FORTY-ONE

Paxx pulled into her driveway, the gravel crunching beneath her tires. The farmhouse stood silent against the afternoon sky, shadows lengthening across the yard. She sat in her Jeep, scanning the property before getting out. The wind rustled through the trees, carrying the scent of impending rain.

Paxx moved through the house, checking each room and window before setting her gun and badge on the kitchen counter. She then pulled Anna's soup from the refrigerator and put it on the stove, turning the burner low. The familiar action calmed her racing thoughts.

Twenty minutes later, the sound of tires on gravel announced Tracie's arrival. Paxx watched through the window as her friend parked beside the Jeep. Tracie's stride was purposeful as she approached the house, a leather messenger bag slung across her body.

"Thanks for coming," Paxx said as she opened the front door.

"Of course," Tracie replied with a smile while walking inside.

After closing the door, Paxx gestured towards the kitchen and said, "Let's set up on the dining table."

With files and laptops arranged across the table, Paxx handed Tracie a beer, and they sat facing each other. Paxx replayed the day's events for the next hour, not leaving out a single bit of information she had gathered or her sudden paranoia.

"I don't know, Trace, do you think I'm overthinking all this? Am I putting trouble where there really isn't any?" Paxx stumbled over her words as her anxiety rose.

Tracie reached across the table, grasping Paxx's hands. "Paxx, take a breath."

Paxx breathed deeply, closing her eyes as she exhaled. "That's better," Tracie said. "Now, besides the new information, what else is bothering you?"

Paxx opened her eyes, her gaze drifting to the window where darkness had crept in. The rain had finally started, pattering against the glass in an uneven rhythm. She pulled her hands away and stood up, pacing the worn floorboards of the kitchen. "It's the timing. Dad's murder, my shooting, the trafficking victim with the black rose... It's all connected, I can feel it."

Tracie leaned back in her chair, sipping her beer. "Your instincts have always been good."

"But I don't know if I can trust anyone in the department now. If someone used a department-issued gun in my shooting, and in the other five murders..." Paxx trailed off, her hand unconsciously moving to the scar beneath her shirt.

Paxx moved to the stove and stirred Anna's soup, the rich aroma filling the kitchen. Reaching up to turn the burner down, Paxx noticed the time on the microwave. Suddenly concerned, Paxx moved to the table and picked up her phone, dialing Jaylee's number. The call went straight to voice-mail, sending Paxx's concern into overdrive.

"What's wrong?"

"Jaylee should have been home by now; her phone is going straight to voicemail."

"Try her again."

Paxx shook her head when, once again, it went to voice-mail. Turning off the burner on the stove, Paxx grabbed her keys. "I'm going to drive into town and see if maybe she has had car trouble."

Tracie was on her feet before Paxx could reach the door. "I'm coming with you," she said, her voice leaving no room for argument.

The rain had intensified, hammering against the wind-shield as Paxx guided the Jeep down the dark country road. Her knuckles were white against the steering wheel, her mind cycling through worst-case scenarios. The wipers struggled to keep pace with the downpour.

"Try her again," Tracie suggested, eyes fixed on the road ahead.

Paxx pressed redial, putting the phone on speaker. The same automated voicemail greeting answered. She slammed her palm against the steering wheel. "Dammit."

"She could just be in a dead zone," Tracie offered, but her tone betrayed her doubt.

Both women jumped when Paxx's phone rang, an un-known number appearing on the Jeep's screen. Pressing the answer call button, Paxx let out an audible sigh when she heard Jaylee's voice.

"Paxx, are you home?" Jaylee talked loudly; Paxx could hear the heavy rain in the background.

"Jaylee? Where are you?" Paxx demanded relief and fresh anxiety battling in her chest.

"My car broke down about two miles out of town," Jaylee explained, her voice crackling through spotty reception. "The battery's dead, and my phone died, too. I'm calling from this old gas station..."

"The Sinclair?" Paxx interrupted, already making a U-turn on the slick road.

"Yes. Believe it or not, there is still a working payphone here. I was going to try walking, but..."

"No!" Paxx and Tracie said in unison.

"Stay there, we're five minutes away."

The call disconnected, and Paxx pressed harder on the gas pedal, the Jeep's tires fighting for traction on the rain-slicked asphalt. "Why would her car break down? It's only two years old," Paxx spat, a fresh fear and anger building up.

"I'll call Jake. He has a car trailer, and he can pick it up and bring it to your house," Tracie said, already dialing the phone.

Tears filled Paxx's eyes as she pulled into the old station lot; Jaylee stood in the doorway, her arms wrapped around her, trying to stay dry and warm. Pulling close to the building, Tracie got out and let Jaylee into the front seat. Paxx turned up the heat, leaning over to press her lips against Jaylee's. "Are you alright?"

"Just cold and wet," she replied.

Once Tracie was settled in the back seat, Paxx pulled out of the parking lot, driving slower as the rain intensified. "Where is your car?" Tracie asked.

Jaylee leaned forward, trying to see through the downpour. "It shouldn't be that far up the road."

"What happened?" Paxx asked.

"About two miles out of town, it started sputtering like it was out of gas. I filled up yesterday, so I know it's not. Then the instrument panel started flickering, and everything went dead; I had to fight to get it off the road." Jaylee replayed the harrowing ordeal, her tone fearful and angry.

"It could be several things, which make little sense given how new it is," Tracie responded from the back seat. "Jake will come get it and bring it to the house."

"It needs to go to the dealership," Jaylee replied. "I have Triple A; they can arrange for it to be towed."

"If it's alright, I'd like Jake to look at it before it goes to the dealership," Tracie said.

Jaylee looked over at Paxx, confusion filling her eyes. "What's going on?" she asked.

Paxx's grip tightened on the steering wheel. The windshield wipers struggled against the downpour, creating a hypnotic rhythm that couldn't calm her racing thoughts. She glanced at Jaylee, noting how her wet red hair clung to her pale face and how she shivered despite the Jeep's heater.

"We want to be sure that your car breaking down is an accident," Paxx said finally, her voice low and measured. "Especially with everything else that's happening."

Through the rearview mirror, she caught Tracie's slight nod of agreement.

"What do you mean?" Jaylee asked, her green eyes widening. "Paxx, you're scaring me; it's just bad luck, right?"

Paxx spotted Jaylee's Camaro ahead, abandoned on the shoulder, and slowed the Jeep. She pulled over about twenty yards away and set the hazard lights blinking. Paxx reached across the console to squeeze Jaylee's hand, her thumb tracing small circles against cold skin. "I'm sorry. Maybe I am being paranoid, but I want to be sure."

"Okay," Jaylee murmured, grasping Paxx's hand tightly.

They only had to wait ten minutes before Jake and Paul arrived. Paxx and Tracie pushed the Camaro onto the trailer, but they were drenched and shivering when they returned to the Jeep. Once Paul and Jake secured the car, Paxx followed them to the house.

The convoy pulled into Paxx's driveway, rain drumming against metal roofs as the vehicles came to a stop. Jake backed the trailer close to the barn while Paul parked his truck beside Paxx's Jeep. They gathered in the garage, water dripping from their clothes onto the concrete floor.

"Let's get inside and dry off," Paul said, placing a protective hand on Paxx's shoulder. "Then we can figure this out."

Twenty minutes later, they sat around Paxx's kitchen table, mugs of hot coffee and bowls of hot soup warming their hands. Jaylee had changed into sweatpants and an oversized sweatshirt, her damp hair in a loose ponytail. She looked smaller somehow, vulnerable in a way that made Paxx's chest tighten.

"Are you going to tell me what's really going on? Why are you acting like my car breaking down is some kind of conspiracy?" Jaylee asked, breaking the silence that had settled over them.

Paxx exchanged glances with Tracie, who nodded. The kitchen fell silent except for the persistent rain drumming against the windows and the occasional rumble of thunder.

"I hope I'm just overreacting," Paxx replied as calmly as she could manage, "because of my return to the precinct and the flood of new information I've received this past week." She paused, pinching the bridge of her nose. "I need everyone to be on their toes and be aware of their surroundings." Paxx said, taking Jaylee's hand in hers, "I can't lose any of you."

Jaylee's fingers tightened around Paxx's, her expression shifting from confusion to determination. "Tell me everything," she said, her voice stronger now. "I deserve to know what we're up against."

Paxx nodded, feeling the weight of responsibility settle across her shoulders. She met Jaylee's gaze, finding unexpected strength in those green eyes.

"I think my father's murder, my shooting, and these trafficking cases are connected," Paxx began, her words measured. "And I believe someone in the department is involved."

Thunder rolled overhead as Paxx laid out the evidence, the department-issued gun, the black rose tattoos, and the timing of each incident. Jaylee listened intently, her face paling, but her posture remaining straight and resolute.

Paxx's phone buzzed on the table; picking it up, she looked at Paul. "It's Anna," she said as she answered it.

"Hey, you," she greeted.

"Hey, you, can I talk to my husband, please?" Anna asked, her voice was light yet concerned voice.

"Yeah, he's right here," Paxx replied, handing Paul the phone.

Paul stopped patting his pockets and took the phone from Paxx. "Hey, babe," he said sheepishly. "I left my phone in the truck. Sorry." After a minute of conversation, Paul handed the phone back to Paxx.

"Everything alright?" she asked Anna.

"Yes, everything is fine," she responded. "I'm not used to being in this old house alone. Luckily, Embry is engrossed in her favorite show. I am trying to figure out something for dinner."

"I heated your vegetable soup and will send some home with Paul." Paxx smiled, standing and walking into the kitchen.

"That sounds great, thank you."

"How did you know Paul was here?"

"We have a location-sharing app, so we know where each other is,"

Looking around the room, Paxx raised her eyebrows and asked, "Is everyone okay sharing their locations?"

After exchanging glances, they all agreed, "Great." Paxx smiled, a wave of relief flooding her. "Anna, can you add Jaylee, Tracie, Jake, and me to that app?"

"Sure, I need Tracie and Jake's contact information," she replied.

Paxx shared Tracie and Jake's information with Anna. Moments later, their phones rang, and each received a text message with an invitation to the app.

"Thank you," Paxx said into the phone. "Hopefully, that will give me some peace of mind."

"Paxx, honey, is everything alright?"

"Yeah, and Paul can explain everything when he gets home."

Ending the call, Paxx poured soup into a go container and sent Paul on his way.

A few minutes after Paul left, everyone's phones blared, warning them of a severe thunderstorm warning.

"Mind if we hang out here for a bit?" Tracie asked as they sat at the table drinking coffee.

"Why don't you stay? You two can sleep in the spare bedroom."

Tracie looked at Jake. "Want me to call Ben and tell him you won't be home?" Jake asked.

Tracie shook her head, "No, I will call him." Excusing herself to the living room, Tracie made the call.

Paxx disappeared upstairs, returning moments later with a pair of sweats and T-shirts for Tracie and Jake.

"I don't think your clothes will fit me," Jake laughed.

Paxx chuckled. "These are Paul's. He left them as a just-in-case change of clothes. You two are about the same size."

"Thank you."

When Tracie returned, Jake handed her clothes and asked if Ben was good. Tracie nodded as she took her change of clothes.

"There are clean towels in the bathroom and clean sheets on the bed," Paxx informed them. "Make yourself at home, and anything goes," she winked at Tracie.

Tracie grinned and disappeared down the hall with Jake, leaving Paxx and Jaylee alone in the kitchen. The storm continued its assault on the farmhouse, with rain hammering against the windows and wind howling through the eaves.

"Come sit with me," Jaylee whispered, wrapping her arms around Paxx from behind.

Paxx turned in Jaylee's embrace, studying her face. Despite everything she'd learned, Jaylee's expression held no fear, only determination and something else that made Paxx's heart skip. "I'd rather take a bath or shower with you."

Jaylee smiled, her green eyes darkening as she brushed her lips against Paxx's. "I think that can be arranged."

They moved up the stairs, Paxx holding Jaylee's hand as if afraid to let go. In the bathroom, Paxx turned on the faucet. Steam soon filled the space as water filled the deep claw-foot tub.

Jaylee stood behind her, arms encircling Paxx's waist, chin resting on her shoulder. "You're carrying too much."

Paxx closed her eyes, leaning back into the embrace. "Maybe I am," Paxx admitted, her voice barely audible above the rushing water. "But I've never known how to put it down."

"Let me help," Jaylee whispered, her fingers finding the hem of Paxx's shirt. They undressed one another, letting their fingers linger on every inch of exposed skin, relishing each touch and kiss that followed.

Once they stepped into the hot bath, their slick bodies pressed against each other beneath the water's surface. Paxx guided Jaylee to straddle her lap; their mouths danced together as their hands resumed their exploration.

"I was so scared when I couldn't reach you..." Paxx confessed against Jaylee's collarbone, her voice shaky.

Jaylee cupped Paxx's face between her palms, forcing their eyes to meet. "I'm right here," she whispered. "And I'm not going anywhere."

FORTY-TWO

By five a.m. the following day, Jake was under the hood of Jaylee's Camaro, Tracie was making breakfast, and Paxx was poring over the files on the dining table. Jaylee entered the kitchen around six, her face ashen and eyes bloodshot.

When she looked up, Paxx asked, "Jaylee, you don't look so good. Are you sick?"

Jaylee coughed, her hand pressing against her forehead. "I have a terrible headache."

Standing, Paxx pressed her palm against Jaylee's forehead. "Honey, you're burning up. You must have gotten chilled last night out in the rain."

Jaylee sat at the table. "You actually can't get sick from being in the cold and rain. One of my clients the other day was just getting over the flu; I should have worn a mask around them."

Paxx's hand lingered longer, brushing back the stray hairs clinging to Jaylee's damp forehead. "Flu or not, you need to rest. Going out in that downpour couldn't have helped."

Tracie appeared at Jaylee's other side, spatula still in hand. "I've got some zinc and elderberry tablets in my bag. My mother swears by them." She studied Jaylee with narrowed eyes. "You look like death warmed over. Bed is where you belong."

Jaylee laughed, wincing at the pain in her head. "Thanks."

"Honesty is the best policy," Tracie chuckled as she returned to the stove.

"Let me get you some hot tea," Paxx whispered, pressing her lips to Jaylee's forehead.

Tracie called Jake and asked him to bring her bag from the truck. Paxx heated water and made tea, and Jaylee disappeared into the living room. With pills and tea in hand, Paxx entered the living room; her heart sank at Jaylee's small, pale form curled up under a blanket on the couch.

"Do you want me to call and make you a doctor's appointment?"

"No, I just need to rest."

"Did you call into work?"

"Yes, I took today off."

"Want me to stay home with you?"

Jaylee's eyes fluttered open, the fever making them shine unnaturally. "No, you need to keep working on this. I'll be fine." She reached for Paxx's hand, her grip weaker than usual.

Paxx hesitated, torn between duty and desire. The case files spread across the dining table contained desperately needed answers, but leaving Jaylee alone in this state felt wrong. Thunder rumbled in the distance, a reminder that the storm hadn't fully passed.

"I'll check on you every hour," Paxx finally conceded, brushing her lips against Jaylee's burning forehead. "And if you get worse..."

"You'll be the first to know," Jaylee finished, attempting a smile that didn't quite reach her eyes.

"I'll let Anna know you are home; she is closer than I am if you need something."

"Paxx, I've just got a cold, the flu at worst; I will be fine," Jaylee assured, touched by Paxx's concern.

"Just like I have had no one to worry about me, I have never had someone to worry about."

Touching Paxx's cheek, Jaylee whispered, "I love you for worrying about me."

Paxx turned toward the kitchen when she heard Jake's voice, and the door to the garage close. Stepping into the living room, Jake said, "I've got good news and bad news."

"Let's start with the good news," Paxx suggested.

"The good news is no one tampered with the car."

"And what's the bad news?" Jaylee inquired, her voice low and raspy.

"The bad news is your brain's fried."

"I know I look rough, but that wasn't very nice," Jaylee joked with a grin.

They all chuckled as Tracie brought in a steaming bowl of cereal and a plate of toast.

"My ex-brother-in-law is the General Manager at the local Chevy dealership," Jake said, wiping his hands on a rag. "Is that where you purchased the car?"

Jaylee nodded while accepting the food. "Yes, I bought it new almost two years ago."

"Then it should still be under warranty. I'll take it to the dealership and speak with Henry. I'll make sure he looks after you," Jake promised.

"You don't have to do that," Jaylee smiled, "But I appreciate it."

"My pleasure," Jake replied, kissing Tracie as he left the room.

"I'm going to clean up the dishes and head to the office," Tracie said before returning to the kitchen.

"You have some great friends," Jaylee said to Paxx as she set the bowl of cereal on the coffee table.

Paxx grinned as she cupped Jaylee's cheek, "We have some great friends," she replied, "I promise they will be there for you any time you need them."

Jaylee's eyes glistened, though Paxx couldn't tell if it was from fever or emotion. "I'm not used to this," she admitted, sinking deeper into the couch cushions. "Having people rally around me."

Paxx tucked the blanket more securely around Jaylee. The intimacy of the moment, caring for someone in their time of need, felt both foreign and achingly right.

"Well, get used to it," Paxx whispered, pressing her lips to Jaylee's forehead. "Because none of us is going anywhere."

A knock at the front door broke the moment. Paxx frowned, not expecting visitors. She cast a questioning glance at Jaylee, who shook her head, showing she wasn't expecting anyone.

Opening the door, Paul stood on the porch, empty container in hand. "Anna wanted me to bring this back before it got lost in our cabinet." Paul smiled.

"Thank you," Paxx replied, stepping aside to let him in.

His gaze landed on Jaylee. "Are you sick?"

Jaylee nodded her head, her eyes heavy.

Paul walked through the living room, motioning for Paxx to follow him to the kitchen. "I heard from my contacts in Chicago about Eliza Monterben," Paul started, accepting a cup of coffee from Tracie. "Her sister reported she was missing ten weeks ago when she didn't come home from school."

"Sister, what about her parents?" Paxx asked.

"That's the worst part of all of this," Paul frowned. "Her father is Nemesio Guzman."

"Fuck me," Paxx gasped as she melted into a chair.

Tracie looked between Paxx and Paul, her gaze questioning.

"Nemesio Guzman is South America's second-largest Cartel boss," Paul explained. "He moved his daughters to the States to give them a better education and to keep them out of harm's way."

"What are the chances that her being taken and killed are just coincidental?"

"Do you believe in coincidences?"

"No."

"Then you already know the answer," Paul replied. "My contact said Guzman's men are already in Chicago, turning the city upside down. They're operating quietly, but..."

"But they'll leave bodies in their wake," Paxx finished, rubbing her temples. The magnitude of what they'd stumbled into was staggering. A cartel boss's daughter murdered in their small town wasn't just a homicide; it was the potential catalyst for a bloodbath.

They heard Jaylee cough from the living room. Paxx's gaze darted toward the sound, her chest tightening with concern.

"How bad is this going to get?" Tracie asked, her voice barely above a whisper.

Paul set his coffee cup down. "If Guzman finds out his daughter's remains were discovered here, he'll descend on this town with a vengeance. We have no way to stop."

Pulling out her phone, Paxx dialed a number.

"Who are you calling?" Paul asked.

"Captain Kimble, he has to know not to release her name yet," she replied as the call was picked up. "Captain Kimble," she began, filling him in on the information Paul had given her. "Yes, sir, I will be in as soon as possible," she replied, ending the call. "Okay, he is going to hold back the announcement as long as possible; in the meantime, he will call in the Feds; he knows we cannot handle this alone."

"I will call Anna and see if she will check on Jaylee a few times today," Paul said, making the call.

Paxx nodded as Paul stepped into the hall to speak with Anna. The enormity of what they'd discovered pressed against her chest like a physical weight. She'd been prepared for corruption, even trafficking, but cartel involvement changed everything.

"I need to grab my gear," Paxx said to Tracie, who was leaning against the kitchen counter, face drawn with concern.

"This is bad," Tracie said, voice low. "Worse than we thought."

"It's like we've been investigating a house fire and just realized the whole damn town is on fire behind us," Paxx confirmed, gathering her notes from the dining table. "The department can barely handle what we've uncovered already. If Guzman's men decide to make an example of Chandler County..." She didn't need to finish the thought.

399

"Okay, Anna will be over in a bit to stay with Jaylee," Paul said as he reentered the room.

Paxx entered the living room and found Jaylee lying on the couch, her eyes heavy with fatigue and her forehead creased with concern. "Paxx, I overheard you all talking, and it doesn't sound good."

"You just worry about resting and getting better. Anna will be over in a bit to check on you."

"She doesn't need to; I have cared for myself most of my life. And I don't want her or Embry to get sick."

"You can tell her to go home when she gets here," Paxx smirked, holding her hands up in surrender.

Jaylee sighed, "You're right, it won't do any good."

"I love you, and I will call to check on you later," Paxx whispered, kissing her forehead.

"Love you too, and please be careful."

❓ ❓ ❓
FORTY-THREE

Paxx walked into the precinct at ten after eight, the bullpen already bustling with activity. After dropping her bag at her desk, Paxx crossed the room to Captain Kimble's office. He motioned her in as he finished up a phone call. "Yes, sir, I will let her know," he told the person on the other end of the call.

"Have a seat," he suggested as he crossed the room and closed the door. "Well, if this isn't a shit show." he breathed out, sitting heavily in his chair.

"When are the Feds going to be here?" Paxx asked, leaning forward.

Kimble slid his hand down his face, trying to wipe away the anguish. "They have their hands full with multiple crises across the country, so they will send somebody as soon as possible."

"So we are just supposed to sit back and wait for the head of the second-largest cartel in South America to rain down revenge on us?" Paxx gasped angrily.

"No, we need a plan. We have to find out who killed Eliza Monterben and why, and we have to do it fast," Kimble demanded.

"Then we are going to have to take our chances and loop everyone in," Paxx spat, "We are going to need everyone's help if we have any chance of bringing Eliza's killer to justice and avoiding a bloodbath with her father."

"I agree," Kimble nodded. "I am going to let you take the lead on this. Are you ready?"

Paxx took a deep breath, knowing this would put an even bigger target on her back. "We must keep this city safe, so yes, I am ready."

"Good," Kimble nodded. "Then I will talk to the Chief and have him send out a precinct-wide email, having all available personnel meet this afternoon at three in the main conference room."

"Ask him if we can bring the county in as well; my brother Paul transferred there from Chicago," Paxx said, pausing before continuing. "He is the one who gave me the information about Guzman."

"Okay," Kimble agreed, "I'm sure that won't be an issue."

Settling at her desk, Paxx called Jaylee.

"I'm feeling better," Jaylee assured, "My headache is gone, and Anna brought over some cough syrup that has eased the coughing."

"I'm glad," Paxx said, relief softening her voice. "You get some rest. I'll be home as soon as possible; I love you."

"Love you too," Jaylee replied.

After hanging up, Paxx turned to her notes, but a knot of tension had settled between her shoulder blades. She sat at her desk for the following five hours, organizing her thoughts and notes. Once an hour, she called Jaylee, who assured her she was okay each time.

At ten o'clock, Rowan walked in, looking haggard and tired. His normally clean-shaven face showed a days-growth of stubble, and his eyes were dim.

"You look like shit," Paxx assessed as he sat at his desk. "Are you sick?"

Without making eye contact, "Rough night" was all he said.

"Can I get you some coffee?" Paxx asked as she stood and picked up her cup.

"Sure, thank you," He replied, handing her his cup.

Upon returning with the coffee, Paxx leaned against his desk and said, "Rowan, what's going on? In almost three years, I have never seen you unshaven and looking like you spent the entire night on a bender."

Rowan sighed, finally looking up to meet her gaze, "My wife," he paused as he sipped his coffee, "She left me last night, actually this morning around three."

Paxx knew he was married, but had never heard him talk about her. "Rowan, I'm so sorry."

Rowan shrugged. "It's been coming for a while; being a cop's wife is hard; we all know that when we ask innocent women to marry us."

Paxx sighed, thinking of Jaylee and how hard she knew it had been on her for the last couple of months. "Maybe you will work it out; I have to believe couples make it through the long haul. How long have you been married?"

"Almost four years ago, we married a few months before moving here." He replied.

"If there is anything you need, let me know," Paxx said, her voice steady as she returned to her desk. As she observed the disheveled man sitting opposite her, a flurry of conflicting thoughts invaded her. Could it be that Rowan's nonchalance about her shooting and rough demeanor was a facade, masking nothing more than his marital troubles? Or was she correct in thinking there was something deeper, something more unsettling, lurking beneath his exterior? She couldn't quite decide, torn between suspicion and empathy.

Paxx wrestled with whether she should loop Rowan in on the identification of Eliza Monterben and who her father was, or wait and let him find out with everyone else. Paxx's fingers hovered over her keyboard as she stole another glance at Rowan. His shoulders slumped forward, eyes fixed on his computer screen without really seeing it. The decision weighed on her: should she go with her gut and be cautious, or should she have some basic human decency and inform her partner before the bomb dropped?

"Rowan," she said finally, keeping her voice low. "I'm going to tell you something, but I need you focused. The department's about to be in deep water, and personal stuff aside, I need to know if you're with me."

He straightened, something flickering behind his tired eyes. "What's going on?"

"There's a meeting at three. Kimble's calling everyone in." She leaned closer, lowering her voice further. "We ID'd the victim from the house raid; her name is Eliza Monterben."

Rowan's brow furrowed. "Should I know that name?"

"No, but her father is Nemesio Guzman," Paxx said flatly, letting the name hang in the air between them.

Rowan's remaining color drained from his face, turning his complexion ashen. "The cartel boss?" Rowan hissed, his troubles forgotten. "Jesus Christ, Paxx. Are you absolutely certain?"

"Paul's contacts in Chicago confirmed it," Paxx replied, observing his reaction. "Ten weeks ago, her sister reported she was missing when she didn't come home from school. Guzman sent both of his daughters to the States to keep them safe and to have a chance at a better education."

Rowan ran a trembling hand through his disheveled hair. "This changes everything. If Guzman discovers his daughter was murdered here..."

"He'll burn this town to the ground looking for answers," Paxx finished. "His men are already tearing through Chicago. It's only a matter of time before they trace her here."

Looking up, Rowan took a deep, ragged breath. "I need to talk to you and Captain Kimble right now."

? ? ?
FORTY-FOUR

P axx stood and followed Rowan across the room to Captain Kimble's office. After a quick knock on the door, Kimble motioned them inside, and Rowan closed the door behind them. "Captain, I need to talk to you and Detective Algatta."

Paxx shuddered at the formality with which he referred to her. "Spill it, Rowan."

Rowan paced the small office, running his hand through his hair several times before he spoke.

"Get on with it, Taylor," Kimble spat.

Rowan stopped pacing as he stood and moved his gaze from Paxx to Kimble. "What I am about to tell you cannot leave this room," he said. "I am Special Agent Rowan Taylor, part of the FBI's anti-corruption unit."

Captain Kimble stiffened in his seat, and Paxx felt a sense of calm come over her. She stared at Rowan, her mind racing. The revelation explained so much, including his sudden appearance in their department almost three years ago, his detachment, and even his convenient absence during critical moments.

"You've been investigating us?" Kimble asked, his voice dangerously quiet.

"Not you specifically," Rowan clarified, loosening his tie. "We've been tracking a network of corrupt officials across several counties with ties to trafficking and drug distribution. When Eliza Monterben's name came up in our investigation six months ago, we had no idea of her connection to Guzman."

"So, the wife leaving..." Paxx began.

"It's true, unfortunately. The cover becomes your life. She couldn't take the lies anymore. But that's not important right now."

Kimble leaned forward, hands clasped on his desk. "You didn't think to mention this before now? Even after one of my detectives was nearly killed?"

"I couldn't compromise my position," Rowan countered. "And frankly, Captain, until last week, I couldn't be sure if all the information I had was legit."

"What happened last week?" Paxx asked.

"You came back to work," he shrugged.

"What does Paxx's returning to work have to do with anything?" Kimble demanded.

"Nothing at first," Rowan replied, "But then you began digging into your shooting, purposefully leaving me out of the loop. I knew then that you could be trusted."

Paxx sat still as confusion filled her. "I don't understand."

"Paxx, your father, he is the one who called us and sent us files full of discrepancies and related cases no one seemed to be able to tie together."

"If my father is the one who called you, then why would you think I couldn't be trusted?" Paxx asked, almost afraid of the answer.

Rowan's expression darkened. "Because your father's files also contained evidence that suggested someone close to you was compromised. Someone on the inside who knew your movements."

The room seemed to shrink around Paxx, and the air was suddenly thin. Her hands gripped the edge of her chair until her knuckles whitened.

"That's absurd," Kimble interjected, but his voice lacked conviction.

"Is it?" Rowan pulled a small flash drive from his pocket. "Your shooting wasn't random, Paxx. Someone told them exactly where you'd be that night."

The revelation hit her like a physical blow. She thought of all the people she trusted, colleagues she'd shared drinks with, friends she'd confided in. Her throat constricted. "Who?"

"That's what we're still trying to determine," Rowan replied, placing the drive on Kimble's desk in front of Paxx. "The last message I received from your dad before his death said, and I quote, "She's surrounded by wolves in sheep's clothing. Trust no one around her until you verify them personally."

Paxx felt as though the floor shifted beneath her. Her father, whom she had spoken to very rarely in the two years before he was murdered, had been watching her, protecting her from afar. The realization sent a chill down her spine.

"So, you've been vetting everyone in my life?" The violation stung, even as she understood the necessity. "That day at my house, the conversation between you and Paul, does he know who you are?"

"No, he has no idea. I was pushing him to clarify why he suddenly returned to Chandler County after ten years away."

Paxx stood, stepping too close to him as she spat, "You think my brother is dirty?"

Rowan took a step back, holding his hands up in surrender. "No, I, I don't anymore," he stammered. "After you were shot, he said he realized how much time he had lost with you, and his wife had been pressuring him for years to move back so she could be closer to you. The shooting helped push him into the move."

Paxx returned to her seat, a new gratefulness toward Paul and Anna settling on her. "Do you have any leads on the dirty cops?"

Rowan sat in the empty chair, a weight pressing down upon his shoulders. "I do, and you will not like who is involved."

"Let's have it," Kimble said, breaking his silence.

Pulling a notepad from the inside pocket of his jacket, Rowan began reading off names: "Ian Pazinski, your dad's partner, Gabriel Hallman in Narcotics, Allan Gregory in evidence, and..." He paused and looked at Paxx. "Shannon Darby in Special Crimes," he sighed.

"What?" Paxx gasped..

"I'm sorry, Paxx; I know you trust her."

"Ian doesn't surprise me," Paxx nodded, "But Shannon, she told me she thought Thompson was involved in something," Paxx replied, her mind suddenly consumed with every conversation they had had over the past three years. "She has always had my back, fed me information occasionally. She fed me information, fuck." she spat, "the file, your statement.

The statement you gave me yesterday, that is your original statement, isn't it?"

A look of relief crossed Rowan's face as he nodded, "Yes."

"That bitch, she has been feeding me half-truths for years," Paxx fumed as a sudden burst of anger spilled out.

"Detective," Kimble growled, standing abruptly. "You have got to keep your cool; we can't afford any of this information getting out until we have concrete proof."

Paxx swallowed hard, forcing the rage back down. Kimble was right. If Darby really was dirty, tipping her off would be catastrophic. She glanced at the flash drive on the desk, imagining all the evidence it contained, evidence her father had died collecting. She forced herself to take three measured breaths before nodding at Kimble. "Yes, sir."

"Let me be clear, we have substantial evidence against Pazinski, Hallman, and Gregory. With Darby, it's more circumstantial. Unexplained deposits, calls to burner phones, being conveniently absent during certain operations, discrepancies in case files."

"But enough to put her on your list," Paxx said, fighting to keep her emotions in check. The betrayal cut deep, deeper than she wanted to admit. Darby had been her confidante, the one person in the department she thought had her back.

"Yes," Rowan confirmed. "Enough to put her on the list."

"We have this meeting in an hour, and I need to brief the Chief," Kimble interrupted, his complexion pale. "How am I going to explain that most of our major departments have been compromised?" Shaking his head, he looked up at Rowan, "Now that we have this information, how do you want to handle it?"

Rowan stood, slipping his hands in his pockets, "Just continue like before, dirty or not; we need all hands on deck to find Guzman's daughter's killer."

"If Darby's involved," Paxx said, her voice steadier than she felt, "she might be feeding information about our investigation to whoever's pulling the strings."

"Yes," Rowan replied, "But my guess is that no one involved knows who Eliza Monterben is. Once you make the announcement, I suspect all hell will break loose amongst those involved. It will be difficult, and your current reaction is precisely why we don't typically inform officers about ongoing corruption investigations. Your performance moving forward has to be flawless."

Kimble cleared his throat. "Taylor's right. This is bigger than personal feelings. Darby's been the lead on three major drug busts in the last year. If she's compromised..."

"Those busts could all be compromised," Paxx finished for him, the realization making her stomach turn. "This is a fucking mess." she spat.

"We must maintain appearances until we have enough to move on all of them simultaneously." Rowan interjected, "Paxx, can you keep your composure and act like nothing has changed?"

Paxx nodded confidently, but inside, she felt like she was crumbling. "I can handle this."

Rowan cautioned. "These people know you, your habits, your tells. Especially Darby."

"All the more reason I won't slip up," Paxx replied, her jaw set in determination. "They'll expect me to act a certain way. I'll give them what they're looking for."

Kimble rechecked his watch. "We have forty minutes before the meeting. I need a minute with Special Agent Taylor. Detective, go get yourself together."

Paxx recognized the dismissal. She rose from her chair, legs feeling oddly numb, and headed for the door. As she returned to her desk, she thought about all the times she and Shannon had talked about cases over a beer and Shannon's interest in her personal life. Her persistence in trying to get into an intimate relationship. Paxx sat hard in her chair, fighting the bile that kept rising in her throat. She closed her eyes and finally admitted that she had kept Shannon at arm's length for a reason, and it had nothing to do with keeping things professional between co-workers.

Shannon had been a cop just a little longer than Paxx, and they had become fast work friends, but it wasn't until Renee died that she began pushing their friendship further. Then, after her dad's death was when she started flirting, suggesting they "hook up." 'Fuck' Paxx cursed under her breath; she was hoping to get information about how much Dad knew about their operation.

Paxx stared at her computer screen, unseeing. Her thoughts spiraled through memories of late nights with Shannon, the confidential files shared over whispered conversations, and the seemingly innocent questions about her father after his death. Every interaction is now tainted with suspicion.

Her phone vibrated against the desk. Jaylee's name flashed on the screen. "Are you alright?"

"Yes, I'm fine," she assured, "But you don't sound like you are."

Paxx shook herself mentally; she had to get a grip and keep it together. "No, I'm fine. I'm just nervous about this meeting. I don't like talking in front of a lot of people. How are you feeling?"

"Better; I am beginning to think it was just a twenty-four-hour bug or something." Jaylee replied, "Are you feeling okay? I would feel bad if you caught something from me."

"I am feeling fine, but I would gladly stay home sick with you anytime. Although I would prefer to stay home sick when neither of us is actually sick."

Jaylee's soft laugh filtered through the phone, soothing Paxx's frayed nerves. "I like the sound of that," she murmured, her voice equally as sultry. "When do you think you'll be done today?"

Paxx glanced at the clock on her computer, reality crashing back. In twenty minutes, she'd be in a room with people who might have orchestrated her shooting, people she'd trusted with her life.

"Hard to say," she answered, keeping her tone casual despite the knot in her stomach. "This meeting could run long, and I might have follow-up work after."

"I understand, just... be careful, okay? Something about your voice doesn't sound right."

Paxx swallowed hard. Of course, Jaylee would pick up on her tension; the woman seemed to read her like an open book. "I'm fine. Just stressed about the case."

"Alright, call me when you leave, and I will start dinner."

"I will; I love you."

"I love you, too."

Jaylee will start dinner. Paxx smiled at the thought of Jaylee cooking in their kitchen when she got home. She let her mind wander, imagining Jaylee pressed up against the counter as she brought her to.... 'Holy shit Algatta,' Paxx smirked under her breath, the heat between her legs causing her heart to race.

"What are you thinking about?" Rowan's voice pulled her out of her erotic thoughts.

Standing abruptly, she pushed her jeans down her hips a little, trying to relieve the building pressure. "Nothing," she muttered, avoiding his gaze.

"Right, look, I need to know you'll be able to handle this. Especially around Darby."

Paxx's momentary distraction evaporated at the mention of Shannon's name. The betrayal fresh again, cutting deeper now that she'd had time to process it.

"I'm fine," she insisted, straightening her shoulders.

"Okay, then. You're up in ten," he said, gathering papers from his desk and leading the way to the conference area.

???

FORTY-FIVE

P axx met Paul and Jake in the hallway, where they stood talking. "Hey, guys."

"You look like you've seen a ghost," Paul replied. "You're not getting sick, are you?"

Paxx shook her head. "No, but that's as good an excuse as any if someone says something. We have all got to talk sooner rather than later."

"Paxx," Jake started, concern etched on his face. "What's going on?"

Paxx glanced over her shoulder, scanning the hallway for unwanted ears. "Not here," she whispered as they entered the half-full conference room where officers and detectives were milling about with coffee cups in hand. Paxx scanned the room, her gaze landing on Shannon Darby across the space. The woman smiled warmly at her, raising her coffee mug in greeting. The familiar gesture, one Paxx had seen hundreds of times before, now made her skin crawl.

Paxx smiled before turning her attention back to Paul and Jake. "Do not talk to anyone in this precinct until we have had a chance to talk," She said. Then, she left them standing just inside the door and made her way to the front of the room.

Kimble appeared at her side, his presence solid and reassuring. "Ready?" he asked under his breath.

"As I'll ever be," Paxx replied, watching Shannon sit beside Pazinski. Their heads bent together briefly in conversation, and Paxx forced herself to look away.

By three o'clock, every chair was filled, and additional officers were standing and leaning against the walls. Paul and Jake took their places in the back, wearing guarded expressions. Meanwhile, Rowan sat in the front row, his posture seemingly relaxed.

Kimble cleared his throat. "Alright, listen up. Detective Algatta has information on Jane Doe from the raid last week. This is sensitive intel, so I expect everyone's full attention."

The room fell silent as Paxx stepped forward. She felt dozens of eyes on her, including the four pairs belonging to people who had moved deceptively amongst their fellow officers undetected for many years.

Paxx took a steadying breath, the weight of every gaze in the room pressing against her skin.

"Our Jane Doe from the raid has been identified," she began, her voice carrying across the silent room. "Her name is Eliza Monterben. She is sixteen years old and reported missing from Chicago over two months ago." Paxx paused, letting the information settle. "She is, was, the youngest daughter of Nemesio Guzman."

The reaction was immediate. A collective intake of breath rippled through the room, followed by murmurs and curses. Paxx watched, her eyes flickering between Darby, Pazinski, Hallman, and Gregory. Darby's face had gone perfectly still while Pazinski's hand tightened around his pen so hard Paxx thought it might snap. Both Hallman's and Gregory's complexion paled as they sank into their seats.

"For those unfamiliar with the name, Nemesio Guzman runs the second-largest cartel in South America." Another round of gasps and curses surged through the room. Paxx held up a hand, "Listen up," she demanded, "Within a week of Eliza going missing, Guzman had boots on the ground in Chicago, searching for his daughter, and if we are not yet on their radar, we soon will be." Paxx let this land before adding, "We have reason to believe whoever kidnapped and killed Eliza didn't know who she was."

Paxx scanned the room, taking in the reactions. Shannon's right hand trembled slightly before she tucked it under her thigh. Pazinski's jaw clenched rhythmically. They were rattled, just as Rowan had predicted.

Paxx continued, "Guzman will not just want revenge; he will make an example of whoever is responsible. He will burn this county to the ground if that's what it takes to find his daughter's killer."

"What do we know about how she ended up here?" Officer Gregory asked, his voice remarkably steady despite the sweat beading at his temples.

"Little to nothing," Chief Morrison spoke from the back of the room. With a confident gait, the six-foot-five, two-hundred-fifty-pound man made his way to the front of the room. Thanking Paxx for her information, he took her place at the podium when she stepped aside. "That is why we need everyone digging into this. Anyone with a CI needs to reach out to them. Narcotics, reach out to your recent arrests and see if they know anything about products coming in connected to Guzman. Homicide: dig deeper into all victims with the black rose tattoos."

Several homicide detectives exchanged confused looks. "Eliza had a black rose dipped in red tattooed on her right shoulder when she was found. This cannot be a coincidence, and honestly, I am mad as hell that someone in narcotics connected the dots and not homicide."

Paxx noticed Shannon shift uncomfortably in her seat. Her eyes darted toward Pazinski, who stared straight ahead, his expression neutral.

"This investigation takes priority over everything else," Morrison continued, his voice resonating harshly. "I want daily reports from each department head. Captain Reynolds with homicide and Captain Kimble with narcotics. We need to find out who killed this girl before Guzman's people descend on this town."

The Chief's eyes swept across the room. "And make no mistake, his people will come. If they're not already here. So find the bastard who has put us all in danger, and I want them found yesterday." He slammed his fist down on the podium, causing everyone to flinch.

As the Chief walked away, Captain Kimble stepped forward, "What the hell are you waiting for?" he shouted.

Suddenly, the room became a flurry of movement and soft conversations as it emptied, leaving chairs and empty coffee cups scattered around. Paxx watched as officers and detectives filed out with a purpose in their steps. Shannon lingered, taking her time gathering her things while casting furtive glances toward Gregory. When their eyes met briefly across the room, Paxx caught the subtle nod between them.

"That went as planned," Rowan murmured, appearing at her side. His voice was low, meant only for her ears. "They're rattled."

"Yeah," Paxx replied, maintaining her professional demeanor despite the thundering of her heart. "Did you see Gregory's face? I thought he might pass out right there."

"We've got them on their heels. Now we watch where they run," he replied.

"I have a thought," Paxx said, turning her back to the near-empty room. "The gun, it had to come from evidence? If it belonged to a retired officer, then it was one submitted to be destroyed?"

Rowan's expression darkened as he considered her question. "It would explain why we haven't been able to trace it through normal channels," he murmured, eyes narrowing.

"Evidence lockup maintains logs of destroyed weapons, but we both know how easily paperwork gets lost. Especially if someone with the right clearance is involved," she growled, referring to Officer Gregory.

"And the perfect place to liberate a weapon that's already documented elsewhere," Rowan added, "I will check cases where weapons were seized or decommissioned, but never made it to destruction."

"I need to talk to Paul and Jake before they leave," Paxx said, scanning the room for Paul and Jake.

"Go. I will go down to the evidence locker and see what I can dig up," Rowan replied, picking up his files and walking away.

Paxx gathered her things and walked to the back of the room, where Paul and Jake waited patiently. "Do you have time for a quick cup of coffee?" she asked.

Looking at one another, Jake and Paul both nodded in agreement. They chose a small coffee shop three blocks from the precinct, far enough to avoid casual drop-ins from colleagues but not so distant as to raise eyebrows about their absence. The place was nearly empty, with only an elderly couple in the corner and a college student typing furiously on a laptop near the window. Paxx chose a booth at the far end, positioning herself to face the door.

"So," Paul said after they'd ordered coffees, "you want to tell us what the hell is going on?"

Over the next twenty minutes, Paxx filled them in on who Rowan really was, their dad's involvement, and the dirty cops Rowan had uncovered.

"Jesus Christ," Jake muttered, running a hand through his hair. "But you have suspected Ian for quite a while," he continued as he leaned back against the booth. His coffee sat untouched, steam no longer rising from the surface.

"I know, and it pisses me of that they've been hiding in plain sight, building relationships, creating trust all this time." Paxx leaned forward. "The evidence against Darby is circumstantial, but Rowan's evidence is otherwise solid. Bank records, burner phone patterns, absences that align with major trafficking movements."

"And Dad knew," Paul said, not a question but a statement.

Paxx reached across the table, grasping his hand. "It is most likely what got him killed."

Paul's jaw tightened as he absorbed her words. For a moment, he looked like their father, the same rigid set to his mouth, the same flicker of determination in his eyes. Tightening his fingers around Paxx's hand, he said. "That's why he was acting so strange those last few weeks." He shook his head. "I thought maybe he was working a tough case."

"He was, the toughest one of his career. Taking down fellow officers."

Jake set his coffee cup down with deliberate care. "So, where do we stand now? Who else knows about this besides us and Rowan?"

"Chief Morrison and Captain Kimble," Paxx replied. "Tight circle, for obvious reasons. We don't know how deep this goes or who else might be involved."

"We will go back to the county office and see what we can dig up," Jake replied, taking the last drink of his coffee.

"I will call my contact in Chicago and see how things are going there," Paul assured as he stood, pulling a few bills from his pocket and tossing them on the table.

Paxx slid out of the booth, grateful for Paul and Jake's help. "Let's touch base tonight, even if it is by phone." She hugged Paul and Jake and then returned to the precinct.

The walk back to the precinct gave Paxx time to breathe and process the weight of what they were facing. Four dirty cops. Her father's murder. A cartel that would soon come hunting. She quickened her pace against the chill that suddenly crept in.

❓ ❓ ❓
FORTY-SIX

B ack at her desk, Paxx found a message from Rowan asking her to meet him in the evidence lockup. She took the stairs down two flights, badge ready, as she approached the secured area. The clerk, a middle-aged man named Hawkins, whom Paxx had known for years, buzzed her through with a nod after she signed into the visitors' log.

"Taylor's in the back," he said, not looking up from his computer.

Paxx stepped into the evidence lockup, the air thick with the smell of stale cardboard and metal. Rows of shelves towered above her, filled with boxes and bags of evidence from countless cases. The soft hum of fluorescent lights echoed in the silence, creating an almost sterile atmosphere. Rowan stood by a desk cluttered with files, his brow furrowed in concentration as he flipped through pages. At the sound of her footsteps, he looked up, his expression shifting from troubled to relieved. "You made it."

"Did you find anything on the gun?"

Rowan nodded, gesturing to a file spread out on the desk. "I pulled some records from cases that were supposed to go to destruction but never made it there." He tapped a finger against one of the documents. "We could have a match. This weapon, a Glock .45, was retired by Ellen Montgomery six years ago after a perp disarmed her then shot her with it."

"I remember this, she is now in a wheelchair." Paxx frowned as she scanned the details. "So, it's possible it was never entered into evidence properly?"

"Exactly. And there's no record of who had access to that evidence lockup during that time frame."

Paxx crossed her arms, processing the implications. "That could explain how someone on the inside got their hands on it without raising any red flags."

"Right," Rowan said, his voice steady as he leaned over the file again. "Besides the Glock, several other weapons and drugs are missing."

A chill ran down Paxx's spine. "How many?"

"Do you remember the drug raid we conducted about eighteen months ago?"

"Yes, that was our first major bust in this area. We seized over two million dollars' worth of heroin and enough firearms to outfit a small nation."

"This location was a stopover before they transported them south," Rowan elaborated. "And now, all those weapons and drugs are missing."

Paxx's eyes narrowed, and she swallowed hard. "What? How can so many drugs and weapons disappear?"

"That's what I've been trying to piece together. According to the official logs, everything was accounted for and scheduled for destruction, but here's the kicker. According to the computer log, everything was destroyed on order from the DA's office after the case closed." He tapped the signature line. "Signed off by Officer Allan Gregory."

"But the drugs and weapons were never actually destroyed," Paxx stated, her voice hardening as the implications crystallized.

"No, and I cross-referenced with the destruction facility. They have no record of receiving this evidence. The paperwork exists, but the actual destruction never happened."

Paxx ran her fingers through her hair, mind racing. "So they intercepted the evidence before destruction, falsified the paperwork, and now have millions in drugs and untraceable weapons at their disposal. What are the chances they are still here in Ivan Hope? Or Chandler County?"

"With that many weapons and drugs, it would take several small loads to get them out of town without someone noticing." Rowan breathed. "And whoever is behind this, if they have any brains at all, they would sit on them for a while before trying to move them."

Paxx sat in a chair across from Rowan, her mind working as she played out scenarios and probabilities. "If Gregory signed that everything had been delivered and destroyed, then he has to be the one here in evidence who handed everything over."

"Okay, you sure Hawkins wasn't involved also?"

Paxx shook her head. "Remember, Hawkins was out almost a month after having his knee replaced."

"That's right, I remember. Which made it the perfect time to move everything."

"And Gregory was working evidence during that time," Paxx said, the pieces clicking into place. "He volunteered for it and said he wanted the extra hours. He had full access and no oversight. It wasn't until about six months ago that he was put on full-time down here. So, we have Gregory linked."

"But what's their endgame?" Rowan wondered aloud, leaning against the evidence table. "Stealing weapons and drugs is one thing, but trafficking? Murder? That's escalating fast."

Paxx's eyes darkened. "Maybe they didn't start out planning to go this far. Maybe it began with skimming a little product here, a few weapons there. Then they realized the potential profit."

"And where did it start? Who started it?" Rowan spat out questions with no answers. "And how are Darby, Hallman, and Pazinski connected?"

"Pazinski and Hallman have to be the ones hiding the murders or deaths of the trafficking victims, and Shannon, well, she could be involved in all of it." Paxx sighed. "Being in Special Crimes gives her unique access to every case that comes through our department. I remember her telling me once that she was constantly fixing detectives' and officers' mistakes on reports."

"That would explain how she could manipulate evidence across multiple cases. The perfect position to coordinate everything."

Paxx felt her stomach tighten as another thought surfaced. "What if the warehouse shooting wasn't just about silencing me? What if they thought I'd discovered something about the missing evidence or the trafficking?"

Rowan's eyes met hers, sharp with realization. "The timing would make sense. Eliza Monterben went missing approximately two weeks before you were shot."

"I remember requesting additional evidence files on the warehouse that week. Shannon offered to help me track down some records. Said she knew shortcuts through the system."

"She was checking what you knew. Monitoring your progress."

"I don't believe it's a coincidence that she volunteered to accompany me to the warehouse last Sunday. I think she was aware those men would be there. Her analysis of the shooter's position and her insistence that you fabricated your statement were too precise." Paxx rubbed the bridge of her nose as a headache set in. "She knew precisely what went down."

Rowan's expression darkened as he leaned forward, lowering his voice even though they were alone. "Then she's not just involved, she's coordinating. That level of manipulation requires someone with authority and access."

"And trust," Paxx added, the realization hitting her like a physical blow. "Everyone trusts Shannon. She's got connections throughout the department. People talk to her, confide in her."

"The perfect position for gathering intelligence."

"We need to figure out how Eliza fits into all this. A cartel boss's daughter doesn't just end up dead in Chandler County by accident." Glancing at her watch, Paxx was surprised to see it was already five-thirty. "Right now, I am going home; I need to see Jaylee, and I need food, a shower, and a good night's sleep.

"Agreed," Rowan replied as he gathered up papers and placed them back in an evidence box. "I will see you in the morning.

The drive home was a blur, each traffic light stretching into eternity as Paxx's mind churned through the day's revelations. The late afternoon sun cast long shadows across her windshield, painting the world in amber and gold. Her knuckles whitened around the steering wheel as she replayed the conversation with Rowan. A horn blared behind her, jolting Paxx back to reality. The light had turned green. She accelerated through the intersection, trying to focus on the road rather than the betrayal gnawing at her insides. By the time she pulled into her driveway, exhaustion had settled deep in her bones. She rested her forehead against the steering wheel, drawing a long breath before gathering her things and walking up to the front porch. The front door opened before she reached it. Jaylee stood in the doorway, her red hair catching the last rays of sunlight, turning it to flame. The sight of her, beautiful, genuine, untainted by the corruption Paxx had been wading through, brought tears to Paxx's eyes.

"You look like hell," Jaylee remarked, her voice soft and soothing despite the harshness of her words. Her eyes were filled with concern as she extended her arms wide, offering Paxx a warm and comforting embrace.

Paxx dropped her bag and melted into Jaylee's embrace. "How are you feeling?"

"Tired but much better," Jaylee replied, picking up Paxx's bag as she led her into the living room.

Paxx froze her eyes wide with regret, "Shit, Jay, I forgot to call you when I left work."

"That's all right. I knew you were busy, so I've been watching your location. I knew when you left the office."

Paxx wrapped her arms around Jaylee's waist, bringing their bodies closer. She could feel Jaylee's heartbeat through her chest, steady and strong. "Can I kiss you?"

Running her fingers through Paxx's hair, Jaylee whispered, "Yes, please."

Paxx smiled, feeling both relieved and excited. She leaned in and pressed her lips against Jaylee's, moving with a slow, deliberate tenderness. The sensation overwhelmed Jaylee; even with the time she had been with Paxx, she had never experienced such a delicate and passionate kiss before.

"Wow, do that again."

This time, Paxx's hands roamed. They skimmed over Jaylee's hips, her fingers dipping into the waistband of Jaylee's jeans before sliding up her sides, feeling the curve of her ribs through the thin fabric of her shirt. Her thumbs brushed against the underside of Jaylee's breasts, teasing, torturing, and she felt Jaylee shudder against her. "How are you feeling?" Paxx murmured against her lips, her voice thick with lust.

"I want you to continue, but I need to go stir dinner."

Releasing her, Paxx followed her to the kitchen. As she watched Jaylee at the stove, stirring the contents of the pot, the vision from earlier that day flashed through Paxx's mind. Grinning wickedly, Paxx crossed the room and turned off the stove before pressing Jaylee against the counter. Her hands found Jaylee's hips, and she leaned in close, her breath hot against Jaylee's ear. "Dinner can wait."

Jaylee moaned, her head falling back against the cabinets as Paxx's lips trailed down her neck. Her hands fisted in Paxx's hair, pulling her closer, and Paxx's hands slid lower, cupping

Jaylee's ass through her jeans. Their passion consumed them as they explored each other's bodies with hunger and need, fingers tracing lines of desire, mouths leaving heated kisses on exposed skin. They lost themselves in one another, willingly surrendering to temptation and lust. Later, Paxx watched Jaylee move around the kitchen, her hair now pulled up in a messy bun. The domesticity of the moment surreal amidst the events of the day.

"You're staring," Jaylee said without turning around, smiling as she grabbed two glasses from the cabinet.

"Can't help it, you're beautiful."

Jaylee placed the glasses on the table and leaned over, pressing a kiss to Paxx's lips. "Smooth talker." She grinned as they settled at the table with their dinner reheated and steam rising from their plates. "Now eat before it gets cold again."

Following dinner, Paxx stayed seated at the dining table and called Paul before connecting with Tracie and Jake, placing the call on speakerphone. The group delved into the latest information while Jaylee cleaned up the dishes. Although she appeared focused on her task, Paxx noticed the subtle tilt of her head and the occasional pause in her movements, indicating she was listening intently to the conversation.

"And you're sure about Gregory and Hallman's involvement?" Tracie asked, her voice carrying skepticism mixed with growing concern.

"Their signatures are on the paperwork," Paxx confirmed. "Gregory had full access to evidence during Hawkins's absence, and Hallman signed off on destruction that never happened."

Jake's deep voice interrupted, "I don't understand why take the risk. Shannon's been with the department for what, fifteen years? Why throw away a career for this?"

They all went silent, as if waiting for someone to answer the question. Jaylee moved silently to the table, setting a cup of tea in front of Paxx before sitting across from her.

"Money," Paul said, breaking the silence. "It always comes down to money. The question is: how much?" His voice carried through the speakerphone, filled with disgust.

"That still doesn't explain how they got involved with human trafficking," Tracie said. "That's a whole different level of criminal enterprise."

Paxx wrapped her hands around the warm mug, drawing comfort from its heat. "I've been thinking about that. What if they were only moving drugs, skimming products, and selling weapons on the side? Then, someone higher up, the person pulling the strings, figures that a seemingly nowhere town in Nebraska is a good place to hide women. There is plenty of open country, a few abandoned farmhouses, and since the grain factory closed, there are several vacant buildings on the outskirts of town.

"I think we should do a county sweep of all abandoned property," Jake said. "Sure, the hell couldn't hurt."

"Yeah, maybe we will get lucky," Paul agreed.

"I will talk to the Sheriff first thing in the morning and see if we can get warrants started," Jake replied.

"And I will do the same with Captain Kimble." Paxx agreed.

After a round of goodbyes, Paxx ended the call.

Jaylee's hand found Paxx's across the table, her touch grounding. "You don't think they'll find anything."

Paxx exhaled deeply, holding Jaylee's hand. "To be honest? No. If Shannon is as involved as we suspect, she'll know about the sweep before the paperwork is even submitted." She abruptly sat up and grabbed her phone, texting Paul, Jake, and Tracie. 'Jake, we need to keep the warrant requests under wraps, then release the information an hour or two before we act. If we handle this correctly, we might just catch a rat.' Paxx sighed again as she put her phone down, watching as each replied in agreement.

"You're exhausted, and carrying too much."

Paxx looked up, meeting Jaylee's concerned gaze. "I'm fine."

"Liar," Jaylee countered with a gentle smile. "I can see it in your eyes. The way you're holding yourself." Her thumb traced small circles on Paxx's skin. "This case is eating you alive."

Paxx sighed, her defenses crumbling under Jaylee's perceptive gaze. "It's not just a case anymore. It's..." She struggled to find the words. "These are people I've worked with for years. People I trusted."

"That's what makes lies and betrayal so painful," Jaylee replied. "Come on, let me run you a bath, and you could use a massage," she smiled seductively.

"You do remember what happened the last time you gave me a massage, don't you?"

"Oh, yeah, I owe your other cheek a hickey."

"I don't know what kind of medicine Anna brought you today, but remind me to thank her."

? ? ?

Forty-Seven

The intimacy of the previous night had been a momentary escape from the chaos. But now, in the quiet, she lay awake, watching Jaylee sleeping peacefully. Her mind returned to the events of the previous day and the revelations that had shaken her to her core.

Shannon. The name tasted bitter in her mouth. A trusted colleague, someone she'd confided in, shared drinks with after complex cases, and even considered a friend. All the while, Shannon had been watching her, manipulating her, possibly orchestrating the very attack that had nearly killed her.

Forcing herself to stop thinking, Paxx turned over and placed her arm around Jaylee, who, at the touch, nestled closer.

Hours later, in the dim morning light, Paxx awoke to the gentle sound of Jaylee's breathing beside her. For a moment, she watched the rise and fall of Jaylee's chest and the way her lips parted slightly as she slept.

Careful not to disturb her, Paxx slipped from the bed and padded to the bathroom. Placing her hands on the sink, she looked in the mirror. She barely recognized the woman looking back. She winced at her eyes shadowed with exhaustion despite the night's rest and tension etched on her face. She took a quick shower, trying to wash away the unease that had settled into her bones.

Once dressed in jeans and a teal button-down shirt, with her badge on her hip and her gun secured in her shoulder holster, she emerged from the bathroom to see Jaylee sitting up in bed, her hair tousled and her eyes still heavy from sleep.

"Morning, gorgeous," Paxx smiled, sitting on the edge of the bed, pressing a soft kiss to her lips before slipping on her boots.

"Morning," Jaylee replied, her voice soft and inviting. She reached out, her fingers gently grazing Paxx's back. "You're leaving already?"

Paxx nodded, trying to mask the dread that tugged at her. "I need to get to the station. I have to get the warrants started."

Jaylee sat up straighter, the sheet falling to her waist as she tucked her fiery hair behind one ear, the movement revealing her naked torso. Paxx smiled as she admired the soft curves illuminated by the morning light.

"Sure, you can't stay a little longer?" Jaylee purred seductively as she leaned against Paxx's back, slipping her hands down the front of her shirt, caressing her breasts.

For a moment, Paxx wavered, the pull of desire washing over her like a physical force, and it was almost impossible to resist. Almost.

"God, I wish I could," Paxx said, her voice rough with regret. She turned and pressed her forehead against Jaylee's, breathing in the scent of lavender and something uniquely Jaylee that made her heart constrict.

Jaylee's expression shifted, and her playfulness gave way to understanding as she cupped Paxx's face between her palms.

Her thumbs traced along Paxx's lips, the touch soothing and grounding.

"You can't blame a girl for trying."

"How about we take a long weekend away when this is over?"

"I think that sounds like a great idea."

"We will take a nonwedding honeymoon."

"MMM, I like the sound of that."

Pulling her in for a kiss, Paxx whispered, "Decide where you want to go, and we will spend it wherever and however you want."

"What I want means we pack light."

"The lighter, the better."

The drive to the station seemed longer than usual, each mile stretching as Paxx replayed conversations and evidence against people she had known most of or all of her career. The Black Rose victims, Eliza Monterben, Shannon's carefully crafted lies, and the warehouse shooting that should have killed her. They were all connected somehow, and she needed to find out how before more bodies turned up.

When Paxx entered the precinct, the early morning shift was changing. A few officers nodded in her direction, but she noticed the whispers that followed her down the hallway.

Captain Kimble was already at his desk when she knocked on his office door.

"Come in, Detective," he said, not looking up from the file he was holding. The circles under his eyes suggested he'd had a sleepless night.

Paxx told him about her conversation with Paul, Tracie, and Jake last night and asked about search warrants for all abandoned houses and industrial buildings.

"It will take some time, but I will get started on them. The buildings should be fairly easy since the bank owns most of them." He responded approvingly.

Paxx nodded and left, pausing before returning to face him. "Did you think my dad was dirty?"

Surprised, Kimble met her gaze, "No, Paxx, I never thought he was dirty, but I think the person you should really ask if they believed he was is yourself."

She forced a smile as she turned and walked away, pondering how many times she had asked herself that question throughout her life. At her desk, her father's ghost loomed more prominently in her thoughts than it had over the last two years. Had she ever truly believed he was corrupt? Or had the whispers of others planted seeds of doubt she'd never fully confronted? She dropped into her chair, rubbing her temples. The question Kimble posed gnawed at her. The answer wasn't as simple as she wanted it to be.

Her phone buzzed with a text from Jaylee: 'Be careful today. I've got a bad feeling. I love you.'

Paxx stared at the message, her thumb hovering over the screen. Finally, she typed back: 'Always am. I will check in later. I love you too.'

"Good morning, Detective."

She looked up to find Rowan standing by her desk with two cups of coffee.

"Thank you, good morning."

"Got anything?"

"Kimble has put in the paperwork for warrants on all abandoned buildings, houses, and property in Ivan Hope," she replied, sipping the coffee. She sighed at its boldness before continuing. "Jake has done the same for everything in the County outside of Ivan Hope."

Rowan nodded a smile that met his eyes, brightening his face. Paxx leaned back in her chair as she assessed his mood.

"Did you and your wife make up, or have you already found a girlfriend?"

"Rachel and I have not made up, but we did talk for a long time last night," he said as he settled into his chair. "When I told her this case was almost over and we could move back to Denver, she agreed to try and give it another shot."

"I am happy for you, Rowan; hopefully, we can wrap this up soon."

By nine a.m., three warrants had been issued for the County and two for the city. At 9:15, Kimble held a brief meeting, setting up two teams to execute the warrants.

"Detective Algatta will lead team one at the house on Harver St, and Detective Taylor will take the home on Juniper." Captain Kimble informed the squad. "We are looking for any signs of drug manufacturing, evidence connected to the Black Rose victims, or anything linking back to Eliza Monterben's murder. Stay in contact, report anything suspicious, and for God's sake, be careful."

As the room cleared, Rowan asked Paxx and Kimble, "Have you seen Gregory this morning?"

Paxx and Kimble both shook their heads. "No, why?" Kimble asked.

"He was supposed to leave some paperwork on my desk this morning by seven concerning the next shipment of narcotics to be destroyed," Rowan replied.

"Maybe he is just running late," Paxx responded, unconvinced.

"I'm going to call downstairs before we leave," Rowan said as he hurried to his desk. A moment later, his brow furrowed, and he returned. "He didn't come to work today."

"Did he give a reason when he called in?" Paxx questioned.

"He didn't call in; he just didn't show up."

"Well, we will have to worry about him later," Kimble growled. "You need to clear the houses before the next round of warrants comes through."

The team dispersed, and Paxx headed toward her assigned location with four uniformed officers. As they drove to Harver Street, the morning sun struggled to break through gathering clouds. As they approached, Paxx sighed at the abandoned three-story house standing like a sentinel at the end of a weed-choked driveway. Its gray exterior was coated in peeling paint and overgrown vines. The boarded-up windows and sagging porch gave the impression of a long-forgotten place.

"Charming place," one of the officers muttered as they approached, weapons drawn.

Paxx signaled for three officers to take the back while she and the fourth approached the front; the wooden stairs creaked and groaned under their weight as they made their way up to the porch. "Ready?" Paxx asked into her mic, checking her weapon one final time.

A musty, damp smell filled the air, a reminder of the house's neglect. Once the officers at the back door settled into position, Paxx pushed open the front door, wincing as it creaked, the sound echoing through the deserted house. Paxx toed the floor ahead of her, cautiously stepping inside and testing the floor's strength with each step. As the team slowly made their way through the house, it was evident by the layers of dust and lack of signs of anything being disturbed for decades that the house was not being used for anything sinister.

Thirty minutes after entering the house, the team exited and gathered in the driveway. Pulling her phone from the back pocket of her jeans, Paxx read off the address of the next house that had been approved. Ten minutes later, they repeated the process and again for the following three locations. By the time they arrived at their sixth house, Paxx was beginning to have doubts about finding anything, especially after the text she had received from Rowan and Jake saying they were not having any luck either.

Driving slowly down the half-mile, tree-lined driveway of their final location, Paxx stopped the car just as the house came into view. The large, two-story farmhouse with peeling white paint and boarded-up windows gave it an eerie and ominous appearance. Beyond the house, overgrown grass fields stretch as far as the eye can see. "Looks like there has been some traffic here recently. Keep your head on a swivel," she said over the radio to the officers in the car behind her.

As the unit slowly approached, the unmistakable smell of marijuana filled the air, pungent and earthy, indicating recent activity at the house. But underneath that was a putrid, rotting smell. Paxx directed the officers to spread out and approach the scene. As they neared the porch, the stench grew more pungent, causing one of the younger officers to gag. Paxx recognized that smell now, and a sudden dread filled her. Death had a distinct odor, one she'd encountered too many times in her career.

"Team ready at the back," came the whispered confirmation through her earpiece.

"IHPD! We have a warrant to search these premises!" she called out, her voice slicing through the silence. When there was no response, Paxx nodded to the officer beside her, a young man named Draken. She tried the door handle, opening the door easily.

"Stay tight," she whispered into her mic as they entered, weapons raised.

As they stepped into the house, the putrid smell was overpowering; the younger officer gagged, unable to entirely suppress his reaction.

"Breathe through your mouth, not your nose," Paxx instructed Draken and the other officers over the coms. Continuing the walk-through, Paxx was not surprised when she opened a bedroom door and found three lifeless, decomposing bodies. "I've got three bodies," she informed.

"I've got two," a voice replied.

"There are five more upstairs." Another officer replied.

"Awe Fuck," Officer Shaw spat, "Detective, you better come here; I'm in a small room off the kitchen."

Retreating to the kitchen, Paxx met Officer Shaw's distraught gaze. "What is it?"

Swallowing the bile that was rising in his throat, he replied, "It's Officer Gregory."

Pushing past Shaw, Paxx gasped when she saw the young officer slumped against a washing machine, a single bullet wound to the head. "Fuck," she screamed, pressing two fingers to his neck, even though she knew he was dead. "Everybody out of the house," she growled into her mic. Exiting the house, she called Captain Kimble, the Crime Scene Unit, and Rowan.

FORTY-EIGHT

An hour later, Paxx stood in the open field behind the house, watching as the coroner's van arrived and Crime scene techs swarmed the property. Rowan approached, his face ashen, jaw clenched tight.

"Thirteen bodies and Gregory," Paxx said, voice low and rough with emotion. "The bodies appear to be Black Rose victims. They have the same signature marks and appear in the right age range. Some have been here a while."

Rowan nodded, unable to tear his gaze from the house. "Gregory was killed execution-style. Recently, probably within the last twelve to fifteen hours."

"Maybe he wanted out," Paxx responded, her voice hard. "He was visibly shaken yesterday after the meeting."

"I think Alan Gregory was a good cop who got in over his head," Kimble said, joining them. His face was drawn with fatigue and anger as he surveyed the scene. "Preliminary search of his phone shows multiple calls to Brant Coleman in the past week. The last one was yesterday evening."

Paxx's stomach clenched. "Somehow, this Brant knew we were getting close."

"Alan was a loose end," Rowan added.

The wind picked up, carrying the scent of death from the house. Paxx turned away, focusing on the distant tree line instead of the procession of body bags being carried out. Each victim represented a failure: girls and young women she should have saved, a killer she should have caught sooner.

"We need to find him," she said, her voice steady despite the rage building inside her. "he's going to disappear if we don't move fast."

"I already have forensics running the number," Kimble replied. "I have also requested a warrant for Alan's home, so you two get over there and secure the location until the warrant comes through. I will text you the address."

Nodding, Paxx, and Rowan hurried to his Tahoe. Once on the road, Paxx texted Jaylee.

Looks like it may be a late night. I will eat something at the precinct.'

Moments later, Jaylee replied. 'I am home; I could fix dinner and have Anna bring you some.'

Paxx sat confused before she remembered Jaylee's car was in the shop. Instead of texting back, Paxx called her.

"Hey, gorgeous," Jaylee answered.

"Hey, beautiful, I'm so sorry. I forgot about your car being in the shop. I should have left you my Jeep and driven the truck." Paxx apologized.

"No worries. Three of my appointments were canceled because of illness, and the fourth is still recovering from the flu, so they were happy to postpone another day," she replied. "How is your day going?"

Paxx sighed, debating on what to reveal. "It has been a bitch of a day so far, and I don't want to go into it right now."

"Okay."

"I will call Jake and see if he has heard anything about your car."

"Thank you, I will talk to you later; I love you."

"I love you, too. Talk to you soon," Paxx said as she disconnected the call and dialed Jake's number.

"Braddock," Jake answered.

"Hey, Jake, it's Paxx. Got a minute?"

"Sure, what's up?"

"First, how have your searches gone so far?"

"We have been to three places, and so far, nothing. How about you?"

Paxx filled him in on the farmhouse and its contents.

"Holy shit," Jake breathed.

"Yeah, tell me about it," Paxx agreed. "Rowan and I are on our way to Allan's house to see if we can find some answers. On a different note, any news on Jaylee's car?"

"I haven't heard anything. Give me a few minutes, and I will call you back," Jake said, ending the call.

Pulling up to a small house in a neighborhood in the middle of town, Paxx and Rowan sat silently as they waited for the warrant.

Ten minutes later, Paxx's phone rang, Jake's name on the screen. "That was fast," Paxx greeted.

"Well, the news is not good," Jake replied.

"Okay."

"The mechanic was working on the car this morning, and something sparked and caught the car on fire. Luckily, they could put the fire out before it set the shop on fire."

"Holy shit," Paxx gasped.

"Anyway, Henry said he would take care of everything, and Jaylee just needed to go and pick out another car; he would sell her whatever she wanted at cost."

"I will call her and let her know. Maybe Anna can take her."

"Sorry," Jake apologized.

"Not your fault. Thank you for all of your help."

"My pleasure."

Ending the call, Paxx called Jaylee and filled her in on the news.

"Well," she replied, "I was thinking of trading it in for something more suited for the country. Looks like I got the push I needed." She laughed.

"I wish I could go with you, but I don't know when I will be free long enough during their business hours."

"I will call Anna and see if she can take me."

'If she can't, you might try Tracie, she has an office here in town; she may be able to run you over, then go back to the office. I will send you her number."

"Okay, thank you," Jaylee said before ending the call.

Paxx sat for a minute, then texted Jaylee, *I love you,* remembering her promise never to end a call without telling her.

I love you

"Warrants in," Rowan said as he opened his door.

As they approached the ranch-style home, Paxx nodded in agreement when Rowan motioned for her to take the back. Once at the back door, Paxx tried the knob, turning it. Opening the door, she listened before entering. "Back door is unlocked," Paxx said into her coms.

"Front, too," Rowan's voice replied in her ear.

Weapon at the ready, Paxx moved through the dimly lit back of the house, searching each room and closet methodically as she cleared them one by one. The floor was littered with scattered papers, photographs, and broken glass. "Someone has torn this place apart," she remarked to Rowan when they met in the middle of the house.

Rowan shook his head at the overturned chairs and shattered dishes in the dining room. "Whoever did this was pissed. Let's see if there's anything they missed."

Paxx moved through the living room, stepping over broken furniture and litter on the floor. The coffee table was flipped, and its glass top shattered across the hardwood floor. Books had been pulled from shelves, their pages ripped out and scattered.

"Looks like our guy was in a hurry," she said, slipping on latex gloves and crouching to examine a pile of papers. "And he didn't want anyone else to find whatever he was looking for."

Rowan nodded, moving toward a desk in the corner where the drawers had been emptied onto the floor. "Computer's gone. Cords are still here, but no laptop or desktop."

Turning up nothing as they searched the house's main rooms, they moved on to the bedrooms. The search of the main bedroom, including the closet and bathroom, turned up nothing.

Paxx cursed when she hit her shin on the corner of the bed in the spare bedroom. "Damn, that hurt," she growled, rubbing her leg.

Rowan grinned as he winced. "That must be a heavy bed; it didn't even budge."

"No, it didn't," Paxx grumbled, looking at the small frame bed. "Rowan, do you have hardwood floors at your house?"

"Yes," he answered.

"And when you bump the furniture, does it ever move? Even just a little?" she asked, pressing against the bed frame, unable to move it.

Realization dawned on Rowan. "Yeah, it's incredibly annoying."

They worked together to slide the mattress off the bed, uncovering a large piece of plywood atop the box springs. Together, they lifted one end of the wood. Underneath, hidden inside the box springs, were several guns and rows of narcotics.

"I'll be damned," Rowan exclaimed, astonished.

Paxx stared at the cache, her pulse quickening. "Automatic weapons, handguns... and what looks like heroin, meth, and ..." she picked up a small bag of blue pills, "...some kind of synthetic I don't recognize." Stepping back, she pulled out her phone to document the find before calling Kimble. While she waited for him to answer, she noticed a small gap at the side of the box spring's wooden frame, wider than the rest of the seam.

"Kimble," he answered on the third ring.

"We've found drugs and weapons at Gregory's place," Paxx reported. "And it looks like someone searched for them before we arrived."

"Shit. Stay put. I'm sending forensics and backup."

After ending the call, Paxx knelt beside the bed frame again. "Rowan, hand me your flashlight."

She directed the beam into the narrow gap she'd spotted, revealing a stack of cash and a flash drive. Moving drugs away from the corner, she pulled up a makeshift trap door, revealing several more stacks of money, a black notebook, and two more flash drives. Paxx took several photos before picking up the flash drives and notebook. Pulling an evidence bag from her back pocket, she slipped the flash drives into it before returning it to her pocket. Opening the notebook, she scanned a few pages before dialing a number on her phone.

"Paul, have you heard anything from the two Detectives we met in Pennsylvania?" she asked, stepping out of the room.

"No, why?"

Paxx explained what they had found before saying, "I found a notebook. It's filled with names and information. One of the names is Bailey Rosalba Hines. Do you think that is the lady cop we met?"

"It's possible. Rosalba is not a very common name," Paul replied. "Does it reference why she is in the book?"

"No," Paxx answered, flipping through more pages. "It just lists her name and the word 'clean' next to it." She turned another page. "Her partner, Coleman Brandt, is also here with 'payment due' written beside his name."

"Does it say how much is owed?" Paul asked.

"Fifty thousand," Paxx answered, her voice tightening. "There are other names too, some with 'PAID' and others with 'DUE' beside them."

"Could be a blackmail ledger," Paul suggested.

"Or payment records for corrupt officers," Paxx added, flipping through pages. "There's a section labeled 'Product Movement' with dates, locations, and initials."

Rowan appeared in the doorway, his expression grim. "Forensics is ten minutes out."

Paxx nodded as she snapped pictures of each page in the notebook, her eyes resting on the name Coleman Brandt once more. Turning to Rowan, she asked, "Rowan, what name did they find on Allan's phone?"

Rowan paused to think. "I believe it was Brandt Coleman."

"Paul, Allan had several calls to and from a Brandt Coleman over the past few days, including last night before he was murdered. What are the odds that the Brandt Coleman he spoke with is the same as the Coleman Brandt we encountered in Pennsylvania?"

"I think it's too much of a coincidence not to be."

"I think we just stumbled into something much bigger than anticipated. If Allan was keeping track of dirty cops across state lines..."

"Then the Black Rose murders might be connected to a multi-state trafficking operation," Rowan finished, his expression grim. "The victims could be collateral damage, or worse, deliberately targeted."

"And Eliza Monterben turning up here no longer looks like an accident," Paul growled. "I think I'd better do some digging into Coleman Brandt."

"Okay, but be careful," Paxx replied before disconnecting the call.

Forensics arrived moments later, swarming into the house with equipment cases and evidence collection kits. Paxx handed the notebook to the lead CSU tech, watching as she bagged and labeled it.

"I need copies of every page in that book as soon as possible," Paxx instructed.

The technician nodded. "I will get them to you as soon as possible, Detective."

Paxx stepped outside, needing fresh air to clear her thoughts. She leaned against Rowan's Tahoe, watching as more police vehicles arrived.

"You okay?" Rowan asked, joining her.

Her voice low and steady despite the adrenaline coursing through her, Paxx said, "If Allan was tracking dirty cops across multiple jurisdictions, and if those cops are connected to the Black Rose killings..."

"Then we're in the crosshairs of people with badges and guns who don't want to be exposed," Rowan finished, his eyes hardening. "People who've already killed at least one cop."

"Two, if you count my dad," Paxx replied, "And attempted to kill a third if you count me. If we're right about this, we're dealing with a network, not just individuals. And they've already proven they're willing to kill to protect themselves." Paxx said, lowering her voice further.

Her phone vibrated with an incoming text. It was from Paul: 'Looked into Coleman Brandt. He's been with the Pennsylvania State Police for 15 years. Clean record and multiple commendations. Nothing suspicious on paper.'

She showed the message to Rowan. "Too clean?"

"Maybe. Or maybe he's good at covering his tracks." Rowan replied, "What about the flash drives?"

Paxx patted her pocket. "I'm keeping these close until we can check them somewhere secure. Not at the station."

They stood silently, watching crime scene technicians carry evidence bags from the house. Kimble's car pulled up, and he stepped out, his expression grave as he approached them.

"Tell me you have something concrete," he said without preamble.

Paxx filled him in on the notebook and their suspicions about the connection to Pennsylvania, careful to keep her voice low. She deliberately omitted mentioning the flash drives tucked safely in her pocket.

"Jesus," Kimble muttered, rubbing his forehead. "This just keeps getting bigger." He looked around at the growing number of officers on the scene. "Who else knows about this theory?"

"Just us and Paul," Rowan answered.

"Keep it that way for now," Kimble replied.

? ? ?

FORTY-NINE

Kimble's phone rang. He checked the screen and stepped away to answer it, his posture tense as he spoke in hushed tones. When he returned, his expression was even grimmer.

"That was the ME." Kimble said, stepping back to them, "Gregory's time of death has been narrowed down to between 9 PM and midnight last night.

Paxx nodded, her mind racing. "Gregory was killed shortly after his last call to Brandt Coleman. What about the women?"

"It looks like most of them were killed approximately the same time frame, maybe a few hours earlier, others two or three days ago," Kimble replied.

"Do you think Gregory killed them or helped kill them before he was killed?" Paxx asked, bile rising in her throat.

Rowan shrugged. "I think whoever killed them was trying to get rid of evidence."

"But why just leave them here? Why not bury them or burn the house down?" Paxx asked as she began to pace.

Kimble rubbed his chin thoughtfully. "Maybe they were interrupted before they could dispose of the bodies properly.

Or maybe there are more women, and they are not done. Or maybe they wanted us to find them."

"A message?" Rowan suggested.

"If so, to whom?" Paxx asked, her eyes narrowing.

"That's what we need to figure out," Kimble said. "You two should head back to the station. The Chief wants to be briefed on everything, and I mean everything."

She felt a chill run down her spine. Did he suspect she was withholding evidence? The flash drives now heavier in her pocket. "We'll be there in forty-five."

As Kimble turned to coordinate with the forensic team, Paxx glanced at Rowan. His eyes met hers, and she saw the unspoken question there. They walked together toward his Tahoe, maintaining professional silence until they were safely inside with closed doors.

"You're holding something back," Rowan said, not starting the engine yet. It wasn't an accusation, just an observation.

Paxx gripped the door handle, her knuckles whitening. "I need to trust you, Rowan. Really trust you."

Rowan sighed, the weight of his deception for the past three years heavy, "I know you feel like I have betrayed you, but I assure you, Paxx, you can trust me."

Paxx released her hold on the door handle, removing the flash drives from her pocket. "I need to see what is on these before I turn them over to forensics."

"My laptop is in the backseat. Copy the files onto it, then take the drives to CSU. We can look at them when we get to the precinct. It will take hours, perhaps even tomorrow, before anyone looks at them," Rowan suggested.

Pulling Rowan's computer onto her lap, Paxx copied each flash drive into different folders, labeling each with nondescript headings. Once complete, she returned to the house, handing the evidence envelope to the first CSI she found.

Once Paxx was back in the car, Rowan started the engine and pulled away from Gregory's house. Their silence was heavy with unspoken words.

"You know, if I'm caught with copies of evidence, I could lose my badge."

"If we're caught," Rowan corrected, eyes fixed on the road. "But we won't be. And sometimes you have to bend the rules to get to the truth."

"That's rich coming from you."

Rowan's grip tightened on the steering wheel. "I deserved that."

"Yes, you did." Paxx stared out the passenger window, watching the suburban landscape melt into downtown Ivan Hope. "Thirteen girls, Rowan. Thirteen girls who might still be alive if we'd caught this sooner."

"You can't blame yourself for that."

"I'm not blaming myself. I am blaming every uncompromised cop in Ivan Hope. How does somebody bring thirteen girls into a town the size of Ivan Hope without anyone noticing?" Rowan knew she wasn't looking for him to answer, so he kept quiet. "Whoever kept them had to feed them and supply basic hygiene products. If the ultimate goal were to sell them, they would need to be clean, well-groomed, and fed. Am I right?"

This time, Rowan answered, "Let's run Darby, Pazinski, Hallman, and Gregory's financials and see if any of their grocery bills have increased over the past several months."

Paxx called Jake and asked if he would run the financial reports on their dirty cops. "I think it's best we keep this out of the precinct," Paxx told him.

Jake agreed. "I'll let you know as soon as I have them."

They pulled into the precinct parking lot, the midday sun casting harsh shadows across the concrete. Paxx glanced at the laptop bag containing their illicit copies, her stomach knotting with anticipation and dread.

"We need to review these files before the briefing," she said, checking her watch. "Twenty minutes."

Rowan nodded, grabbing the laptop as they hurried inside. They bypassed the busy bullpen for the relative privacy of Interview Room 3, the one with the faulty security camera that maintenance had been "planning to fix" for months.

"Here," Rowan said, pulling the door closed behind them and setting up the laptop.

Paxx clicked through files, finding mostly mundane documents until she opened a spreadsheet labeled "Inventory." Her breath caught.

"Jesus," she whispered. The spreadsheet contained rows of ages, races, heights, weights, and hair colors.

Rowan gazed over her shoulder, a shudder running through him. "There must be a hundred girls listed."

"There are no names," Paxx growled, feeling tears in her eyes.

Rowan pulled out a chair and sat beside her. "Easier to treat them like objects than people if you don't know their names."

Paxx scanned down the columns, looking for patterns. "Look at this; they're categorized by 'grade.' A through D."

"Quality ratings," Rowan said, disgust in his voice. "The higher grades would fetch more money."

Paxx clicked through more files and found another spreadsheet with dates, locations, and dollar amounts. "This is a ledger. Transactions." Her finger traced across the screen. "These must be sales."

Paxx scanned further down the spreadsheet, her jaw clenching tighter with each entry. "Look at this column, 'Status.' Most say 'In Transit' or 'Processing,' but these thirteen..." Her finger traced down the screen to where thirteen consecutive entries were marked Compromised."

"The thirteen victims at Gregory's," Rowan confirmed, his voice hollow. "They were killing their merchandise."

"Not merchandise," Paxx snapped. "People. Girls. Children." She scrolled back up, studying the data more carefully. "There's a pattern to the shipments. Every three weeks, like clockwork."

"We need to cross-reference the dates with any reports about missing persons," Rowan suggested. "That might give us actual names to attach to these... girls."

"There's another delivery scheduled for tomorrow night," Paxx interjected as she continued to read.

Rowan leaned closer. "Coordinates. That's a location."

Paxx copied the numbers into her phone's map app. "It's a warehouse on the edge of town, just south of the Chandler County line."

Looking at her watch, Paxx shut the laptop. "We have to meet with Chief Morrison in three minutes. I think we'd better loop him in. If there is a chance this shipment comes in tomorrow night, we need to be ready."

"Agreed." Rowan nodded as he placed the computer in his bag, and they left the room.

As they walked toward the Chief's office, Paxx felt her phone vibrate. A text from Jake: "Financials coming through. Something's off with Darby's accounts. Multiple cash withdrawals, $500-1000 each, every Tuesday for the past eight months."

She showed Rowan the message, keeping her voice low. "Tuesday grocery shopping for captives?"

"Or payment for services," Rowan muttered.

Paxx stopped as someone stormed out of the Chief's office, nearly colliding with them. It was Detective Darby, her face flushed with anger.

"Shannon," Paxx called out, but Shannon ignored her. "What was that about?" Paxx murmured as they continued toward the door.

"Not sure, but she's not in a good mood," Rowan replied.

They reached Chief Morrison's door, and Paxx knocked firmly. "Come in"

Morrison's gruff voice came from the other side.

The Chief sat behind his desk, shirtsleeves rolled up, tie loosened. The blinds were half-drawn, casting striped shadows across his weathered face. He gestured to the chairs opposite him without looking up from the file he was reading.

"What do you have?"

"We found something significant," Paxx replied, taking a breath to steady herself. She glanced at Rowan, who nodded for her to continue. "It relates to Gregory and the victims."

The Chief leaned back in his chair, arms crossed tightly over his barrel chest. "Go on."

She recounted their discoveries, the time of death, the connection between Gregory and the unknown women, and most importantly, what they'd uncovered on the flash drives.

Morrison listened intently as she described the spreadsheet and its chilling implications. When she mentioned the scheduled shipment for tomorrow night at the warehouse, his expression shifted from skepticism to concern.

"How reliable is this information?" Morrison asked, rubbing his temple. "And how did you come across this information?"

Paxx shifted in her seat. "We found three flash drives hidden in Gregory's home. We found them during our search." It was not a lie, but it was not the whole truth, either.

Morrison's eyes narrowed slightly. "And you've already examined the contents?"

"We needed to understand what we were dealing with," Rowan interjected. "Knowing the possible involvement of Darby, Pazinski, and Hallman, I thought it best we see the information before word got around of their contents."

Morrison studied them both for a long moment, his expression unreadable. Finally, he nodded slowly. "You made the right call. If those flash drives had gone straight to evidence, they might have disappeared." He leaned forward, lowering his voice. "But I don't need to tell you that copying evidence without authorization is a career-ending move."

Paxx felt her muscles tense. "Sir..."

Morrison held up a hand. "I didn't hear you confess to anything, Detective. And I don't want to." He stood up and moved to close the blinds completely, plunging the office into shadowy privacy. "We need a plan that doesn't tip off whoever's running this operation."

"We need to surveil that warehouse," Rowan said. "Set up a sting for tomorrow night."

"Gather a team you both trust," Morrison replied, "I will loop in Kimble."

As she stood, Paxx asked, "May we use county officers and local ones?"

"Anyone you trust, Detective. This is no time for politics."

Standing to leave, Paxx asked, "What was Darby so upset about when she left?"

Rubbing a hand over his face, Morrison said, "She turned in her retirement papers."

"She's retiring? Now?"

Morrison's expression darkened. "Said she's been planning it for months. But now a family emergency has deemed it necessary to relocate out of state." He met Paxx's eyes. "Effective immediately."

"That's convenient timing," Paxx said, unable to keep the edge from her voice. "I've known Shannon for fifteen years. She's ambitious, driven, and never talked about her family."

"Unless she knows we're closing in," Morrison said. "She could be planning to disappear before we can connect her to the trafficking operation."

"Or she's preparing to move a large shipment and doesn't plan on returning," Rowan added.

Paxx paced the office, her mind connecting fragments of information. "The Tuesday cash withdrawals, the scheduled delivery..." Paxx's pulse quickened. "She knows we're onto her."

"Chief, we need to put surveillance on her," Rowan said.

Morrison agreed, his jaw tight. "I've already flagged her passport, along with Pazinski's and Hallman's. I will call Captain Kimble and have him assign two officers to keep an eye on Darby."

Paxx couldn't sit still, as her mind raced. "I'm going to text Jake. He's been running financials on all of them. We need to know if there have been any unusual transactions in the last few hours." Paxx said, already pulling out her phone. "Chief, if she's planning to run, she might accelerate the timetable. What if tomorrow's delivery gets moved up?"

"You think they'd change plans this late?" Morrison frowned.

"If Darby suspects we're onto her, absolutely," Rowan said, exchanging a glance with Paxx. "These people have contingency plans for their contingency plans."

Morrison sighed. "Let me make a call. We need to get eyes on that warehouse tonight, not tomorrow." He reached for his phone.

As they left the Chief's office, Paxx felt the weight of what they were dealing with settle in her chest. Human trafficking, Corrupt officers, and a network that had operated under their noses for months, maybe years.

Paxx's phone rang; Jake's number appeared on the screen. "Darby's account shows a wire transfer of fifty thousand dollars to an offshore account about thirty minutes ago."

"Shit," Paxx muttered. "She's running."

"Let's get to Captain Kimble, see what he wants to do," Rowan suggested, picking up the pace.

? ? ?

FIFTY

As they walked past their desks, Paxx saw a white envelope with large, bold letters written in black across the front sitting on her desk. A shiver ran down her back, and she halted abruptly. Snatching it up, her heart pounded as she read: URGENT! With a quick breath, she tore it open, revealing a neatly typed note that demanded her attention with ruthless clarity: If you want to keep Jaylee, Anna, and Embry Alive, drop the investigation! Her breath caught in her throat as the weight of the chilling words threatened everything she held dear.

Rowan halted when he saw the expression on Paxx's face. "Paxx, what is it?"

Paxx handed him the letter as she pulled out her phone. "I need to call Jaylee."

"Go ahead," Rowan agreed after reading the note.

Stepping away for privacy, Paxx dialed Jaylee's number, fear gripping her with each unanswered ring. On the fourth ring, Jaylee picked up.

"Hey, gorgeous?" Jaylee answered, her voice warm and seductive.

"Hey, beautiful," Paxx exhaled, not realizing she'd been holding her breath. "Did you get in touch with Anna?"

"Yes, I did. She'll be here to pick me up shortly," Jaylee answered. "Paxx, is everything okay? You sound tense."

"It's been a long day," Paxx replied, trying to calm her voice. "Do me a favor, stay inside, and keep the doors locked."

"Paxx, you're scaring me."

"I just need to know you're safe. I'll explain everything later, I promise." Paxx replied as she struggled to keep her voice steady. "I am going to have Jimmy come get you, and he will take you to Paul and Anna's."

"Paxx, please tell me what is happening."

Paxx told her about the events of the day and the note left on her desk. "Jay, do you know how to use a gun?"

"Yes, I am also a black belt in Jujitsu."

"My badass girlfriend."

"Yes, I am," she smirked. "I'll wait for Jimmy."

"There is a gun safe in the bedroom closet," Paxx said, giving her the combination. "There are a couple of pistols, a shotgun, and plenty of ammunition; I need you to help Jimmy keep everyone safe."

"Don't worry; we will be fine. Go do your job, Detective, and come home to me safe."

"I will," Paxx promised, her voice thick with emotion. "I love you, Jaylee."

"I love you, too," she whispered. "Now go catch these bastards."

Paxx ended the call and turned back to Rowan, her expression hardening as she dialed Jimmy's number. "We need to warn Paul and Anna."

"Already on it," Rowan said, holding up his phone. "Paul's going to meet Jimmy at your place. Have an officer take them all to a safe house. Not his home, somewhere off the books."

"Is there someplace people in the department don't know about?" Paxx asked, holding up a finger when Jimmy answered.

She felt a little more at ease after explaining the situation to him. His military background gave her a sense of security. "We'll be fine, Paxx."

Turning to Rowan, she said, "Jimmy's on his way to the house."

"Good, and Paul said he has access to a cabin," Rowan explained, lowering his voice. "His friend from Chicago owns it. No paper trail connects it to him or you. It's about an hour north, near Chadron State Park."

Paxx nodded, relief seeping through her. "Good. That's good, let's find Kimble."

They located Captain Kimble in the conference room. Maps of the warehouse district were spread across the table. As several officers watched, Kimble was marking potential entry points on a specific building.

"Detectives," he acknowledged as they entered. "We're setting up surveillance teams for the warehouse."

"There's more," Paxx said, handing him the note.

Kimble scanned it, his expression darkening.

"They are safe and, on their way out of town," Paxx said, struggling to steady her voice.

"This confirms we're getting close, and they're scared." Kimble spat.

"And they are getting desperate. Which makes them dangerous." Rowan added.

Kimble nodded. "I've got plainclothes officers monitoring Darby's residence and vehicle. These two teams will set up surveillance on the warehouse. "

"What about Pazinski and Hallman?" Paxx asked.

"Already covered," Kimble replied. "Pazinski's at home, according to his GPS, and Hallman left the precinct twenty minutes ago, heading east."

"I think it is safe to say the roaches are scattering now that the lights are being turned on," Rowan spat as he answered his ringing phone.

Paxx watched Rowan's face intently as he listened to the caller, noting how his expression shifted from concern to focused intensity.

"Send it to my phone," Rowan commanded before hanging up. He turned to Paxx and Kimble. "That was Forensics. They found something on the hard drive from Darby's computer, deleted emails between her and Hallman discussing a shipment coming in tonight."

"Tonight?" Kimble's eyebrows shot up. "What time?"

"Midnight," Rowan said, tapping rapidly on his phone as an email notification came through. "And they've got coordinates. It's not the warehouse we've been watching; it's an abandoned farm five miles south."

"They're using a decoy location. We'd have been watching the wrong place while they moved their product." Kimble said, picking up his phone.

Paxx felt her pulse quicken. "Hold on," she said, holding up her hand. "It doesn't make sense for them to email each other on work computers, knowing we had access to them."

Rowan's eyes met hers, understanding dawning on his face. "It could be a trap."

"Or they wanted us to find it," Kimble added, his jaw tightening. "But why?"

Paxx paced the small area, her mind racing through possibilities. "To get us all in one place. If they know we've discovered them, they could be setting us up. These are seasoned cops who know procedure. They wouldn't make such a basic mistake unless they were setting us up."

"The language here is too explicit. 'Shipment coming in at midnight' and 'Make sure everything's ready for distribution.' It's like they wanted to spell it out for anyone reading." Rowan commented.

Kimble set his phone down, his weathered face grave. "Team One, you go to the original location. Team Two, I want you at this new location. Gear up, tactical vests, and full comms. Once you arrive, I want a full report from each team."

Rowan motioned for team two to gather around as he pulled up the coordinates on his tablet, zooming in on the satellite view. "This location is isolated. Limited entry points, surrounded by open property. Perfect spot for an ambush."

Jackobson, the team leader, nodded, then led his team out of the room.

Paxx watched them go, but something kept nagging at her. She turned to Kimble. "Captain, they're trying to divide our resources. That's what they want."

"I agree," Kimble said, rubbing his chin. "But we can't ignore either location," his expression hardening with resolve. "I want eyes on both locations before we commit any officers inside. Drone surveillance first, and I want a third team ready to move at my command."

A knock at the conference room door caused them to turn around. A female officer stood in the doorway, "Detective Algatta, there is a Detective Rosalba from Pennsylvania here to see you."

Looking at Rowan and Kimble, Paxx nodded to the officer, "Bring her back."

Moments later, the slender woman with blonde hair pulled back in a tight ponytail and blue eyes entered the conference room. Her black slacks and white blouse were neatly pressed, and her badge was displayed on her hip beside her sidearm.

"Detective Algatta?" she smiled, her gaze sharp and assessing as she surveyed the room.

"Good to see you again, Detective Rosalba," Paxx replied, extending her hand. "This is my partner, Detective Taylor, and Captain Kimble."

"Detective Bailey Rosalba, Pennsylvania State Police," she said, her handshake firm. "I've been tracking a human trafficking ring with ties to the el aniquilacion organization for the past eighteen months."

Kimble gestured toward an empty chair. "Your timing is interesting, Detective."

Rosalba stayed on her feet. "We arrested a minor player two days ago who began talking to avoid the death penalty. He admitted to being involved in several shipments of girls being moved from Canada and Mexico to various states. Ian

Pazinski's name surfaced, and after we looked into him and then my Chief received a call from your brother Paul about Coleman. That's how I ended up here."

"Do you think your partner is involved in all of this?" Paxx asked.

"Unfortunately, yes." Bailey replied, "I wasn't sure until you and Paul showed up to question Clancy Devonshire. Once Coleman found out, he was insistent that we escort the two of you to the prison, and then when he got the call about Clancy's attack," she paused, meeting Paxx's eyes. "His reaction confirmed my suspicions."

"What happened after Clancy was attacked?" Kimble asked, leaning forward intently.

"Coleman made an urgent call to someone. When he got off, he told me he needed to return to the station, citing a development in another case. But he was sweating, agitated." Bailey's eyes narrowed. "I checked his phone records later. The call went to a burner."

Paxx exchanged a glance with Rowan. "And you believe Coleman is connected to Pazinski?"

"I know they are." Bailey pulled out her phone, swiped through a few screens, then turned it toward them. "This was taken six months ago at a hotel in St. Louis."

The photo showed Coleman and Pazinski smiling together at what appeared to be a hotel bar, Hallman visible in the background.

Paxx's jaw tightened. "So, Coleman's definitely connected to Darby and the others."

"I don't know about anyone named Darby, but I believe he is connected to Pazinski," Bailey nodded. "When I confronted him about his unusual behavior after you left, he claimed he was just stressed about a personal matter. But I've worked with him for three years, I know when he's lying."

Rowan crossed his arms. "What made you decide to come here now?"

"Because Coleman disappeared last night," Bailey said, pulling out her phone and showing them a text message. "He sent this claiming a family emergency, but when I checked with his sister, his only family, she hadn't heard from him in weeks."

Kimble's eyes narrowed. "You think he's here?"

"I think the fact that your father was killed after investigating Clancy Devonshire and you were shot after asking questions is no coincidence. I also don't believe Nemesio Guzman's daughter being kidnapped and ending up dead in your town is random." Bailey stated.

Paxx looked around the room, gauging Rowan and Kimble's reactions to Bailey's information, "How the hell do you know all of that?" Paxx spat, her eyes narrowing at Rowan.

"The FBI has been following this situation for years, and for the past eight months, I have been a liaison between them and our station," Bailey confessed.

Rowan's phone buzzed with an incoming message. "Surveillance team reports movement at the warehouse. Three SUVs just arrived."

"And Team Two is reporting no activity at the farm location," Kimble added, checking his own device.

"I think something big is happening tonight," Bailey confirmed. "I also have intel that Guzman's men are on their way here."

"We don't have the manpower to prevent a cartel war," Kimble barked.

"Knowing Guzman has moved out of Chicago, the FBI director is sending agents to assist." Baily nodded at Rowan.

"They will be here within the hour," Rowan replied, rechecking his phone.

Anger filled Paxx as she crossed the room, and shoved Rowan, "You fucking knew all of this?" she shouted.

Rowan staggered back a step but quickly regained his footing, his hands raised defensively. "Paxx, I couldn't tell you. I was under orders. And I didn't know about Bailey or Coleman specifically. This is as new to me as it is to you."

"Orders?" Paxx growled, her blue eyes blazing. "My family is being threatened, and in danger, and you've been holding back?"

Captain Kimble stepped between them. "Detective, stand down. That's an order."

Paxx backed up, her chest heaving, but she maintained her composure.

"Detective Algatta, I understand your anger, but Rowan was under strict orders. The cartel has informants everywhere, including police departments." Bailey said from behind her.

Paxx whirled around to face Bailey, "When Paul and I were in Pennsylvania, you knew all of this?"

"Detective," Kimble's voice cut through the tension. "We don't have time for this. Whatever Agent Taylor and Detective Rosalba knew or didn't know can be addressed later. Right now, we have three SUVs at the warehouse and potentially Guzman's men en route."

Paxx stepped back, her chest heaving with barely contained fury. She knew Kimble was right, but the betrayal stung deep. "Fine. But this isn't over," she said, fixing Rowan and Bailey with a cold stare.

"It's been a long time coming, Paxx," Rowan said quietly. "And when this is over, I'll explain everything. But right now, we need to focus on stopping these bastards and keeping this town and your family safe."

Paxx clenched her jaw but gave a curt nod. "So what's the plan, Captain?"

Kimble turned to the map on the table. "We need to co-ordinate with the FBI agents when they arrive. In the meantime, we'll maintain surveillance on both locations but won't engage. Bailey, what else can you tell us about Guzman's movements?"

"Our intelligence suggests he's personally coming to handle this situation," Bailey replied, pulling up an image on her phone. "This was taken at a private airfield outside Chicago six hours ago."

The grainy surveillance photo showed a distinguished older man with salt-and-pepper hair boarding a private jet.

Rowan looked at his phone. "Team One reports at least twelve individuals entering the warehouse. Heavily armed." He pointed to the warehouse schematic. "We need to move now, before this turns into an all-out war zone with civilians caught in the crossfire."

"Rowan, can you find out the agents' ETAs?" Kimble asked as a knock came from the door.

The four of them looked over, the same officer as before standing in the doorway.

"What is it?" Kimble nodded.

The officer's face was pale, and she looked frightened. "Sir, there is a gentleman here to see Detective Algatta."

"Who is it?" Paxx asked.

"He says he is here to collect his daughter's body," she continued, "Eliza Monterben."

The room fell silent, the tension palpable as Paxx locked eyes with Rowan.

"Nemesio Guzman is here?" Kimble asked.

Bailey's hand instinctively moved to her weapon. "He wouldn't come alone."

"No, he wouldn't," Paxx agreed, her mind racing. "But if he's walking into our station instead of sending his men to burn it down, he wants something beyond revenge."

"Where is he?" Kimble asked the officer.

"In the lobby, sir. He has four men with him. They're all armed," she stammered.

Kimble's expression hardened. "Tell them to surrender their weapons or they don't come any further into this building."

"With all due respect, Captain," Bailey interjected, "that's Nemesio Guzman. He's not going to disarm."

"This is our station," Kimble said. "Everyone plays by our rules."

Paxx took a deep breath. "I'll talk to him."

"Absolutely not," Rowan stated.

Kimble straightened his shoulders, his expression hardening with resolve. "Officer Jenkins, escort Mr. Guzman to interview room three. Tell him Detective Algatta will be with him shortly."

The young officer nodded nervously before disappearing.

? ? ?
FIFTY-ONE

"**I**'m going to talk to Mr. Guzman," Paxx said as she walked to the door. "Bailey, you listen in the observation room, and Rowan, you get a timeline for the feds' arrival. Looking at Kimble, Paxx shrugged. Sorry, sir, I didn't mean to take over.

Kimble shook his head. "No problem, Detective, I will update the Chief.

Paxx and Bailey left the room. Bailey stopped at the observation room while Paxx continued to the interview room next door. Opening the door, Paxx tried to keep calm when a large man pushed her up against the wall and patted her.

"Emilio," Guzman spat, "This is her house; we are guests."

Emilio stepped back, "Sorry, ma'am."

Paxx straightened her shirt, then took the seat across from Guzman. The man sitting across from her looked tired and worn despite the firm set of his jaw. Despite the graying of his hair, she guessed him to be in his late forties.

"Mr. Guzman, my name is Detective Paxxton Algatta. How can I help you?"

Meeting her gaze, Guzman sighed, "I have come to collect my daughter's body. I understand you are the officer who found her and killed the man responsible for her death."

Paxx's throat tightened as she studied the man before her. Nemesio Guzman, the second most powerful cartel leader in South America, was sitting across from her like any grieving father.

"Yes, sir. I'm very sorry for your loss." Her voice remained professional despite the surreal nature of the moment. "Your daughter's case is... complicated."

Guzman's eyes narrowed. "Complicated, how, Detective? Was she not murdered by this animal you shot?"

"Yes, sir, we believe so." Paxx placed her hands flat on the table. "But there's more to the story. Your daughter's death appears connected to a larger trafficking operation. She had a black rose tattoo on her shoulder. Does that mean anything to you?"

A flash of something, pain, recognition, or rage, crossed Guzman's face before his expression hardened again. "El Aniquilacion."

Emilio shifted uncomfortably behind his boss. Paxx noted the movement but kept her focus on Guzman.

Guzman looked at Emilio and nodded.

Emilio stepped out of the room with a look of understanding.

"May I ask how you knew she was here? We haven't released her identity to the public." Paxx asked, glancing up at the two-way mirror.

Guzman's jaw tightened. "My people have connections. When Luciana didn't come home, her sister called their mother. When she called, I sent people looking."

"Luciana, that was your daughter's name?"

"Named after my mother," he replied as he crossed himself in reference. We changed her and her sister's names when they came here for school, thinking it would keep them safe." He admitted sadly.

Standing, Guzman straightened his jacket, "I would like to see my daughter now, Detective."

"Of course," Paxx replied, stepping to the door. As they walked to the elevator, Paxx texted Dr. Margon, asking her to have Eliza's body ready for viewing and informing her about the situation of Eliza's father being present.

The elevator ride down to the first floor was silent and tense. Paxx could feel the weight of Guzman's grief filling the small space. Despite knowing who this man was and what he had done, she couldn't help but see the father beneath the criminal. Death was the great equalizer, stripping away titles and reputations, leaving only raw humanity.

"This way," Paxx directed when the doors opened, guiding Guzman down the corridor and across the short distance between buildings.

Dr. Margon was waiting outside the viewing room, her typically vibrant demeanor subdued. She nodded respectfully to Guzman.

"Mr. Guzman, I'm Dr. Margon."

"Doctor, is my daughter ready to go?"

Looking at Paxx, Dr Margon replied, "I just need Detective Algatta to sign release papers."

Paxx nodded, agreeing to the release. Stepping into the room, Guzman knelt beside the metal table that held his daughter's body and murmured what Paxx figured was a prayer. Paxx stepped back, giving the man privacy with his grief. Dr. Margon caught her eye and motioned toward the hallway.

"I'll be just outside," Paxx said, though she doubted Guzman heard her.

In the hallway, Dr. Margon handed Paxx a clipboard with release forms. "This is surreal," she whispered. "Nemesio Guzman himself in my morgue."

"I know." Paxx sighed as she signed the forms. "But right now, he's just a grieving father saying goodbye to his daughter."

The door opened, and Guzman emerged. His expression hardened again, grief locked away behind a mask of control. His eyes, however, remained red-rimmed.

"I have arranged transport," he said. "My people will handle everything from here."

Paxx nodded. "Of course."

"Detective, I would speak with you privately before I leave." Guzman nodded, his eyes harder now, calculation replacing grief.

Paxx exchanged a look with Dr. Margon, who discreetly stepped away. "Of course, Mr. Guzman."

Guzman's posture changed once they were alone, becoming more rigid and dangerous. "I want the cops responsible for my daughter's death."

Paxx's eyes widened. "How do you know officers are involved?"

"I have eyes and ears everywhere, Detective."

"I understand your grief, sir; I also understand the need for revenge. But I ask that you let us handle this. I do not want to put the innocent people of our town in danger by having a cartel war break out."

Guzman studied her face for a long moment, his dark eyes calculating. "You speak of innocent people, yet my innocent daughter is dead." His voice remained low but carried the weight of promised violence. "What justice can you offer that would satisfy me?"

Paxx met his gaze steadily. "Complete justice. Not just the trigger men but everyone involved, from top to bottom. I give you my word."

A humorless smile crossed Guzman's face. "Your word? What value does the word of a police detective hold against the life of my child?"

"I understand your skepticism," Paxx replied, not backing down. "But I'm not asking you to trust the badge. I'm asking you to trust the person wearing it." She took a breath. "I lost my father to corruption. He was a cop, too. His killers walked free because the system protected them. The same person responsible for his death is responsible for your daughters, and I will not let them go free again."

Guzman's expression shifted, something unreadable passing behind his eyes. "You speak of personal vendetta, Detective. This I understand." He stepped closer, lowering his voice. "Twenty-four hours. I will give you twenty-four hours to show me progress. After that..." He left the threat unspoken.

"I appreciate that, Mr. Guzman," Paxx said, maintaining her composure despite the implicit danger. "But I need something from you as well."

"And what would that be?"

"Information. You mentioned 'el aniquilacion when I told you about the black rose. What does it mean?"

Guzman's jaw tightened. "It is not a what, Detective. It is a who. A group that operates beyond borders, beyond laws." His voice dropped even lower. "Aniquilacion means annihilation in Spanish; these monsters are ruthless; all they care about is money and power."

Paxx met his gaze, and he smiled at the accusing words she did not say.

"I know what people say about me, Detective. I am ruthless and a killer, but I never hurt children or women. I deal in products and currency. Women and children are neither."

Paxx nodded, understanding the distinction he was making. "Do you have any names? Contacts? Anything that could help us track them?"

"These people hide in plain sight, Detective. They operate through legitimate businesses, politicians." Guzman's eyes darkened. "My daughter was studying political science at the university. She was... idealistic. Wanted to change the world." A brief flash of pain crossed his face. "I believe that is how they found her. They target those with connections, with potential influence." The words came out like poison. "My Luciana went to school here to have a legitimate life, away from..." He gestured vaguely to himself. "Her sister said she'd met someone, the daughter of a police officer."

Paxx's stomach tightened. "Do you know her name? Were they romantically involved?"

"No, and I don't know. Luciana was private about her relationships." His eyes hardened. "But I will find her. With or without your help."

Before Paxx could respond, the door opened, and Emilio returned with four men in dark suits. They carried a simple wooden casket.

Her stomach churned, but she maintained her professional demeanor. "Please contact me if you have any further information," Paxx said, handing Guzman her card.

Taking the card, he opened his coat and pulled a card from the inside pocket. "You do the same, Detective, and again, thank you for bringing justice to one of the men who killed my daughter. I am in your debt."

Guzman and one of his men disappeared out the door while three more carefully laid his daughter in the casket.

"I didn't know the man you shot was the one who killed her," Dr. Margon said as she stepped up beside Paxx.

Paxx shrugged, "I don't know that he is, but I also don't know that he isn't."

"Holy, shit Paxx, you lied to Nemesio Guzman?" Elizabeth whispered.

Paxx and Elizabeth nodded to the three men as they carried the casket through the door, disappearing outside.

"I want him out of our town as soon as possible," Paxx said once the door closed.

"I don't blame you," Dr. Margon replied, her eyes still fixed on the door where Guzman's men had disappeared. "How'd you manage to keep your cool through all that?"

Paxx let out a breath she hadn't realized she was holding. "Practice. Lots of practice." She checked her watch, aware that Guzman's twenty-four-hour countdown had already begun ticking.

Dr. Margon let out a slow breath. "You think he's going to cause trouble?"

"I think he's already causing trouble," Paxx said, watching through the window as the men loaded the casket into a sleek black SUV. "But not in the way you might expect."

"What do you mean?" she asked.

Paxx turned the business card over in her hand. It was cream-colored with embossed gold lettering. Simple, elegant, and terrifying in what it represented. "He gave me twenty-four hours to show progress before he takes matters into his own hands."

Dr. Margon's eyes widened. "Jesus, Paxx."

"Yeah." She pocketed the card. "I need to get back upstairs. Thanks for handling this."

"Of course. And Paxx, be careful."

"Always," Paxx replied, exiting the building.

During the elevator ride, Paxx's mind raced through the new information: Aniquilacion, the daughter of a police officer. When the doors opened, Rowan was waiting, arms crossed over his chest.

"How'd it go with the cartel boss?"

Leading him to the broken camera interview room, Paxx filled him in on everything Guzman had told her.

"What will you do about giving him Hallman's and Pazinski's names?" Rowan asked once Paxx had finished.

She leaned against the table and said, "I can't tell him who they are. I mean, we don't know which one or if either of them is responsible for his daughter being taken. For all we know, Shannon set the whole thing up."

As they sat in silence, Paxx's phone buzzed. Pulling it from her back pocket, she read a text from Paul: 'Can you meet me and Jake across the street at the library?'

'Be there in three,' Paxx responded, pushing off the table and reaching for the doorknob. "I need to run an errand. Be back in thirty," she told Rowan as she opened the door.

As she entered the library, Paul met her outside one of the private reading rooms.

"What's going on?" she asked when he guided her inside and closed the door.

"She's here, Trace," Jake said into his phone before putting it on speaker.

"Hey, Paxx," Tracie greeted.

"Hey, what's up?"

"Tracie is meeting Jimmy and the girls in Bringham," Jake responded.

"Okay, is something wrong?" Paxx questioned.

"No, nothing is wrong," Tracie replied, "But I did find something in your dad's notes that urged me to make sure Anna and Jaylee could not be tracked, so I am taking them my Jeep and burner phones."

"What did you find?" Paxx asked, trying to keep the fear out of her voice.

"If I read the connections your dad made correctly, he believed Shannon Darby is Nemesio Guzman's niece," Tracie said.

"What?" Paxx spat, "How is that possible?"

"I don't know," Tracie replied, "But your dad was pretty certain."

"I will have Rowan do a deep dive on her when I return to the station," Paxx commented. "Speaking of Guzman, I just talked with him at the precinct."

In unison, they all said, "WHAT?"

Paxx nodded. "He came to claim his daughter's body," she continued, filling them in on the conversation and information they had exchanged. "So I guess we can rule Shannon out as the person who arranged Eliza's kidnapping," she finished.

"Holy shit," Tracie said through the phone.

"That doesn't necessarily rule Shannon out," Paul interjected. "Family ties don't always mean loyalty. She could be working against her uncle."

"If she's related to Guzman, why is she here in Ivan Hope? It can't be a coincidence." Jake added, running a hand through his hair.

Paxx leaned against the table, her mind racing. "If Shannon is Guzman's niece and Eliza Luciana was dating the daughter of a police officer..." She trailed off, the implications settled heavily between them.

"You think Shannon set up her own cousin?" Paul asked, his voice low.

"I don't know what to think anymore," Paxx admitted, glancing at her watch. "Guzman gave me twenty-four hours to show progress before he takes matters into his own hands. We need to work fast."

"Do you have a bead on Shannon?" Jake asked.

"No," Paxx replied. "She took a large sum of money from her bank account and hasn't shown up at home. We cannot track her phone; it must be turned off, and her car is at her house."

"Has anyone done a well check at her house?" Paul asked.

Paxx shook her head, "I don't think so, you don't think?" She couldn't finish the sentence. Even though Paxx knew Shannon was somehow involved, it didn't negate the fact that she had known her for seventeen years.

"If whoever is in charge is cleaning house, I am sure Allan will not be the last person we find that they have eliminated." Paul sighed.

"Paul and I will go by her house," Jake interjected.

Paxx nodded in agreement.

"I should be back in about an hour," Tracie said from the phone. "I will drop off phones for Paxx and Paul so you can keep in touch with Anna and Jaylee."

"Thank you, Tracie. I very much appreciate you," Paxx replied.

"Me too," Paul added.

"I'm happy to help," she replied. "I will talk to everyone soon." Then the line went dead.

Paxx stood, glancing at her watch again. "I need to get back to the station. Rowan and I need to track down this el aniquilacion group."

"Be careful, Paxx," Paul said, his expression solemn. "If Shannon really is Guzman's niece, and she's involved in all this…"

"I know. We've got corruption in the department, a cartel boss giving us ultimatums, and a trafficking ring possibly connected to another cartel. Just another day in Ivan Hope."

Jake's mouth turned up in a humorless smile. "We'll call as soon as we check Shannon's place."

Paxx nodded, then headed for the door. "Thanks. Both of you."

Paxx gave her brother a quick hug before heading back to the station. The weight of Guzman's deadline pressed down on her, a constant reminder of how quickly things could spiral out of control.

FIFTY-TWO

When she returned to the precinct, Rowan was waiting at his desk, his face unreadable.

"The feds will be here in three hours," he said as she approached. "Kimble's been calling every fifteen minutes for updates."

"Great." Paxx sat down, pulling up Shannon's personnel file. "I need you to call your buddies at the bureau and have them do a deep dive into Shannon."

"Okay, why?" Rowan asked as he picked up his phone.

"My friend Tracie, a PI, has been looking into my father's old notes and case files. In my dad's notes, she found references about Shannon possibly being Nemesio Guzman's niece." Paxx watched Rowan's expression go from curiosity to understanding.

"If she is, that would explain so much." He replied, dialing the phone.

Once he hung up, Paxx asked, "What would it explain?"

Rowan leaned forward, lowering his voice even though they were alone. "Shannon's file never quite added up. Her background is too clean, too perfect. The kind of record you see when someone's had professional help constructing it."

He tapped his fingers against the desk. "If she's connected to Guzman, it would explain her rapid rise through the ranks."

"And her access to sensitive information about operations across multiple jurisdictions," Paxx added, the pieces clicking into place. "What I don't understand is, if Hallman or Pazinski were involved in Eliza's kidnapping and ultimately her death, why didn't she intervene? Not just because it was her cousin, but Guzman despises human trafficking, and by the way he talked about it, I am sure he was being truthful."

"Maybe she couldn't," Rowan suggested, his brow furrowed in concentration. "If Shannon is playing both sides, she'd have to be careful about showing her hand. Intervening directly could have exposed her position."

Paxx nodded slowly, considering the possibility. "Or maybe she was the one who arranged it in the first place. If she's connected to this Aniquilacion group and not just her uncle..."

"It would be the perfect cover," Rowan finished. "A respected officer with connections to law enforcement and two of the most powerful cartels in South America."

Paxx's phone buzzed with a text from Jake: 'At Shannon's. Door unlocked. The house is clear, but signs of struggle in the living room. Blood on carpet.'

"Shit," Paxx muttered, showing Rowan the message.

"You think they got to her?" Rowan asked.

"Maybe, but the bigger question is who?" she replied as she responded to Jake's text, 'How much blood? Did you find her phone?'

Jake sent a picture of a large blood stain on the carpet a moment later. 'No phone, lots of blood.'

Showing Rowan the photo, Paxx stood, "I need to show this to Kimble.'

Paxx raced down the hallway to Kimble's office, Rowan close behind. Without knocking, she pushed open the door, finding Kimble on the phone. He held up a finger, signaling for them to wait.

"Yes, sir. I understand the urgency... No, sir, I'm not suggesting we delay, just that we proceed cautiously..." Kimble's expression tightened. "Of course. We'll be ready."

He hung up, looking at Paxx and Rowan with tired eyes. "That was the Chief. The FBI's ETA has been moved up. They'll be here in an hour."

"Sir, we have a situation," Paxx said, holding out her phone with the blood-stained carpet photo. "This is from Shannon Darby's house. My brother and his partner just checked it out—door unlocked, signs of a struggle, blood on the carpet."

Kimble's face paled. "Christ." He took the phone, studying the image more closely. "That's a lot of blood."

"There's more," Paxx said, glancing at Rowan. "We have reasons to suspect that Shannon Darby could be Nemesio Guzman's niece.

Kimble slammed his hand on the desk, exclaiming, "Can we not catch a fucking break?" His face turned a deep shade of red with anger.

Paxx worried that he might suffer a stroke or a heart attack if he didn't calm down. "Jacob, take a breath," she advised him soothingly.

Kimble shut his eyes, taking several deep breaths in and out. "Thanks, Paxxton," he said, locking eyes with her.

"Your wife would have our heads if you keeled over," Paxx joked.

Kimble laughed, "Indeed, she would, and her temper makes the cartel look like kittens."

"Yes, sir," Paxx replied, returning to a professional tone. "We really need to know if Shannon is related to Guzman," Paxx continued. "If she is, and he finds out she is missing, possibly hurt or dead, what is already a bad situation will get a hell of a lot worse."

"I'll call my guy and see if he has found anything, maybe light a fire under his ass to hurry up," Rowan said as he left the room.

"How did our quiet town turn into a drug, weapons, and trafficking hub?" Kimble asked Paxx, not expecting an answer.

"Complacency," Paxx replied.

Kimble nodded. "You're right. We got comfortable and thought we were immune to the big-city problems. Meanwhile, they were setting up shop right under our noses."

"And we have to consider that Shannon might have been helping them all along," Paxx said, the weight of the betrayal settling in her chest. "If she's been feeding information to Guzman or el aniquilacion or both..."

Kimble leaned back in his chair, his shoulders sagging.

The door opened, and Rowan stepped back in, his expression grim. "My contact at the Bureau just sent over some preliminary findings. Shannon Darby isn't her real name. She was born Alonsa Ortega Riviera."

"So not Guzman?" Paxx questioned.

"Guzman's wife is her mother's sister." Rowan replied.

"We really need to find..." Paxx started and then paused when her phone buzzed. Looking at the screen, she saw a text from an unknown number. Opening the text, she was surprised to see Shannon's name. "It's a text from Shannon."

'Paxx, I know you think I am involved in all of this, and I am, just not in the way everyone thinks. Meet me at the coffee house on the corner of Hill and Blane; I will explain everything.'

"What does it say?" Kimble asked.

"She wants me to meet her, and she says she is involved, but not how everyone thinks," Paxx replied, rereading the text.

"I'm going with you," Rowan demanded.

Paxx took a minute to think, running scenarios over in her mind. "No," She replied, then texted Tracie.

'How far out are you?'

'Fifteen minutes.'

'Meet me at Jillian's Coffee House.'

'Be there ASAP.'

"You're not going alone," Kimble interjected.

"No, I'm not going alone, but we need information, and I think if I go as a friend, I will get some."

"I will be in a car down the street," Rowan said, leaving no room for discussion.

"Okay." Paxx agreed, texting Shannon back, telling her she would arrive in fifteen minutes.

Paxx drove to Jillian's Coffee with her mind racing. Could Shannon really be innocent in all this? Or was this an elaborate trap? Either way, she needed answers, and this might be her only chance to get them directly from the source.

She parked half a block away, scanning the area for anything suspicious before heading inside. The coffee shop was nearly empty, just a barista wiping down the counter and an elderly couple in the corner sharing a pastry.

Paxx ordered a black coffee and chose a table with her back to the wall, giving her a clear view of both entrances. She checked her watch. Five minutes until Tracie would arrive, and Rowan was already positioned in an unmarked car down the street.

The bell above the door jingled, and Shannon walked in. She looked nothing like the polished, confident detective Paxx knew. Her hair was pulled back in a messy ponytail, her clothes rumpled, and a large bandage was above her right eyebrow. She scanned the room, spotting Paxx and making her way over.

"Thanks for meeting me," Shannon said as she slid into the seat across from Paxx.

"Want some coffee?" Paxx asked when she saw the barista look over at Shannon with a frown.

Shannon turned and looked at the counter. The barista pointed at a sign that read, 'Everyone must make a purchase; this is not a gathering place.'

"How does this place stay in business?" Shannon sighed as she stood and walked to the counter, returning with a cup of black coffee. "Five bucks for a cup of coffee, Christ."

Paxx surveyed the area, uncomfortable with Shannon's lack of unease. A minute after Shannon returned to the table, Tracie walked through the door, stopping at the counter, then sliding in beside Paxx with a cup of something that smelled like vanilla and had a heap of whipped cream on the top.

"Shannon, this is my friend, Tracie," Paxx introduced, once again uneasy that a stranger did not seem to bother her.

Shannon nodded at Tracie before turning her attention back to Paxx. "Nice to meet you, but I hoped we'd talk alone."

"Tracie stays. She's been helping me with my father's case."

Something flickered in Shannon's eyes, uncertainty, maybe even fear. She took a sip of her coffee, grimacing at the taste. "Fine. I don't have much time anyway."

"What happened to your head?" Paxx asked, gesturing to the bandage.

Shannon's hand unconsciously went to the wound. "That's part of why I'm here. Three men broke into my house last night. I managed to fight them off, but not before one of them got me with the butt of his gun." She leaned forward, lowering her voice. "They were el aniquilacion, Paxx. They came for me."

"Why would they come after you if you're Guzman's niece?" Tracie asked bluntly.

Shannon's eyes widened before narrowing. "I see you've been busy."

"Shannon, I need you to tell me what the hell is going on," Paxx demanded. "How are you involved?"

Shannon took a deep breath. "Yes, my uncle is Nemesio Guzman, and no, I am not involved, at least not in how you think."

"Yeah," Paxx spat, "And how do I think you are involved?"

"You think I am part of Pazinski and Hallman's operation," she replied.

"What is their operation?" Tracie asked.

"They look the other way when el aniquilacion runs drugs, guns, or girls through here," Shannon responded, unconcerned.

"How long have you known about this?"

"I stumbled upon the information a little over three years ago."

"Is this why my dad was killed?"

Shannon's expression darkened. She stared into her coffee for a long moment before meeting Paxx's gaze. "Yes. Your father was investigating Pazinski and Hallman. He didn't know about me or my connection to Nemesio, but he knew something wasn't right with the department."

Paxx's hands clenched around her coffee cup. "So, you knew who killed my father all this time?"

"It's not that simple. I suspected, but I didn't have proof. And I couldn't go around accusing fellow officers without evidence."

"Bullshit, you're Nemesio Guzman's niece. You could have gotten the proof."

"That's exactly why I couldn't! Do you have any idea what position I'm in?"

"Why don't you tell me!"

"I came to the States for a better life," Shannon replied, "A life away from drugs and guns. By the time I was old enough to leave home and attend college, I had seen enough bloodshed to last a lifetime. I wanted to make a difference I could never make back home, so I went to college and got a degree in forensic studies. When my parents learned I was an American cop in a small town, Uncle Neme demanded I find a way to use this place as a depot for his product."

"So, you told him to find someone else?" Paxx asked, skeptical.

Shannon let out a humorless laugh. "You don't tell Nemesio Guzman 'no.' Not even family. But I could stall, redirect. I convinced him I could be more valuable as a clean law enforcement officer who could warn of investigations and provide intelligence." She leaned forward. "I fed him just enough to keep him satisfied while ensuring his operations stayed out of Chandler County."

"Until they didn't," Tracie observed.

"Until el aniquilacion moved in," Shannon corrected. "That changed everything. My uncle may be a cartel leader, but he has a code. Human trafficking violates everything he stands for."

"So, what do Hallman and Pazinski have to do with all this? How did they get involved with el aniquilacion?" Paxx asked as her unease continued.

"I don't know how it started, but I do know Pazinski is the one who brought Hallman and eventually Gregory in," Shannon said, checking her watch.

Paxx looked around the room and nudged Tracie's leg with her knee. Tracie nudged her back, understanding her concern.

"Do you want another coffee?" Tracie asked as she stood, drawing Shannon's attention away just long enough for Paxx to remove her gun from her shoulder holster, holding it under the table out of sight.

"No, I'm good," Shannon replied, returning her attention to Paxx.

Tracie walked to the counter, and Paxx watched as she typed on her phone before removing her jacket, then her pistol from its holster, placing her jacket over her forearm and hand.

Paxx squeezed the grip of her weapon beneath the table, keeping her face neutral as she asked, "Who else besides Pazinski, Hallman, and Gregory are involved?"

Shannon's eyes darted to the door again before returning to Paxx. "There are at least a dozen officers across four departments, judges, and prosecutors across three states. It's a network, Paxx. That's why I couldn't just go to the Chief or Internal Affairs."

"And my father figured it out," Paxx said, the realization heavy in her voice.

"He was getting too close. Your father was meticulous, Paxx. He'd been collecting evidence for months before they killed him."

"Then why didn't you come to me with this information?" Paxx demanded, her finger resting beside the trigger guard.

Shannon's eyes hardened. "Because I was trying to protect you."

As Tracie returned to the table, Paxx noticed a black SUV pulling up outside, its windows tinted too dark to see inside. Her instincts screamed danger.

"Time's up," Shannon muttered, glancing toward the window. "I can't be seen with you any longer."

"You're not going anywhere until you tell me who killed my father," Paxx said, her voice low and threatening.

Shannon's eyes darted between Paxx and the door. "It was Hallman. At least I was told he was the one who pulled the trigger, I was also told that Pazinski ordered it. Your father had evidence connecting them to el aniquilacion, financial records, and meeting logs. He was going to take it to the FBI."

"And you let them kill him," Paxx accused, tightening her grip on the concealed weapon.

"I didn't know until it was too late," Shannon insisted.

"You're going back to the precinct with us," Paxx demanded. Tracie took the hint and stood, blocking the view from the road.

"I can't go back, Paxx, I'm already dead if I do," Shannon said, fear evident in her eyes. "The men who came to my house weren't just after me, they were sent to silence me. Hallman found out I've been feeding information to my uncle about their operation."

The black SUV's doors opened, and three men in dark clothing stepped out.

Paxx glanced at the SUV again. "Who's in the vehicle?"

"My uncle's men," Shannon replied, her expression shifting to something Paxx couldn't quite read.

"If they're your uncle's men, why do you look so scared?" Tracie asked, her hand tightening around her concealed weapon.

Shannon's composure faltered. "Because they're not here to save me. They're here to take me back to him."

"I thought you said your uncle had a code," Paxx said, watching as the men approached the coffee shop door.

"He does. But in his world, family betrayal is the worst offense." Shannon's voice trembled. "I've been playing both sides too long, Paxx. Nemesio found out I was withholding information about el aniquilacion's operations here."

The bell above the door jingled as two of the men entered. The barista took one look at them and disappeared into the back room. The elderly couple hurriedly gathered their belongings and shuffled out.

"Look, I've prepared a file with everything I know, names, dates, locations. It's taped to the bottom of the third drawer of my desk."

"Why are you telling me this now?"

"Because someone needs to finish what your father started, and I won't be able to."

Tracie and Paxx stood, but as Paxx lifted her weapon, Shannon stepped in front of her. "Paxx, don't please, they will not hesitate to kill both of you, I made my choices and now I have to answer for them. "

Paxx holstered her weapon, then pulled Shannon into a firm embrace. "You have always been a good friend to me, Shannon. I just wish you had come to me." Paxx whispered against her ear.

Shannon hugged Paxx, gripping the back of her shirt. "So do I, Paxx, so do I." Leaning back, Shannon covered Paxx's mouth, kissing her. "I wish we could have had at least one night together," she whispered as she turned and walked away, letting the two men lead her to the SUV.

Paxx watched as Shannon was led into the SUV, her heart pounding with conflicted emotions. The third man lingered at the door, making eye contact with Paxx before following his companions. The message was clear: don't follow.

"Holy shit," Tracie muttered beside her. "Are we just going to let them take her?"

"We don't have a choice," Paxx replied, her voice hollow. "If those are Guzman's men, interfering would only get us killed." Paxx stood frozen in place, the taste of Shannon's kiss still lingering on her lips as she watched the SUV pull away. Her mind raced with conflicting emotions, betrayal, confusion, and an unexpected ache that felt dangerously close to regret.

Paxx pulled out her phone and dialed Rowan. "Did you see that?" she asked when he answered.

"I saw it," Rowan confirmed, his voice tight with tension. "Black SUV, three men, they took Shannon. I've got the plate."

"We need to get back to the precinct," Paxx replied, walking to the door.

"What happened in there?" Rowan demanded, meeting them at the door. "Who were those men?"

"Guzman's people," Paxx said, her voice tight. Turning to Tracie, Paxx said, "If you come upstairs with me, I will get you the file Shannon said she has."

Tracie nodded as she placed her gun in its holster and slipped on her jacket.

Looking at Rowan, she demanded, "Find out what is going on at the warehouse."

? ? ?
FIFTY-THREE

T he three of them hurried to their vehicles. As Paxx slid behind the wheel, her mind replayed the last few minutes with Shannon. The fear in her eyes, the unexpected kiss, the resignation in her voice. Had Shannon truly been trying to play both sides? Or was there something more she wasn't telling them?

Ten minutes later, they pulled into the precinct parking lot. The FBI would be arriving soon, and Paxx needed to find that file before anyone else did. She led Tracie through the building, avoiding as many people as possible. Once at Shannon's desk, Tracie stood watch as Paxx pulled out the third drawer on the left, finding nothing, then the one on the right, "Shit," Paxx spat, finding only remnants of tape.

Looking over at her, Tracie said, "Pull the drawer all the way out, see if it's lying on the floor."

After fighting to get the drawer out, Paxx sighed at seeing a dark blue plastic envelope. Picking it up, she slid the drawer back into place. Then, leading Tracie to the nearest women's restroom and checking that all the stalls were empty, Paxx slid it into the back of Tracie's jeans, covering it with her shirt and jacket.

While in the privacy of the bathroom, Tracie took a phone from the inside pocket of her jacket and handed it to Paxx. "Jaylee, Anna, and Jimmy's numbers are all programmed in, I told them you would call once you had the phone. I will take Paul's to him as soon as I leave here."

Paxx hugged Tracie, "I can never thank you enough for all you have done these past few days."

Tracie returned the embrace, "You would do the same for me."

"Always."

They hurried out of the bathroom and to the nearest elevator. Paxx rode down with her and outside to Jimmy's truck. "Be careful, Tracie," Paxx urged.

"You too, and call me if you need anything else," Tracie replied before climbing into the truck.

Paxx watched her drive away as she called Jaylee.

"Paxx?" Jaylee answered.

"Yeah, beautiful, it's me," Paxx replied, relieved to hear her voice.

"Oh, thank God," Jaylee's voice cracked with emotion. "Are you okay? What's happening?"

"I'm fine," Paxx assured her, scanning the parking lot for any signs of surveillance. "But things are getting complicated. I need you to stay put until I tell you otherwise. The FBI is about to arrive, and I don't know how this will play out. How are you and Anna holding up?"

"We're managing. Paxx, I love you."

"I love you too," Paxx replied, fighting to keep her voice steady. "Listen, Jaylee, I need you to stay put until I give the all-clear."

"I understand, but when this is over..."

"When this is over, I am going to make love to you every day for a week."

"Twice on Saturday and Sunday?"

"As many times as you want, my dear. I promise."

"I am going to hold you to that."

"Please do. I have to go. Give Anna and Embry hugs for me, and I promise to call as soon as I can." Paxx began walking back to the entrance when she saw five black SUVs with government plates pull up in front of the building. "I love you so much. Don't ever forget that."

"I love you, too, and Paxx, please be careful. You promised always to come home to me."

"I will come home to you, Jay, I promise." With those words, Paxx ended the call and rushed into the building, taking the stairs two at a time to try to beat the elevator.

Paxx burst onto the fourth floor, breathing hard from the sprint up the stairs. She spotted Rowan standing near Kimble's office, his back rigid as he watched the elevator doors. When he turned and saw her, relief washed over his face.

"They're here," he said as the elevator doors opened, revealing three men and two women in dark suits. Their expressions were grim, their movements precise as they entered the hallway.

Leading them was a tall woman with sharp features and perfect posture who surveyed the room with calculating eyes.

"Captain Kimble," she asked as Kimble emerged from his office. "I'm Special Agent Vivian Martin, FBI Public Corruption and Civil Rights Task Force. We spoke on the phone."

Kimble stepped forward, extending his hand. "Agent Martin. We've been expecting you."

"I understand you've had quite the situation developing here," Martin said, her gaze sweeping across the room before landing on Paxx. "And you must be Detective Algatta."

Paxx straightened her shoulders, meeting the woman's penetrating stare. "Yes, ma'am."

"I've heard a lot about you." Martin nodded, extending her hand. "Special Agent Taylor speaks very highly of you."

Shaking her hand, Paxx looked at Rowan, his cheeks flushed red. "Really? And here I was thinking he thought I was as big a pain in the ass as he is."

Vivian laughed, a hearty sound that caught Paxx off guard. "She is just as you described her, Agent Taylor."

Rowan cleared his throat. "We should move this to the conference room, ma'am."

"Of course," Agent Martin nodded, turning to Kimble. "Captain, I'd like Detective Algatta to brief my team immediately. We are not here to take over and blow up your case. We are here to support and fill in any way needed."

"Thank you, ma'am," Paxx nodded in appreciation.

"Please, detective, call me Agent Martin or Vivian. We are on the same side, and I am sure you have worked as hard for respect as I have, so we are on the same level." Agent Martin replied.

"Thank you, Agent Martin," Paxx replied.

The conference room was filled with FBI agents and select IHPD officers. Paxx noticed how the federal agents positioned themselves, always maintaining sight lines to the doors and never clustering together too closely. These weren't regular field agents; they moved with the practiced caution of people who had worked dangerous undercover operations.

"Detective Algatta," Martin began once everyone was seated, "I understand you've uncovered evidence of a significant trafficking operation connected to your department. Can you give us a rundown on the players and where we stand with the surveillance at the warehouse?"

Paxx nodded as she stood in front of the room and confidently relayed all that had happened in the past month and what she knew of her father's investigation into the Black Rose killings and trafficking ring. Thirty minutes later, Chief Morison entered the room, his expression bleak.

Paxx watched as Morrison and Kimble spoke. Glancing up at her, Kimble frowned, then nodded to Morison before approaching the front of the room.

"The Chief just received a call from his brother-in-law. He lives a few miles from the warehouse on old Route 246," Kimble began. "On his way home, he noticed a lot of activity, so he pulled over and watched for a few minutes. He says several vehicles were going in and out of the building."

"We need to move now," Paxx replied.

"The Chief is already calling team 2 and sending them over," Kimble said as he pulled out his phone. "You take everyone here to the warehouse. I will have team 1 stand by where they are."

Turning to face the room, Paxx announced, "Everyone, suit up. We are leaving in five."

Every eye in the room locked on Paxx. The FBI agents were already standing, hands instinctively checking weapons and comms. Rowan moved to her side, his presence steady and reassuring.

"We'll take my team's vehicles," Agent Martin announced, her voice calm but carrying the unmistakable edge of someone accustomed to running high-stakes operations. "Detective Algatta, you ride with me and Agent Taylor. I want to hear every detail about this warehouse on the way."

Paxx nodded, her heart pounding in her chest, her side aching with the memory of nearly dying on the cold concrete floor of the very warehouse she was about to revisit. 'You've been back there, you've faced your demons; you can do this,' she reminded herself.

The next few minutes passed in a blur of controlled chaos, agents checking tactical gear, officers coordinating with dispatch, and weapons being distributed.

In the precinct parking lot, Paxx climbed into the back seat of Martin's SUV and listened as Rowan told Martin everything they knew about the warehouse and operation.

"Why didn't you have this warehouse under surveillance?" Martin asked, looking at Paxx through the rearview mirror.

"It was a crime scene a little over a month ago; we didn't think they would return," Paxx explained. "We weren't expecting them to be so bold."

"What kind of crime scene?" Martin asked.

Paxx paused before answering, "I was shot. If Rowan had not been there, I most likely would have died."

Martin met Paxx's eyes in the mirror. "Them returning is bold and stupid."

Paxx stared out the window as they sped through town, the flashing lights of the convoy reflecting off storefronts and parked cars. Her thoughts drifted to Jaylee, to the promise she'd made to come home. The weight of that promise settled heavily on her chest, mingling with the familiar burn of adrenaline.

"I need to know what we're walking into," Agent Martin said, her voice cutting through Paxx's thoughts. "You've been inside. What's the layout?"

Paxx leaned forward. "The main entrance leads to a large open area, two corridors branch off—one connects to an adjoining smaller building, and the other to small rooms. There are three floors; the upper floors used to be offices, and each floor has a landing or mezzanine that overlooks the floor below."

"What kind of business did it used to be?" Martin asked.

"A hub for online stores. It only lasted about five years before they realized a place where the winters weren't so harsh would be a better fit for easy shipping. It was a major loss for our town." Paxx recalled.

"Large loading docks at the rear, steel catwalks, and plenty of blind spots. The upper floors have large windows, but most are boarded or painted over." Rowan continued.

"Sounds like a tactical nightmare," Martin muttered, turning onto the highway. The convoy of black SUVs and unmarked police vehicles stretched behind them, lights flashing. "How many entrances and exits?"

"Three that we know of," Rowan interjected. "Main entrance, loading dock, and a side door that leads to what was once the employee parking lot."

"Any idea where they would house people?" Martin asked

"The small rooms would be my best guess." Paxx answered, "We didn't find evidence that they had been holding people there."

"They could have moved them once they thought there wasn't a threat of you coming back," Martin replied.

"That's probably what Shannon and I stumbled on last Sunday when we were there." Paxx sighed, mentally kicking herself.

"What do you mean?" Rowan asked.

"I wanted to come back out here, face my mortality," Paxx explained. "Anyway, when I mentioned it to Shannon, she offered to come with me. When we got there, there were three men already in the building. We never got a look at them, but one of the voices was familiar. That night, I finally realized the voice was from the man who shot me. I don't know who he is, but I will never forget that voice."

"We're coming up on the turn," Rowan interrupted. "About half a mile ahead. There's an access road that cuts through the woods, gives us cover to approach from the east."

"I want drones in the air as soon as we're within range," Martin instructed through her radio. "And thermal imaging. I need to know how many bodies we're dealing with before we make a move."

"Copy that," came the immediate response over the radio.

The convoy slowed as they approached the turnoff, headlights cutting off in sequence. Paxx felt her pulse quicken as the warehouse came into view through the trees.

Martin pulled onto the access road, tires crunching over gravel and fallen branches. The thick canopy of trees shielded them from view as they advanced toward the warehouse.

Through gaps in the foliage, Paxx could see lights blazing from the building's windows.

"They're not even trying to be subtle," Rowan muttered, checking his weapon.

"Arrogance or urgency," Martin replied.

"There hasn't been power out here for years," Paxx said as she looked out the window. They must have generators running lights."

Within minutes, the tactical teams were deployed around the outskirts of the warehouse. Drones hummed softly overhead, their cameras feeding real-time images to tablets in the command vehicle. Paxx stood behind Martin, watching heat signatures bloom across the screen, at least twenty figures moving inside the building.

"Multiple subjects on all three floors," the tech operator reported. "Heaviest concentration in the northeast corner of the main building."

"That must be where they are keeping the girls," Paxx replied as she tightened her vest and readied her weapon.

"This is your show, Detective. How do you want to proceed?" Martin asked, pulling on her vest and preparing her rifle.

Paxx studied the thermal imaging pattern of movement. Her mind raced through tactical possibilities, weighing risks against the situation's urgency.

"Three teams," she decided, her voice steady. "One through the main entrance as a distraction, one through the loading dock to secure the victims, and a small team through the side entrance to cut off any escape routes." She pointed to the screen. "I want snipers positioned here and here to cover the upper floors."

Martin nodded approvingly. "Clean and direct. I like it."

"The northeast corner is our priority," Paxx continued. "That's where the victims are likely being held. We need to secure that area first, before anyone can use them as hostages or worse."

Rowan stepped forward, checking his tactical gear. "I'll lead the team through the side entrance."

"And I'll take point on the main," Kimble's voice boomed behind them.

Paxx swung around. Captain Kimble and Reynolds from Homicide stood behind them in full tactical gear.

"You didn't think we would let you have all the fun, did you?" Kimble chuckled.

Paxx smiled, although it felt more like a grimace. "Sir?"

Kimble nodded toward the warehouse. "This is still your show, Detective. Please continue."

Paxx nodded, turning back to the tactical plan. "I'll take the loading dock team. That's where the victims will need immediate assistance."

"I'm with you," Martin said, checking her weapon one final time.

"All teams, check comms," Paxx instructed, pressing her earpiece in place. A series of confirmations echoed through the channel.

❓❓❓
FIFTY-FOUR

The teams dispersed to their positions, moving through the afternoon light. Paxx led her group around the warehouse's perimeter, keeping low as they approached the loading dock.

"All teams in position," came the whispered confirmation through her earpiece.

"On my mark, three... two... one... execute."

The coordinated assault began with precision. Flash-bangs detonated at the main entrance as Kimble's team stormed in, their shouts echoing through the cavernous space. Simultaneously, Paxx's team breached the loading dock, spreading out in sets of two and covering as much area as possible.

Gunfire erupted from the upper floors, bullets pinging off metal surfaces and embedding in concrete.

"Multiple armed suspects on the catwalks," Rowan's voice crackled through her earpiece. "We've got movement toward the northeast corner."

"They're trying to reach the victims," Paxx responded, signaling her team to advance.

"Movement to your right," Martin whispered into her comm.

Paxx pivoted, catching a glimpse of a figure darting between crates. "Police! Don't move!"

A burst of gunfire erupted from behind a stack of pallets. Paxx and Martin dove for cover as bullets splintered the wooden crate beside them.

"Two shooters, northeast corner," Paxx reported into her comm. "Cover me!"

Martin nodded, raising her rifle and providing suppressive fire as Paxx sprinted across the open space toward a hallway. The familiar layout of the warehouse gave her an advantage; she knew where she needed to go. The northeast corner had once been administrative offices, later converted to storage rooms with heavy doors. Perfect for holding captives.

"Shots fired, east corridor," Kimble reported, his voice strained.

"We have to get to the victims before they do," Paxx barked into her comms, an urgency settling in her chest.

"I'm right behind you, Algatta," Martin called out.

As they emerged from the corridor, gunfire erupted down the hallway further away, but still too close for comfort.

Paxx and Martin pressed their backs against the wall, crouching low. "There are several offices in both directions," Paxx motioned.

"We will go right; you go left," Rowan said from behind them.

"Be safe," Paxx nodded, watching Rowan and another FBI agent move to the other side of the corridor.

Rowan and Paxx glanced down the adjoining hallway in opposite directions. Once they were certain they were clear, they nodded to one another. Paxx and Martin moved to the left, staying low and close to the wall. Rowan and the other agent did the same. As they moved off in different directions, Paxx grimaced when she heard gunfire from down the hall in the same direction Rowan had gone.

Paxx's heart raced, but she forced herself to stay focused. The lives of innocent victims depended on her actions in the next few minutes.

"First door on the left," she whispered to Martin, who nodded and took position on the opposite side of the doorway.

Paxx tested the handle, but it was locked. She signaled to Martin, who positioned herself to cover while Paxx prepared to breach. With a swift, powerful kick, Paxx crashed through the door, her weapon raised.

The small office was empty except for a mattress on the floor and chains bolted to the wall. The stench of human waste took her breath away.

"Clear," Paxx called, her stomach turning at the evidence of human suffering. "But someone was here recently."

At the next office, Paxx moved into position, weapon ready, as Martin tested the doorknob. Locked. Without hesitation, Martin stepped back and delivered a powerful kick near the lock. The door splintered open, revealing an empty office with scattered papers and abandoned furniture.

"Clear," Martin called, moving toward the next door.

They rapidly cleared two more rooms, finding nothing but dust and debris. The fourth door was different; it was reinforced with a padlock.

"This is it," Paxx whispered, her pulse racing.

Martin nodded, pulling a small breaching tool from her tactical vest. "Stand back."

The lock gave way with a metallic snap. Paxx moved in first, sweeping her weapon across the darkened space. The stench hit her, sweat, fear, and blood. Gathered at the back of the room, at least twenty young women stood frozen in fear.

The women huddled together, eyes wide with terror, some clutching each other, others shrinking back against the wall. Their clothes were filthy, torn in places, and many bore visible bruises.

Paxx slung her rifle strap over her shoulder and cautiously stepped forward, hands visible. "My name is Detective Algatta. We're here to help you."

One woman, barely more than a girl with hollow cheeks and matted blonde hair, stepped forward. "Are you real?" she whispered in broken English. "Not like others who promise help?"

"We're real," Paxx assured her, her voice gentle but firm. "Medical teams are on their way. No one's going to hurt you anymore."

Martin still stood in the doorway, partially outside the room, when a sudden burst of gunfire had her turning to look down the hallway. Paxx gasped when she saw her drop to her knees, with visible pain on her face. Shouting at the girls to get down low, Paxx quickly moved to Martin, pulling her inside the room before firing several shots down the hall.

"Vivian," Paxx called out.

"The bullets hit my vest. Fuck that hurts."

"Can you move?" Paxx asked, still watching the hallway.

Martin struggled to her feet, and two of the women hurried over to help her.

"We have approximately twenty women in the east corner office," Paxx said into her comms.

"What floor?" a voice asked.

"First," Paxx replied.

"Move everyone away from the outside wall. We're coming in," the voice responded.

"Roger that," Paxx responded, turning to the women. "Everyone, move away from that wall," she commanded, pointing to the exterior wall of the warehouse. "Stay low and move quickly."

The women hesitated, fear evident in their eyes.

"Please," Paxx softened her tone. "We're getting you out of here."

The blonde woman who had spoken earlier nodded and began ushering the others toward the opposite side of the room. "Do as she says," she urged in multiple languages.

An explosion rocked the building as the tactical team blasted through the exterior wall. Concrete dust billowed through the room as armored officers poured in, forming a protective barrier around the victims.

"This way," a female agent called, gesturing toward the newly created exit. "We have medical standing by."

Paxx stood by Martin, supporting her weight as they supervised the evacuation. The women moved with surprising speed, desperation fueling their exhausted bodies as they scrambled toward freedom.

"Get them to safety," Paxx told Martin. "I need to find Rowan."

Martin grabbed Paxx's arm. "Be careful. These aren't street thugs we're dealing with."

"I know, and I will," Paxx replied as she left the room, Martin sending two officers with her.

Moving down the corridor, Paxx kept her weapon at the ready. The sounds of gunfire had diminished, but sporadic shots still echoed through the warehouse. Her earpiece crackled with tactical updates from the other teams.

"Suspects down in west corridor," came Kimble's voice. "Third floor secured," another officer reported. "Rowan, report status," Paxx called into her comm. The silence that followed made her stomach clench. "Rowan, do you copy?" Paxx spoke into her comm, her voice low but urgent.

Static crackled in response, and then Rowan's strained voice came through. "Northeast corridor, second floor. Two shooters have me pinned down. Could use backup."

"On my way," Paxx replied, gesturing to the officers with her. "Second floor. Move."

They found the nearest stairwell and ascended cautiously, checking corners and blind spots. The second floor was darker, with fewer operational lights, casting long shadows across the open spaces.

One of the officers tapped Paxx on the shoulder, motioning to their left. Paxx looked over and saw Pazinski crouched behind a barrel, his lips moving. Paxx held up two fingers, signaling the officers he wasn't alone.

"FBI, we have you surrounded," one of the officers yelled. Pazinski turned and locked eyes with Paxx.

"You're just like your old man Algatta, don't know when to leave well enough alone," Pazinski growled.

"You left the note on my desk?" Paxx asked, her eyes narrowing in anger.

"No, it wasn't me," he broke eye contact, turning to say something to the person beside him. "This goes deeper than you can imagine, Paxx. You will never tie up all the loose ends."

"I will keep digging until I do," Paxx spat. "You have nowhere to go, Pazinski. Give yourself up."

Pazinski laughed bitterly. "You think I care about getting out of here? It's too late for that."

The figure beside him shifted in the shadows. "No more talking, Ian."

Paxx recognized that voice instantly; it was the same voice that had taunted her as she lay bleeding on the concrete floor, little more than a month ago. The same voice that had haunted her nightmares. Her grip tightened on her weapon.

"Show yourself," she commanded, her voice steady despite the rage building inside her.

"Detective Algatta," the voice replied. "We meet again. Though you were in a much more... vulnerable position last time."

A flash of movement to her right caught Paxx's attention. Rowan was crouched behind a stack of crates.

"You know," the voice continued, "I had such high hopes you'd die that night. Messy but effective. Just like your father."

The mention of her father sent a bolt of white-hot fury through Paxx's veins. She forced herself to breathe, to think. Getting emotional was exactly what he wanted.

"Was that supposed to get a rise out of me?" Paxx called out, her voice steady despite the fury coursing through her.

"Because all it's doing is confirming what I already know, you're a coward who hides in shadows."

The man stepped partially into view; she recognized his face, even in the dim light.

"Ian was right about one thing," the man said. "This does go deeper than you know. Your father discovered that, too. Such a shame he couldn't keep his moral outrage to himself."

Paxx caught Rowan's eye across the space. He gave her a subtle nod, indicating he was moving into position. She needed to keep them talking.

"Mr. Hines, you set your brother–in–law up to take the fall for my dad's murder and tried to do the same with my shooting. Too bad you didn't know he was locked up when you shot me." Paxx said teasingly.

"An unfortunate setback," he replied.

"You're a low-level dealer, Hines. How did you end up here?" Paxx questioned, watching Rowan and the two officers get into position.

"Just lucky, I guess," Hines chuckled. "Right place, right time. And when a member of el aniquilacion allows you to work for them, you don't turn them down."

"Well, I'm curious," Paxx said, trying to keep him occupied. "When this day is over, are you going to be the highest-ranking person on site, or is someone else here in charge?"

"No, I am not in charge here," Hines replied, "But I am sure the others are long gone."

"You know what I think, Hines?" Paxx kept her voice steady, buying time as she saw Rowan shifting into a better position. "I think you're expendable. Just like you were when you helped kill my father. Just a tool to be used and discarded."

"You don't know what you're talking about," Hines snapped, his composure cracking.

"I know what I'm talking about," Paxx continued, her eyes darting between Hines and Pazinski. "You think you matter to el aniquilacion? You're nothing to them. Just another body to throw in the way when things get hot."

Hines shifted uncomfortably, doubt flashing across his face before hardening into resolve. "I know my place in the organization."

"Your place?" Paxx scoffed. "As a sacrificial pawn?"

Pazinski suddenly moved, grabbing Hines's arm. "We need to end this now."

The movement triggered a flurry of action. Rowan burst from his position, weapon trained on the two men. "FBI! Drop your weapons!"

In that split second, Pazinski made his choice. He shoved Hines forward and raised his gun, not toward Rowan or Paxx, but toward Hines's back, shooting him once in the head before disappearing back behind the barrels.

Paxx stood frozen, her eyes on the dead man on the floor, a pool of blood forming around his head. Movement beside her brought her back from her trance. Captain Kimble appeared, eyes on Paxx, his expression unsettling.

"Who's over there?" he questioned, peering around a stack of pallets.

'Pazinski," Paxx replied. "He just shot T.J. Hines."

Kimble nodded, no questions about who T.J. Hines was or why Pazinski shot him.

"I need all teams to report status," Kimble called into his comm, his eyes never leaving the spot where Pazinski had disappeared. "Secure all exits and establish a perimeter. No one leaves this building."

Rowan moved forward, his weapon trained on the barrels where Pazinski had taken cover. He exchanged a glance with Paxx, silent communication passing between them. She nodded, understanding the plan without words.

"Pazinski," Paxx called out, her voice firm. "It's over. You've got nowhere to go."

Silence followed, broken only by the distant sound of tactical teams securing other parts of the warehouse. Kimble moved to Paxx's side, his weapon drawn.

"I'll flank him," Kimble whispered. "Keep him talking."

Something in his tone made Paxx glance at him. His eyes were too focused, too determined. She recognized that look, it wasn't the concentration of an officer about to apprehend a suspect. It was the calculation of someone about to eliminate a loose end.

"He's making a run for it," Rowan said, spotting movement behind the barrels. "East stairwell!"

Paxx took off, with Kimble close behind. She made it to the doorway just in time to see Pazinski disappear, and then two shots rang out from behind her. Whirling around, Paxx saw Kimble leaning over the mezzanine rail, a smug smile on his face.

"Captain?" Paxx said, her voice tight with suspicion.

"Sorry, Algatta. He was going for his weapon," Kimble replied, holstering his gun.

Paxx moved to the railing, looking down to see Pazinski sprawled on the concrete floor below, blood pooling around him. A bullet was lodged in the back of his vest, and a large hole was in the back of his head. The placement of the shot, the timing. None of it felt right.

"You shot him in the back," she said, her eyes narrowing as she turned back to face Kimble.

The captain's expression hardened. "He was a dirty cop who just executed someone in front of you. I made a split-second decision to protect my officers."

Rowan appeared beside Pazinski, taking in the scene with a quick, assessing glance. Looking up, his eyes met Paxx's, a silent question passing between them.

Kimble's calm demeanor sent alarm bells ringing in Paxx's head. This wasn't right. None of this was right.

"He was running down the stairs," Paxx said, her hand instinctively griping the butt of her weapon. "He was running away; he wasn't an immediate threat."

"He was armed and dangerous," Kimble replied, moving his hand to his hip, resting his palm on the butt of his gun.

"Captain," she said, keeping her voice level despite the alarm bells ringing in her head. "I need to check on the victims we recovered. Make sure they're getting proper care."

Kimble's eyes hardened. "That can wait, Detective. We need to secure the scene first."

The tension between them stretched taut. Paxx noticed his hand hadn't moved from his weapon. She kept her own stance casual but ready, years of training kicking in as her instincts screamed danger.

"With all due respect, sir," she countered.

"I said it can wait," Kimble snapped, his professional mask slipping briefly.

Rowan's voice came through her earpiece, low and urgent. "Paxx, we've got a situation downstairs. Need you here now."

She maintained eye contact with Kimble. "I've been called downstairs, sir. Agent Taylor needs assistance." Paxx turned away, her mind racing.

? ? ?
FIFTY-FIVE

S he kept her movements casual as she descended the stairs, fighting the urge to look over her shoulder. Rowan was still crouched beside Pazinski's body, his expression unreadable as he examined the fallen officer.

"Vest stopped one round," Rowan murmured as she approached. "The head shot killed him instantly."

Paxx crouched next to him, whispering. "That wasn't a defensive shot."

"I know," Rowan responded, locking eyes with her. "Shot to the back of the head."

"Kimble executed him," Paxx murmured, feeling a knot in her stomach.

"Stand up calmly and walk to the outer door."

Paxx searched Pazinski's pockets and retrieved his phone. With deliberate calm, she walked toward the exit, aware that Kimble was watching her every move from above.

"He's watching us."

"I know," Rowan replied, matching her stride.

They moved together as they crossed the warehouse floor. The tactical teams were still securing various areas, but the gunfire had stopped. Medical personnel were tending to the rescued women and a few officers and agents near the entrance, the flashing lights of ambulances visible through the open doors.

As they moved away from Pazinski's body, Rowan leaned in close. "We've got a major problem."

"No shit Sherlock," Paxx spat.

Stepping through the open doors, Paxx spotted Martin sitting in the back of an ambulance, her vest removed as a medic examined her bruised ribs. "You good?" Paxx asked, stepping up to the open door.

Martin smiled. "Takes more than a couple of rounds to the chest to keep me down."

"I think we stumbled into something much bigger than we expected," Rowan said from behind Paxx.

"What do you mean?" Martin questioned as she shooed the paramedic out of the ambulance.

"Captain Kimble is part of this," Paxx whispered.

"What?" Martin gasped, pulling her shirt down and exiting the ambulance.

As the three stood together, Paxx laid out the events that had happened upstairs, ending with Kimble shooting Pazinski.

Martin's face drained of color. "It makes a sick kind of sense," Martin said, her voice barely audible over the surrounding chaos. "With as much corruption as is in this department, someone with authority would have to run interference."

"We need to be careful here," Rowan cautioned, his eyes scanning the chaotic scene around them. "If Kimble's involved, we don't know who else might be."

"What about the women?" Paxx asked, glancing toward the group of rescued victims being loaded into ambulances. "They could be in danger if Kimble tries to tie up loose ends."

"I've already contacted the FBI field office," Martin replied. "We're arranging secure transport and protective custody. No local involvement."

"Good," Paxx nodded. "I want to talk to them before they're moved."

Martin grimaced as she took a step.

"It won't hurt so bad in a few days," Paxx commented, understanding Martin's pain. "A warm bath and gentle hands will help, too."

"If you're offering, I will have to decline," Martin grinned. "My husband might have an issue with it."

"I'm not offering," Paxx laughed, "And I'm certain my girlfriend would have an issue with it."

The three shared a moment of levity before Rowan's expression turned serious again.

"We need to secure Pazinski's phone before Kimble realizes you have it," he whispered. "And we need to figure out what to do about Kimble without tipping our hand."

Paxx nodded, slipping the phone into her pocket. She scanned the scene, finding Jake and Paul across the structure. From a pocket on her vest, she retrieved her phone to call Paul.

After a brief conversation, Paul headed their way, Jake joining him. Paxx slipped Pazinski's phone to Paul as they approached. As they stood close, she summarized Kimble's situation to them.

Jake's brow furrowed as he growled, "That bastard! All the conversations and planning we have had with him over the past week."

"We have to handle this with kid gloves," Agent Martin replied, trying to keep them calm. "I think the best way to move forward is for us to take over," she said, looking at Rowan.

Rowan turned to Paxx, a questioning look in his eyes. "Paxx?"

Paxx sighed. "Maybe the only way to get to the bottom of all of this," she replied, "He can't stop you from investigating in any way you deem necessary."

"Okay, Rowan, I want you to find Jackson, Harris, and Klein and start ushering local police off the scene." Martin directed.

"Yes, ma'am," Rowan nodded before walking away.

As Paul surveyed the area, he asked Paxx about Detective Rosalba's location. "I think she returned to Pennsylvania. I left her with Kimble and Rowan when I met you at the library." Paxx replied,

"I'll ask Rowan," Paul said as he and Jake turned away and returned to the other county officers.

"I want to check on the girls," Paxx told Martin.

They approached the makeshift triage area where the rescued women were being evaluated. The blonde woman who had spoken to Paxx earlier sat wrapped in a thermal blanket, her hollow eyes fixed on the ground. When she noticed Paxx approaching, something like recognition flickered across her face.

"How are they doing?" Paxx asked the FBI agent, oversee-ing the medical response.

"From what we can see, most have minor injuries, dehy-dration, malnutrition," the agent replied. "Psychologically..." She shook her head. "They've been through hell."

Paxx nodded and knelt before the blonde woman. "Do you speak English well?"

The young woman nodded, a slight smile on her lips.

"Can you tell me your name?" Paxx asked.

"Natalia," she whispered in reply. "Natalia Kazakov."

"Natalia, I know this is difficult, but I need to ask you a few questions before you're moved to a secure location. Anything you can tell us might help catch the people responsible."

Natalia's eyes darted around the scene, pausing at the ware-house entrance where officers were still coming and going. "They will kill me if I talk," she whispered.

"We're going to protect you," Paxx assured her. "All of you. No one will know what you've told us."

The young woman hesitated, then leaned closer. "There was man... not like the others. He wore suit. Expensive. He would come to inspect us." Her voice trembled with fear.

Paxx felt her blood run cold. She exchanged a quick glance with Martin before turning back to Natalia. "Do you think you would recognize him?"

Natalia nodded slowly. "He would have me talk to girls for him." Averting her gaze, she continued, "Sometimes, when he wanted one of them, I would have to stay with them so I tell the girl what he want."

Paxx swallowed the bile as it rose in her throat. "I'm so sorry you have gone through all of this."

"Can you tell me how long you've been here, Natalia?" Martin asked.

Natalia's eyes darted around nervously. "Three days here. Before that, another place, and before that, a long ride, I don't know where. They move us at night, in trucks with no windows."

"How long have you been with them?" Martin asked.

Natalia thought for a moment. "When is this?"

"It's June eighteenth, twenty twenty-four," Paxx replied.

"I was taken on my sixteenth birthday," Natalia replied as tears filled her eyes. "That was September, one."

"September first, but what year?" Paxx asked, her heart constricting at Natalia's revelation.

"Two thousand twenty-one," Natalia whispered, a tear sliding down her dirt-streaked face. "I nineteen now."

Martin and Paxx exchanged glances, the weight of Natalia's words hanging heavy between them. Three years in captivity. Three years of unimaginable horror.

"They keep me because I speak English."

"Natalia," Paxx said, "would you be willing to work with a sketch artist to help us identify this man in the suit?"

The young woman's shoulders tensed, but she gave a slight nod. "If you promise they will not find me."

"I promise," Paxx said. "We're going to make sure you're safe."

As Paxx stood, she saw Kimble emerge from the warehouse. With eyes on Natalia, Paxx said, "Natalia, look at me."

Natalia looked up at Paxx, her eyes filled with hope.

"I promise you I will protect you. Do you trust me?" Paxx asked.

Natalia nodded, "Yes."

Paxx leaned to the left, unblocking Natalia's view of Kimble. Natalia's face faded into horror when she saw him. Paxx moved back, blocking her view once more before kneeling before her.

"Look at me; you are safe," Paxx assured.

Natalia's eyes were wide with fear, her body trembling beneath the thermal blanket. "That's him," she whispered. "The man in suit. He come to inspect girls."

Paxx kept her expression neutral despite the rage building inside her. "You're sure?"

"Yes," Natalia nodded frantically. "He is one who give orders."

Paxx's blood ran cold. She fought to keep her expression neutral despite the shock coursing through her system. Kimble wasn't just corrupt; he was directly involved in the trafficking operation. "Thank you for telling me, you're very brave. Listen to me carefully," Paxx said, making sure her body still blocked Natalia from Kimble's view. "Don't look at him again. Don't let him see you recognize him. Agent Martin is going to take you somewhere safe right now."

Martin nodded, grasping the meaning. "I'll handle this." She spoke into her comm, requesting immediate transport for a high-priority witness.

"Detective Algatta!" Kimble's voice boomed from behind them.

"Get her out of here now," Paxx murmured to Martin.

With an arm around Natalia's shoulders, Martin guided her away from the other girls and into a nearby federal vehicle.

Paxx straightened her shoulders and turned to face Captain Kimble, forcing her features into a neutral expression despite the revulsion churning in her stomach.

"Sir," she acknowledged, her voice controlled.

Kimble approached with measured steps, his face a mask of professional concern. "I need a full report on the victims we've recovered. How many are there? What's their condition?"

"Twenty-three women total, sir," Paxx replied, watching his eyes for any reaction. "Most are suffering from malnutrition, dehydration, and various injuries. FBI is coordinating secure transport to medical facilities."

"Good work," Kimble nodded, his gaze shifting to the departing federal vehicle containing Natalia. "Where's that one going?"

Paxx's pulse quickened. "She was shot, sir. Agent Martin is taking her for immediate medical attention," she lied.

"Why isn't she going in an ambulance?" he questioned.

"The ones on sight are full, and the fastest way to get her to the hospital was for Martin to take her," she replied.

Kimble looked at her, his gaze skeptical. "Have you seen Hallman?"

"No, sir," she replied. "Have you seen Detective Rosalba?"

"Who?"

"Detective Rosalba from Pennsylvania State Police. She was here this morning," Paxx replied, confused by his question.

"Oh, her. I have no idea where she went when she left this morning," he said dismissively.

Paxx nodded, filing away this information. Something wasn't adding up. Rosalba had been with Kimble when she'd left them, and now he claimed she'd departed this morning.

"We need to process these arrests quickly," Kimble said, his tone leaving no room for argument.

"The FBI has taken jurisdiction. Agent Taylor has requested I assist with victim interviews." Paxx replied.

Kimble's jaw tightened. "This was a joint operation."

"Yes, sir," Paxx nodded, "Special Agent Martin decided they were taking over due to circumstances she didn't share with me."

Turning away, Kimble shouted, "Agent Taylor."

Paxx watched as Rowan turned to face Kimble, his jaw set in determination.

Rowan approached with measured steps, his expression neutral. "Captain Kimble."

"What's this about the FBI taking over my operation?" Kimble demanded, his voice carrying across the chaotic scene.

"Not your operation, Captain," Rowan corrected. "This was a joint task force, and I'm following procedure. We'll coordinate with your department, but custody of suspects and victims falls under federal purview, so the Bureau assumes primary jurisdiction."

Paxx stood still, watching the exchange while her mind raced.

Kimble's face darkened. "This is my jurisdiction, Agent Taylor. You know, we have been working on this case for months."

"This decision comes from the ASAC. We'll need your officers to complete their reports and submit all evidence to us." Rowan replied.

"This is bullshit," Kimble spat, his composure slipping. "I've got two dead officers and a warehouse full of evidence. My team deserves to be part of this investigation."

Rowan assured him that his officers would receive full credit in the reports. "But given the cross-jurisdictional nature of human trafficking crimes and the international victims, FBI protocol is clear."

"Captain," she interjected, "I can liaise between departments if that helps. Ensure IHPD gets proper recognition while following federal protocols."

"Fine," Kimble conceded, his voice clipped. "But I expect you to keep me fully informed of all developments."

"Of course," Rowan replied.

Paxx watched as Kimble stalked away, his body language betraying his fury despite his attempt at composure.

"We need to talk," she murmured to Rowan once Kimble was out of earshot.

Rowan nodded, leading her away from the chaos toward a quiet corner behind an ambulance.

"One of the girls, Natalia, identified Kimble," Paxx said without preamble, keeping her voice low. "He's not just corrupt; he's directly involved in the trafficking operation. She called him 'the man in suit' who inspects the girls."

Rowan's expression hardened, a muscle in his jaw twitching. "Jesus Christ," he whispered. "Are you certain?"

"Absolutely. She nearly had a panic attack when she saw him." Paxx struggled to keep her voice steady as rage and disgust churned inside her. "Martin moved her to a secure location."

"We need to get these girls out of here and to a safe location," Rowan replied as he surveyed the scene around the warehouse. Paxx followed his gaze, watching as the County Sheriff's officers cordoned off the area with police tape. She saw Paul talking with an officer, pointing toward a third-floor window, his brow furrowed in concern. Paxx saw Hillman in a window, a look of defeat on his face. "Rowan, there's Hallman," Paxx said as she tapped his shoulder, urging him to follow her to where Paul was standing.

Rowan nodded, his eyes narrowing as he spotted Hallman in the window.

"Something's not right," Paxx muttered, quickening her pace.

As they approached Paul, Paxx noticed his tight expression. "What's going on?" she asked.

"Hallman's refusing to come down," Paul explained in a low voice. "He's barricaded himself up there. Won't respond to radio calls, and when an officer tried to approach, he threatened to shoot."

"I'm going up," Paxx said, running inside the building before anyone could stop her.

❓ ❓ ❓
FIFTY-SIX

P axx raced up the metal stairs, her footsteps echoing in the stairwell. She could hear Rowan behind her.

"Paxx, wait!" he called, but she didn't slow down.

When Paxx got to the third floor, she paused at the stairwell door, listening. There was nothing but silence. With a deep breath, she opened the door and surveyed the hallway.

"Hallman?" she called out, her voice steady. "It's Detective Algatta."

No response.

Moving down the hallway, Paxx approached the room where she'd seen Hallman from outside. The door was ajar. Sunlight filtered through dirty windows, spilling into the corridor.

"I'm alone," she lied, knowing Rowan was behind her. "Talk to me."

"That's far enough, Paxx," Hallman's shaky voice came from across the room. "I didn't want any of this, Paxx. You have to believe me."

"Tell me what happened, Gabe. How did you get involved in all of this?" She replied, pulling out her phone, opening the recorder app, and opening the mic on her comms.

531

"I was following orders," Hallman replied, his voice breaking. "At first, it was looking the other way, drug shipments, and evidence that went missing. Small stuff, you know? But then..."

"Then what, Gabe?" Paxx kept her voice gentle, encouraging him to continue while she inched forward slowly.

"They brought in the girls." Hallman's face contorted with anguish. "I told Kimble I wanted out, but he said I was in too deep. Said they'd pin everything on me if I tried to walk away."

"How long has this been going on?" Paxx asked, getting a clear view of him. He sat slumped against the wall, his service weapon in his hand.

A bitter laugh escaped his lips. "Four years." He whispered.

"Who else is involved?" she asked, watching him.

"Pazinski, Issacs from County, Detective Brandt from Pennsylvania, Officer Graham from Chicago. Hell, there are judges and lawyers from here to Texas." He chuckled. "I don't know everyone involved."

Paxx closed her eyes at the list of names. "Is Darby a part of this?"

"She was until the girls started showing up; then, she refused to take part."

"How could she walk away and not you?"

Hallman chuckled again, this time fear seeped through the sound. "She told Kimble who her uncle was. Did you know her uncle is Nemesio Guzman?"

"I didn't," Paxx lied.

"Yeah, well, she threatened Kimble. If he didn't get rid of the girls, she would call him."

"Who is the supplier you work for?"

"Originally it was Guzman, but Kimble got greedy and started taking girls from el aniquilacion. Shannon told him he was dealing with the devil, but Kimble didn't care."

"How long has Kimble been working with el aniquilacion?"

"For about two years now. That's when things got really bad. The cartel doesn't just traffic drugs; they traffic people. Young women, mostly. And Kimble... he got a taste for the power."

Paxx felt sick. "Gabe, you need to come with me. We can get you protection if you testify."

Hallman shook his head, tears welling in his eyes. "You don't understand, Paxx. There's no protection from these people. They'll find me."

"The FBI can protect you," she insisted, taking another cautious step forward. "Your testimony could bring down this entire operation."

"Like they protected your father?"

"Gabe, Pazinski told me you killed my father."

Hallman's head snapped up, meeting her gaze. "Paxx, I didn't kill your father. I swear it."

Paxx believed him; the sadness in his eyes twisted her gut. "Who killed him, Gabe?"

"Kimble," he replied, breaking eye contact. "He killed them both, James and Allan."

Paxx felt her knees weaken and pressed her hand against the wall to steady herself.

"Why?"

"Your father found out about the operation. He'd been collecting evidence for months. He was going to take it to the FBI. Kimble couldn't let that happen."

"And Allan?"

"He put it together after James was killed. Came to me. I tried to warn him to back off, but he wouldn't listen. For the past two years, I have been holding him off, trying to get him to stop collecting evidence."

"But he wouldn't stop."

Hallman shook his head. "Your dad is dead. Allan and Ian are dead. I am the last loose end here, because we both know Kimble will never get to Shannon."

"Let me help you, Gabe."

"I won't be able to save you, Paxx, and you can't save me," Gabe said, raising his service weapon to his temple.

"Gabe, no!" Paxx lunged forward, pushing his arm up as the shot rang out.

She pulled the gun from his hand, the echo of the gunshot reverberating through the empty room. Rowan burst through the door, weapon drawn. "Paxx!" His eyes darted from her to Hallman's body, assessing the situation.

Paxx pulled Hallman into her arms, his sobs racking his body. She handed the gun to Rowan, shaking her head when he pulled out his handcuffs. With her comms off, she instructed Rowan, "Get a vehicle to the door downstairs. Let's get him out of here."

Rowan nodded, securing the weapon before calling an agent and requesting an unmarked vehicle at the side entrance.

"We have approximately five minutes before someone comes looking," he warned, helping Paxx get Hallman to his feet.

"My career is over," Hallman mumbled, his body trembling. "My life is over."

"Not if you help us bring them down," Paxx said, supporting his weight as they moved toward the door. "We need everything, you know, Gabe. Names, dates, locations—all of it."

They navigated the empty corridor, Rowan taking point while Paxx guided Hallman. The floor had emptied as officers processed the scene downstairs, focusing on the rescued women and securing evidence.

Hallman's bloodshot eyes found hers. "Why are you helping me? After everything..."

"Because you're our best chance at bringing Kimble down. And because it's what my father would have done."

???
FIFTY-SEVEN

T hey reached the stairwell without incident. Hallman's breath came in ragged gasps, whether from exertion or the crushing weight of his situation, Paxx couldn't tell.

"Vehicles in position," Rowan murmured as they approached the ground floor. "Agent Mercer is driving. He's clear on the protocol."

Paxx nodded, grateful for Rowan's efficiency. "Gabe, listen to me. You're going to a secure location. No paperwork, no processing. You will be safe, and we will figure this out."

"Kimble has eyes everywhere. He'll know I'm missing."

"Let us worry about that," Rowan assured him, checking the hallway before gesturing them forward.

Once Hallman was secured in the vehicle, Agent Mercer drove away, with a second unmarked federal vehicle close behind. Paxx released a heavy breath and looked around for Paul. She found him standing by the command center, talking to Jake. Crossing the parking lot, she joined them.

"Did you hear all of that?" Paxx asked, pulling out her phone.

"Yes, and I recorded it on my phone," Paul confirmed.

"Me too," Paxx nodded as she compressed the file and sent it to Special Agent Martin. "Have you seen Kimble? I thought he left, but if someone told him Hallman was still here, I suspect he will return."

Jake nodded toward the warehouse. "Inside, he's been asking about you."

"I bet he has," Paxx muttered, her mind racing.

"Where's Hallman?" Kimble's voice boomed from behind her. Paxx turned to face him.

"I haven't seen him," she lied.

Kimble's eyes narrowed, studying her face. "I thought you went upstairs to talk to him?"

Paxx shook her head, "No, sir, I was just helping to clear the last few offices."

Kimble's jaw tightened. "I want every inch of this place searched. He's involved in this, and I want him found and in cuffs."

"Yes, sir," Paxx responded, maintaining eye contact despite the rage burning inside her. This man had murdered her father and had orchestrated a criminal enterprise that trafficked young women. Had betrayed everything the badge stood for.

Kimble stormed off as more of his calm demeanor fell apart.

Paul's hand brushed Paxx's arm. "Easy," he murmured, sensing her tension. "We need to play this smart."

"I know," Paxx replied through gritted teeth. "But knowing what he did to dad..."

"We'll get him. But we need to be careful. If he suspects we know anything..."

Paxx nodded, watching Kimble from across the parking lot as he barked orders at a group of officers. His composure was cracking, and that made him dangerous. Paxx surveyed the warehouse, watching officers move in and out with evidence bags. Paramedics transported the rescued women to the hospital; their haunted expressions burned into her memory.

Her phone vibrated. A text from Rowan: 'Package delivered. Safe house secure. No tails.'

"How much longer will we be on scene?" Paxx asked Jake.

"Another hour, maybe two."

"I should go back in and help," Paxx said, though her mind was elsewhere. She needed time to process what Hallman had told her about her father.

"I'll come with you," Paul offered, falling into step beside her. "Paxx, how are you doing? Really?"

Paxx reached over and squeezed his hand. "I always felt that more than just revenge from Mr. Black was behind Dad's death, and I was furious when Shannon told me Hallman had killed him. Do you think she lied to me, or did she not know the truth?"

Paul gripped her hand tightly. "Sis, I don't think she would lie to you. I don't know her, but Tracie told Jake and me about the kiss she planted on you at the coffee shop. I don't think she knew it was Kimble."

Paxx chuckled, "She told you?"

"In the strictest of confidence," Paul assured. "I promise not to tell Jaylee."

Paxx continued walking, releasing his hand. "I will tell Jaylee. I would never keep something like that from her."

They entered the warehouse again, and the activity inside was still frantic, but more organized now. Evidence technicians in white coveralls processed the scene, documenting everything. The air still carried the faint metallic scent of blood mixed with dust and mold.

Her phone vibrated again. A text from Jaylee: 'Are you okay? The news is reporting a massive smuggling operation takedown. Call when you can.'

"Did you see any news crews?" Paxx asked Paul.

"No, why?"

"Jaylee texted. She says the news is reporting a large smuggling operation takedown." Paxx frowned, showing him the text.

Paul shook his head, scanning the parking lot through the open warehouse door. "That's not right. There shouldn't be any press releases yet. We haven't even finished processing the scene."

"Someone leaked it," Paxx muttered, typing a quick response to Jaylee: 'I'm fine. Will call soon. Love you.'

"Who?" Paul spat as he pulled out his phone and called Jake.

Paxx's eyes narrowed as she scanned the warehouse. "Someone who wants to control the narrative."

She spotted Kimble across the room, huddled with two other officers, his phone pressed to his ear. Anger flushed his face.

"Someone leaked the takedown to the press," Paul said into his phone.

"We just heard," Jake replied, "I'm here with Rowan; he is trying to shut it down."

Paul ended the call by saying, "The FBI is aware of the leak. Rowan is trying to get the coverage off the wire."

As a chopper approached, Paxx answered. "I'd say it's too late."

Outside, they observed a news chopper hovering over the warehouse.

"Shit," Paxx spat, "There will be twenty news vans here within the next thirty minutes."

With a loud, urgent voice, Rowan rushed to the warehouse and called out, "We need to pick up the pace, people. We are already on the news." Pausing, he scanned the large space, his eyes settling on the corner where Kimble and the two officers stood. "And when we find out who leaked this to the press, we will have your badge."

Kimble's face darkened as his eyes locked with Rowan's across the warehouse. The tension between them was palpable. Kimble muttered something to the officers beside him without breaking eye contact, then strode toward the exit.

Paxx felt her muscles tense as he approached. He stopped a few feet away, his expression composed again, though his eyes betrayed his fury.

"Agent Taylor," Kimble addressed Rowan with forced politeness. "I assure you, no one from my department would leak information to the press. We understand protocol."

"Yet here we are," Rowan replied coolly. "With a helicopter overhead and evidence still being collected."

Kimble's jaw tightened. "Perhaps the FBI should look to its own house before casting accusations."

"We will find the source, and quickly." His expression was smug and confident.

"You have no authority to invade these officers' privacy," Kimble boomed, realizing the FBI was running phone records.

"Don't I?" Rowan said. "Someone has put this entire investigation in jeopardy, so I have every fucking right to invade."

Kimble stepped closer to Rowan, his voice lowering to a threatening whisper. "You're overstepping, Agent Taylor."

"Am I?" Rowan didn't back down. "Last I checked, compromising a federal investigation is a felony."

Paxx glanced between the two men, watching the power struggle unfold. She caught Paul's eye, silently communicating that they needed to stay alert.

An Agent approached, her expression grim. "We've got a match on the leak. The call came from a burner phone, but we've triangulated the location." She handed Rowan a tablet showing a map with a blinking dot.

"Technology moves quickly these days, Captain," Rowan said smugly.

Kimble's face remained impassive, but Paxx noticed the slight twitch in his jaw.

As Rowan examined the warehouse, he shouted, "Everyone, stay put!"

Paxx watched as Rowan looked at the tablet and then walked to the corner where Kimble and the two officers had been talking. One officer fidgeted, his face ashen, and his eyes locked on Kimble. Rowan approached the young officer, whose Adam's apple bobbed nervously in his throat. The warehouse had fallen silent, and everyone was watching the scene unfold.

"Officer Henry, isn't it?" Rowan asked, his voice calm.

The officer nodded, unable to speak.

"Empty your pockets, please."

Officer Henry's face drained of color as all eyes turned to him. He darted a look at Kimble, who gave an almost imperceptible shake of his head.

"Now, Officer," Rowan demanded.

Henry pulled out his wallet, keys, and then a cheap burner phone. Rowan examined it before handing it to the female agent.

"Check the call history," he instructed.

"Captain Kimble told me to call it in," the officer blurted, his voice cracking.

The warehouse went still. All eyes turned to Kimble, whose face had hardened into a mask of controlled rage.

"Officer Henry," Kimble's voice was dangerously soft, "you're mistaken. I gave no such order."

"But sir, you said...." Henry's protest died in his throat as Kimble's glare cut through him.

Paxx watched the betrayal unfold, her stomach churning with disgust. Kimble was throwing one of his own officers under the bus without hesitation. Rowan stepped between them, blocking Kimble's view of the officer. "We'll sort this out at the field office. Officer Henry, you're coming with us for questioning." He nodded to two agents who moved forward to escort the shell-shocked officer outside.

"This is ridiculous," Kimble snarled. "You can't possibly believe..."

"Captain Kimble," Rowan interrupted, "I'd like you to come with me as well."

A bitter smile spread across Kimble's face. "On what grounds, Agent Taylor?"

"Obstruction of justice, for starters," Rowan replied evenly. "We can discuss the rest at the field office."

Kimble's hand moved subtly toward his hip, and Paxx felt her breath catch. Every instinct screamed danger.

"I wouldn't," she said, her hand hovering near her weapon. "Not with so many witnesses, Captain."

Kimble's eyes locked with hers, and in that moment, Paxx saw the raw hatred behind them, the same hatred that must have been there when he murdered her father.

"Detective Algatta," he said, his voice dripping with venom, "always the crusader. Just like your father."

"Is that why you killed him?" The words left her mouth before she could stop them.

Kimble's expression remained icy and unflinching, devoid of shock or remorse, and at that moment, both Paul and Paxx knew with certainty that Kimble was their father's killer. A dangerous silence filled the warehouse as the accusation hung in the air. Kimble's eyes narrowed, calculating, his hand still hovering near his weapon.

"You should be careful with unfounded accusations, Detective," Kimble said, his voice eerily calm. "They could damage your career."

"They're not unfounded," Paxx replied, taking a step forward. "Hallman told us everything before he disappeared."

Kimble's composure slipped, a flash of panic crossing his features before he regained control. "Officer Hallman is unstable and faces serious charges. His word means nothing."

"We have recordings," Paul interjected, moving to stand beside his sister. "And evidence that corroborates his statement."

Kimble's face hardened as he assessed the siblings standing before him. "You're bluffing," Kimble said, his voice low. "You have nothing."

"We have everything," Paxx countered. "The evidence our father collected before you killed him. The evidence Allan gathered. Your connection to the trafficking operation. The names of every officer on your payroll."

Rowan pressed closer, his hand now on his weapon. "Jacob Kimble, I'm placing you under arrest for the murder of Detective James Algatta, obstruction of justice, and conspiracy to engage in human trafficking. You have the right to remain silent—"

Kimble drew his weapon in one fluid motion, but Paul lunged forward, driving his shoulder into his chest while gripping his wrist. The gun clattered to the ground as Paul wrestled Kimble down. Officers scattered, some drawing weapons, unsure where to point them in the chaos.

"Don't move!" Rowan shouted, his weapon trained on Kimble as Paul pinned him to the concrete floor.

Paxx kicked Kimble's gun away and drew her weapon. "Everyone, stay calm," she commanded, scanning the warehouse. Some officers looked shocked, others confused, and a few, Paxx noted, appeared more calculating, their eyes darting between Kimble and the exits.

Rowan handcuffed Kimble while Paul maintained pressure on his shoulders. "You're making a mistake," Kimble growled, his face pressed against the cold concrete. "You do not know who you're dealing with, or what you've done."

Paxx knelt beside him, her voice low and dangerous. "I know exactly what I've done. I am finishing what my father started."

Rowan approached, handcuffs at the ready. "Jacob Kimble, you're under arrest. You have the right to remain silent."

As Rowan recited the Miranda rights, Paxx stood, holstering her weapon. Paul got to his feet, his eyes meeting hers in a silent exchange of relief and shared resolve.

"You okay?" he asked quietly.

Paxx nodded, taking a deep breath. "Yeah. You?"

"I'm good," Paul replied, rubbing his shoulder where he'd tackled Kimble.

Kimble's voice cut through their moment of respite. "This isn't over, Algatta. You have no idea how deep this goes."

Paxx turned to face him, her expression hardening. "Then we'll keep digging until we root out every one of you."

Rowan gestured to two agents, who moved to escort Kimble out of the warehouse. As they led him away, Kimble's eyes locked onto Paxx one last time, filled with a mixture of hatred and something else, fear.

Paul turned to his sister, his face etched with concern. "Paxx, are you sure you're alright?"

She nodded, her breathing ragged. "I will be," she said, watching Kimble being escorted out of the warehouse. "We got him, Paul. We finally got him."

Paul squeezed her shoulder. "Dad would be proud."

Paxx felt tears prick at her eyes, but she blinked them back. There would be time for that later. Right now, they had work to do.

"Let's finish processing this scene," she said, her voice steady. "There's still a lot more to uncover."

As they returned to the task at hand, Paxx couldn't shake the feeling that Kimble's words were more than desperate threats of a cornered man. This was just the beginning, and the road ahead would be long and treacherous. But she felt a glimmer of hope for the first time in years. Justice for her father was finally within reach.

? ? ?

FIFTY-EIGHT

Can there ever truly be closure?

Deep wounds, leave permanent scars.

? ? ?
FIFTY-EIGHT

Three months later ......

Paxx stood at the kitchen sink, her fingers drifting over the cool surface of the gold badge in her palm. Number 1002—etched into burnished gold of the enameled emblem of the city police department, caught the morning sun through the window. For a moment, she remembered her father's deep voice as he pinned this same badge to his uniform each day. Three years had now passed since his murder, and though the hollow ache in her chest still flared sometimes, holding his badge no longer felt like clutching at a wound. Instead, it was a reminder of everything she'd lost, everything she'd gone through, and everything she'd become.

"Hey, you alright?" Jaylee asked, placing a steaming mug of coffee on the counter next to Paxx.

"Yeah," Paxx replied, looking up and catching Jaylee's reflection in the window. The two had been through a lot together over the past six months, healing through a near-fatal gunshot wound, Paxx reconnecting with her mother, and navigating the turbulent waters of a police department plagued by corruption. Jaylee's support had been unwavering through it all. "Thinking about how much has changed."

Jaylee wrapped her arms around Paxx from behind, resting her chin on her shoulder. "Your dad would be proud of you. Of both of you."

Paxx leaned back into the embrace, savoring the warmth and stability Jaylee provided. The department was still in disarray, struggling to cleanse itself of the corruption left by Kimble and his cronies. "The department's still a mess. Removing all of Kimble's people is taking longer than we hoped."

Jaylee tilted her head, brushing a strand of hair behind Paxx's ear. "But it's happening, one corrupt officer at a time,"

Paxx set the badge into its cherry-wood display box, a gift from Paul. "Twenty-three so far. Each confession leads to another name. If this pace continues, by the time I sit for the Captain's exam, there might not be a force left." She turned, meeting Jaylee's supportive gaze. "I worry about what we still haven't found."

"You can't fix everything at once. Rowan and the FBI are still investigating the cartel connections ..."

"And dragging their feet while they're at it," Paxx interjected with a frustrated huff.

Jaylee raised an eyebrow but didn't take the bait to argue. "Paul and Jake are handling the county departmental clean-up," she continued, refusing to let Paxx spiral into frustration just yet. She tapped Paxx in the chest, glancing at the pile of law-enforcement textbooks stacked on the counter. "And you," Jaylee added with mock sternness, "need to focus on studying for the Captain's exam."

Paxx groaned at that and rolled her eyes, though there was no real annoyance behind it. "God help me, you sound like my brother."

"Well, he's not wrong. You've already done so much, Paxx. More than anyone else could've managed in your position."

"Still can't believe the Chief wants me to take Kimble's spot."

Jaylee reached for Paxx's hand, intertwining their fingers and giving them a reassuring squeeze. "You deserve this." Paxx stared at their joined hands for a moment before nodding, some of the tension easing from her shoulders again. She squeezed Jaylee's hand, smiling at the matching tattoos on their ring fingers.

The soft buzz of Paxx's phone cut between them. Paul's name lit up the screen. "You're on speaker," she said, keying the call.

"Morning, ladies," Paul's voice crackled in. "Big news—Shannon Darby's agreed to testify against Kimble and the el aniquilacion cartel. Prosecution's confident."

Shannon had once been their ally inside the department, until the day Paxx learned she'd been feeding intel to both her uncle Guzman and the el aniquilacion cartels. "She cut a deal?"

"Partial immunity, she's giving names, dates, operations. FBI says her access to the cartel's inner workings is unprecedented."

Jaylee squeezed Paxx's shoulder. "That's...good."

"It is," Paxx agreed, though an icy knot of betrayal coiled in her stomach. At times, she still saw Shannon's face that afternoon in the coffeehouse: regret tangled with resolve as the truth unfolded.

Paul's tone grew cautious. "She wants to talk to you before the grand jury convenes in November."

The kitchen suddenly felt too small. "Why now?"

"She says there's something about Dad's case she didn't share, wants to tell you in person. I've got a burner number she'll use. It's only active for a few minutes each day."

"When?"

"Right now, I'll text you the window. After that, it shuts off."

"Today?"

"Her request, I guess that's life as a cartel boss's niece. She won't even be in the country until she testifies."

Paxx pressed her lips together, her thoughts racing back to the night someone shot her, to the parts of her father she still didn't understand. If Shannon was reaching out, it had to matter. "Okay. Send it. I'll call."

"Let me know the day and time. I'll come with you."

"Thanks."

When the call ended, Paxx stood by the window and brushed her fingers along the scar on her side, the souvenir of the bullet that almost killed her. Jaylee's concerned expression met hers. "I thought I was done with this chapter."

Jaylee looped an arm around her waist. "I'm not going anywhere. Whatever she has to say, we face it together."

Paxx tilted her head into Jaylee's shoulder, inhaling the familiar scent of lavender. "I don't trust her, I still feel like she's playing us."

"Then go prepared, listen, but keep your guard up."

A buzz caught Paxx's attention, a text from Paul with the burner number and its fifteen-minute window. Paxx tapped the contact, heard Shannon's tentative greeting come through. They spoke just long enough to set a date: November third, at the courthouse. After the brief call ended, she looked at Jaylee, telling her the details.

"That's forever from now."

"It's either then, or I fly to South America."

"November third it is."

Paxx offered a small, wry smile. "Just keep my mind off it until then."

With a playful purr, Jaylee slid her hands beneath Paxx's shirt. "Every day, and twice on weekends."

Paxx laughed, lifting Jaylee onto the counter. Their lips met in a warm, urgent kiss. Outside, the world hustled onward. But here, for now, with Jaylee's legs curled around her, Paxx let herself believe that nothing else mattered.

But November crept closer with unnerving speed.

???
FIFTY-NINE

Two months later ......

Paxx stared at the framed photo of her and Jaylee on her desk, the morning light catching on the glass. She ran her finger along the edge of the frame, a ritual that had become a comfort and motivation since becoming captain.

A soft knock on her door broke her reverie. She looked up to see Rowan leaning against the doorframe, two coffee cups in hand. She hadn't realized how much she had missed him until this moment. His hair looked freshly cut, and the cleanly trimmed beard he now wore suited him.

"Look at you, in your dress blues, Captain Algatta. I thought you might need this," he said, offering her a coffee. "Court days are always rough."

"It's been too long, Rowan. Thanks." She accepted the cup with a grateful nod. "Any updates on the witness list?"

Rowan settled into the chair opposite her desk. "Agreed. Five months is too long, and yes, the DA confirmed Shannon Darby will testify today. She's been prepped, but..."

"But she's still walking a tightrope with her uncle," Paxx replied as she leaned back in the chair she was still trying to get used to sitting in.

"Shannon Darby always has an angle," Rowan said, his jaw tightening. "Even now, with immunity on the table."

Paxx took a sip of coffee, grateful for its warmth. "She requested to speak with me before her testimony."

Rowan raised an eyebrow, his intense blue eyes studying her with concern. "You sure that's wise?"

"Probably not," Paxx admitted, fingering the silver captain's bars on her collar, still unfamiliar after only a month. "She says she has information about my father's case that wasn't in her official statement."

"Want me to come with you?"

"Paul will be there." She checked her watch. "I need to get going. Will you walk with me?"

"That's why I am here. To escort you to the courthouse."

"You think I need protecting?"

"Unfortunately, yes, today especially."

As they walked down the station corridor, officers nodded respectfully at Paxx. The transition from detective to captain had brought a different kind of attention: respect tinged with wariness, loyalty mixed with scrutiny.

"The courthouse will be crawling with Guzman's people," Rowan said, matching her stride. "And not just in the gallery. Some are still wearing badges."

Paxx kept her expression neutral, though her stomach tightened. "How many of our people do you think remain compromised?"

"Fewer than before you cleaned house. But corruption has deep roots."

They pushed through the glass doors into the bright morning sun. Paxx slipped on her sunglasses, scanning the parking lot with practiced vigilance.

———◆———

The courthouse buzzed with activity as Paxx made her way through security. Rowan walked beside her, his presence a steady comfort as they navigated the crowded hallways.

Paul met them outside a small conference room, one floor above the courtroom.

"You ready for this?" he asked.

Paxx nodded, though her stomach churned with apprehension. "As I'll ever be."

"Shannon's already inside," Paul added, his voice low. "She seems nervous."

"Wouldn't you be?" Rowan asked. "Today, she publicly admits to being a dirty cop and a family member of one of the most notorious cartel bosses in history."

Paxx straightened her uniform jacket. "Give us fifteen minutes."

Paul nodded, placing a reassuring hand on her shoulder. "I'll be right outside."

Shannon sat at the conference table when Paxx entered. She had pulled her dark curly hair back in a professional style that matched her navy suit. Her striking blue eyes lifted to meet Paxx's, and a soft smile lifted her mouth at the corners.

"Hi, Paxx, I mean Captain Algatta."

Paxx closed the door behind her, the soft click emphasizing the sudden privacy. "Shannon. It's been a while."

"Captain suits you," Shannon said, her fingers fidgeting with a pen on the table. "Though I never thought you'd take a desk job."

"Neither did I." Paxx remained standing, maintaining the height advantage. "You said you have information about my father?"

"Straight to the point," Shannon frowned.

"I didn't think this was a social visit. Did you think I would just forgive you for what you did?"

"I didn't think you ever gave me a second thought."

Paxx took a step forward and gripped the back of a chair. "I considered you a friend, Shannon. Just because I wouldn't sleep with you didn't mean I didn't care about you. That's why I wouldn't sleep with you; I didn't want to lose you as a friend."

Shannon looked up, shock in her eyes. "You thought I wouldn't be your friend if we had sex?"

Paxx averted her gaze this time, "I wouldn't have."

"Paxx, why didn't you ever tell me that? I would have backed off."

Paxx met her eyes again. "You would have?"

"Hell no, I wouldn't have. You're too fucking hot."

Paxx chuckled, not able to suppress a smile. "Still relentless."

"And I will be until you agree."

"I'll never agree," Paxx responded, raising her left hand with a smile to show off the tattoo encircling her ring finger.

"You got fucking married?" Shannon exclaimed.

Paxx shrugged, concealing that she and Jaylee weren't married, but were just as dedicated to each other for life.

"I'll be damned. A lot has changed over the past five months."

"We don't have much time. What is it you wanted to tell me?"

Shannon leaned forward, her expression softening. "Before your dad died, he asked to meet with me. I thought it was about an investigation, but it was personal."

"Personal?"

"He knew he was in danger. He'd been compiling evidence against corrupt officers for months. But what ate at him most wasn't the danger. It was you."

Paxx swallowed hard. "Me?"

"He regretted how he treated you when you were younger and then how he pushed you away even farther after you came out. Said it was the biggest mistake of his life. He knew he'd hurt you and was trying to figure out how to make amends."

"Why did he talk to you?"

"He knew I was gay, and despite everything, he trusted me. After Renee died, he thought you would quit, turn in your badge, meet a nice guy, get married, have kids, the whole thing." Shannon chuckled, "But you didn't, you lost yourself for a while, but you hung in there. He didn't see how you were away from work, like some did, but he saw you in the field, plowing forward."

Paxx's heart hammered against her ribs. She sank into the chair across from Shannon, all pretense of authority forgotten.

"He respected you. Dare I say he was proud of you." Shannon continued.

Paxx swallowed hard, fighting the burn behind her eyes. "Why are you telling me this now?"

"Because I'm about to testify against my family. And I needed you to understand that family... It's complicated. Your father loved you, Paxx. He didn't know how to show it, or say it, but he loved you."

Paxx felt a tightness in her chest, a complicated ache that had been her constant companion since her father's murder. "He had a funny way of showing it."

"Yeah, well," Shannon leaned back, "not all of us had great role models for expressing emotions." Her eyes met Paxx's, a shared understanding passing between them. "Before he died, he gave me something for you. Said if anything happened to him, I should make sure you got it."

"What was it?"

Shannon reached into her jacket pocket and pulled out a small leather pouch. "I've kept it hidden ever since. Couldn't risk it being found during the investigation."

Paxx took it, her fingers trembling. Inside was a pair of silver keys and a folded piece of paper with an address and a brief note written in her father's handwriting. 'For Paxxton and Paul.'

A soft knock at the door interrupted them before the door opened, and Paul stepped in. "We need to go, Paxx."

Paxx nodded, then turned back to Shannon, reaching across the table and squeezing her hand. "Thank you, Shannon, and good luck today and with everything that life brings you."

"Thank you," Shannon replied, tears glistening in her eyes. "Paxx, remember that no matter what they say in there today, or accuse me of. I had nothing to do with your father's death. I swear."

Paxx stood and walked out into the hallway, surprised to see Jaylee standing beside Rowan.

"Hey, sweetie, I didn't know you were coming." Paxx smiled, pressing a kiss to Jaylee's lips.

"I wanted to be sure she didn't lay another kiss on you." Jaylee laughed.

"My lips are only for you, my love."

"Good," Jaylee whispered.

Paxx looked around, frowning at Anna's absence. "Where's Anna?"

"She wasn't feeling very well this morning," Paul replied, stepping up to join them. "Mom is watching Embry so she can rest."

"Hopefully this baby will come in the next few weeks," Paxx replied as they made their way to the elevator.

"I hope she feels better soon," Jaylee said, her voice warm with concern. "Anna's been so uncomfortable these last few weeks."

"The doctor said everything looks good, though," Paul replied, checking his watch. "Just the usual third-trimester complaints."

Rowan glanced at his watch. "We should head to the courtroom. The DA texted that they're almost ready to start."

"I can't believe we're finally here," Paul said as they entered the elevator. "Dad would be proud of what you've accomplished, Paxx."

"What we've accomplished," she replied, looking at Paul and Rowan. "Teamwork made it possible."

The courthouse's main courtroom was already full when they arrived. Journalists filled the back rows, their expressions hungry for the day's testimony. Paxx spotted several officers she'd worked with in the gallery, some she trusted, others she still had questions about. The four of them slid into a seat in the third row next to Tracie and Jake. As they settled in, Paxx's eyes met Kimble's, who sat at the defense table, his eyes red with hate and anger.

The courtroom fell silent as Judge Harriet Wallthorn entered, her stern expression betraying nothing, signifying today's proceedings. After completing the formalities, the DA, Mary Chandler, stood.

"The prosecution calls Shannon Darby to the stand."

A ripple of whispers swept through the gallery as Shannon entered from a side door, escorted by two U.S. Marshals. Her navy suit and composed demeanor couldn't mask the tension in her shoulders as she moved to the witness stand. After being sworn in, she sat, her shoulders squared and her expression neutral. It was a measurable moment: Shannon choosing to risk being hated by every cop in the room rather than let Kimble's empire claim one more body.

Chandler's questions started simple. Shannon's title, department, her service record, and years on the force. But soon, they pivoted, as Chandler gestured toward a mountain of evidence, some of it sealed in plastic, some projected onto a screen for the jury.

"Ms. Darby, please tell the court your relationship to Nemesio Guzman?" Chandler's voice was almost gentle. The air in the courtroom shifted, as if everyone leaned forward at once.

"I am his niece."

"Explain to the jury, as concisely as you can, how your relationship to Guzman factored into your involvement with Captain Jacob Kimble, and the charges brought before him."

"I was a pawn." Shannon's jaw flexed. "My uncle made contact once I became a detective and moved to the Special Crimes Unit. I declined, but then, a month later, a woman from his legal team showed up at my door. She said, 'Family first, Shannon. You do what you're told, or your mother's house in Tucson burns tonight.' I was trapped. I fed them crumbs, nothing real at first, but then he demanded more. Gun seizures. Names. Who was moving the evidence, and when. Every call was a threat. Every text, a reminder of what would happen if I said no."

Chandler's eyes flicked to the jury, then back. "Why didn't you report it?"

"Do you know who Nemesio Guzman is?" Shannon's lips twisted, almost bitter. "His threats are not idle. My mother received letters warning me to follow instructions. My father's car windows were shot out while he was inside."

"Detective Darby, can you clarify for the court what knowledge you have of the cartel operations within the department?"

Shannon leaned forward, her voice low but carrying. "I joined the police force to make a difference. I wanted to separate myself from my family."

"Ms. Darby, please answer the question."

Shannon's lips parted, but her answer caught in her throat. She glanced at Paxx, at the familiar, wry compassion, and drew a slow breath. "The Guzman organization, my uncle's organization, had at least three active sources within law enforcement here in Ivan Hope."

"And these sources, how high up did it go?" Chandler pressed.

Shannon's gaze flickered toward the defense table, where Kimble wore an impassive veneer so complete it appeared cut from stone.

"I knew of Captain Kimble and one officer on the street level." Shannon's voice didn't waver, but her hands gripped the wood on either side of the microphone, whitening at the knuckles. "Kimble was the critical piece. Kimble knew the evidence's location, who signed the logs, which units would respond to an arrest, and the timing of those responses. He ran interference, shifting suspect priorities off cartel threats and onto rivals or unsanctioned street gangs."

A collective intake of breath washed through the rows behind her.

"Did Captain Kimble contact you directly?"

"He did, twice. First was in an official capacity, to warn me about leaks in my department. The second was before the shooting of Detective James Algatta. He made it clear that if I didn't follow his orders, he had the means to make my uncle second-guess my loyalty. He implied there were files to 'prove' I was feeding information to both my uncle and El Aniquilacion."

"And were you giving information to both your uncle and El Aniquilacion?"

"I never fed information to El Aniquilacion," she said, voice steady now, gaze boring straight ahead. "I was born a Guzman, but I didn't choose that life. My uncle, Nemesio, is obsessed with keeping the family bloodline useful, but I drew the line at dealing death. I never moved drugs, never helped them kill anyone. I only... I only ever passed along inventory lists. Guns, evidence runs, and confiscations that showed up on the news were always the highest priority. Kimble would send me a burner, tell me what to forward up the chain. I did it because I thought the alternative was waking up in a body bag, or worse, getting one of my colleagues or family members killed as a message."

"Do you have evidence of Captain Kimble's involvement?"

Shannon nodded. "Every time I fed a detail to my uncle, Kimble's team would get the case file to me first. Sometimes the original paperwork was missing; sometimes I'd get two copies of a report, one clearly doctored. I started logging the discrepancies. I have burner phones and text logs, and a ledger Kimble kept in his old office safe. He called it the Black Bible."

A murmur rippled through the courtroom at that. Even Wallthorn arched a brow.

"Detective Darby, please direct your attention to the exhibit marked 'D.' What is this?" Chandler placed a binder on the stand.

Shannon scanned the paper, the lines of text etched in her memory. "It's the shift calendar for the Evidence Unit from sixteen months ago. The color coding shows when cartel inventories coincided with police busts."

"And the annotations BRN, Rose Red, and Midnight Delivery?"

"The Black Rose Network." Shannon's jaw clenched. "Those were trafficking runs, timed to happen when the fewest officers were watching."

Paxx watched Kimble, whose unreadable glare seemed to liquefy behind the defense table. He remained motionless, his dawning awareness of impending doom palpable. An audible gasp came from one juror, a middle-aged woman with a floral scarf knotted at her throat. Chandler pressed the next question like a thumb against a bruise. "Did you conspire with Jacob Kimble in the murder of Detective James Algatta?"

Shannon managed a single, sharp inhale. "No. I never knew that was coming. I was told to avoid Detective Algatta. I thought it was for my safety, but now I know it was because he was getting too close. They knew he was going to blow the whole thing wide open."

"And afterwards?"

"Afterwards," Shannon whispered, and for the first time, her voice broke, "I began collecting more evidence. I tried to convince my uncle that Kimble was bad for business."

"Why was Captain Kimble bad for business?"

"Because he was also involved with the El Aniquilacion cartel."

"What was it he did for the El Aniquilacion cartel?"

"He trafficked and exploited women. Something my uncle despises."

Chandler's pacing stilled. "Were you ever compensated for your involvement by Nemesio Guzman or anyone else?"

Shannon shook her head. "No, I never took a dime."

A silence followed as Chandler let it hang, then turned to the judge. "No further questions, Your Honor."

Now the defense. Kimble's attorney, a silver-haired man in an ill-fitting suit, rose and adjusted his glasses.

"Detective Darby, isn't it true that you were under review for prescription drug theft at the time of these alleged events?"

"I was under review for taking two Vicodin after I broke my hand in the field. I self-reported, sir. I passed the tox screen." Her tone was ice.

"And yet you've admitted to leaking police reports to a major cartel. Why should we believe you now?"

Shannon smiled, but her eyes were dead. "Because you're asking for the truth. You didn't say I had to like it."

Kimble's attorney circled. "You claim you hated every second, but you stayed. Why?"

"Because if I left, my family would be dead."

"So you expect this court to believe your testimony, knowing you held back evidence for years, participated in felonies, suppressed information, and only now, facing charges of your own, decided to cooperate?" His tone dripped with contempt.

Shannon nodded. "Yes."

"Why?" he sneered. "Why not run? Why not disappear and spare the city this circus?"

She leaned in. "Because even dirty cops tire of being blackmailed and threatened."

The defense tried to rattle her with details, but Shannon parried: every question about conflicts of interest, every reference to her uncle's bloody reign, Kimble's coercion, every aside about her orientation designed to paint her as deviant or unstable, she answered with pinpoint accuracy, never once breaking the icicle calm.

By the time Chandler passed the witness, even the journalists in the back row had traded pointed glances.

Shannon's voice wavered at times, but she maintained her composure under the intense scrutiny. Once the Judge released Shannon from the witness stand, he announced a recess until the following day, when closing arguments would begin.

? ? ?
SIXTY

"Think the jury bought it?" he said.

"I think the jury knows a survivor when they see one," Paxx replied, as she stood outside the courthouse, the midday sun warm on her face as she waited for Jaylee to finish speaking with someone from work. She was still processing Shannon's testimony, how she'd dismantled the defense's attempts to discredit her and laid bare the intricate web of corruption without flinching. It had been both impressive and unsettling to watch. Then her mind turned to the pouch and keys Shannon had given her.

"You, okay?" Jaylee asked, appearing at her side and sliding her hand into Paxx's.

"Yeah," Paxx nodded, showing Jaylee the leather pouch. "Shannon gave me something from my father."

Jaylee's eyes widened. "What is it?"

"I'm not sure yet," Paxx admitted. "Keys to something, and an address."

Paul approached, his expression curious. "What's that you've got?"

"Dad left something for us," Paxx explained, showing him the note. "Shannon's been holding onto it since before he died."

Paul looked at the address on the note, his forehead wrinkling. "I know this place. It's that old hunting cabin Dad bought years ago, the one out by Lake Whittshum."

"Hunting cabin?" Paxx frowned. "I didn't know he had a cabin."

"He bought it the year I moved to Chicago," Paul explained. "I only went there once with him. He said it was where he went to think. I thought he sold it years ago."

"Paul, do you remember where exactly this cabin is? Could you find it again?" Paxx asked.

Paul nodded, studying the address. "It's pretty remote, but yeah, I could get us there. About two hours north, tucked away in the woods. Dad liked the privacy."

Paxx glanced at her watch, then at Jaylee, a silent question in her eyes.

"Go," Jaylee said, understanding immediately. "You need to see what's there. Just be careful, both of you."

Paxx kissed her, "I'm not going without you," then looked at Paul. "It's ten after twelve. We need to go home and change, but we could be there by three."

"Let's go home and change; I need to check on Anna, see if she is okay with me going," Paul replied.

"Of course." Paxx agreed.

An hour later, they were traveling north in Paul's SUV. Anna was in the front passenger seat, while Paxx and Jaylee sat in the back. Paxx held the leather pouch on her lap, her hand intertwined with Jaylee's, resting on Jaylee's leg. Meanwhile, Paxx and Paul's mother stayed home with Embry.

The cabin wasn't what Paxx had envisioned; she had pictured a quaint, weathered structure hidden among towering pines, its wooden frame aged by time and weather. As they pulled into the gravel driveway, the sight that unfolded before her took her breath away: a grand two-story log cabin, its walls crafted from thick, sturdy logs. A charming wrap-around porch embraced the entire structure, offering a panoramic view of the shimmering expanse of Lake Whittshum. The cabin exuded a sense of elegance and warmth, its commanding and inviting presence amidst the natural beauty surrounding it.

"Is this how you remember it?" Paxx asked Paul as they got out of the SUV.

"Not even close," Paul chuckled. "When I was here, it was a one-room hunting shack."

Jaylee squeezed Paxx's hand. "You, okay?"

Paxx nodded, her eyes fixed on the cabin. "Just trying to picture him here. Alone. Thinking." She fingered the keys in her pocket. "It's hard to imagine."

They approached the cabin, the gravel crunching beneath their feet. A layer of leaves covered the porch; otherwise, the place seemed well-maintained.

Paxx withdrew the key from her pocket, her hand trembling as she approached the front door. She hesitated, feeling a strange sense of trespassing despite the key in her palm, a physical invitation from her father from beyond the grave.

"It's okay," Paul said, placing a steadying hand on her shoulder. "He wanted us to come here."

Paxx nodded, inserted the key, and turned it. The lock clicked open easily, as if someone had recently oiled it. The door swung inward on silent hinges, revealing a spacious living area bathed in the golden afternoon light filtering through large windows.

"It's beautiful," Jaylee whispered, stepping inside behind Paxx.

The interior was immaculate, not the abandoned, cobweb-filled space Paxx had expected. The main room featured a stone fireplace, comfortable-looking furniture, and walls lined with bookshelves.

Anna walked to the nearest chair and sat down, her baby belly stretching her maternity clothes.

"Sweetie, are you alright?" Paxx questioned as she moved a nearby footstool over and lifted Anna's swollen feet.

"I'm fine; I'm just ready for this little one to be out," she smiled as she rubbed her belly.

"Soon," Paxx grinned as she bent over and kissed Anna's stomach, a ritual she had started several months ago, once she had started showing.

"This doesn't feel like Dad," Paxx murmured, stepping inside. The cabin smelled of pine and something else, paper, perhaps, or old leather. "It's too..."

"Organized," Paul finished, running his finger along a shelf of alphabetized books.

"That's what he pays me to do," a voice interrupted from the front door.

Paxx and Paul grabbed for their holsters, then grimaced when neither found the holstered weapon they usually had.

The older man at the door held his hands up in surrender and chuckled. "Just like your old man."

"You knew our dad?" Paul asked as he approached the man.

"I did," he nodded, then extended his hand. "My name is Charlie Grumen. I live in the next house over." He nodded to the south. "Your father and I became friends over the past ten years. I even helped him build this place."

"The two of you built this?" Paxx asked, stunned as she looked around.

"Me, him, and about ten other men from around here," Charlie replied. "He said he had been an absolute bastard of a father, so he wanted to leave his kids something nice. Anyway, I was beginning to think you two would never show up, at least not while I was still alive."

"I just received this today," Paxx said, holding up the leather pouch.

Charlie nodded. "It seems you're not sure why you're here?"

"I'm sorry," Paul said, walking over to Anna. "I should introduce all of us."

Charlie smiled, "Well, you are Paul, and you are Paxx," he said, pointing at them. "You must be Anna, Paul's wife, and I'm sorry, but he never showed me any pictures of you," he said, looking at Jaylee.

"This is my partner Jaylee," Paxx replied, stepping close and placing her arm around Jaylee's waist.

Charlie nodded, "Oh yes, that's right, you're one of them lesbians, no offence."

"None taken," Paxx smirked.

571

"Your daddy talked about you often; he would curse and carry on. But the guys and I would tell him, as long as she finds someone who loves her and makes her happy, does it matter if they are a man or a woman? He fought us at first, but eventually he agreed that as long as you were happy, that was the most important thing." He looked at Jaylee and Paxx for a long moment before continuing. "And you are happy, aren't you?"

"Very," Paxx agreed, pulling Jaylee closer.

"Okay, then let's get to it so you can start enjoying this place," Charlie said, holding out his hand to Paxx.

Paxx handed him the keys.

Charlie looked at the keys, selecting the smaller of the two. "This one's for the safe room. Your father had me build it special, and he said someday his kids might need what's inside."

Jaylee stayed with Anna as Charlie led Paxx and Paul down a hallway adorned with framed landscapes to what appeared to be an ordinary closet door. When Charlie inserted the key into a keyhole beneath the doorknob, the entire panel slid sideways, revealing a steel door behind it.

"Your father was a cautious man," Charlie said, returning the key to Paxx. "The combination is your birthdays. Month, day, year for each of you. Paul first, then you."

Paxx stared at the keypad, a strange tightness in her chest. Their birthdays. The most basic information a father should know about his children, yet it felt strangely intimate that he'd chosen this as his secret code. She glanced at Paul, who nodded encouragingly.

With steady fingers, she punched in Paul's birthday—05-15-89—followed by her own, 10-02-87. The keypad beeped softly, and the steel door clicked, swinging inward on silent hinges.

"I'll leave you folks to it," Charlie said, backing away. "I'll be next door if you need anything. Your daddy said this was a private family business."

The two of them stood as Charlie's footsteps receded down the hallway. Paxx reached for the light switch, illuminating a room the size of a small bedroom. Filing cabinets lined the walls instead of furniture; a large safe stood in one corner, and a desk dominated the center of the space. A large manila envelope with Paul and Pax's names was on top of the desk.

Paul picked it up, opened it, and pulled out several papers and documents. "It's the deed to the house and banking account information."

Paxx stood beside Paul, looking over the papers as Paul handed them to her. "This explains why there was no will and no assets left," Paxx said.

The last page was a typed letter, signed by their father.

"Let's take this to the living room, read it with Anna and Jaylee," Paul suggested.

Paxx nodded in agreement.

Once they were all seated, Paul began reading.

"Dear Paul and Paxxton,"

Paul began, his voice catching. *"If you're reading this, then I'm gone, and Shannon has passed along what I entrusted to her. I know I wasn't the father you deserved. I made choices that hurt you both, choices I've regretted every day."*

Paul paused, clearing his throat before continuing.

"This cabin and everything in it represent my attempt to make things right, not just with you, but the world. The deed is

in your names, and there are three trust accounts set up, one for property maintenance and one for each of you. Charlie will help with anything you need. The filing cabinets contain evidence I've been gathering for years, proof of corruption within the department, connections to organized crime, and the names of everyone involved. I couldn't bring it forward while I was alive. They would have killed me before I could testify, and then they would have come for you."

Paxx felt Jaylee's hand tighten around hers as Paul read on.

"'Now, for the hard part. I should have told you this years ago, face to face. My cowardice robbed us of that opportunity, and I'm deeply sorry for that. First, I want to assure you that every penny used to build this house, and the trust is clean, hard-earned money.

I want you both to know how proud I am of the people you have become, despite my shortcomings. Paul, I know you and Anna have a great life, and I regret I will not be there to meet your children and witness what a great father I know you will be. Paxx, I apologize for all the hurt I caused you, and I hope you find someone to love and who will love you the way you deserve.

I know I've made many mistakes, but the biggest was letting my work consume me. I thought I was protecting you by keeping you at a distance when the corruption infiltrated the department. That decision cost me my relationship with both of you.

The safe contains files about Nemesio Guzman and his organization. Things I never reported, things I should have. My silence cost lives. Don't make the same mistakes I did. Use this information wisely, and above all, watch out for each other.

Whatever you decide to do with the evidence I've collected is your choice. You can turn it over to the authorities or burn it all.

I did not want to leave this burden to you, but I trust you both to make the right decision.

I love you both more than I ever had the courage to say.

Dad

The room fell silent as Paul finished reading and handed the letter to Paxx. She stared at it, her vision blurring with unexpected tears. Jaylee's arm tightened around her.

"I never thought..." she began, then stopped, unsure how to articulate the storm of emotions crashing through her. "All these years, I thought he was just disappointed in me."

Paul leaned back, rubbing his eyes.

Jaylee squeezed Paxx's waist. "But he cared. Enough to build all this. Gather evidence, and think about your futures."

Anna shifted uncomfortably in her seat, one hand resting on her swollen belly. "What are you going to do with all that evidence?"

Paxx stared at the letter in her hands, tracing her father's signature with her fingertip. "I don't know," she admitted. "Part of me wants to march into the FBI field office tomorrow and dump it all on their desks. But..."

"But we need to be smart about this," Paul finished. "If what Dad says is true, and these files contain what he claims they do, we could put ourselves in danger by coming forward."

Jaylee squeezed Paxx's hand. "Not to mention what it could mean for your case against Kimble and the cartel. If there's evidence in those files that wasn't properly obtained..."

"It could compromise everything," Paxx said, her voice hollow.

"Folks, I don't want to end this abruptly," Anna said, grimacing, "but we should probably return to Ivan Hope."

Paul stood there, his face going pale. "Are you...?"

Anna nodded. "It might still take some time, but yes, I think we're nearing that point."

"Isn't it too soon?" Paxx exclaimed, seized by panic.

"It's a few weeks early, but the doctor said it could happen any time after thirty-six weeks," Anna explained, her face contorting with another wave of discomfort. "Nothing's imminent, but I'd rather be close to the hospital when things progress."

Paul went into action mode, helping Anna to her feet while Paxx gathered their belongings. Jaylee moved to the door, already pulling out her phone.

"I'll call your mom," she told Paxx. "Let her know we're on our way back and what's happening."

"We need to lock up the safe room," Paul reminded them, his voice steady despite the panic in his eyes.

Paxx nodded, torn between the urgency of Anna's situation and the weight of what they'd just discovered. "You get Anna to the car. I'll secure everything."

Paxx rushed back to the safe room, scanning the space one last time. The filing cabinets stood like silent sentinels, holding secrets her father had deemed important enough to preserve but too dangerous to reveal while he lived. She hesitated, then, on impulse, grabbed the manila envelope containing her father's letter and a small stack of files labeled "Guzman" from the desk, tucking them under her arm before closing the steel door. She heard the automatic lock engage and watched as the outer panel slid back into place, transforming once again into an innocuous closet door.

? ? ?

SIXTY-ONE

S he went back to the front of the cabin, confirming the lights were off before locking up. Paul already had the SUV running, with Anna in the front passenger seat, breathing through another contraction. Paxx slid into the back seat beside Jaylee, the manila envelope clutched to her chest.

"Did you get everything?" Paul asked, already backing out of the driveway, his knuckles white on the steering wheel.

"Just this for now," Paxx replied, showing him the envelope. "The rest will be there when we come back."

Anna let out a slow breath as another contraction passed. "How far apart are they?" Jaylee asked, her voice calm as she reached and took Anna's wrist in her hand, checking her pulse.

"About fifteen minutes," Anna replied, her hand protectively cradling her belly. "We have time, but not a lot."

Paul navigated the winding country roads while Jaylee tracked Anna's contractions on her phone. Paxx found herself caught between the immediate urgency of her niece's or nephew's impending arrival and the weight of what their father had left them.

As the SUV sped down the highway, Paxx ran her thumb over the edge of the manila envelope. Her father's secrets, their inheritance, felt heavy in her lap. She glanced at Jaylee as she focused on timing Anna's contractions, her medical training clear in her calm demeanor.

"Eight minutes now," Jaylee announced, looking up at Paul in the rearview mirror. "We need to call ahead to the hospital."

Paul nodded, his jaw tight with concentration as he navigated a sharp curve. "Paxx, can you make the call? My phone's in my jacket pocket."

Paul reached over to squeeze his wife's hand, his expression a mixture of excitement and fear. "You're doing great, honey. We'll be there soon."

"I'm okay," Anna breathed, her hands gripping the door handle as another contraction passed. "Just... focused."

Paxx made the call, her voice steady as she explained the situation to the hospital staff. When she hung up, she caught Jaylee's eye, finding strength in her partner's calm presence.

"They will be ready for us," she reported. "Dr. Hadleman is on call. They said to come straight to the maternity entrance."

"Thank God," Paul muttered, pressing harder on the accelerator.

"You, okay?" Jaylee whispered, her hand finding Paxx's knee in the dim interior of the SUV.

"Yeah," Paxx nodded.

Paxx squeezed Jaylee's hand, leaning in to whisper, "It's just... everything's happening at once. Dad's files, the trial, and now the baby."

"Life doesn't wait for convenient timing," Jaylee murmured back, her thumb tracing circles on Paxx's palm. "But we'll handle it. All of it."

Paxx nodded, grateful for Jaylee's steady presence. She tucked the folder into her bag and leaned forward between the front seats. "How're you doing, sweetie?"

Anna let out a sharp gasp, clutching her belly.

"Six minutes," Jaylee announced, her voice remaining calm despite the quickening pace of events.

"Almost there," Paul assured, his knuckles white on the steering wheel as he navigated through traffic with increasing urgency.

The hospital came into view just as Anna's contractions hit five minutes apart. Paul pulled up to the maternity entrance, where a nurse rushed out with a wheelchair. The transition from car to hospital happened in a blur. A nurse, with Paul beside her, whisked Anna away, while Paxx and Jaylee trailed behind.

"Family can wait in the labor suite," the nurse instructed, leading them through the automatic doors.

"They go with me," Anna demanded.

"Mrs. Algatta, they need to..." the nurse began.

"They are coming with me," Anna growled. Paxx smiled at the change in Anna's normally calm demeanor.

The nurse hesitated for just a moment, then nodded. "Alright then, everyone, follow me."

Nurses led them to a spacious labor suite with natural light filtering through large windows. Nurses helped Anna onto the bed while they began hooking up monitors and taking her vitals. Paul stood by her side, holding her hand and whispering encouragement.

Paxx and Jaylee positioned themselves near the window, trying to stay out of the medical staff's way while remaining close enough for Anna to see them. The manila envelope sat forgotten in Paxx's bag, eclipsed by the miracle unfolding before them.

"Dr. Hadleman will be here shortly," a nurse informed them, adjusting the fetal monitor. "You're at six centimeters, Mrs. Algatta. Things are progressing nicely."

Anna nodded, her face contorting as another contraction hit.

Paxx watched Anna's face relax as the contraction eased, amazed at her sister-in-law's strength. Paul wiped Anna's forehead with a cool cloth, his expression a mixture of awe and concern.

"You should call your mother," Anna said to Paul and Paxx between breaths. "She'll never forgive us if she misses this."

"Already texted her," Jaylee said. "She's on her way with Embry."

Paxx moved to Anna's side opposite Paul, taking her free hand. "You're doing amazing, Anna."

Dr. Hadleman arrived, a tall woman with silver-streaked hair and a commanding presence that put everyone at ease. "Hello, Anna. Looks like this little one is eager to get here."

"Yes, they are," Anna smiled, then grimaced, and cried out as another contraction hit. "Paxx," she said after the contraction passed.

Paxx squeezed her hand and placed a hand on her forehead. "I'm right here."

Anna looked at Paxx, then Jaylee, finally focusing on Paul, who nodded at the unasked question. "Paxx, will you and Jaylee be Embry and this little one's godmothers?"

Paxx couldn't stop the tears from sliding down her cheeks. Jaylee grinned and nodded. "Of course we will. Can we be both aunts and godmothers?"

"You can be whatever these kids need," Paul replied, the smile on his face causing his eyes to squint.

Anna's grip tightened on Paxx's hand as another contraction hit. "Oh God, this one's stronger," she gasped.

Dr. Hadleman checked the monitors, then examined Anna again. "You're progressing quickly now. Eight centimeters."

The next hour passed in a blur of activity. Nurses moved around the room, checking vitals and adjusting equipment. Paul remained steadfast at Anna's side, his normally composed demeanor replaced by a mixture of worry and excitement. Jaylee had taken up position near Anna's head, coaching her through breathing techniques.

Paxx stepped back slightly, giving the medical staff room to work. As she watched her family in this intimate moment, a wave of emotion washed over her.

Anna reached for her, "Paxx,"

"I'm here," Paxx replied, gripping her hand.

"Don't leave," Anna begged.

Paxx looked at Paul, a sudden sense of fear overcoming her.

"I'm not going anywhere, sweetie," Paxx promised, squeezing Anna's hand as she moved closer. A lump formed in her throat at the vulnerability in her sister-in-law's eyes.

Dr. Hadleman looked up from between Anna's legs. "It's time to push, Anna. On the next contraction, I want you to bear down."

Paul wrapped his arm around Anna's shoulders, his face a mixture of terror and awe. "You've got this, baby. We're all here with you."

The next contraction hit with full force. Anna's face contorted as she pushed, her grip on Paxx's hand tightening to the point of pain. Paxx didn't flinch, keeping her eyes locked on Anna's face, whispering encouragement alongside Paul and Jaylee.

"Good, Anna. I can see the head," Dr. Hadleman announced.

"You're doing great," Paxx encouraged, her voice strong despite the emotions threatening to overwhelm her. "Just a little more."

Anna's face flushed crimson as she bore down with renewed determination, her knuckles white as she gripped both Paul's and Paxx's hands.

"I see shoulders!" Dr. Hadleman announced, her voice steady and confident.

Paxx held her breath, watching in awe as new life entered the world. The room seemed suspended in time, the beeping monitors and bustling nurses fading into background noise.

"One final push, Anna. You're doing beautifully," Dr. Hadleman coached.

Anna let out a primal cry, her entire body tensing with effort. Then, release, followed by the unmistakable sound of a newborn's first angry wail.

"It's a boy!" she exclaimed, then asked. "Dad, do you want to cut the cord?"

"Paxx, will you?" Anna whispered.

Paxx swallowed hard as she moved to take the scissors a nurse offered her. As she cut the cord, separating mother from child, she cried, tears of joy streaming down her face. A nurse placed the tiny, squirming infant on Anna's chest, his skin still slick and mottled pink. Paul leaned over, his tears falling as he gazed at his son.

"He's perfect," Paul whispered, touching the baby's tiny hand with his finger. The newborn's fingers curled around his father's, drawing a choked sob from Paul.

Jaylee moved beside Paxx, slipping an arm around her waist. Paxx leaned into her, overwhelmed by the miracle they'd just witnessed. For a moment, everything else—the trial, her father's files, the corruption, all faded into insignificance.

"Have you chosen a name?" Dr. Hadleman asked as she and the nurses worked to complete the delivery process.

Paul and Anna exchanged glances, and Paul answered, "Keegan Jaymes."

Paxx grinned, "Dad would appreciate that."

"It's not just for Dad." Paul added, looking at Jaylee, "We want to spell Jaymes as J-A-Y-M-E-S, in honor of both dad and Jaylee."

Jaylee's eyes widened, tears welling up. "Really?"

Anna nodded. "We named Embry after Paxx, and we want you always to be a part of this family."

Jaylee pressed her hand to her mouth, tears streaming down her face as she looked from Anna to Paul and back again. "I don't know what to say," she whispered.

"You don't have to say anything," Paul replied, his voice thick with emotion. "Your family."

Paxx wrapped her arm around Jaylee's shoulders, pulling her close as they both gazed at little Keegan Jaymes. The baby's tiny features were scrunched in concentration, his dark hair plastered to his head.

"Would you like to hold him?" Anna asked, looking at Jaylee.

Jaylee nodded, carefully accepting the swaddled newborn. She cradled him against her chest. "Hello, little one," she whispered. "Welcome to the world."

Paxx watched Jaylee with the baby, her heart swelling with love. Jaylee's nurturing nature shone through as she spoke softly to him, gently rocking him. The way Jaylee's face softened as she gazed down at Keegan stirred something profound in Paxx's chest.

"He's got your eyes," Jaylee said to Paul, who beamed with pride.

"And Anna's nose," Paxx added, touching the baby's cheek with her finger.

"Your turn," Jaylee said, carefully transferring the newborn to Paxx's arms.

Paxx hesitated for just a moment before accepting her nephew. As she cradled him, feeling his warmth and weight against her chest, a fierce protectiveness surged through her. Keegan's tiny face relaxed, his eyes opening to reveal dark blue eyes.

"Hey there, little man," she whispered. "I'm your Aunt Paxx." The words caught in her throat. "I promise I'll always be here for you."

A soft knock at the door announced their mother, with three-year-old Embry in tow. The little girl's eyes widened at the sight of the baby.

"Is that my brother?" she asked, her voice hushed with wonder.

Paul lifted her to see better. "Yes, sweetie. This is your baby brother, Keegan."

Embry studied the newborn with serious eyes. "He's very small."

"Yes, sweetheart," Anna smiled tiredly. "But he'll grow, just like you did."

Embry nodded, satisfied with this answer. She reached out, her small finger brushing against her brother's cheek. "Hello, Keegan. I'm your big sister."

The room fell quiet as everyone watched the touching moment between siblings. Paxx felt her mother's hand on her shoulder and looked up to see tears in her eyes.

"Would you like to hold him, Nanna?" Paxx asked, already moving toward her mother.

The older woman nodded, accepting Keegan with practiced ease. "Oh, he's beautiful," she whispered, rocking him. Without looking up, she asked, "Paxx, when are you and Jaylee going to make me a nanna?"

Heat rushed to Paxx's face as she glanced at Jaylee, whose mouth dropped open in surprise. Over the past five months, Patsy had made great strides in accepting Paxx and Jaylee's relationship. Not that they had not had disagreements and heated discussions, but they never failed to talk through them.

"Mom," Paul warned, giving her a look.

"What?" their mother replied innocently, still gazing adoringly at her grandson. "It's a legitimate question."

Paxx stood stunned at her mother's question.

"Mom," Paxx choked out, "we don't—I mean, we're not—"

"What your eloquent daughter is trying to say," Jaylee interjected, taking Paxx's hand, "is that we're taking things one step at a time."

Patsy looked up from the baby, her expression innocent. "Well, at my age, I don't have time for you two to dawdle."

"Dawdle?" Paxx sputtered. "Jaylee, help,"

"Let's focus on Keegan and Anna right now," Jaylee said.

? ? ?

SIXTY-TWO

T wo months later....

Paxx sat on the cabin's porch swing, watching the sunset paint the ice-rimmed lake in shades of gold and crimson. The Kimble trial had ended with a conviction, but the sentencing was proving to be a drawn-out process, with multiple appeals already filed. She and Jaylee had been spending most weekends at the cabin, processing her father's files.

"Coffee?" Jaylee appeared in the doorway, holding two steaming mugs. She wore one of Paxx's oversized sweatshirts and leggings, her hair pulled back in a messy bun.

Paxx accepted the mug, the warmth seeping into her hands. "Thanks, love."

Jaylee settled beside her on the swing, tucking her feet underneath her as she nestled against Paxx's side. "Any revelations today?"

Paxx shook her head, taking a sip of coffee. "Not exactly, but I'm seeing patterns. Names that keep appearing together, dates that align with certain departmental changes." She sighed, leaning her head against Jaylee's. "Dad was meticulous. He built this case for years."

"How many files do we have left to go through?" Jaylee murmured, pulling a blanket over their laps as the evening air grew colder.

"Maybe a dozen more in that second cabinet," Paxx replied, absently tracing circles on Jaylee's shoulder. "But the real question is what to do with all this information."

They'd been having this conversation for weeks now, weighing their options. The evidence revealed a shocking web of corruption involving judges, politicians, and high-ranking officers, spanning decades. Some were still in positions of power; others had died or retired. el aniquilacion and the Nemesio Guzman organizations connected all of them.

Jaylee nodded to the question that seemed to have no answer. The past two months had brought a strange new rhythm to their lives, weekdays filled with their respective careers, weekends split between visits with baby Keegan and Embry, and hours spent in the safe room, piecing together the elaborate web of corruption her father had documented.

"Do you mind if we take a break from all of this tomorrow?" Jaylee asked.

Paxx smiled, wrapping her arm around Jaylee's shoulders. "Only if we can spend the whole day in bed."

Jaylee's eyes lit up with a mischievous glint as she set her coffee mug on the small table beside the swing. "I think we can arrange that, Captain."

Paxx's heart fluttered at the title, still not used to it after four months in the position. "Is that so?"

"Mmmm," Jaylee hummed, leaning in to kiss Paxx's neck. "You've been pushing yourself too hard."

The warmth of Jaylee's lips against her skin sent a pleasant shiver down Paxx's spine. She set her mug down and turned to face Jaylee, cupping her face in her hands. "Have I told you today how much I love you?"

"You have," Jaylee smiled, her eyes crinkling at the corners. "But I will never tire of hearing it."

Until next time......

M. Lea discovered her love for mysteries in the mid-1980s when a family friend gifted her *B Is for Burglar* by Sue Grafton. That moment sparked a lifelong passion for clever plots and strong female detectives. At eighteen, she began writing her first novel and has been crafting stories ever since.

A dedicated single mother from Missouri, M. Lea balances full-time work with her creative pursuits. She's an avid book collector with a personal library of more than 1,000 titles and shares her home with her son and four spirited Chiweenie dogs. When she's not reading or writing, she enjoys Jeeping, golfing, kayaking, and camping.